Fatal
Rebounds

Part I of the Fatal Trilogy

Fatal Rebounds

Part I of the Fatal Trilogy

A fictional story with a mixture of drama, mystery and romance, and is full of unexpected twists and turns in rebound relationships. As the three main characters transition from their late teens to adulthood, they experience growing pains that only add fuel to the fire. The question of *'Who did it?'* leaves you in suspense until the very end.

Written by

Dorothy J Morris

Library of Congress Control Number (LCCN): 1-354717043

Fiction: Contemporary

ISBN: 978-0-61537914-2

Published by:
Dorothy J Morris
www.dorothyjmorris.com
contactme@dorothyjmorris.com

Printed in the USA

First Edition - Paperback and Electronic

Acknowledgements

Thank you God, for giving me the desire and ability to write, even though it was during a tumultuous period in my life. Thank you to my family, Keirra, Vicky, Nicky and Andrew, for believing in me and helping me realize my dreams. I love you with all my heart. Thank you to my wonderful big sister, Cassandra Johnson. When I told you about my dream of writing, you told me to stay away from negativity, because not everyone will be as supporting. You are wise beyond your years. Thank you to my little brothers, Nathaniel and Peter Johnson, for inspiring me to pursue my dreams. Too numerous to list by name: descendants of my grandparents (Ida Mae & James Burger and Rosa Lee & Daniel Johnson); five god-daughters; and extended family (Giwa-Osagies, Kamaras, Kennedys, Morris/Mitchells) - *I love you so much*. My adopted parents: Errol & Emma Simmons, Gracie & Luis Kennedy, and Rosa & Gus Mackey - thank you for always being there for me, and for helping me raise my daughters.

Thank you to my friends for your love and support. Willie Banks, you will always have a special place in my heart. You read my manuscript (twice) without reservations, and provided invaluable feedback. Nancy McCreary, my best friend of 25+ years, and author of *These Beautiful Brown Eyes,* thank you for your advice. My Baltimore posse: Mary Steward, Lavern Munroe, Linda Scott, Laurie Williams, Ernestine Braswell, Earlene Whitworth-Hill, Sherry Yachera, Alecia Daye, Teresa Webster, Joyce Franklin, Lisha Tucker, Leslie West, O'Lillian Johns, Rosalie Colvin, and Leslie Watley. Thank you for your daily advice, and for keeping me focused on my goals. Lastly, thank you to my friends and colleagues at the Social Security Administration. Thank you for spreading the word about my first novel. I am overwhelmed by your love and support.

A Special Thank you to my silent readers: Andrew Morris, Linda Braswell, Christin Braswell, Ernestine Braswell, Willie Banks, Keirra Kennedy, Victoria Mackey, Teresa Webster, Marchand Bey-McQueen, Felicia Boatwright, Monique Johnson, Kara Colvin, Jerald Sampson, and Wanda Russell. Thank you for providing invaluable feedback after reading my first draft. Thank you to Esauren Phyer, Author of *"Tahitian Pearl"*; Marian L. Thomas, Author of *"Color me Jazzmyne"*; and Nikkea Smithers, Author of *"On the Flipside"* and President of "Readers with Attitude" book club, for being the first to reach out to me and give me guidance on self-publishing.

To all readers, in general, thank you for picking up my first novel. I hope this book will inspire you to read the sequels, *Fatal Vengeance* and *Fatal Blow*. Thank you in advance for your support.

This book is dedicated to my beautiful daughters, Keirra and Vicky. We have had good times and bad times, but through it all, we had one another.

I love you so much.

Chapter 1

Pandora's Box

Charlie Simmons, a millionaire by marriage, was in the mall shopping for an anniversary gift for his wife when he spotted a young lady sitting alone on a bench, crying. He overheard her talking to herself as he slowly approached her.

"I don't know what I'm going to do," the young lady sobbed, oblivious to Charlie's presence.

"Hey pretty lady, are you okay?" Charlie asked with genuine concern.

The young lady looked up and saw the most gorgeous man she had ever seen. "I need to find a job," she whispered, while wiping her tears away.

Charlie sighed before asking, "What's your name?"

"Dottie Smith," she softly replied.

Charlie shook his head and bore a worried expression after observing her fragile appearance. "Have you eaten yet?"

She shook her head, confirming his suspicion.

Charlie held out his hand. "Come with me to the food court." Reluctantly, Dottie placed her small hand in his and followed him.

While eating a burger and fries, Dottie told Charlie her mother had passed away, and she and her sister, Mercy, were struggling to make ends meet.

Charlie sat up in his chair and clasped his hands, mulling over her dilemma. "I'm going to help you and your sister," he finally said.

Dottie smiled, for the first time in a long time. She paid close attention to Charlie's well-groomed appearance, including the diamond rings he wore on every other finger, and sized him up as the 'answer to her prayers.'

"Where do you live?" Charlie curiously asked, observing Dottie's beautiful smile.

"My sister and I live in a shelter," Dottie shyly admitted, as she held her head slightly downward, avoiding his questioning gaze.

Charlie instantly pulled out his wallet and gave her five one-hundred dollar bills, along with his business card. "You and your sister go stay in a hotel tonight, and call me tomorrow."

Desperate to get out of the shelter, Dottie called Charlie the very next day. He picked her and her sister up from the shelter and took them shopping. He was smitten with Dottie, because she was not polished or stuck up like his wife. He even underutilized proper English and his expansive vocabulary in her presence.

Two weeks later, Charlie moved Dottie and her sister into a fully furnished two-bedroom apartment. Initially, they were his charity case; his way of giving back. After spending some time alone with Dottie, Charlie started seeing her in a different light. He never intended to pursue an intimate relationship with her, and felt guilty the night it happened. He vowed that it would not happen again, but his promise was short-lived after he impregnated her.

Charlie was excited when Dottie gave birth to a baby boy. They decided to name him Guy, after Charlie's deceased grandfather. Living with the presumption that his wife never wanted children, he looked at his son's birth as a blessing. Charlie wanted to tell the world he had a son but was afraid of the repercussions, especially since he depended on his wife for his livelihood.

Four years later, Dottie and Charlie had another son, and named him Alex. Subsequently, Charlie moved the three of them into a five-bedroom house, which was a lot smaller than the mansion he and his wife lived in. When he told Dottie's sister he could no longer support her, Mercy married Nate Johnson, the next man who walked into her life.

For six years, Charlie cleverly covered his tracks to ensure his wife never found out about his children, and his affair with Dottie. However, he walked into their house one day and found Jeanine sitting alone on the sofa in the living room, with the lights turned off.

"Honey, what are doing home from work so early?" he cautiously asked, noticing how the burning candle revealed her red teary eyes.

Jeanine did not respond. Instead, she slowly tilted her head toward the pictures strewn across the coffee table. Following her gaze, Charlie gasped at the sight of random pictures of himself and Dottie with their kids. Suddenly, he felt someone breathing down his back, so he quickly turned around, bumping into Jeanine's father, who was much bigger and taller.

Charlie shivered in response. "Mr. Benedict, um…what are you doing here?"

"Get out of this house!" Mr. Benedict exploded. "My daughter is through with you!"

Charlie flinched, then quickly turned to Jeanine. "Let me explain…."

"There's nothing to explain!" Mr. Benedict barked, pointing to the pictures on the cocktail table. "The proof is in the pudding!"

Charlie fell to his knees in front of Jeanine, clasping his hands. "I promise, I'll do right by you," he pleaded. "Please let me make it up to you."

"How?!!" Mr. Benedict angrily questioned. "You're a disgrace to this family!" he yelled, as he aggressively grabbed Charlie by his shirt and punched him in the face.

Charlie dropped to the floor, feeling the stinging pain from the fist to his right eye. He slowly stood up, but did not retaliate. He understood Mr. Benedict's anger.

Jeanine stood up and rushed to her father. "Father! Go home!"

"Are you sure?" Mr. Benedict hesitantly asked. "I'd be more than happy to throw this buzzard out of here."

"Father, trust me," Jeanine pleaded, firmly grabbing her father's hand and guiding him to the foyer. "I'll take care of this."

Mr. Benedict sighed. He never liked Charlie, which is why he forced him to sign a prenuptial agreement, and recently had him investigated. When the investigation revealed Charlie's second family, Mr. Benedict decided to deliver the news and the pictures to Jeanine himself. He figured it was the only way to prove to her that she deserved better.

"Call me if you need me," Mr. Benedict said, after kissing Jeanine on the forehead. He turned and stared at Charlie with contempt before walking out the front door.

As soon as Mr. Benedict left the house, Jeanine turned to Charlie with a cold demeanor. "Are you in love with her?" she firmly asked, still hurt by his unfaithfulness.

"No," Charlie lied. In fact, he *was* in love with Dottie and knew that her feelings were mutual. Though, he wondered if Dottie's feelings would remain the same if he could not maintain the lifestyle he provided for her, at Jeanine's expense.

"If you continue sleeping with her," Jeanine sharply stated, "this marriage is over." Then she walked toward their bedroom, leaving Charlie to ponder his predicament.

Charlie continued taking care of Dottie and the kids, who were six and two at the time, but kept his visits with them short. He also brought his sons home with him to visit Jeanine, who was introduced as a "*family friend*," at her insistence. She was very friendly toward them during each visit, so they thought nothing of it.

For approximately three years, Charlie stopped seeing Dottie and remained faithful to his wife. Their marriage seemingly returned to normal. Initially, Dottie was upset, but she eventually became excited with the prospect of dating other men. Charlie even promised to double her allowance, as long as she kept the men she dated away from their children.

Everything was fine until Charlie freaked out one day, while pulling into Dottie's driveway with his sons in tow. He witnessed Dottie on the front porch having a seemingly intimate conversation with a much younger man. He slammed his foot on the brakes and gripped the steering wheel when the young man grabbed Dottie's butt and held her close to him. Charlie was so distracted, he did not notice his sons when they exited his car and said "goodbye."

Dottie noticed Charlie as soon as he pulled into the driveway. She wanted to show him what he was missing. After she welcomed her sons home and watched them enter the house, she put her arms around her friend's neck and pulled him closer to her. Then Dottie briefly glanced in Charlie's direction before giving her friend a long seductive kiss.

Charlie hastily put his gear in reverse, backed out of the driveway, and sped off. After grilling his sons, he learned that the young man spent the night with Dottie almost every night. He confronted her the next day.

"I'm not married to you!" Dottie said with an attitude. "I do what I *damned* well please, and there's nothing you can do about it!"

Charlie angrily shoved Dottie, then pinned her against the wall. "I'm not going to take care of you...and your man!" he shouted, as his hands and voice trembled. "You're going to show me some respect!"

Dottie yanked herself from his grip and pouted. "I have a life too," she professed, while rubbing her sore arms. "Oh, it's okay for you to go home every night to your wife, but you expect me to be alone," she sarcastically remarked. "It's not fair!"

Charlie balled up his right fist and pulled back to hit her, but backed off when Dottie put her hands on her hips, as if daring him. He sighed as he regained his composure. "Well, you have to make a choice right now!" he harshly said, "either him or me!"

Dottie stared at Charlie in disbelief. "You're still married, re-member?"

"I'll work on that," Charlie hesitantly admitted. "Just give me time." It dawned on him that he may have just reopened Pandora's Box. *What's wrong with me? I know she needs a companion, but I can't let go...not yet.*

Dottie thought about it and decided to give Charlie a chance, for the sake of the children. "Okay, but you need to make time for me," she firmly stated, refusing to comprise. "I need to feel loved, and you need to spend more time with me."

Charlie began spending the night with Dottie every other week-end, and would often show up unexpectedly during the week. When she became pregnant two years after their reunion, he had doubts about his paternity. He kept going over the timetable in his head, but came up empty. There was never a question when Dottie was preg-nant with Guy and Alex, but this time it was different.

Charlie tossed and turned in bed during one of his overnight vis-its, before shaking Dottie awake. "Hon', we need to talk."

Without opening her eyes, Dottie groggily asked, "What's the matter?"

"Um...I don't know...how to ask this any other way," Charlie stuttered, "but...I need to know...who the father is."

Dottie quickly opened her eyes and turned to face him. "What the hell do you mean, 'who's the daddy?' You're the daddy!"

"Dottie, it's just not making any sense."

"I tell you what!" Dottie snapped, "I'll agree to a paternity test after I have the twins! I can't deal with your doubts right now," she added, before rolling over and turning her back to him.

The truth was, Dottie did not know who had impregnated her. She was intimate with the young man Charlie questioned her about, and she would make love to Charlie at the same time. Consequently, the young man did a *"disappearing act"* once he found out she was pregnant.

Charlie's frown softened as he lightly placed his right hand on her shoulder. "Baby, I'm sorry," he cooed. "I want to be here for you and our children." He kissed her lightly on the cheek and snug-gled up next to her. Minutes later, he was sound asleep, snoring. However, Dottie remained awake, thinking about Charlie's ques-tion.

When Dottie gave birth to the twins two months later, doubts about Charlie's paternity resurfaced. It was obvious; the twins were biracial. Their complexion was practically fair, their eyes were green, and they had silky light-brown hair. Their appearances were the complete opposite of Charlie's and Dottie's, who were both dark skinned, had dark brown eyes, and tight curly hair.

Charlie wanted the twins to be his. He had always wanted a daughter; now he had two. He decided to keep his doubts to himself as he fell madly in love with them. They instantly became "*Daddy's little girls.*"

Dottie, on the other hand, was worried. She feared Charlie would leave her if he ever learned the truth about the twin's biological father, a green-eyed, fair-skinned gentleman, whom she met by chance.

Chapter 2

Twisted Fate

*C*harlie woke up in a good mood. He was supposed to take Dottie shopping but was stalling because his wife was still home in bed. He thought it was strange that Jeanine did not get up early and go to work like she normally does.

Charlie shook her awake. "Hon', are you feeling okay?"

"Yes honey, I'm fine," Jeanine said, after yawning. "I see you're up early, looking dapper as usual," she indicated, after noticing he had on a suit and tie.

Charlie averted his eyes away from her. "I have a business meeting to attend."

"Will you be home tonight?" Jeanine casually asked.

Charlie stood up and walked to the closet to retrieve his shoes before responding. "Um…I'm not sure," he stuttered. "I have to go out of town to meet with some investors."

Jeanine mumbled, "*Liar,*" under her breath.

Charlie looked up after putting on his shoes. "What did you say, hon'?" he asked, after it dawned on him that Jeanine may have called him a liar.

"I said have fun!" Jeanine joyfully replied.

"Oh, um, I'll do that," Charlie timidly said, avoiding eye contact with Jeanine.

Jeanine threw the covers back and got out of bed, when Charlie stood up to leave their bedroom. "Did you get everything?" she asked with a smirk on her face.

Charlie turned back and gazed at her with puckered brows. "What do you mean?"

"Your clothes and other personal things," Jeanine said, pointing to his closet.

Puzzled, Charlie asked, "What are you talking about?"

"I'm just kidding," Jeanine said with a wicked grin, while slipping on her robe. "I'm going to eat breakfast. Have a nice day," she added, after giving him a big wet kiss and heading toward the kitchen. She knew Charlie was confused, because they had not kissed or made love in over a month.

Charlie was stumped as he put his hands to his lips. When he walked outside, he became instantly alarmed at the sight of three moving trucks. That is, until it dawned on him that Jeanine was always giving furniture and clothes to charity. Charlie assumed this was one of those days.

Then Charlie saw Jeanine's real estate agent pulling into the driveway. He anxiously waited for her to get out of her car. "Hi Allie," he said, as he greeted her with a handshake. "What are you doing here?"

"I just came by to get some measurements."

Charlie raised a brow as he watched Allie remove her briefcase and measuring tape from the trunk of her car. Before he could question her further, Jeanine sprinted out the front door toward them.

"Hi Allie!" Jeanine breathlessly said, reaching out with both arms. "It's so good to see you! How are you, dear?!" she asked with a big Kool-aid smile, embracing Allie with a warm hug.

"I'm fine," Allie stammered, wondering why Jeanine was treating her as if they were best friends.

Perplexed, Charlie turned to Jeanine and asked, "What's going on?"

"Oh, it's nothing," Jeanine nonchalantly replied. "Allie dropped by today for a visit. Come dear; let's go inside so we can talk." She quickly guided Allie toward the front door.

Pressed for time, Charlie refrained from asking additional questions. As soon as he pulled away, Jeanine called for the movers to come inside and pack up everything.

Allie turned to Jeanine with a questioning gaze. "Does your husband know you sold the mansion?"

"Not yet," Jeanine mischievously replied, "but I'm looking forward to telling him in person."

"What?" Allie asked, bewildered by Jeanine's response.

Jeanine bore a wide fake smile before responding. "Honey, it's not meant for you to understand," she firmly stated. "Will you do me a favor by making sure the house is locked up after the movers leave?" She headed inside the house without waiting for Allie's response.

✺

Charlie thought about Jeanine's unusual behavior during his drive to Dottie's. He knew she was up to something, but he could not put his finger on it. It was at that moment that Charlie decided to end the affair with Dottie. He did not think it was worth the risk of possibly losing everything, including the prestige that comes with marrying an heiress. He pulled into Dottie's driveway and sat in his car for fifteen minutes, trying to figure out a way to break up with Dottie for good.

Dottie was livid. She had been waiting for Charlie all morning. She was in the kitchen putting groceries away when she heard the front door open and close. She slammed the box of cereal on the countertop and rushed toward him.

"Charlie! How long do I have to put up with your broken promises?! It's been fifteen years! And when are you going to divorce your wife like you promised?! I'm tired of lying to the kids, telling them you're out of town on business when you live less than thirty minutes from here."

Sensing the beginning of a heated argument, Charlie walked to the sofa, hunched over with his head held down. He mumbled to himself, "Here we go again. I would've left her a long time ago if it weren't for my kids."

Dottie stomped over to the sofa and stood in front of him with her hands on her hips. "Charlie! Are you listening to me?!!"

"Listen, I think we better cool it," Charlie softly admitted. "What I'm doing with you…it's not right." Then he looked into her eyes and clasped his hands, as if pleading for her understanding.

"Oh, now you're remorseful," Dottie mocked. "Why didn't you have a conscience before I started having your babies?"

Charlie did not respond. He figured this overdue conversation would yield an unpleasant outcome, regardless of any reasonable explanation. He drooped back further into the sofa, covering his eyes with his hands.

"Oh, you forgot what you told me," Dottie condescendingly said. "You complained about your wife not wanting to give you any babies because she didn't want to mess up her precious body."

Charlie jumped up from the sofa and stood eye-to-eye with Dottie. "Don't you dare say one word about my wife!" he shouted to the top of his lungs.

Dottie did not back down. She rushed over to the front door and threw it open. It bounced back leaving a three-inch gap. "Just get out of my damn house!" she ordered. "Me and my kids will do just fine without you. Go home and take care of your precious wife," she added with malice.

Charlie sighed as he slowly walked toward Dottie with a grim outlook. "Don't worry about the kids," he said with assurance. "I'll continue to provide for them."

"Oh, but I'm not worried!" Dottie viciously replied. "First thing Monday morning, I'm going to the courthouse to file for child support. And while I'm there, I'm filing a restraining order against your trifling behind!"

Charlie opened his mouth to respond but closed it when his oldest child, Guy, appeared in the hallway of the living room. Looking into his son's eyes, he saw anger and tears. Charlie's heart ached when Guy quickly turned his back on him and retreated to his bedroom.

Charlie turned to Dottie and grumbled, "Why didn't you tell me the kids were here?!"

"They got out of school early today!" Dottie snapped. "Besides, Guy is old enough to watch the kids."

Charlie did not like Dottie leaving the kids with Guy, and made a mental note to hire a nanny. He also did not want his wife to find out about the twins. A court order would definitely alert her.

Charlie turned to Dottie with fear in his eyes. "You know I take good care of you and my kids. Please don't do this. It's not necessary."

"Just leave!" Dottie yelled, opening the door wider. "I can't stand looking at you any longer!" Then she balled up her fists and had a burning desire to punch him in the face.

Charlie reached for her, but Dottie held her hand up and said through clenched teeth, "Don't even try it."

Charlie put his hands down and gave up on trying to reason with Dottie. He knew if he pressed the issue, she would do something irrational. Dottie slammed the door behind him as soon as he walked out the door.

Blindly heading toward his car, Charlie's knees buckled when he saw his wife's limo. He was struggling to think of a good lie for showing up at Dottie's house, to cover up the lie he told her earlier about heading out of town to meet with investors.

Jeanine peered out the back passenger window and shook her head in disgust. "Just look at him. He's such a scumbag!" she said aloud, as she put on her sunglasses and waited for the chauffeur to open her door. She exited the limo and marched toward Charlie with an attitude.

Charlie stood still as the blood drained from his face. "Jeanine, what are you...?"

Jeanine held up her right hand to silence him. "Don't! No more lies! Just tell me the truth."

Charlie opened his mouth to speak, but nothing came out but hot air.

Jeanine sighed before asking, "Is it true you have twin daughters from the woman you promised to stop sleeping with?"

Charlie grabbed her hands and pleaded with her. "Jeanine, listen baby. I'm not even sure if the twins are mine." He knew it would have been easier to tell her the truth, but he loved the twins as if they were his.

Jeanine yanked her hands from his grasp. "Your uncertainty leads me to believe you're still sleeping with her."

Charlie's voice trembled. "But I broke it off today," he said, wondering if it was too late to save their marriage. "Let me prove it to you."

"Tell me," Jeanine thoughtfully said, "how can I compete against your children? I accepted Guy, and later Alex. I forgave you because you told me Dottie was just a fling. And now…twins? You've gone too far." She briefly turned her back to him, struggling to hold back her tears.

Charlie took a deep breath and exhaled, then started sweating profusely. He knew she was fed up with his shenanigans.

Jeanine turned around and stared at Charlie with contempt. "I filed for a divorce," she sharply announced, "something I should've done a long time ago. Don't bother returning home; your things were packed and placed in storage."

Charlie gasped with astonishment as tears welled up in his eyes. He even stretched out his arms to Jeanine, but she was unmoved by his gesture.

"Here's the key to your storage unit," Jeanine said, as she retrieved it from her purse and handed it to him. Then she turned and swiftly walked to her limo while Charlie followed her, begging for forgiveness. Her chauffeur quickly opened the door and waited for her to get inside, then smiled as he closed the door in Charlie's face.

Charlie lifted the door handle, but Jeanine quickly locked it and turned her head away from him. She closed her eyes and reflected on how she came to the decision to leave Charlie for good.

After Charlie begged for forgiveness and asked for a second chance, Jeanine hired a private investigator, Tim Carter, and ordered twenty-four-hour surveillance on Dottie's home for one year. She was hopeful and relieved when Tim told her he did not find any evidence that Charlie had resumed his affair with Dottie.

Unfortunately, three years later, Jeanine suspected Charlie was sleeping with Dottie again, especially when he claimed he was going out of town every other weekend for business. She rehired Tim to follow Charlie again, and her suspicions were confirmed. Devastated by this second act of betrayal, she sold her mansion, filed for divorce, and made arrangements to relocate to Sunrise, Florida to be with her father, who had fallen ill.

While on the way to her father's home, Jeanine had a gut feeling that she would never see Charlie again. Strangely, she concluded, there was no love lost between them.

Charlie backed away as the limo pulled off. Looking back at the house, he was not surprised to find Dottie observing the scene from her living room window. Then he looked toward the front bedroom window and was shocked to see his sons, Guy and Alex, gazing at him.

He shook his head and muttered, *"Look at this mess!"* Sadly, he walked to his car and unlocked the door, but paused when he saw Dottie running out the front door toward him.

"Wait!" Dottie breathlessly called out. "Look at it this way. She's finally out of our lives. We can finally live as husband and wife," she added with a wide grin. Dottie put up her arms to embrace Charlie, but he pushed her away. With tears in her eyes, she weakly said, "You promised me."

Exasperated, Charlie tried to walk around Dottie to open his car door, but she forcefully stood in front of him, blocking his path. "Dottie, I don't have time for this. I have to go home and repair my marriage."

After Dottie refused to get out of his way, Charlie aggressively grabbed her arms and shook her. "You don't get it, do you?! My wife was my life! She meant everything to me!" he added with conviction, as he forcefully shoved Dottie out of his way.

Dottie was surprised to hear Charlie's confession. He had always talked negatively about his wife in her presence. She crossed her arms while a river of tears flowed down her face.

"You need to be honest with yourself," Dottie sobbed. "You were only with her for the money."

Charlie winced because Dottie's reasoning partially rang true.

Dottie wiped away her tears with the back of her hands. Then she gazed into Charlie's eyes and asked in a soft whisper, "Are you...telling me...you never loved me?"

Seconds went by before Charlie finally answered her. "I love you...but not in the same way I love her." He wished he could have told Dottie he loved her more than she would ever know.

"My heart is broken," Dottie mumbled, as she turned and quickly walked inside her house.

Charlie slowly got into his car and started the ignition, but turned it off when he saw Dottie rushing back out the front door without closing it.

"Watch the kids!" Dottie yelled in Charlie's direction, while dashing to her Mercedes Benz, a gift Charlie purchased for her thirtieth birthday. "I'll be back," she added in a soft whisper.

"Wait! Where are you going?!" Charlie asked, quickly exiting his car to approach hers. "Please don't do anything crazy," he said, after noticing the smirk on Dottie's face.

He reflected on the previous time Dottie had threatened to take her life if he did not leave his wife. He found her half-conscious after she had overdosed on pills. The paramedics saved her life. Now Charlie was worried Dottie would do something to harm herself again. He was kicking himself for not convincing her to go see a therapist.

Sprinting to her car, Charlie opened the front passenger door and jumped in before Dottie floored the accelerator. "Dottie, slow down!" Charlie shouted, while quickly fastening his seatbelt.

Bracing himself as Dottie swerved around cars going ninety miles per hour, Charlie fearfully hollered, "Please, Dottie! You're going to kill us!"

Dottie looked at Charlie and chuckled, then pressed down on the gas pedal while gazing into his eyes. They were only inches from rear-ending the car in front of them.

"Dottie! Pay attention to the road!" Charlie frantically pleaded.

"Oops," Dottie said, laughing softly as she quickly made a sharp turn to avoid a collision. "Don't fret, I gotcha," she added with a wicked grin. Dottie was not herself. She no longer cared about her life.

Charlie tried to convince her to slow down, to no avail. He even grabbed the steering wheel, but it was too late. Dottie turned toward him and softly whispered, "I loved you," before making a sharp turn off the highway, crashing through the guardrail and descending the steep mountainside. The car rolled several times before igniting into a ball of fire.

On December 19, 1997, the local media headlines read: *"Murder-Suicide - Fatal Twist with Married Lover in Tow."* The news also reported Dottie and Charlie had four children together while Charlie was still married to Jeanine Benedict, heiress of Trowne Key Estates, five-star resort hotels and condominiums around the world.

Dottie was 35 and Charlie was 50 at the time of their deaths. They left behind their children: Guy, 15; Alex, 11; and twin daughters, Dana and Cassandra, 4. Since Dottie's sister, Mercy, was her sole family member, she was granted legal custody of the children.

Chapter 3

Life after Death

Charlie's funeral service took place the following Sunday at Mount Olive Methodist church in Miami, Florida. Dottie and Charlie's children attended the service with their Aunt Mercy. Jeanine sat in the front row, softly crying with her head held down. As mourners lined up to pay their respects, Mercy maneuvered her way to the front of the church and sat next to Jeanine.

"Hi Mrs. Benedict," Mercy whispered, as she patted Jeanine's leg. "I hope you don't mind me bothering you, but I'm going to need some money to take care of the kids."

Jeanine slowly lifted her head, put her hand on her chest and gazed at Mercy in disbelief. She was instantly distressed by Mercy's boldness. She had already paid for Dottie's funeral and burial expenses after Mercy complained about not having any money, *and now this.*

An usher witnessed their exchange and approached Mercy. "Ma'am, you need to return to your seat," he firmly said, "or you will be escorted out of here."

"You don't have to be pushy!" Mercy complained, as she forcefully stood up and faced him. "Humph…I know my manners!"

The usher was going to respond, but stood back after smelling alcohol on Mercy's breath. He covered his mouth as Mercy brushed past him, almost knocking him over in the process.

After the service ended, Mercy looked on in disdain as Jeanine walked over to Guy and Alex and hugged them. Jeanine was struck by their resemblance to Charlie. Guy had inherited his father's tall, slender build and dark complexion, while Alex had his deep dimples and charming persona. She looked down at the girls and noticed they did not resemble Charlie at all. She knew the twins were not Charlie's, when she had asked him about them, earlier. Her private investigator gave her a picture of their biological father, who disappeared shortly after Dottie became pregnant. She understood why Charlie treated them as if they were his; they were beautiful.

Next, Jeanine approached Mercy with her head held high. "I have taken measures to ensure that the children are financially supported," she firmly stated. "My attorney will draw up the necessary paperwork next week." Jeanine retrieved an envelope from her purse and handed it to Mercy. "Hopefully, this will be enough until Charlie's will is executed." Without waiting for a response, Jeanine turned and walked away.

Mercy hurriedly opened the envelope and was amazed to discover a check for ten thousand dollars. She had never seen that much money in her life. She instinctively concluded that it would be in her best interest to keep the children with her.

Mercy hired an attorney at the urging of her husband, Nate. He knew Jeanine was worth millions, and guessed they stood to get more money than she was willing to offer. In anticipation of Charlie's will, Nate had already picked out a brand new silver Cadillac from a local dealer. Mercy was also anxious. She had commissioned a real estate broker to find a six-bedroom house in a new housing development.

Mercy and Nate were asked to be present during the reading of Charlie's will. They anxiously sat in the conference room waiting for their attorney, while Jeanine waited with her attorney in his office.

Mercy kept looking back at the conference room door. "Where is he?"

Nate also wondered what was taking their attorney so long. "He will be here soon," he said, briefly glancing toward the conference door. "Don't worry; he's not going to miss out on a deal like this."

Mercy crossed her arms and sat back in her chair. "Humph....I just hope we get our fair share of the money."

"Baby, we hit the lottery this time," Nate cheerfully said with a wide grin.

Mercy held her head down in despair. "Yeah, but at the expense of my sister," she sadly admitted.

Nate put his hand on Mercy's shoulder. "I'm sorry," he sympathetically replied. "I didn't mean to sound insensitive. I loved Dottie, but Charlie was always looking down his nose at us. He never gave you the respect you deserve."

"I know," Mercy somberly replied, as she gazed into Nate's eyes. "But let's not get carried away until we find out how much money is at stake, okay?"

"I can tell you for sure," Nate said, while rubbing his hands together with excitement, "we're going to get paid big time!"

An hour later, all parties were seated at the conference table. After Jeanine's attorney made the introductions, Mercy and Nate eagerly listened for the amount they would be receiving on behalf of the children.

"Charlie's estate is worth $100,000," Jeanine's attorney announced, while gazing in Mercy's direction. "Mrs. Benedict has graciously signed over the entire amount to the children, of which they will each get $20,000 on their eighteenth birthday. The difference of $20,000 will be payable to you, Mrs. Johnson, on behalf of the children today."

Mercy banged her fists on the table, then bolted out of her chair. "What exactly does this mean?!!" she exploded, directing her anger toward Jeanine. "I need more money to take of care of these damn kids!"

Jeanine remained speechless, while her attorney sharply retorted, "The children are not Mrs. Benedict's responsibility. When they turn eighteen, they will have access to their trust accounts. In the meantime, make use of the $10,000 Mrs. Benedict gave you earlier from her own personal account, the $20,000 you will be receiving today, and the Social Security benefits the children will be entitled to as a result of Charlie's death. Mrs. Benedict has agreed to vouch that the children are Charlie's, if necessary."

Mercy's attorney was at a loss for words. After reviewing the will, he realized Jeanine was absolved of further financial obligations to Charlie's children. He turned to Mercy and said, "I'm sorry, Mrs. Johnson, but Mrs. Benedict was appointed executive of Charlie's estate, and as such, the terms of this financial arrangement cannot change."

"Can we sue for more money?" Nate eagerly asked.

Their attorney simply said, "No."

Mercy was exasperated as she flopped down in the chair and began whimpering. Nate put his arms around Mercy, listening to her complain about not receiving more money.

Nate was also upset knowing $20,000 was not enough to buy his $40,000 Cadillac, especially since he did not have a job. He felt bitter about lowering his standards, and opted for a used Cadillac instead.

Early on, Jeanine had learned from her private investigator that Mercy and her husband were chronic drug and alcohol abusers, which is why she established trust accounts for the children. She thought about seeking custody of the children, but knew Mercy would fight her tooth and nails. She had also feared the children would be a constant reminder of her late husband's infidelity.

From a young age, Guy knew his family was not normal. All of his friends lived in two-parent households, but his father was just a visitor who rarely spent the night.

When Guy was twelve years old, he walked into the laundry room where he found his mother, and had a heart-to-heart conversation. "Ma, why do you have a different name from us?"

"Because...just because," Dottie said, averting her eyes away from him, while trying to think of a good explanation. She never answered Guy's question, and filled the void by folding the laundry.

"Ma, why doesn't he spend Christmas with us?"

"Your dad works out of town," Dottie lied. She was too ashamed to admit he was out of the country with his wife during the holidays.

All of Guy's questions came to light when he overheard his parents arguing about his father's absence from his twin sisters' birthday party. He was in his bedroom when his parents stormed into Dottie's room, slamming the door behind them. He put his ear to the door, eavesdropping.

"Dottie, I can't be everywhere at the same time," Charlie harshly admitted. "Why are you complaining anyway?! I do everything around here. I pay the bills. I bought this house. I bought you a brand new Mercedes. And I take care of my kids. What do you bring to the table? Nothing! You don't even have a job," he said, while pacing back and forth, wondering why she chose today to nag him.

Dottie's voice cracked when she finally spoke. "About this house, it's not even in my name, and neither is my car. What if something happens to you? Your wife will get everything. Have you thought about that?"

Charlie's frown softened, after mulling over Dottie's concerns. "I promise...I'll make some changes," he said, as he pulled out his wallet and gave her ten $100 bills. "I'm tired of arguing. Go buy you something nice." He kissed her on the forehead after successfully squashing their argument with money.

From that argument, Guy discovered his father was already married to the lady introduced to him as a "*family friend*," and his mother did not have a high school diploma. The latter surprised him because Dottie was always on his case about getting good grades and doing well in school.

Dottie's concerns about her house proved valid, especially since she did not know it was listed solely in Jeanine's name. Charlie could not buy any big-ticket items without his wife's financial backing, so he had convinced her to purchase the house as an investment.

Jeanine discovered early on that Dottie and her children were the occupants, but decided to let them continue residing there. For one thing, she did not want anyone to know her husband had a mistress and had fathered children outside their marriage. Secondly, she did not want the children to suffer, despite their parents' indiscretions.

Several days after Charlie and Dottie died, Mercy asked Jeanine if she and Nate could stay in the house with the children. "Of course, we'll pay you rent," Mercy added, to sweeten the deal.

Jeanine eyed Mercy suspiciously, while considering her answer. "Fine," she finally said. "Just make sure you adhere to the community association's rules."

"You know we will," Mercy casually replied with a fake smile.

Jeanine did not get upset when Nate and Mercy did not pay the rent as agreed. She just wanted to make sure her stepchildren's lives remained as normal as possible. However, she soon realized her generosity proved fruitless when she began receiving complaints from nearby neighbors. She immediately called Mercy in response.

"I don't know what those bougie people are talking about!" Mercy shouted with gusto. "I mind my business, and they should mind theirs!"

Jeanine knew Mercy was lying. Her heart was racing as she closed her eyes and silently counted to three. Then she firmly ordered, "Keep the yard cleared of debris, keep the lawn furniture in the backyard, stop having weekend parties, and keep the music volume down. Am I making myself clear?!" she asked in a stern but measured voice.

"Yeah, whatever," Mercy casually replied, before slamming the phone on its cradle.

Shortly afterward, Mercy and Nate made matters worse. Their weekend parties turned into daily occurrences, and their visitors were hanging out in the street harassing the neighbors. After dealing with their nonsense for almost two years, Jeanine sent an eviction notice.

In response, Mercy immediately picked up the phone and dialed Jeanine's number. When Jeanine answered on the second ring, Mercy yelled, "We're not leaving! How are you going to just throw us out on the streets like this?!"

Jeanine calmly but firmly replied, "I warned you, but you wouldn't listen to reason. I want you out of that house in one week!"

"I don't care what you say!" Mercy angrily replied. "We're not going no damn where!" she added, before realizing Jeanine had already hung up on her.

Nate and Mercy thought Jeanine was bluffing. They knew she had a soft spot for her stepchildren, and believed they could always use them as leverage.

They were sitting on lawn chairs in the front yard, drinking and smoking, when the local sheriff showed up a week later. Their nervousness showed as the sheriff approached them.

"Ma'am," the sheriff said with a southern drawl, as he looked at Mercy, "we're giving everyone in this house one hour to pack up and leave the premises."

Mercy panicked, nearly falling out of her chair. "What are you talking about?" she asked, as she quickly stood up and approached him.

"This here is a court order," the sheriff said, while showing Mercy the document. "Your landlord wants you off the property."

Nate sat up in the lawn chair looking crazy, while Mercy ran into the house to call Jeanine. She hung up the phone when she could not reach her, then came back outside several minutes later, feeling deflated.

"Ma'am," the sheriff said, while looking at his watch, "you all now have fifty minutes to leave the premises. You should retrieve your personal belongings. The furniture and appliances stay in the house."

Nate grabbed Mercy's hand and guided her into the house. "Come on, baby," Nate said. "Let's go pack our things."

"Where are we going to live?" Mercy worriedly inquired, while Nate quickly grabbed a box of garbage bags to pack their belongings.

"We can go to St. Petersburg, Florida to live with my sister and her family," Nate confidently answered. "We'll hit the road after we pick up the kids from school."

They packed their essentials and loaded them in the trunk of Nate's car, then headed to the twins' school first. When they arrived at Guy's school, Guy looked at Nate and Mercy with a questioning gaze. "What's going on?" he asked, as he opened the car door and got into the backseat.

"We're moving to St. Petersburg," his Aunt Mercy explained.

"But why?"

"Because your stepmother is an evil witch!" Nate shouted, while putting his car in reverse. Then he looked back at Guy and saw his sad face. "What?! You thought you were special? Jeanine Benedict doesn't give a damn about you, boy! You need to get that through your thick head!"

Guy was trying hard to hold back his tears. He thought his step-mother cared about him and his siblings. During the two-hour drive to St. Petersburg, Guy closed his eyes and dreamed this nightmare with his aunt and uncle would end on his eighteenth birthday.

Two weeks after arriving in St. Petersburg, Christin and Tava-rus, Nate's sister and brother-in-law, realized Mercy and Nate were moochers. Tavarus grew angrier by the day, after realizing Nate was not interested in finding a job or contributing to the household. He decided to address his concerns when he caught Nate hiding his crack pipe under his car seat.

"Nate, you need to get yourself together," Tavarus said. "You and Mercy get Social Security checks for those kids. I find it hard to believe that you can't give us anything toward the rent."

"It's not like that," Nate nervously explained, shifting his eyes downward. "That money is for the kids."

Tavarus looked at Nate as if lost his mind. "Do I look like Bo-Bo the Clown to you?!" he asked without waiting for Nate's re-sponse. "You didn't think I'd find out you were on drugs?" Tavarus shook his head, before he continued, "I think it's best if you all get your own place."

Soon after, the livelihood of Charlie and Dottie's children dras-tically changed, from bad to worse. They ended up in an apartment, which was converted from a makeshift motel.

Chapter 4
Life is Not a Bowl of Cherries

*B*eing the oldest, Guy spent all of his spare time studying and taking care of his brother and sisters. His Aunt Mercy made it very clear to him that his siblings were his responsibility. She would pitch in to help when she was not drinking or partying, but for the most part, Guy became a surrogate parent immediately following his parents' deaths.

Guy often took his siblings to the park and to the library, to escape verbal and sometimes physical abuse by his aunt and uncle. They rarely had money to go to the movies, or anywhere else for that matter. Guy knew it would have been easier to find a job, but he also knew he would worry about whether his siblings were being mistreated in his absence.

One day, Jeanine Benedict ordered her private investigator, Tim Carter, to check on Guy and his siblings. Guy was sitting on a park bench watching his siblings play on the monkey bars, when Tim approached him.

"Hi there, young man," Tim said, as he sat down next to Guy. "What's happening?"

Guy chuckled, sensing Tim was trying too hard to be approachable. He simply said, "Hi," before turning away, to avoid a conversation.

Tim probed, "I see you're here with your brother and sisters, huh?"

Guy eyed Tim suspiciously before standing up to leave.

"Wait! Don't leave," Tim pleaded, as he stood up and tried to hand Guy five $100 bills. "This is for you."

Guy frowned as he raised a brow. Then he stood up and walked away. He stopped in his tracks after thinking about the welfare of his brother and sisters. He hesitantly turned back and approached the man. "What's the catch?"

"Nothing," Tim stated. "A friend of mine wanted me to make sure you and your siblings were okay."

"Who's this friend?" Guy curiously asked.

"Someone who cares about your well-being," Tim sincerely admitted. "Please take the money and use it for anything you need."

Guy was skeptical, but took the money anyway. "Thank you," he mumbled.

"Promise you won't tell anyone about me or the money, especially your aunt and uncle," Tim insisted.

"I promise." Guy turned around and headed in the direction of his siblings. When he looked back, Tim was gone. He wondered how this man knew about his aunt and uncle.

Guy did not know his stepmother, Jeanine Benedict, had arranged this monetary payout, along with other similar transactions to come. Jeanine was a force to be reckoned with, especially when it came to her stepchildren. She loved them immensely and cared about their well-being. As their self-appointed guardian angel, Jeanine would resort to the *unthinkable* to make sure no harm ever came to them.

Fall 2000....

By age seventeen, Guy Simmons stood six-two and weighed 180 pounds of pure muscle. His two front teeth were separated by a small gap, which was barely noticeable. He was handsome and the striking image of his father.

He began his senior year at a new school, Calomine Way High. On the first day of school, Guy was in the administration office waiting to be seen by a school counselor when he was instantly awestruck by a young lady, who had just walked into the office. He overheard the receptionist call her by her name: *Justina Reyes*.

Justina was in the office registering for school, after relocating from Miami, Florida. When the receptionist told her to have a seat, Justina glanced over at Guy and thought he was cute. She looked over his attire, then cringed at the sight of his worn-out jeans and wrinkled shirt. Frowning and rolling her eyes skyward, she whispered, "*Loser*."

As luck would have it, they were in the same science class. Initially, Justina was put off when their teacher paired them together to work on an assignment. However, Justina decided her negative disposition toward Guy was not worth a failing grade.

She approached Guy after class, and suggested they meet at her house for dinner, to work on the assignment afterward. Guy was nervous about the visit when he caught the bus to Justina's neighborhood. He realized her home was situated in a new housing development, where the homes were immaculate and worth more than a half-million dollars.

When Guy knocked on the door, he was greeted by Mr. Reyes, Justina's father. Mr. Reyes welcomed Guy inside and introduced him to his wife and younger daughter, Carmela.

"Nice to meet you, Mrs. Reyes," Guy said, as he shook her hand.

"Same here," Mrs. Reyes replied with indifference, looking Guy over from head to toe. "Why don't you wash up in the powder room and meet us at the dining table. I'll tell Justina you're here."

Minutes later, Guy arrived in the dining room to an array of food. He was surprised they were eating so much food in the middle of the week. "Where should I sit?" he asked Mrs. Reyes.

"Have a seat next to Justina."

Guy obliged her request, but instantly felt out of place at the dinner table. He fidgeted with his napkin, before discreetly glancing in Justina's direction, to observe the proper table etiquette.

Justina stared at Guy with her peripheral vision. She thought he looked dreadful, and softly giggled at his expense.

"Son, I'm proud of you and Justina," Mr. Reyes said, holding up his glass of tea to solute them. "May you both have continued success and prosperity." He clicked his glass with Justina's, then with Guy's.

"Ditto," Mrs. Reyes added, after clicking her glass with Guy's. "I'm sure your parents are proud of you."

"My parents…they're deceased," Guy sadly admitted. "They died in a car accident three years ago."

"I'm sorry to hear that," Mr. Reyes sympathetically replied. "If you'd rather not talk about it, I understand."

"Thank you," Guy said. "I must admit, every year that goes by gets a little easier for me to cope. My siblings are still having a hard time, though."

"Can you tell us about your siblings?" Mr. Reyes asked. "That is, if you don't mind?"

"Sure. I have twin sisters, Dana and Cassandra," Guy proudly stated. "They are seven. Dana's a little strong-willed and tries to be independent," he added with a light chuckle. "Cassandra's quiet and shy. And my younger brother, Alex, is fourteen. He's a handful, but I try to keep him focused on his schooling."

"You have a big responsibility," Mrs. Reyes marveled. "Are you the primary caretaker?" she asked without flinching.

"Yes, for the most part," Guy humbly admitted.

"We currently live with our aunt and uncle, but that will change after I graduate."

"Son, in a way, I can relate to you," Mr. Reyes said. "I lived in Cuba until I was seven years old. My parents realized the conditions were not improving, so they decided to send me to live with relatives here in America. Unfortunately, they could not afford to come with me. Life without my parents proved difficult. I went into the workforce after graduating from high school, so I could support my family, and...."

"So Guy," Mrs. Reyes butted in, while rolling her eyes at her husband, "do you have a job lined up?"

"I plan on working for Calvent Lucent Technology, and attending junior college part time," Guy proudly proclaimed. He looked in Justina's direction for her reaction, but she never looked up from her plate.

"I'm familiar with that company," Mr. Reyes thoughtfully said. "My company has a contract with them. They're very competitive. You hang in there. In a few years, Calvent Lucent will be recognized as a Fortune 500 company."

Upon hearing Mr. Reyes' response, Guy breathed a sigh of relief. Six months earlier, his school counselor had called him into the office to inform him that Calvent Lucent Technology was interested in hiring him full time. A week after accepting the job offer, Guy learned he was the youngest and least-qualified employee the company had ever hired. He remembered telling the man he met at the park, that he was interested in working in the computer industry, and wondered if he had arranged for him to get the job.

"I really needed to see a positive in my decision to work," Guy explained, "instead of going to college full time. I need to be financially stable, to care for my siblings."

"That's a smart move," Mr. Reyes said. "However, I don't think you should have to concern yourself with such an enormous responsibility at your age. But I'm sure you have your reasons. I think your goals are admirable."

Guy beamed. "Thank you, sir," he sincerely replied. He looked down at his empty plate, then turned to Justina and asked, "Are you ready to get started on our assignment?"

"Sure. Mom, Dad, may we be excused?"

"But we still have dessert," Mrs. Reyes said, as she stood up and removed the lid from the cake container, which was situated in the center of the table. "I'm sure Guy would like a piece of homemade strawberry cake. Wouldn't you, honey?" she asked, while placing a slice before him.

"Mrs. Reyes," Guy softly replied, "if you don't mind, I'd like to take mine to go."

"Sure, honey. I'm going to give you three extra slices for your brother and sisters."

Guy smiled in response to her thoughtfulness.

Justina and Guy completed their assignment in the library room. After closing the notebook, Justina glanced in his direction. "Enlighten me, Guy. Why is it you never hang out? You're always to yourself."

"It's not that like that." Guy mulling over whether he should explain his situation. "Can I confide in you?" he whispered.

Justina nodded.

"Well, I'm in a very tough situation," Guy struggled to explain. "I spend a lot of time taking care of my brother and sisters, and I plan on seeking custody of them after I graduate."

"Why can't you just let your aunt and uncle continue taking care of them?"

Guy briefly closed his eyes and sighed before responding. "They're not right," he said with sadness in his voice. "My aunt is a straight-up alcoholic, and my uncle is a crack-head."

Justina's eyes grew bigger. "I didn't know," she sincerely admitted. "I'm sorry to hear about your mom and dad. I can't imagine life without my parents, especially my dad."

Guy sighed. "You cannot begin to understand my life. I bet you never had to worry about money, food, or anything. I didn't tell you about my situation to solicit your pity. I told you these things because one day, I will be successful. I will live in a house this size and drive the finest car. I plan on giving the lady of my dreams the world, if she gives me the opportunity," he said, as he gazed into her eyes.

Guy had purposely allowed the last sentence to linger. He wanted Justina to get a clear picture of his goals, with the hope that she would see him in a different light.

Instead, Justina was taken aback. She thought, *I hope he wasn't trying to imply that I'd be that someone.*

"So Justina, what are your plans?" Guy curiously asked.

"They're not important," Justina flatly replied. "I think it's time for you to go home to your family." She quickly stood up and walked to the library door, gesturing for Guy to leave.

Guy was hurt by Justina's dismissive response. He had secretly yearned for her, and made it his mission to capture her heart. He knew Justina would eventually venture on to the finer things in life, including a man that could lavishly provide for her. He wanted to convince her that he would be that man.

After Guy left, Justina immediately called her new best friend, Regine Croswell, who was also a senior at their high school. "Girl, he tried to come on to me," Justina said with disbelief.

"Who?" Regine curiously asked.

"Guy Simmons."

Regine's heart fluttered at the mention of Guy's name. She thought he was the sexiest man alive. *Hmmm, mmm, mmm.... He is every woman's dream: tall, dark and handsome.*

"Regine, are you there?!" Justina asked, after hearing silence.

Snapping out of her daydream, Regine stammered, "Yes,...I'm here. So what happened?"

Justina rehashed the conversation she had with Guy, including the fact that his parents were deceased.

"That's so sad," Regine acknowledged.

"What's sad is that he implied that I would be the person he'd like to spend the rest of his life with."

"He did?" Regine asked with disbelief.

"Girl, have you seen the clothes he wears?"

Regine rolled her eyes skyward. "Yes, but what does that have to do with anything?"

Justina sighed as she briefly removed the phone from ear. "Did you hear a thing I just told you?!"

"Yeah, listen, I gotta go. I'll see you in school tomorrow."

"Oh, okay," Justina hesitantly replied.

Regine hung up without telling Justina she had a crush on Guy. She wondered if Justina read too much into Guy's intentions.

The next day, Regine and Justina saw Guy sitting alone in the school library. Justina turned up her nose, but Regine saw an opportunity. "Justina, I'll catch up with you later."

"But wait...where are you going?" Justina quizzed, as she watched Regine walk away.

Regine briefly glanced back at Justina. "I'll see ya later."

Justina frowned when Regine approach Guy's table.

Since Guy was engrossed in his studies, he did not notice Regine standing in front of him.

"Is this seat taken?" Regine nervously asked.

Guy blankly stared at Regine before answering, "Oh…um…sure. Have a seat. Aren't you Justina's friend?"

Regine smiled. "Yes, is that a problem?"

"No," Guy said, as he perked up with a big smile. "Maybe you could help me get to know her better."

Regine exhaled and rolled her eyes. "I gotta go. I'll talk to you later." She stood up and briskly walked away from the table.

"What's wrong?" Guy asked to her backside.

Regine ignored him as she walked out of the library. It dawned on her that Justina was telling the truth.

Justina watched Regine from a distance. She did not like what she witnessed, so she rushed over to Guy's table. "What did you say to my friend?!" she asked with an attitude.

Without waiting for his reply, Justina put her hands on her hips and swerved her neck back and forth. "Listen, pretty boy! You are not all that! If you were in Miami, you would've been jacked up a second ago. In fact, I should get my posse up in here to rata-tat-tat all over your behind!"

"First of all," Guy explained, "I am from Miami. Secondly, I didn't do anything to your friend. And by the way, I was probably a member of your posse," he jokingly added.

When Guy saw the scowl on Justina's face, he sat up in his chair with puppy-dog eyes. "I really didn't do anything to your friend. Can we squash this animosity, and be friends?"

Justina rolled her eyes and tightened her lips. "Oh, hell no!" she yelled, while throwing Guy's books on the floor. "Just stay the hell away from me, and my friend!" Then Justina looked at Guy with hatred in her eyes, before storming out of the library.

The next day, Regine heard about what Justina did, and thanked her for coming to her defense. She had finally gotten the nerves to tell Justina she had a crush on Guy, from the moment she first laid eyes on him.

"Why didn't you tell me?" Justina asked with a bewildered gaze.

"Because I wasn't sure how you would react, especially since you told me he tried to come on to you."

Justina sighed. "What did he say to you yesterday?"

"He said we could be friends," Regine lied.

"Girl, I must admit your technique to approaching this guy is whack."

Regine was hurt by Justina's relentless honesty. "I gotta go. I have something to do before my next class begins. You don't have to worry about me. I'm never going to approach Guy again." She walked away with her head held down. Regine thought she had something in common with Guy. She even envisioned Guy as the type of man she would like to marry, and have children with some day.

Shortly after the incident with Guy, Regine fell into a deep state of depression. She came in from school one day and walked past her godparents, Judge Bryan and Cecilia O'Neal, without speaking. Her godmother became concerned, and decided to confront her. She found Regine sitting quietly on her bed.

Cecilia bore a worried expression as she walked into Regine's room. "What's the matter, honey? Aren't you excited to be going off to college soon?"

Regine lifted her head. "Yeah, but there's this guy...."

"Oh...brother," Cecilia lamented, as she sat on the bed next to Regine. "What's his name?"

"Guy Simmons, why?"

Cecilia sighed. "I think you should focus on your education. You'll have time for boys later on."

"I suppose you're right," Regine softly admitted.

Cecilia kissed Regine on the forehead before standing up to leave. "Trust me, baby. When you start college, you'll have plenty of guys to choose from. Let's not get distracted, okay?"

Regine was appreciative of Cecilia. Besides her grandmother, she wondered how she would have made it without her godparents' support. She lived with them since she was four years old, but they treated her as if they raised her since birth.

Cecilia returned to her bedroom, troubled by the conversation she just had with Regine. She quietly sat in front of her vanity mirror, brushing her hair and thinking.

"What's the matter, honey?" her husband, Bryan, asked, as he walked into their bedroom and noticed her somber mood.

Cecilia stopped brushing her hair, and responded to his reflection in the mirror. "It's Regine. She's depressed over a boy."

"Don't worry," Bryan said, as he approached her, "the sooner Regine goes off to college, the better. Besides, I don't want her crazy father to hurt this guy."

"That's what I'm afraid of. I still believe we should have told Regine that her father is alive and well."

Bryan sighed. "Honey, you know what he does for a living. Regine doesn't remember him, and he prefers it that way."

"I suppose you're right," Cecilia replied, still not convinced.

Bryan sensed that his wife was still worried. "Hon', how can we tell her gently, about what her father does for a living?" he asked, then pretended how the conversation would go. *"Regine, your dad is not only alive, but he's also a famous drug lord and a murderer."*

Cecilia shivered at the thought. "Honey, please stop talking like that."

Bryan walked over to her and placed his hand on her shoulder. "Now you see why it's important she never finds out."

Cecilia stared into her husband's eyes. "Yes, I do. Do you think her grandmother told her about her father?"

"I doubt it. Bessie has more to lose than we do, especially when Regine finds out who she really is."

"Poor thing," Cecilia said, as she shook her head, not knowing who she felt sorrier for - *Bessie or Regine*. "I'm so glad Justina convinced Regine to attend Central Tillman University with her. I can only imagine what would've happened if a relationship between Regine and this Guy Simmons had materialized. I've had many sleepless nights worrying about any man who, heaven forbid, breaks her heart."

"Me too," Bryan acknowledged. "I fear the guy wouldn't live to see tomorrow if he does."

Chapter 5

Silver Lining

*J*une 2001....

Guy graduated from high school against all odds. After walking across the stage to receive his diploma, he thought he was all alone with his siblings. However, his stepmother, Jeanine Benedict, sat far away taking pictures of them. She watched as one of his sisters donned his graduation cap, and the other played with his tassel. Alex stood idly by, grinning from ear to ear. It was hard to believe Guy's aunt and uncle were not there for him on one of the most important days of his life.

Jeanine suddenly sat up on the edge of her chair, witnessing a beautiful young lady approaching Guy. Watching his reaction made her smile; he lit up like a Christmas tree. She did not know Guy had a crush on the one and only *Justina Reyes*.

Justina had caught a glimpse of Guy and his siblings after the ceremony. She looked around for his other relatives, but there was no one else. After getting her father's permission, she asked Guy if he and his siblings would like to go out to dinner with her family and friends. Reluctantly, he accepted her offer. It was a nice surprise, considering their last conversation had ended on a sour note.

Guy and his siblings were elated when they discovered they would be riding in a limo. Other than riding in one when their parents died, they had never experienced luxury like this.

The limos stopped in front of Shell's Seafood restaurant, which predominantly catered to the affluent. The chef and the owner of the restaurant eagerly greeted everyone as they walked inside.

Regine pulled Justina aside after they exited the limo. "What's going on?" she curiously asked Justina. "Why did you invite him? I thought you didn't like him."

"I felt sorry for him. Didn't you notice no one else was present for him during the graduation ceremony?"

"Yes, I did," Regine sadly admitted.

"Well, I wanted to do something nice. Poor thing doesn't have much," Justina said in a patronizing manner.

"I know, but one day he's going to be successful, and I plan on helping him make his dreams come true."

Justina frowned. "You do know he's a package deal, right? For God's sake, he's talking about taking care of his brother and sisters. I don't think you're prepared for his baggage."

"But I am. I'd love those kids as if they were mine."

Justina looked at Regine and wondered if her friend's head was screwed on tight.

Regine became annoyed with Justina's reaction. "You'll never understand if you've never been in love," she explained.

"I could never love someone who doesn't love me back," Justina frankly replied. She embraced Regine and wished her luck.

The host escorted Justina's party to the back room, which was beautifully decorated with colorful balloons and streamers. There was also a live band playing as they entered the room, which was surrounded with an array of appetizers, exotic entrees, and delightful sweets.

During dinner, Regine sat next to Guy and his siblings. She also graciously volunteered to help Guy with his sisters. Guy could not help but notice his sisters' positive reaction to Regine. Though, his eyes kept wandering in Justina's direction.

Regine's godmother, Cecilia, glanced at her husband, discreetly alerting him of Regine's unusual behavior. He had already noticed, and asked himself, *How am I going to explain this to her father?*

After dinner, Regine and Justina were surprised with brand new BMWs; Regine's was black, Justina's was red. They were both ecstatic.

Regine turned to Guy, dangling her new car keys. "So, Guy, do you want me to take you and your brother and sisters home?"

Guy bit his bottom lip, mulling over whether he should tell her where they lived. "No thank you," he finally said. "We'll catch the bus."

"Regine's driving skills are limited anyway," Justina teased.

Regine was not amused. She crossed her arms and pouted in response.

Justina playfully hugged Regine. "Girl, you know I'm just kidding." Then she turned to Guy. "Why don't you all go home in one of the limos?"

Guy did not say a word. His eyes told Justina how much he appreciated the offer. But, he stood still when the chauffeur asked him for his home address, then cringed when his brother blurted out that they lived on the South side.

Justina knew why Guy was deeply embarrassed. She had taken the liberty of discreetly following him home from school one day. She was baffled when she saw drug dealers and drunkards loitering in front of his apartment building.

Before he entered the limo, Guy told Justina he would call. Sadly, he did, nonstop, for two weeks until she left for college. Unfortunately, she never returned his phone calls.

Chapter 6

What Gives?

*A*s the limo pulled up in front of their apartment building, Guy and his siblings' excited disposition turned gloomy. They dreaded returning home, never knowing what to expect from their aunt and uncle.

Guy purposely kept his siblings behind him as he opened the door and peered inside. His Uncle Nate was nodding in the recliner with his shirt off, and a rubber contraption was wrapped around his arm. Guy also spotted a used syringe and crack pipe on the cocktail table. Across the room, his Aunt Mercy was sprawled out on the sofa with an empty bottle of gin resting on her stomach. Guy looked back at his siblings and held his finger to his lips, gesturing for them to remain quiet as they entered the apartment.

Nate instantly opened his eyes when he heard the door close behind them. He quickly sat up in his recliner and directed his gaze at Guy. "So you think you better than me, boy?!"

Guy braced himself for another argument. "No," he flatly said, then walked toward his room.

Suddenly, Nate stood up and charged at Guy. "Boy, don't walk away from me when I'm talking to you!" he yelled, before he pushed Guy to the floor and straddled him, repeatedly punching him in the face and chest. Guy tried fighting back, but his arms went limp after being overpowered by Nate's strength.

"Leave my brother alone!" Alex yelled, while Dana and Cassandra helplessly looked on, crying profusely.

Guy struggled to get up, but Nate wrestled him to the floor again.

"Get off my brother!" Alex demanded, as he jumped on Nate's back trying to pull him off Guy.

Nate was much bigger and stronger than Guy and Alex put together. With one arm, he pulled Alex to the ground and put his hand on the back of his neck, then forcefully pummeled his face onto the floor.

Guy wiggled out from underneath Nate's weight and jumped up. He instinctively put his arms around Nate's neck and started choking him. "Let my brother go!" he demanded.

While Nate was swinging his arms around, trying to maneuver out of Guy's grasp, Alex rolled out from under Nate and stood up.

"We're tired of you bullying us," Guy breathlessly said, struggling to keep Nate in a chokehold. "You're going to leave us alone!"

Nate suddenly stopped swinging his arms and started shivering.

Alex got scared and panicked. He grabbed Guy's arm and pleaded, "Let him go! He's not worth it!"

Guy let him loose, then stood by as Nate collapsed to the floor. Mercy heard the commotion and woke up from her drunken stupor. She sat up and saw Nate hunched over, vigorously coughing. "Y'all better...leave...my husband...alone," she slurred, then slumped back onto the sofa and passed out.

Guy rushed into his bedroom, pulled out his duffle bag and began packing his personal belongings. His siblings followed him into the bedroom and sat on the bed, saddened by what just transpired.

Alex stood up and walked over to Guy. "Take me with you," he pleaded.

Guy stopped packing and turned to his little brother. "I wish I could, but I need you to stay here and look after the twins until I can find a place for us to live. I promise, I'll be back to get all of you."

While touching his neck, Nate regained his composure and sauntered to the doorway of Guy and his siblings' bedroom. He looked at Guy with disdain, before he yelled, "Get out of my damn house!"

Guy did not say anything. He threw his duffle bag over his shoulders and quietly walked out the front door. He was not sure where he was going but had enough money saved up for a day like this. He thanked God for the man who occasionally gave him money. He had managed to save over twenty-five hundred dollars.

When Guy first met Jeanine's private investigator, Tim Carter, he thought he looked too young and hip to care. He wished he had asked more questions. He did not even know his name. Each time he asked, Tim would always reply, "*I'm a friend of a friend.*" Unbeknownst to Guy, that same man was sitting in front of their apartment in a car with heavily tinted windows, when he walked out the front door.

Tim picked up the phone and made an important phone call. "Mrs. Benedict, there's a problem."

"What's going on?" Jeanine fearfully asked.

"Guy looks pretty beat up. I believe Nate jumped on him again. This time he was carrying a duffle bag when he walked out of the apartment. I'm guessing, but it looks like Guy is moving out on a permanent basis."

"Good. He's a tough kid. Once he gets settled on his new job, I'm certain he'll be back for his siblings."

"What do you want me to do about Nate?"

"I don't care what you do. Just make sure he regrets putting his hands on Guy. Am I clear?"

"Loud and clear."

The next day, Tim waited until Nate walked up the street to the corner store before he approached him. "Hi there, can we talk for a minute?"

Nate eyed Tim suspiciously before asking, "Who in the hell are you?"

Tim ignored Nate's question. "What if I pay you $1,000 for your time?" he asked, as he held up ten one-hundred dollar bills.

Nate's eyes lit up at the sight of the money. He grabbed it from the Tim's hand and counted it. "What can I do for you?" he eagerly asked, after putting the money in his wallet.

"I need you to come with me to drop off a package. My car is up the street. It's nothing illegal."

Nate did not care if it was illegal or not. He had already spent the money in his head. He was rubbing his hands together as the stranger opened the rear passenger door for him.

As soon as Nate stuck his head in the car, he was pulled in by a big burly man. He tried fighting back, but he was overpowered by the man's strength. Then he was driven to a vacant lot where he was beaten and bloodied.

Minutes later, Tim stood in front of Nate and threatened, "If you ever put your hands on Guy or his siblings again, you won't survive the next beating. Are we clear?" Tim asked, as he took back his $1000 from Nate's wallet.

Nate nodded before he collapsed to the ground. When he returned home an hour later, Mercy questioned him about his bruised face and bloodied shirt. Nate ignored her and stayed to himself.

Mercy knew something strange was going on when he refused to go anywhere near Alex and his sisters. She approached him and asked, "Are you okay?"

"I'm fine!" Nate snapped. "Just leave me the hell alone!" He placed his hands on his forehead, wondering how this stranger knew Guy. He felt physically and emotionally wounded.

Guy spent his first night of independence at a motel. The next day, he found an affordable apartment to rent. After receiving his first paycheck two weeks later, he took the bus to visit his siblings. He knocked on the door expecting the worse.

Mercy gladly opened the door and greeted him. "Hi Guy. It's so good to see you, suga'. Come on in, honey," she enthusiastically said, as she stood back and motioned for him to step inside.

Guy suspiciously eyed his Aunt Mercy. He had never known her to be syrupy, and thought it was annoying.

"Why don't you have a seat?" Nate nicely suggested.

Guy looked at Nate with a quizzical gaze before responding. "No, I'm not staying."

"Um…Guy," Mercy stammered, "me and your uncle want you to give us some of the money from your trust account."

When Guy raised a brow, Nate chimed in. "After y'all daddy died, his wife put some money in a trust for y'all. When you, your brother and sisters turn 18, y'all get $20,000 each. So, um…I can take you to the bank and help you with the paperwork," he said with forced kindness. Nate timidly approached Guy and handed him the bank statement.

"No thank you. I can handle my own affairs," Guy curtly replied, looking closely at the account balance. Then he looked up at Nate's face and noticed his scars and bruises, and wondered what happened to him.

"So you're not gonna break us off nothing?" Nate asked with a bewildered gaze. "After all we've done for y'all."

"Actually, you made our lives a living hell!" Guy sharply retorted. "We owe you nothing," he said, before he called for his siblings.

Mercy's eyes were filled with fear. "Come on, Guy," she whined, "You know we love you, suga'."

Guy looked at Mercy and Nate with utter hatred in his eyes. "I'm taking my sisters and brother to the movies. I'll bring them back later," he lied. He had no intentions of returning them.

Guy used the money from his trust fund to purchase a used car and enroll in junior college part-time. Six months later, he filed a court order seeking permanent custody of his siblings. Surprisingly, his aunt and uncle were contesting his custody request, even though his siblings were no longer living with them. They also continued receiving Social Security benefits for the children; a provision Guy could live with, as long as his siblings remained in his custody.

Chapter 7

Life Happens

arch 2002....
M During Regine and Justina's second semester in college, Justina was sure she met her soulmate, Cedric Townsend. She thought he was the finest young man in her class. It also helped that he was rich. However, six months into their relationship, she believed Cedric was cheating on her. She was sitting in her dorm room thinking about him, when Regine walked in.

"What's the matter?" Regine asked, noticing Justina's gloomy disposition.

"I believe Cedric is seeing someone else," Justina sadly acknowledged.

Regine sat on the bed next to Justina. "How do you know?"

"Lately, he's been avoiding my calls, and every time we make plans to go somewhere, he always comes up with some lame excuse."

"Oh...I didn't know."

"I need to go over to his apartment to talk to him. Will you go with me?"

"Sure."

When they arrived at Cedric's apartment, Regine stood idly by as Justina knocked on his door. They knew Cedric was home because music was blaring from inside the apartment.

Justina forcefully banged on the door. "Cedric! I know you're in there! Open this door, right now!"

After Cedric did not respond, Regine grabbed Justina's hand. "Come on, Justina," she pleaded. "He's not worth it."

Justina yanked her hand away. "No Regine! I'm not going anywhere! He needs to open this door, or I'm going to take matters into my own hands."

Regine knew she could not reason with Justina, so she stepped aside hoping things would not get out of hand.

Cedric's friend, PJ, walked up next to Justina and asked, "What's going on?"

"Your friend is trifling!" Justina sharply replied.

PJ ignored Justina and knocked on the door. "Cedric, open up! This is PJ!"

Cedric looked through the peephole and saw PJ, but he refused to open the door.

Justina exploded, slapping the door with her open hand. "Cedric! If you don't open this door, I'm going to break every window in your car! Then I'm going to slash your tires!" She knew Cedric had spent thousands of dollars accessorizing his car; more than what it was worth.

Cedric frantically put his clothes on, and yelled through the closed door, "Stop trippin', Justina!"

Justina crossed her arms, and grumbled, "If you don't open this door, I'm going to make your life a living hell!"

Cedric panicked. He opened the door and quickly closed it behind him. His voice trembled. "Baby…what's up? Why didn't you tell me you were coming?"

Justina closed the space between them. "I'm not a fool," she angrily said. "I know you have someone in there." She tried to push her away around Cedric, but he blocked her with the full weight of his body. In response, she began slapping him in the face.

Cedric aggressively grabbed her arms and held her close to him. "Baby, calm down! She's just a friend." Then he turned to PJ. "Man, help me out."

PJ looked at Cedric like he was crazy. "Man, what do you want me to do? She's a wild one," he added with a chuckle. Then he stood back and took pleasure in watching Cedric try to squirm out of the mess he created.

Wiggling to get out of Cedric's grasp, Justina said, "If she's just a friend, I want to meet her."

"Justina, don't do this!" Cedric begged, still struggling to keep her from going inside his apartment.

Cedric and Justina were both surprised when the door slowly opened. Justina came face to face with her classmate, Tamika.

Tamika stepped outside and saw Cedric holding Justina. "Let me explain," she weakly said to Justina.

Justina frowned. "Explain what?! That you took my man!" she exclaimed, trying to break away from Cedric's tight grip.

Tamika became annoyed. She crossed her arms and twisted her mouth, before spouting, "He was my man long before he was yours anyway! You were just his rebound!"

Justina stood still; she was speechless. She knew Tamika was telling the truth, but it did not make her feel better about the situation.

Cedric released Justina, then went over to Tamika and put his arms around her. He turned to Justina, trying to sound hard and in control. "I have needs. You want to play the virgin role, but we're not on the same page."

Justina held back her tears as she faced Cedric. "Don't ever call me again!"

Regine grabbed Justina's hand and pulled her away from the scene. "Justina, it's going to be okay."

Justina let go of Regine's hand and backed away. "Thanks, Regine, but I need some time alone." She began walking in the opposite direction of their dorm.

PJ approached Regine immediately after Justina walked away. "Don't worry about Justina. She'll be okay."

"I know she will," Regine earnestly replied. "She's a lot stronger than you think."

He extended his hand after realizing he never formally met Regine. "By the way, my name is PJ."

Regine cautiously shook his hand and introduced herself.

"I can walk you back to your dorm,' PJ charmingly said, "if you want me to."

Regine frowned. "I don't think so."

"Come on now; don't act like that. We go to the same school. What harm is it for me to walk with you?"

Regine looked skyward as she reasoned that PJ seemed harmless. "Okay, sure," she finally said. "So tell me, why is your friend such a dawg?" she asked, while walking with PJ toward her dorm.

PJ sighed. "I don't want to spend the rest of the evening talking about Cedric. I'm nothing like him. My mom would kill me if I ever disrespected a woman like that."

Regine smiled in response. She thought PJ was cute, and noted he was tall, slender, and had a fair complexion. When she told him he belonged on the cover of a GQ magazine, he blushed before admitting he dabbled in the modeling industry.

PJ was just as enamored with Regine's beauty. He was particularly awestruck by her exotic features - black, thick, shoulder-length hair; dark chocolate, flawless skin; full, thick lips; big, dark brown eyes; and beautiful straight, white teeth. He especially loved her voluptuous figure on her petite body frame.

Upon arriving at her dorm, they exchanged phone numbers, but PJ wanted to get to know Regine in more ways than one. "Would you like to go for a ride?" he eagerly asked, when they approached the dormitory.

"I don't know you well enough," Regine shyly admitted.

"We're just going to get something to eat. What's the big deal?"

Regine liked PJ a lot. Her common sense said 'no' but her heart said 'yes.' "I don't even know your full name," she shyly admitted.

"Baby, PJ is what they call me. If you don't want to go, I understand." He pretended to be disappointed as he looked longingly into her eyes. "It's just that you're so pretty. I don't want this night to end with a simple goodbye," PJ cooed.

Regine blushed. Her gut instinct told her to be leery of PJ's intentions. She smiled back when he smiled. "Okay," she finally answered.

Thirty minutes later, they were in front of a tall apartment building. Regine looked around unfamiliar surroundings, and nervously asked, "Where are we?"

PJ grinned. "Oh, I forgot to get a few things from the crib. I was hoping we could grab them before we go get something to eat."

"Oh...well...I'll wait for you in the car," Regine insisted.

"Baby, what if something happens to you out here in the car? I promise, it won't take more than a few minutes."

Regine pensively looked at PJ, then immediately averted her eyes downward.

PJ noticed her apprehension. "I won't hurt you," he murmured. "I would never ask you to do anything you don't want to do. You can wait for me in the living room," he charmingly added.

Reluctantly, Regine agreed to go with him. She was pleasantly surprised that his apartment was clean and vibrant. The living room consisted of plush pink carpet, pink vertical blinds, and green throw pillows on a pink oversized couch. There were various shades of pink and green decorations throughout the rest of the apartment. She thought it was strange that a man would choose these colors, but guessed his mother might have assisted him with the furnishings and decorations.

"You have a nice apartment," Regine said, as she sat down, staring at a bouquet of pink roses in a green vase on a white coffee table.

PJ smiled and thought, *She can't be that naïve.* He went into the kitchen, grabbed a soda from the refrigerator, and returned to the living room. "I brought you a soda," he said, as he handed it to her.

"Thanks. I thought you were going to grab a few things and leave."

"I am, after I take a shower," PJ replied with a smirk.

Regine grew uncomfortable, thinking, *What if I made a mistake by coming here?* When PJ exited the living room, she remained on the sofa watching TV. Unfortunately, her thoughts were completely focused on how she put herself in this awkward situation.

When PJ finished showering, he walked into the living room with a pink towel wrapped around his waist. He sat right next to Regine on the sofa, but she quickly scooted away and looked at him with a questioning gaze.

PJ scooted closer and held her hands as he spoke. "I know we just met, but can I have one little kiss?"

Regine yanked her hands from his grasp, then abruptly stood up. "No!" she sharply replied. "I think we should leave."

PJ stood up and faced her. "Regine, I fell in love with you when I first laid eyes you. Baby, I love you," he convincingly said, as he cupped her faced and looked longingly into her eyes.

"You do?" she weakly asked.

"Yes, I do. I know this is soon, but I want you to be my girl," PJ said, before he passionately kissed her. Then he persuaded Regine to come with him to his bedroom where the lights were turned off and pink and green candles were lit.

PJ's heart was beating rapidly as he delicately removed her clothes. When he loosened his towel, he was noticeably erect. "Baby, tell me how much you need me," he pleaded, as he kissed along her neck.

"I…I….yeah," Regine breathlessly mumbled.

Regine's admission heightened PJ's desire. He was on fire as he devoured her breasts and kissed every inch of her body. He slowly pulled away and sat down on the bed. "Baby, get on your knees," he softly ordered.

"What…?"

"Just trust me."

When Regine got on her knees, PJ opened his legs and slowly kissed her lips and neck. Then he grabbed the back of her head and forced her face into his lap. She quickly yanked back.

Perplexed, PJ asked, "You're not going to make me feel good?"

"How?" Regine innocently asked, as she stood up and backed away.

Reaching for her, PJ softly said, "Come on, baby. It's not going to hurt you."

"I can't do it," Regine nervously responded.

PJ smiled. "Baby, I won't hurt you; just relax." He stood up and nudged her to lie down on her back. Then he slowly got on top of her and felt how tight she was. PJ looked at her face and saw tears in her eyes.

"Why didn't you tell me you were a virgin?" PJ asked out of frustration.

"Um…I don't know," Regine whimpered.

PJ lightly brushed his hand along her jaw line. "Baby, it's okay. I'll take my time with you." He slowly kissed her lips, and repeatedly whispered, "I love you. I love your body." Then he rubbed and gently kissed her breasts. He was fully aroused when he touched between her legs.

When he finally inserted himself inside her, Regine screamed. She was in enormous pain, but PJ did not care. He was no longer the loving and gentle man she met earlier; he became a beast. He ravaged her body as if it were his last meal, and ignored her cries to slow down.

"PJ… it's hurting!" Regine cried out, trying to push him off her. "You're…hurting me!"

"Baby, just take it!" PJ demanded, as he suddenly started shivering. He climaxed, then crashed on top of her from exhaustion.

Bells and whistles suddenly went off in her head. *He didn't… use a condom. What if I'm pregnant?* Regine conveyed her concerns, but PJ told her he could not have babies. She was relieved and accepted his explanation - *sort of.*

A couple hours later, PJ asked her to get dressed so he could take her home.

"Why can't I stay with you?" Regine shyly asked.

PJ fumbled for the right words. "I don't mean to sound rude, but you can't stay here tonight. I'll pick you up tomorrow, I promise," he unconvincingly said, satisfied he had accomplished his goal.

Regine hoped she did not make a fool of herself. She was having mixed feelings over her first sexual encounter. She wanted her high school crush, Guy Simmons, to be her first, and was disappointed when he did not express an interest in her.

PJ and Regine were quiet during the drive back to her dorm. When they arrived in the parking lot, PJ did not bother walking Regine to her dorm room. Instead, he stayed in his car and left the ignition on, purposely avoiding her flustered gaze.

Regine slowly exited the car, then turned back to PJ and asked, "Are you going to call me?"

"Yeah baby. I'll call you tomorrow," he replied with a poker face.

Justina was up waiting for Regine, worried that something happened to her. Her fear turned into anger when Regine finally entered their dorm room. She jumped out of her bed, and barked, "Ms. Thang! It's about time you came in. Where have you been?!"

Regine did not respond. She bit her bottom lip, averting her eyes downward. She suddenly felt ashamed under Justina's intense scrutiny.

Justina squinted her eyes, then walked over to Regine and pretended to sniff her body. She suspected Regine had had sex, based on her disheveled appearance.

"You skank!" Justina furiously stated. "I didn't realize I had a freak for a roommate. Before you know it, that boy is going to spread rumors about how easy you are. Did you at least use protection?!"

Without saying a word, tears began flowing down Regine's face.

"How could you be so stupid?!" Justina cruelly asked, clearly disappointed in Regine. "You know about STDs. What about pregnancy? I thought you had better sense than that," Justina added, before storming out of their dorm room, slamming the door behind her.

Regine felt humiliated. Almost everything Justina predicted came true. Regine did not get an STD, but she did get pregnant. PJ denied he was responsible, and told all of his friends she was easy. He even stopped taking her phone calls. Considering PJ's negative reaction towards her, Regine decided it would be best not to have the baby.

Her grandmother called her after she had the abortion. "Baby, are you okay?" Bessie asked with grave concern.

"Yes, Grandma. I'm fine," Regine sorrowfully replied.

"Regine, I need to ask you some questions about this PJ character."

Regine frowned. "Why? We're not in a relationship anymore, or whatever you want to call it."

"I know, but I need his address," Bessie insisted. "And I need to know what type of car he drives."

Regine had no idea why her grandmother needed the information, especially since PJ made it clear that he did not want to have anything to do with her. Unfortunately, she knew she could not win this argument with her grandmother.

Regine exhaled loudly, before she said, "His address is 789 SW 7th Avenue, and he drives a white Toyota Celica. But Grandma, why…?" Before Regine could finish her question, she heard the dial tone.

At seventy-five, Bessie Croswell lived alone in Manassas, Virginia, and had always played a major role in Regine's life. Bessie never remarried after her husband died, but she was in a relationship with a Deacon at her church. Sue, Regine's mother, was her only child, and a pleasant surprise at thirty-seven years old. But Regine, her granddaughter and Sue's only child, was her '*heart*'.

Bessie would do anything to ensure no harm ever came to Regine. She was extremely disheartened over Regine's recent situation. As soon as she discovered what PJ did to Regine, she frantically called her best friend, Lucy, to explain what happened.

Lucy said, "You must calm down and try not to worry." Then she gave Bessie a piece of her own advice. "You have to let go, and let God."

After hanging up the phone, Bessie looked at the piece of paper with PJ's information. Then she picked up the phone to make another important call. While dialing the numbers, she mumbled, *"God might need a little help this time."*

Regine did not know PJ, *AKA* Paul James, was involved in a two-year relationship with Ulysses Jones, his childhood friend. She also did not realize he shared his apartment with Ulysses.

Ulysses is a "wanna-be" Alpha Kappa Alpha, which is a sorority established and incorporated by African American college women. He proudly wore and displayed the organization's colors: pink and green. He was openly gay, but PJ was on the 'down low'.

Ulysses found out about Regine and went ballistic. He and PJ got into a physical altercation but made amends soon after. Unfortunately, it did not take PJ long to resume his playboy antics.

One month later, Ulysses caught PJ kissing a young lady in front of their apartment building. This was all the proof he needed.

"I can't believe this crap!" Ulysses screamed in a high-pitched voice. "Tell me I am seeing things!" Then he flamboyantly snapped his fingers twice in the air before getting in PJ's face. "Now what?! What excuses do you have now?!"

PJ was stumped but quickly recovered. "Stop trippin' and don't start anything, Ulysses," he said, trying to sound hard.

With each syllable, Ulysses snapped his fingers in the air, as he said, "Oh…no…you…didn't!" Then he placed his hands on his hips. "Oh honey, you got me confused. Either you tell her the real

deal, or I tell her!" he yelled, as he rolled his eyes in the young lady's direction.

The young lady suspiciously observed their exchange and turned
to PJ. "Are you gay?"

"Nah...how you figure that?" PJ casually replied.

Ulysses could not believe PJ just lied. He turned to the young
lady and said, "That chump is as straight as a circle." Then he turned
to PJ. "Baby, stop playing in the closet. You got one leg in and one
leg out. For once, keep it real," he added, as if daring PJ to deny it.

"I don't have time for games," the young lady replied, then
quickly walked away from the scene.

PJ was furious when he turned to face Ulysses. "What did I tell
you about telling my business?!"

"I wouldn't tell your business if you kept it real!" Ulysses boldly
replied. "You know what, I can't deal with this anymore. It is over!
Get your things and get out of my apartment right now!" he demanded, before he turned his back on PJ and walked away.

"I'm not going no damn where!" PJ yelled, before running up
behind Ulysses and pushing him to the ground.

Ulysses quickly got to his feet and dusted off his tight-fitting
jeans. "What?!! You put your damn hands on me!" he screamed, as
he ran up on PJ, swinging.

PJ fell to the ground and stayed down. Ulysses towered over PJ,
cursing him out and slapping him multiple times in the face. When
the fight was over, PJ looked like a wounded animal. His light-
brown face turned blotchy red. It was at that moment, PJ knew their
relationship was over.

The next day, PJ returned to the apartment to get his belongings,
but he was attacked at gunpoint. His attacker caught him off guard
while he was opening the trunk of his car. He was gagged, blind-
folded, and thrown in the trunk of his own car.

PJ thought Ulysses was behind this, until the attacker commented, "So, you are the punk that messed over Regine?! I bet
you're sorry you picked the wrong girl to screw over." Without
waiting for PJ's reply, he slammed the trunk shut, got behind the
wheel of PJ's car and drove off.

One would call this karma, but PJ knew it was a personal vendetta; one that had him crying and begging for mercy. He felt bad
about the way he treated Regine, and was going to apologize to her.
Now he realized he may never get the opportunity. PJ silently
prayed and wished this nightmare would end soon.

The thirty minutes he was locked in the trunk of the car, felt like
an eternity. He heard the car engine, and felt every lump and bump

in the road. Then he became alarmed when he felt the car going up a long rocky road before coming to a complete stop.

PJ mumbled through the duct tape, "God, please forgive me for my sins," right before the trunk opened. All he could do was cry for mercy as his attacker repeatedly struck his head with a metal pipe. He grew weaker by the second, and his blood splattered every time the pipe came down. On the tenth blow, his life ended.

The attacker emptied PJ's wallet, taking his ID and cash, before slamming the trunk shut. Then he put PJ's car into neutral and pushed it over the ledge into the Atlantic Ocean.

Two weeks later, Ulysses called Regine. "Hi," he said with an attitude. "I just need to know if you heard from PJ."

"Who are you?" Regine asked.

"PJ's lover, have you seen him?"

Regine raised a brow. "His lover?"

"Yes, he is...or was my partner," Ulysses sassily replied, as he twisted his mouth. "You have a problem with that?!"

"No. I haven't seen PJ, and I'd appreciate it if you don't call here anymore," Regine said, before she hung up the phone. She did not know which was more shocking; the fact that PJ was bisexual, or that he was missing. She was mad at him, but not enough to wish him harm. What she did not know was that someone had sought vengeance on her behalf. This person loved her immensely, and was willing to go to great lengths to make her happy.

The police detectives closed the case after failing to find any leads into PJ's disappearance.

Chapter 8
Possibilities

Regine returned to St. Petersburg and chalked up her relationship with PJ as a learning experience. She eventually got over him, but the situation had hardened her heart. Whenever she went on a date, she would put up a barrier no one could penetrate. Her dates never moved beyond a friendly good night kiss.

At twenty-years-old, Regine wanted to pursue her own goals. With financial support from her godparents, she moved into her own apartment. She also enrolled in the St. Petersburg Culinary Arts School to begin her dream of becoming a professional chef and owning her own restaurant one day.

Shortly after settling into her apartment, Regine went grocery shopping and spotted Guy. She slowly pushed her cart next to his and instantly felt a connection.

"Hi Guy," Regine said with caution.

Guy turned around and was truly surprised. "Hello Regine. What are you doing here? I thought you were in college."

"I decided to come back home," Regine said without alluding to the real reason. "College wasn't for me. What about you?"

"I just received a promotion on my job," Guy proudly announced, "and I'll be graduating from community college soon. I'm sort of on a fast track. But, I'm having a hard time gaining custody of my siblings, even though they live with me."

Regine smiled. "It doesn't surprise me that you're fulfilling your goals. What's the hold up with your custody request?"

"My aunt and uncle are contesting it. We go to court again in six months."

"Who's the judge presiding over your case?"

"Judge Nicole West. Why do you ask?"

"I think I can help you. I'll ask my godfather to see what he can do."

Guy's eyes grew bigger. "You would do that for me?"

"Sure. There are no hard feelings between us," Regine softly admitted. *Just the love I have for you. This boy knows how to rock my world. Is it hot in here, or is it me?!*

"I'm glad to know this," Guy said with a smile. "Are you still living with your godparents?"

"No, I rent an apartment on the North side, off Third Avenue."

"You're about thirty minutes away from me," Guy acknowledged.

Regine dug into her purse and retrieved a pen and paper. "You should stop by for a visit if you're in the neighborhood. Let me give you my number," she said, as she wrote her phone number on the paper and gave it to him.

Guy took her number and tucked it in his wallet. "Thanks," he sincerely said. "I'll call you. Oh, by the way, have you heard from Justina?" he asked, hoping there was still a chance to reconnect with her.

"Yeah…she's fine," Regine nonchalantly replied. *After all this time, he is still asking about her. Unbelievable!*

Guy eagerly said, "Tell her I said '*hello*' if you hear from her again."

"Will do," Regine said, before moving in the direction of the cashier. Regine knew she would not relay this message, just like all the other ones Guy asked her to relay to Justina when they were in high school.

☼

Desperate to gain legal custody of his siblings, Guy called Regine the next day. She reassured him that her godfather would help with the legal custody issue. Soon after, they began bonding. Initially, they met at restaurants and other public places to talk about what was going on in their personal lives. Eventually, Guy began seeing Regine in a different light, and learned they had a lot in common.

They also shared family secrets. Regine told him her mother was a crack addict, and Guy admitted that his mom was his father's mistress. Guy frowned as he reflected, aloud, on his most painful memory. "I remember all the nights my mother begged my dad to spend time with her, only to be rejected most of the time," he sadly admitted.

"That must've been hard for you," Regine sympathetically commented.

"Yeah, it was."

Guy looked at Regine and smiled. "I enjoy being with you."

"Me too," Regine said with a wide grin.

"You're so easy to talk to," Guy sincerely admitted. "I never thought I could tell anyone about my past, especially about my parents."

"At least your mom and dad were a part of your lives," Regine said, as she reflected on her life. "I can't even remember what my dad looked like. He died when I was four. And I haven't seen my mom in eight years. She stays in touch with my grandmother, though. That's the only way I know she's alive. She chose drugs over me."

Guy hugged Regine in response. It was therapeutic for both of them to get all of their pent-up emotions out in the open. Regine was especially relieved to find someone she could trust to share certain aspects of her past life with. Some things she had never shared with anyone else, not even Justina.

Over the next two years, Guy and his siblings grew accustomed to Regine's presence and, for the most part, enjoyed having her around. Regine was also happy being a part of their lives. She spent a lot of time with Guy's sisters. They liked her, but were very protective of Guy. Alex's reaction to Regine was the complete opposite of his sisters'; he was distant and cold. Regine was troubled by his disposition toward her, but she smiled every time he ate her home-cooked meals. He especially liked her homemade cakes.

When Regine's godfather, Judge Bryan O'Neal, realized she was spending so much time with Guy, he wondered if he should notify her father. However, Kevin had already found out about Guy. He also knew Regine had dropped out of college and recently enrolled in Culinary Arts School; he personally footed her bills, including her car and other expenses while allowing her godparents to take full credit. He was not surprised to hear about Regine's close connection to Guy's family, especially since she had no connection with her own biological parents.

Kevin had arranged for Regine to be placed in custody of the O'Neal's after her mother became hooked on drugs. Considering his criminal background, Kevin knew the courts would never grant him custody. He had a hard life growing up in shelters and foster homes throughout most of his childhood, and feared Regine would be subject to the same atrocities he encountered.

Consequently, Kevin contacted Bryan O'Neal, the judge who presided over a criminal case against him when Regine was four years old. The judge had placed him on probation for a drug trafficking charge, a much lesser charge for the crime he committed. No one in the courtroom knew they had made a side deal.

The judge agreed to care for Regine after Kevin agreed to pay off his $500,000 gambling debt. Cecilia, his wife, did not know about her husband's gambling habit. She was just overjoyed to be given the opportunity to raise Regine, especially since she did not have any children of her own. Regine never knew about this arrangement, and had assumed the O'Neals were her godparents since her birth.

Kevin had four daughters, including Regine, from four different women. Regine was the oldest. They never met each other, or knew the others existed. Kevin did not visit any of them, but financially supported all of them. He would do anything for his daughters, including the *unthinkable*. Although he was not physically in their lives, he discreetly had someone watching over them. He had instructed these individuals to take matters into their own hands if harm ever came to any one of them.

At Regine's insistence, her godfather reluctantly agreed to assist Guy with his custody request. Judge Bryan O'Neal made a few contacts and arranged for one of his colleagues to preside as judge over the hearing. In addition, an attorney mysteriously appeared at Guy's front door and offered to represent him, *pro bono*. The attorney told Guy he had heard about his custody request, and found it interesting that a young man wanted the responsibility of raising three children.

With the influence of Regine's godfather and the attorney, Guy was easily granted custody of his siblings. Actually, his attorney was not pro bono. He was paid a healthy sum for his legal services, courtesy of Guy's stepmother, Jeanine Benedict. She found out about the custody request and inconspicuously intervened.

Guy breathed a sigh of relief when he won custody of his siblings. He could not believe his Aunt Mercy broke down in the courtroom, begging him to let her continue receiving Social Security checks for the children. She backed down after the judge told her that she could go to jail if she cashed any more checks. Guy knew he and his siblings would never see or hear from Mercy and Nate again.

One-and-a-half-years later, Guy attempted to purchase his first home. He was heartbroken when he received a rejection letter on his loan request. However, Jeanine found out and made a personal phone call to the president of the bank. The very next day, the bank contacted Guy with a change of heart. They approved his loan, and even gave him more than he had asked for.

Jeanine was also partly responsible for Guy's progressive career. He was a good worker and impressed his managers with his skills. But when Jeanine became an anonymous majority shareholder for Calvent Lucent Technology, his career took off. He received three successive promotions within a three-year period, all while attending college.

Guy felt really good about his accomplishments, and realized the only thing lacking in his life was true love. He was not in love with Regine, but grew to love her as a good friend and confidant. The closest he had ever come to being in love was with Justina.

Regine wanted to show Guy she was all he needed. She decided to take their relationship to the next level by seducing him one night while they were watching a movie at his house. It all started with small kisses along his neck and around his mouth, which lead to touching along the crotch area of his pants.

When Regine unzipped his pants and touched his hardness, he did not push her hand away. Instead, he led her into his bedroom where they undressed. Then he put on a condom while she stretched across his bed on her back. Guy slowly got on top of her and entered. There was no foreplay; just a lot of humping, while Regine laid there wishing she had not initiated sex with him. Guy did not kiss her, nor did he tell her he loved her. Within five minutes, he climaxed, turned over and went to sleep.

Guy was not a virgin, but he did not have any good sexual experiences. His take on sex generated from his first encounter with a stripper, when he was fifteen. Nate thought he was too soft, so he took Guy to the backroom of a local strip club where he arranged a '*sex for money exchange.*'

The stripper made Guy sit in a chair while his uncle sat in the back of the room to observe. Guy thought the stripper was heavy and smelled musky as she gave him his first lap dance. Remnants of her sweat soiled his pants when she stood up and juggled her super-sized breasts in his face. He turned away and held his breath.

His Uncle Nate quickly sat up on the edge of his chair and grumbled, "Boy, don't turn away! Touch 'em! Show her you are the man."

Fear of backlash from his uncle encouraged Guy to do as he was told. He looked at the stripper's breasts, and the first thing that came to his mind was cow nipples. Guy yanked on them as if he were milking a cow.

The stripper yelled, "Ouch! What are you doing?!"

His Uncle Nate was laughing so hysterically, he practically fell out of his chair.

"I...I...don't...know," Guy stuttered.

Guy was being honest. At that time, the only time he had ever seen a naked body was on one of those late night soft porn flicks on cable. He found the channel by accident.

His Uncle Nate grew frustrated and pushed Guy aside. "Move over, boy!" Nate demanded, as he unzipped his pants and motioned for the stripper to satisfy his desire. "I gotta get my money's worth."

Guy's other experiences with neighborhood girls ended on the same note - *physical and loveless*. He had always dreamed of making love to Justina, not Regine or any other girl. He knew he could not commit to Regine, because he did not love her - not like she wanted or deserved to be loved.

Regine stayed awake wondering where Guy's heart was. She did not feel the love and passion she anticipated when she initiated sex with him. His body was with her the entire time, but his mind was somewhere else. She believed it was focused on Justina.

Regine decided to address her insecurities by calling Justina one night out of the blue. Justina had just returned from a Sorority party, and was annoyed when the phone rang. "Hello," she hastily answered.

"Oh, hi. How are you?" Regine asked, trying to sound chipper.

"Okay, I just got in. Wassup?" Justina asked, balancing the phone to her ear while undressing herself with her free hand.

Regine's voice trembled. "I hope...I'm not bothering you, but...I need to know...if you're interested in Guy."

"What?! I can't believe you're calling me about that loser!"

"Wait, let me explain."

"No!" Justina exclaimed. "I dealt with your foolish obsession over this idiot back in high school! Now you listen to me, and make sure you get this right. Guy will never meet my standards. I am too good for him!" she sharply added, before slamming the phone down on its cradle.

Regine heard the dial tone and instantly regretted calling Justina. She instinctively called her grandmother to explain her dilemma. Bessie told her to pray about the matter. *"Let go and let God",* was her grandmother's response to all problems. She took her advice.

Chapter 9
Glass Half-Empty

Justina graduated Magna Cum Laude from Central Tillman University with a degree in criminal justice. She also became a member of the Alpha Phi Sigma National Honor Society. She was looking forward to moving to Athens to attend the University of Georgia's School of Law in the fall.

When Justina returned home for the summer, she discovered Guy had left numerous phone messages for her. She did not understand his insistent attempts to contact her, especially since she never returned any of his calls. Unbeknownst to Justina, her father made Guy aware of her visits, and had convinced him that Justina was a *'good catch'* with a big heart. From the first day they met, Mr. Reyes admired Guy's drive and ambition. Unfortunately for Guy, Mr. Reyes was solely looking out for his daughter's best interest.

Justina looked out her bedroom window, which faced the front of the house, and saw Guy pulling up in a nice car. Her heart dropped, but she quickly recovered after taking a closer look at the female passenger. She shook her head in disgust before she went outside to greet them.

"Hey Regine, it's good to see you!" Justina pretentiously exclaimed with a weak hug. Then she checked out Regine's physical appearance, and mischievously added, "I see you've gained some weight."

Regine's spirits were crushed. "I didn't gain too much," she defensively replied. "So, how's life treating you?" she asked, quickly changing the subject.

"Life is good!" Justina cheerfully replied. "I can't wait to start law school." She went on further to explain what her plans were after law school.

Guy stood in the background listening to their animated conversation, with his eyes fixated on Justina.

Justina glanced over at him. "Oh, I'm sorry Guy. I didn't mean to ignore you."

Guy was gloating when Justina acknowledged him. "It's okay," he replied with a light chuckle. "I figured I'd give you ladies enough time to catch up. So how are you, Justina?"

"I'm fine. How are you?" Justina responded with a plastered smile.

Guy unwittingly replied, "Well, considering you never returned my messages, I'm just fine." *I know I sound bitter, but she could have returned at least one of my phone calls. I must admit - she looks good. Wow, her hair has grown, and she put on a few needed pounds in all the right places.*

Regine noticed Guy drooling over Justina, and quickly chimed in. "Yeah Justina, we've been trying to contact you," she said, eyeing Guy with disgust.

"I'm sorry, but I've been busy," Justina explained, turning up her nose. "You know, making sure I study hard, so I can become a successful attorney," she arrogantly added. *What do they want from me?! I still cannot believe Regine became a ready-made mom to Guy's rug-rat siblings.*

Justina turned to Guy and uncaringly asked, "Do you have legal custody of your siblings yet?"

"I received custody two years ago," Guy said, as if he accomplished this goal all by himself. "Yep, life is good. I also purchased a house a couple of blocks from here."

Justina looked at him in amazement. "That's nice. I'm so happy for you." Then she eyed the Mercedes Benz and asked, "Is that your car?"

"Yes, you like it?!" Guy asked, but did not wait for Justina's response. "My job pays me well, so I can afford to splurge a little."

Regine could not believe Guy was bragging. She was unnerved by his cockiness. She had never seen this side of him.

"It's cute," Justina nonchalantly replied. "Are you still employed with that technology company?"

Guy's eyes beamed with excitement, as he proudly said, "Yeah! I was just promoted to Operations Supervisor."

Justina looked up, as if remembering. "Oh yeah, I remember my dad commenting about that company."

"Yes, he did," Guy confirmed. "Your dad is a smart man. Luckily, I purchased stock in the company just before it soared through the roof."

"Justina, it's getting late," Regine interjected, pretending to look at her watch. "We have to pick up the girls from soccer practice. Maybe we can all go out to dinner while you're here."

"Yeah, maybe," Justina all but knowingly replied. She weakly embraced Regine and extended her hand to Guy. It was an awkward moment of silence before Guy and Regine retreated to his car and drove away.

As soon as Guy expressed an interest in going to visit Justina, Regine invited herself along. He told her it was not necessary, but she insisted. She could only imagine what it would have been like had she not accompanied him. Fearing Guy would try to see Justina again, Regine devised a plan to keep him so busy with her and the girls that he would forget about Justina.

After they picked up the girls, Regine decided to put her plan into action. She made sure the twins heard her loud and clear. "Guy, I was just thinking, maybe we should take the girls to Disney World this weekend," she cheerfully announced. Then she briefly glanced in Dana and Cassandra's direction with a smile, and added, "Especially since this weekend doesn't fall on a holiday."

"Way cool!" Dana cheered with excitement. "Please…please can we go?" she asked Guy.

"Yeah, you promised," Cassandra whined. "You told us if we brought home good report cards, you'd take us."

Sensing Guy's reluctance, Regine said, "Guy, you never spend time with the girls, because of your busy job schedule. They've been more than understanding. I think we should take them."

Guy thought about it and decided this trip would also give him an opportunity to get to know Justina better. "Yeah, maybe you're right." he said, as he briefly glanced back at the girls. "Hey, girls!" Guy said loud enough for Dana and Cassandra to hear. "It looks like we're going to Disney World!"

Then Guy turned his attention to the road, still unable to shake Justina from his thoughts. "Maybe I'll give Justina a call later to see if she'd like to go. She'll probably say no, but there's no harm in asking." He purposely avoided Regine's questioning gaze. Dana and Cassandra were excited, but Regine was furious.

Regine could not believe her plan was about to blow up in her face. "Guy, I'm free this weekend," she made known, wondering if he had purposely dismissed her. "I'm sure you're going to need help with the girls."

When Guy did not respond, Regine became furious. "You heard me?!" she asked, unable to suppress her anger.

"Yeah," Guy halfheartedly replied. He heard her the first time, and had hoped she would get the message.

Regine thought, *I just know he didn't dismiss me. Well, I'm going anyway.*

As soon as they arrived home, Regine bid the girls farewell. Then she hastily got out of Guy's car and rushed to hers. She sat there for a few seconds, dwelling upon what had just transpired before backing out of the driveway.

Guy was unfazed by Regine's reaction. As soon as he walked into his house, he picked up the phone and dialed Justina's number.

"Hello, may I speak to Justina?"

Justina instantly picked up on Guy's voice. "Ugh…may I ask who is calling?" she asked in a disguised voice.

"This is Guy."

"I'm sorry, she's not home," Justina said in a deeper voice. "She's out of town and I don't know when she'll be returning."

Guy rolled his eyes and shook his head after detecting Justina's voice. "It'll be before she starts law school, right?" he sarcastically asked.

"She didn't say, but I'll be sure to relay your message." This time Justina forgot to disguise her voice.

"Okay, but make sure you tell her I called, Justina," Guy angrily said, before he hung up on her.

The next morning, Regine was all packed and ready to go with Guy and the girls. She pulled into his driveway just as he opened the trunk of his car. Regine sighed as she walked to his car with her bag. Guy hesitantly stood back as she quietly and boldly put her bag in the trunk. Then she got into the front passenger seat and happily greeted Dana and Cassandra, who were buckled up in the backseat. Unlike Guy, they were happy to see her.

Guy shook his head as he closed the trunk. He opened the door and got behind the steering wheel, briefly glancing in Regine's direction. "Good morning," he tersely said, avoiding eye contact.

"Good morning to you," Regine mumbled.

During the two-hour drive to Orlando, Florida, Guy and Regine were cordial, but their conversation was lighter than usual. When they arrived at the hotel, Guy told Regine it would be a good idea to get two rooms.

Regine rolled her eyes and shook her head, figuring he was still upset with her. *If anything, I deserve to be here. I'm going to have a good time, with or without him.*

Upon entering the main ticket gate at Walt Disney World, Regine thought she spotted someone familiar. She looked again; it was Justina. *No! It can't be! There is no way this is a freakin' coincidence.* She looked at Guy to see if he noticed Justina, but he was preoccupied with his sisters. Quick on her feet, Regine strategically turned Guy and the twins in the opposite direction.

As the day progressed, it seemed as if Regine had gotten her wish to keep Justina at bay. That is, until she spotted Justina with her sister, Carmela, and another little girl, five feet behind them in line to board the skyscraper.

Regine panicked as she put her hand on her chest, feigning sickness. "Guy, I'm not feeling well. I was wondering if we could leave now."

"Regine, I'm sorry to hear this," Guy sympathetically replied. "We'll leave after this ride." He realized he had been acting like a jerk, and felt bad for the way he had been treating her.

"No! No!" Dana and Cassandra yelled, simultaneously.

"We can't leave now," Dana explained. "We want to see the parade."

Guy was exasperated. "Regine, why don't you take the car and go on to the hotel," he suggested, as he took his key out of his pocket and handed it to her. "The girls and I will catch up with you later. We'll take a cab."

At that moment, Justina turned slightly and her eyes instantly connected with Regine's, then she noticed Guy. Deciding that it was too late to pretend as if she did not see them, Justina hesitantly walked in their direction.

Regine grabbed Guy's arm. "I've changed my mind. I think I can stay a while longer."

Guy looked at her with genuine concern. "That's not a good idea," he firmly replied, "especially since you're not feeling well. Go on to the hotel room. I have my cell phone, so you can reach me if necessary."

Justina slipped up on the tail end of Guy's last statement. "Regine, I'm so sorry to hear you're not feeling well," she said with no emotional connection.

Guy was pleasantly surprised to see Justina. "I didn't know you were coming!" he said with great enthusiasm. "When did you get here?!"

"This afternoon," Justina casually replied.

Regine remained speechless during Guy and Justina's exchange. She did not know what to say to convince Guy that she was suddenly feeling better.

"I see we're in the same line to board the skyscraper," Guy acknowledged. "You all can ride with us if you'd like," he happily offered.

"Well, I don't know," Justina said, as Carmela and her little friend got out of line and stood next to her.

Guy turned to them and said, "Hi girls. Wouldn't you like to ride with us? It'll be a lot of fun." The girls responded with excitement and agreed.

Guy looked at Justina with a sly grin. "Sorry, it looks like you're outnumbered. We're up next." *This is too surreal. After that trick she played over the phone, Justina is the last person I thought I would see. But here she is; in the flesh.*

Justina was having a difficult time thinking of a good excuse to get out this situation. "I suppose one ride is no harm," she concluded, "but afterward, we're going to watch the parade."

Regine walked away, overwhelmed with grief. *Oh God, where did these tears come from?*

After Regine left, Justina initiated the introductions. "Guy, you remember my sister, Carmela. And this is her friend, Alyssa."

Guy smiled. "It's nice to see you again, Carmela; and it's nice to meet you Alyssa," he said, while shaking their hands. Then he introduced and distinguished the twins. "Girls, say hello." Dana and Cassandra waved their hands instead.

Guy was not worried about this awkward moment. He figured once Dana got to know them better, she was going to talk their ears off. He laughed at the thought. It also helped that the girls were all preteens, which would make it easier for them to bond.

"Come on girls!" Justina said with a jolly attitude. "Let's take the seat up front so we can see the action!"

"That's a great idea!" Guy responded in kind. "Maybe afterward we can all watch the parade together."

Justina pretended to ignore him. She watched the girls get into the ride, then made sure they were safely secured in their seats before taking the seat next to Guy.

Guy watched with amazement as he witnessed Justina's nurturing side. He was beginning to think her dad was right about her.

During the ride, the jerky movements pushed Justina and Guy closer together. He was ecstatic. She was unsure. It was then, Justina realized, for the first time, Guy was really handsome. *God, look at this semi-chocolate man. He has flawless skin, a beautiful smile, and beautiful dark brown eyes. Was I this blind before? Why did it take me so long to realize this man is a Prince?*

When Guy reached for her hand, Justina cautiously placed her hand in his and did not let go until the ride was over. He smiled and became hopeful that they could be together forever.

Justina reflected on this moment with Guy. *Wow, I feel like melted butter. No! No! No! Where did these feelings come from?! Let me just sit back and enjoy the ride, so we can part and go our separate ways.* She slowly pulled her hand away from Guy's grasp when the ride came to a stop.

"Guy, it's been real," Justina said, as she exited the ride.

"Where are you going?" Guy quizzed. "I was hoping we could get together and have dinner after we watch the parade."

Justina looked perplexed, but the girls overheard Guy's request and giggled with excitement. She looked at Carmela's pleading eyes and reluctantly agreed.

"After the parade, we're leaving," Justina firmly stated.

"You mean after dinner," Guy insisted, eyeing the girls for assistance.

Their whining pleas unnerved her. Justina did not want to disappoint her sister, so she went along with Guy's plans.

After the parade, Guy thought he would impress Justina by taking her and the girls to an expensive Chinese restaurant. It worked, because Justina's eyes lit up with excitement. She was beginning to view Guy as a potential mate.

The pleasantries at dinner invoked laughter. Justina seemed to enjoy herself, and Guy felt like he was on cloud nine. He thought this day would never happen. It was awesome spending time with the woman of his dreams.

Justina noticed the restaurant was rather elegant. *Can Guy afford to pay for our meals? I'm sure the bill is well over four hundred dollars. I should offer to go Dutch, but I want to see if he can work to be in my presence.*

After dinner, Guy ordered desserts for the girls. He was caught off guard when Justina told him that she needed to speak to him in private. He readily agreed. They stayed close to the front entrance, to keep an eye on the girls.

"I just wanted to tell you I had a really good time today," Justina shyly admitted. "And to let you know…you're okay."

"Just okay?" Guy jokingly asked.

Justina lightly giggled. "You know what I mean. I saw a different side of you today. Thank you for making today special."

"You're welcome," Guy smoothly replied. "Do you think we'll be able to do this again? Not Disney World, but maybe an actual date."

"Maybe," Justina said with a smile that hinted it was highly possible. Then she leaned over and kissed him. She looked up and smiled as Guy stood still with his mouth wide open.

Guy quickly recovered from shock and kissed Justina back, pulling her closer to him. This time the kiss was long and seductive. Justina felt like she was in heaven. Guy was right up there with her.

In the confines of her hotel room, Regine waited patiently for Guy and his sisters' arrival. A thousand probabilities of what happened between Guy and Justina flashed before her eyes. She had a feeling she lost the battle to gain his love. While whimpering, she dialed the number of the woman she can always rely on.

"Hello…Grandmother," Regine said in an almost inaudible voice.

"Regine, is that you?" Bessie knowingly asked.

"Yes, it's me, Grandma," Regine sobbed, still unable to stop the tears from flowing. Now her voice was barely a whisper. "Grandma, I lost him. I lost him to Justina."

"Baby, it's going to be okay," Bessie said with assurance. "There's a better man out there for you. You deserve so much more than he's willing to give you."

Regine's voice cracked. "But…I can't live without him. I need him…in my life."

"Baby, let's pray. When all else fails, we gotta try Jesus." Bessie prayed over the phone with Regine for the next ten minutes.

Regine felt better but was suddenly tired and overwhelmed by the day's events. After she hung up the phone, she laid across the bed and drifted into a dream. Her knight in shining armor was there, but he was faceless. She interpreted the dream as God's way of replacing Guy with a man who truly loves her.

Bessie's heart was heavy because Regine was hurting. She wished Regine's father could be there for her, especially during times like this. After she hung up with Regine, she dialed Kevin's number. He answered on the first ring.

"It's Bessie. I just got off the phone with Regine. She was crying." Kevin did not respond right away, so she asked, "Did you hear me?!"

Kevin's heart was crushed. He was trying to do everything in his power to control his temper. "Yeah, I heard you."

"Your baby is hurting!" Bessie frantically stated. "She needs you now more than ever. You need to tell her you're alive."

"You know I can't do that. What's going on with her?

Bessie sighed. "It's over a boy. She's taking it hard."

"What's his name? Never mind. I think I know who it is."

Bessie heard a click on the other end of the phone, then suddenly became worried. *Oh God, what have I done?*

When Justina dropped Guy and his sisters off at the hotel, he pulled out his cell phone to call Regine. But there was no answer. He was sure she was awake because the lights were on in her hotel room. Since he was not able to reach her, he told the girls they would be staying in his room.

The next morning, Guy knocked on Regine's hotel door and invited her to breakfast.

"Okay, I'll be ready in ten minutes," Regine glumly responded.

Guy picked up on Regine's solemn mood, and could not understand why she seemed so upset. He found a parking space right in front of the restaurant, where Regine instantly spotted Justina standing near the entrance.

Regine was livid. Within a split second, her disposition ranged from anger to confusion to bitterness.

"Hello Regine. I hope you're feeling better," Justina mischievously said, as Regine exited Guy's car. She wanted to reassure Regine that it was nothing personal.

Regine remained mum as she walked past Justina into the restaurant. There was awkward silence between the three grown-ups throughout breakfast. But the girls were unfazed by their behavior; they entertained themselves.

After breakfast, Justina and Regine parted without saying goodbye. Regine felt betrayed, but Justina had no remorse for what happened between her and Guy the previous night. She enjoyed herself and could not stop thinking about him.

Chapter 10

Sacrifices

The drive home from Orlando seemed longer than usual. Guy and Regine were not speaking. He had never seen her so quiet and distant. He wondered what he could possibly say to her to make things better between them.

Regine pretended not to notice Guy's fleeting glances in her direction. She used the time to focus on her future. Regine knew she was ready to leave Florida, and was at peace with her decision.

When they arrived home, the ice between them cracked a little; at least Regine was talking to the girls. She loved them and it was obvious that they loved her. She hugged Dana and Cassandra, then quickly grabbed her things from Guy's car and headed for hers.

Guy dropped his keys, rushing after her. "Regine, hold up! Why are you leaving so soon? I was hoping we could talk."

Regine turned around and came face to face with Guy. "Talk about what?!" she snapped. "Please don't insult me. You know, I hope you and Justina stay together for your sake. You never gave me a chance to be a part of your life after all these years, but you're in for a rude awakening. It didn't take me long to figure out Justina is all about Justina, and what people can do for her. You may not understand now, but I guarantee you will. Have a good life without me."

As she turned to leave, Guy grabbed her arm. "But wait! Let me explain!"

Regine snatched her arm away. "Explain what?!" she angrily questioned. "That you're just like your father!"

"I'm nothing like him!" Guy countered with a hint of agitation.

Regine frowned. "In a way, I agree with you," she smugly replied. "I will never give you the opportunity to use me the way your father used your mother."

"Why are you bringing my parents into this?" Guy asked, perplexed by Regine's rude remarks. "They have nothing to do with us!" he sharply stated.

Regine sighed. "I beg to differ," she confidently replied, then turned and walked toward her car.

"Wait! Let's talk about this!" Guy insisted, as he digested her remarks. *What is she talking about? Oh, she's just jealous. She'll come around, I hope. What did I do?*

Regine ignored Guy as she got into her car and drove off, never looking back. She was overwhelmed by the weekend's events. *I can't believe the sacrifices I made! To think, I went out of my way to make sure he got custody of his siblings! Though, in a way, I feel relieved for this break. I love his sisters and brother, but they are extremely demanding. No more washing clothes, cleaning, cooking, and allowing Guy to enjoy my body without his love, is a refreshing thought.*

The next morning, Guy woke up with a burst of confidence. He had a restless night thinking about his future with Justina. He was sprung, and could not stop smiling. Eagerly, he picked up the phone and dialed her number. Justina answered on the second ring.

"Hello, is this Justina?" Guy hesitantly asked, fearing she may have changed her mind about him.

Justina smiled before responding. "Why yes!" she jubilantly answered, swirling the phone cord with her free hand. "Hello Guy! How are you?"

Guy thought, *Wow! She's actually happy to hear from me!* "I'm okay," he guardedly said. "I was curious to know if you'd be interested in letting me cherish you today."

"That sounds like a big request, but I think I can handle it. What time will you come by to pick me up?"

"How about noon?"

"That's fine. I'll be ready!" Justina happily replied.

Three hours later, Guy promptly arrived at Justina's house. He was nervous when he knocked on the door.

"Hello, Guy," Mr. Reyes happily greeted with a strong handshake. "It's good to see you! Come on in and have a seat. Justina should be down shortly." Then he instinctively sat next to Guy, and asked, "So, how's it going?"

"Everything is well," Guy cautiously replied, fully aware of Mr. Reyes' exaggerated kindness.

"I'm happy you and my daughter are spending time together," Mr. Reyes explained, but refrained from saying more when Justina came downstairs, looking refreshed.

Justina had on a strapless yellow sundress and matching sandals. Her face was adorned with bronze and gold eyeshadow and clear lipgloss. Her naturally wavy, shiny hair flowed down her back. Guy thought Justina looked absolutely stunning.

Mr. Reyes greeted Justina with a kiss. "Have a good time, baby." Then he turned to Guy. "Son, take care of her."

Guy smiled after realizing Mr. Reyes referred to him as his son. "Will do," he said. "I'll have her home on time."

"Don't worry about the time," Mr. Reyes said with a wink. "Just enjoy yourselves."

Justina was surprised by her father's reaction. In the past, he was always overbearing with her other male companions. She wondered what made Guy the exception, and questioned her father's motives.

Justina walked with Guy hand in hand to his car. "What are your plans for us today?" she asked, eagerly looking forward to a fun-filled afternoon.

"I was hoping we could visit the St. Petersburg Fish Aquarium and take a walk along the pier," Guy explained. "Maybe later, we can have lunch at Coquinas. They have the best Bahamian conch fritters and baby-back ribs. After that, we could wind down at my place and watch a movie with my sisters," he added, as he opened the passenger door for her.

Guy walked around to the driver's side, got in, and looked over at Justina. That's when he noticed the frown on her face. "What?" he finally asked, confused about Justina's sudden change in attitude.

Justina remained mum as she crossed her arms and pouted.

"You don't like my plans?" he finally concluded, when she did not respond. "I tell you what… whatever you'd like to do, we'll do it."

"Are you sure?!" Justina asked with a burst of excitement.

Guy smiled. "Sure, your wish is my command."

"Well, if that's the case, let's go on a day cruise!" Justina ecstatically stated. "You can purchase tickets from the tollbooth at the pier. Since the yacht docks at the pier, we'll still have time for a little sightseeing. Oh, by the way, the yacht has a restaurant. They serve scrumptious gourmet food," she explained, before noticing Guy's blank expression. *Why is he looking at me as though I lost my mind!? Why surely he can see that I'm worth every one of his hard-earned pennies.*

"Sure, Justina," Guy reluctantly agreed. He thought, *I feel another hole in my pocket. Maybe it wasn't a good idea for me to stash most of my savings in my wallet during the Disney World trip. Justina thinks I make mad dough.*

They walked around the yacht talking about everything under the sun. Justina was giddy with excitement, and Guy acted like he won a million dollars. Only three other couples were on the same yacht, which gave them more than enough space to talk privately and take in the Gulf Coast scenery.

They ventured to the top deck when Justina turned to face Guy. "Do you like it so far?!" she cheerfully asked.

Guy smiled in response.

"Look at you!" Justina playfully teased. "I knew you would!"

Guy looked into her eyes. "It's beautiful just like you." Then he leaned over and kissed her, ever so gently on the lips.

Receptive to his kiss, Justina wrapped her arms around Guy's neck and engaged in a long, passionate French kiss. They were oblivious to their surroundings. Then Guy looked into her eyes, before he rested his head on her chest, immersing himself in her beauty. Justina rubbed the back of his head and lost control. Opening her legs, she guided Guy's hand up her sundress, giving him consent to slide his hand between her legs.

"I need you now," Justina breathlessly declared.

Guy stared into her eyes and asked, "Are you sure? I wanted our first time together to be special."

"It's special now," Justina insisted, unzipping Guy's pants and caressing his hardness.

Guy did not want to disappoint Justina. Finding a vacant cabin, he guided her inside. Again, he kissed her with fierce passion and desire. While Justina removed her panties, Guy pulled off his pants and boxers, and put on a condom. In an upright position, Guy picked her up and attempted to enter into her flesh. Justina heaved a sigh of relief, as she seemingly held her breath.

"You're so tight," Guy hungrily moaned between kisses, still struggling to enter her. Slowly, he put her down, realizing Justina was a virgin.

"Don't stop!" Justina pleaded, while reaching for him.

"Baby, I don't want to hurt you."

"Please," Justina begged. "I need this!"

"Are you sure?" Guy softly whispered.

"Yes," Justina cooed, pulling him closer to her.

Obligingly, Guy picked her up and laid her across the bed. Then he lifted her sundress over her head and removed her bra. He kissed her feet, slowly moving all the way up to her lips.

Justina moaned with delight as Guy slowly entered her. "Ooh...aah...," she passionately whimpered.

The rhythm of their bodies moved with the sway of the ocean. As they climaxed at the same time, their bodies collided as one. It was evident - *love was in the air*.

Guy held Justina tightly, feeling good about this moment. He also felt honored to have been her first. For the first time in his life, there was an emotional connection when he made love.

Unfortunately, a cloud of doubt filled Justina's subconscious. She could not get over the fact that Guy was a package deal. Plus, she was not even sure if she liked children. This was definitely a deal-breaker.

An hour later, Guy kissed her on the cheek. "Are you okay?" he softly asked, wondering if Justina had doubts about him.

Justina smiled in response. "I think I'm hungry. We can eat out on the deck or eat inside the restaurant."

"I think the deck is better," Guy suggested. "Let's freshen up first."

Guy sought the waiter and had menus delivered to them on the deck. His eyes instantly grew bigger as he stared at the menu prices. Then he whistled as he put the menu on the table and clasped his hands.

Justina thought, *Oh, I get it! He has the menu with the prices.* "What is it Guy?" she knowingly asked. "Don't you like the entrees?"

"It's just...the prices are ridiculous. The least expensive meal is a salad for $49. Can you imagine spending that much money on a salad?" he asked with a hint of frustration.

Justina abruptly threw her napkin on the table. "Just forget it!" she sharply said with an attitude. "I lost my appetite. When we dock, just take me home!" Justina sat back in her chair, crossed her arms, and pouted.

"Justina, please listen to me," Guy pleaded. "I'm working on another promotion at my job. Soon we'll be able to go everywhere and do anything you desire. Right now, my sisters and brother are my main priority. It's just a little difficult to oblige your every request."

"Fine!" Justina snapped. She was unsympathetic, believing she was worth the sacrifice.

"Come on baby," Guy softly pleaded, "don't act this way. I promise I'll make it up to you."

Instead of ordering food, they sat on the deck looking out into the Gulf Coast. Justina ignored Guy's attempts at making small talk.

She concluded it was a mistake – losing her virginity to Guy, and chalked up the whole experience as a lesson learned.

An hour later, they pulled into Justina's driveway, and were surprised to see Regine's car parked across the street.

Regine waited patiently to talk to Justina, to clear the air so to speak. Even after Guy made it clear that he did not want to be her, Regine cared about his siblings and wanted to know whether Justina would be there for them. When she spotted Guy's car, she got out of hers and walked up the path toward Justina's house.

"Hello," Guy said, as Regine approached him. When Regine did not respond, he asked, "Are you okay?"

Regine looked at Guy with disdain before answering, "I'm fine. I hope life is treating you well. Now if you don't mind, I'm here to speak with Justina."

"Sure…you take care," Guy pitifully responded.

Justina hastily retrieved her things from the trunk of Guy's car, then slammed it closed. She quickly walked past Guy as if he were invisible.

"Justina, I'll call you later," Guy cautiously said, figuring she was still upset with him. When she dismissively waved her hand in his direction, he got in his car and drove off, wondering what Regine wanted to talk to Justina about.

"Hi Regine," Justina said with a fake smile. "I'm so happy to see you."

Regine crossed her arms and frowned. "No you're not! So let's stop pretending."

Justina rolled her eyes. "Regine, if this is about Guy, he's not up for discussion. That jerk couldn't even afford to buy me dinner!"

"Justina, are you finished?!" Regine impatiently asked. "You're the one person Guy has always desired. He's been trying to impress you since high school, even after you made it clear to him that he was beneath you. He doesn't have as much money as you think he should, but one day he will."

Justina shook her head in disbelief. "So basically, you're telling me he's camouflaging," she said with a scowl on her face.

Regine frowned. "You don't get it! You've never heard of savings and a budget. I forgot. Ms. Prissy depends upon her physical assets and her parents' good fortune to maintain her lavish lifestyle. If Guy had the money, he would have given you more than you deserve."

Justina rolled her eyes and exhaled loudly.

Regine unfolded her arms and shook her head. "I came over here to see if you were really into Guy," she admitted, "but my perception of you has been confirmed. It's just a matter of time before Guy realizes you're a ruthless, selfish gold-digger," Regine added, before she turned her back on Justina and walked to her car.

Justina did not know her father was within earshot of their conversation. He was disappointed in his daughter, remembering how his wife had the same snooty *"I'm-too-good-for-you"* attitude when they first met.

Mr. Reyes approached his daughter with great disappointment. "Justina, I would like to talk to you for a minute."

"Okay, Dad. Wassup?"

Mr. Reyes smiled before he said, "You remind me so much of your mother. We met when I was working in the maintenance department of Jackson Memorial Hospital in Miami."

Justina looked surprised.

"Yeah, I worked there after I graduated from high school," Mr. Reyes explained, after noticing Justina's reaction. "Your mother wouldn't give me the time or day. Every day I'd speak, but she didn't show any signs of interest. Finally, I cornered her and asked *'what did I do'* to cause her to dislike me. She simply told me that I was the scum on the bottom of her shoes. She questioned why a nurse, an RN at that, would consort with the likes of me. At that time, your mother didn't realize my maintenance job was just part-time. I was also a full-time manager at a local department store.

I moved on after I summed her up as having a superiority complex. Two days later, your mom had a flat tire. She was standing alone in a barely empty parking lot. I offered to assist her, but she told me she had already called her car insurance company for roadside assistance. I waited with her, because I didn't want to leave her alone in an isolated parking garage. An hour passed and she was still waiting for roadside assistance."

Justina could not wait for her father's lecture to end. She knew, from experience, not to interrupt him, because it would take him longer to make his point. In her mind, she was saying, *Hurry up, already!*

"You see, during those days," Mr. Reyes explained, "we didn't have cell phones, so your mom had to enter in and out of the building to use the phone. Each time she entered the building, she noticed me. The last time she exited the hospital, she reluctantly turned to me and asked for my help. The next day, your mom asked me out for coffee, and learned we had a lot in common. As time went on, we discovered we enjoyed sightseeing, walking, and the same movies. It was a year before she realized I was financially secure. She chided me for concealing this information, but thanked me for allowing her to get to know me, instead of my worth."

Justina sighed, then impatiently asked, "Dad, you're telling me all of this to say what?"

Mr. Reyes exhaled loudly, before gazing into Justina's eyes. "Don't judge a book by its cover. Everyone needs someone. As soon as you realize there are no big *I's* and little *you's,* the better off you'll be. I gave you a good life because I had the financial means."

"Dad, don't take this the wrong way, but I want more. And if you're hinting about Guy, drop it! I have no intentions of getting with that loser! My dreams, my future, and my life are bigger than him. Besides, Regine is into him."

"But he only has eyes for you," Mr. Reyes countered, as he kissed Justina on the forehead, realizing he failed to convince her that Guy would be the perfect man for her.

Regine returned to her apartment and quickly packed, taking just the bare essentials for her impromptu trip to Virginia. Next, she called her godparents, the O'Neals, and told them she was going to visit her grandmother.

"Regine, are you sure this is the right decision?" her godmother, Cecilia asked.

"Yes. I need to get away for a while."

"Maybe this will be for the best," her godfather, Bryan said. "Please keep in touch, and call us as soon as you arrive."

"Will do. I love you both so much."

"We love you too," Bryan and Cecilia said in unison.

Chapter 11

In the Mix

*J*eanine placed a small bouquet of flowers on Charlie's tombstone, then knelt by his gravesite. She reflected on her rocky thirty-year marriage to Charlie. She met him during their junior year at the University of Miami. Initially, Jeanine was not attracted to him, but with time, she grew to love him. Two years after graduating from college, Charlie convinced her to marry him.

Jeanine had moved on to work for her father's hotel chain, Trowne Key Estates, after college. She appointed Charlie as her personal assistant after her father outright objected to the idea of Charlie working for the company. Jeanine worked her way up through the ranks, becoming owner and CEO when her father retired. Two years later, Charlie became unhappy in his role, and expressed an interest in owning his own business. Jeanine helped him by providing business contacts and financial support. When she learned Charlie was mismanaging his business account, she inserted a clause, forcing him to seek her approval prior to any business dealings.

Jeanine was only five feet tall, but considered a shrewd businesswoman with little patience for lies and deception. It often disheartened her to know that the foundation of her marriage was built on lies. She always wondered if things would have turned out differently had she left Charlie the first time he betrayed her.

After Charlie died, Jeanine became comfortable being alone. Initially, she did not regret her decision to remain childless. She would not have wanted her child to witness their loveless marriage. However, Charlie's revelation about his sons sparked her interest.

To this day, Jeanine kept a picture of Guy and Alex on the mantel in her living room. She smiles every time she looks at it. In her heart, they were her sons. Because of this, she thought it is was her job to protect them, and take precautions to ensure their well-being. She even made a strategic decision to relocate to Tampa, Florida, after her father passed away. The Gulf Coast, she discovered, is her favorite place; it is so calm and serene. She also wanted to be close to her stepsons, to keep an eye on them.

Jeanine was excited when she learned Guy formed a close bond with Regine. Though, she grew concerned after her private investigator, Tim Carter, reported that Regine's father was connected to the illegal drug world. It was a relief to know he was a nonexistent figure in Regine's life. That is, until Tim discovered that Kevin and Judge Bryan O'Neal, Regine's godfather, were acquaintances. In response, she arranged a private meeting with the judge.

Judge O'Neal knew Jeanine was a powerful woman. When he was forewarned of her connection to Guy, he became overwhelmed with anxiety. He walked into her office with a heavy heart.

"Have a seat," Jeanine firmly instructed, while walking around her desk to confront him.

"Mrs. Benedict," Judge O'Neal weakly said, as he held out his hand to greet her, "it's so good to see you."

Jeanine ignored his extended hand as she removed her reading glasses. She was in deep thought as she sat on the edge of her desk, staring at the judge with a frown and narrowed eyes. In response, Judge O'Neal swallowed air as he sat down and squirmed in his chair.

After a few seconds, Jeanine leaned toward the judge, gazing into his eyes. "I take it you know why you're here," she said in a sharp but measured tone, "but let me make myself crystal clear. I know about your Swiss bank accounts, your gambling debt, and your personal association with Kevin Graham. If so much as a hair disappears on Guy's body, you're going to wish you were dead. Am I clear?!"

The judge pulled out his handkerchief and started wiping perspiration from his forehead. He knew Jeanine was powerful, and could easily have him unseated as judge. He had Googled her name before their visit, discovering she was one of President Obama's financial advisors.

"Can I ask you a question?" Judge O'Neal nervously inquired.

"Sure."

"Does Guy know what you're doing?"

Jeanine raised a brow. "No, and he better not find out! If he does, you will regret it!"

Judge O'Neal shivered at the thought. In his eyes, Jeanine looked ten feet tall. His gut feeling told him she would follow through with her threat, so he decided to refrain from mentioning Guy to Kevin. He remembered when Kevin called him to inquire about PJ after Regine had the abortion. The thought of what probably happened to PJ still kept him awake at night. He did not have any proof, but he believed Kevin had something to do with PJ's disappearance and ultimate demise.

Jeanine listed Guy and Alex as sole beneficiaries of her estate when she found out she had breast cancer. Although she had undergone major surgery to remove the cancer from her left breast three years earlier, she recently discovered the cancer had re-appeared in her right breast.

She was scheduled for chemotherapy on the same day she received an updated status report from her private investigator, Tim Carter. She asked Tim to meet her at her doctor's office, where they would be able to talk privately in the treatment room.

Tim told Jeanine that Guy's sisters adored Regine. He also explained how she was a great role model and mother figure for them. Jeanine smiled in response. She knew Guy could make it without Regine, but she also believed Regine brought stability into his life. She did not want him to go through the rest of his life only to find out he let *Mrs. Right* get away.

"She left him," Tim reported.

"When?" Jeanine curiously asked.

"One month ago."

"How are the kids adjusting?"

"They're okay. It was his fault. He had taken an interest in another young lady named Justina Reyes. She was Regine's best friend."

Jeanine sighed. "The apple doesn't fall far from the tree," she sadly admitted, reflecting on her late husband's transgressions. "What's going on with Justina?"

"I believe she's gone on with her life," Tim said with confidence. "She started law school in Athens, Georgia."

"Good, there's still hope. We have to keep this young lady preoccupied. If Guy is anything like his father, he'll regret his decision and do the sensible thing by going after Regine. Do you have anything in mind?"

"Leave it up to me."

"Just make sure Justina becomes a figment of Guy's imagination. You get my drift?"

"Yes, loud and clear," Tim affirmed.

Chapter 12

Rainy Days

For three consecutive months, since the day at the pier, Justina had been avoiding Guy's phone calls. The last time he tried contacting her, her mother told him Justina had taken an unexpected trip to Jamaica. Mrs. Reyes felt bad for lying to Guy, but agreed with Justina. She did not think he was right for her daughter.

Justina tried to forget about Guy when she started law school at the University of Georgia. However, the thought of him still sent chills down her spine. She had fallen in love with him that day on the yacht, but was in denial. Their feelings must have been mutual, because Guy drove ten hours to visit her during her first semester in law school.

One day, Justina walked out of her apartment, but quickly turned around after seeing Guy's car parked out front.

"Wait!" Guy exclaimed, as he exited his car and slowly approached her. I just want to talk to you.

Justina turned to face him. "There's nothing to talk about! It was a mistake," she firmly said, while crossing her arms.

Guy sighed. "Why did you up and leave for Jamaica without telling me?"

"Guy...it's hard to explain," Justina timidly replied, realizing her mother had lied for her.

"Try me."

"I'm really confused right now. I'm not supposed to feel this way...about...you," Justina stammered, averting her eyes away from him. She could not ignore the way he made her feel.

Guy rubbed his hand across his head out of frustration. "You still don't think I'm good enough for you." He held her hands and looked into her eyes. "Baby, I need you."

"I'm sorry, but I can't see myself being a ready-made mom to your sisters and brother. I'm not right for you."

"I'm not asking you to be their mother. I just want you to give us a chance," Guy stressed, as he cupped her face, then kissed her gently on the lips.

Justina melted in his arms, wanting him to make love to her again.

"Come with me," Guy requested.

"Where?"

"Just trust me," Guy said, as he guided her back to his car.

Apprehensively, Justina got into his car, but suddenly became overwhelmed with doubts about him.

Guy took her to a five-star hotel, where they dined and danced. Later, he escorted her to his hotel room. Guy was on fire as he quickly removed Justina's clothes, then his. Justina nudged him on, licking his neck and moaning while they made love for the second time. An hour later, they fell asleep in each other's arms.

Justina awoke to find Guy standing over her with dreamy eyes. "What?" she groggily asked. She became alarmed when she saw the ring box.

Guy knelt down on one knee, next to the bed. "I love you. I want you to be in my life, my future." He opened the box, which contained a beautiful two-karat diamond engagement ring. "Will you marry me?"

"What about Regine?" Justina asked, as she slowly sat up in bed.

"I love her as a friend, but I'm in love with you."

"I'm sorry Guy, but I want more," Justina coyly admitted. "What we shared was special, but it's not enough. But can I...?"

"What is it?" Guy eagerly asked, hoping she had a change of heart.

"Can I keep the ring?"

Guy was deeply saddened as he hung his head down in defeat. "Yeah, you can keep it."

Justina was delighted to keep the ring, but Guy walked away with his tail between his legs. He returned home with a broken heart.

Two weeks later, Guy began calling Regine, with no success. He realized things were not the same without her. His sisters also tried calling her, to no avail. It hurt him to know she had broken all ties with them.

Guy was sitting in the recliner in the living room, reading a book, when his brother and sisters approached him. "How come Regine doesn't come over anymore?" Dana boldly asked.

"Yeah Guy, look at this house!" Alex sharply stated. "It's a mess," he added, as he looked at the dirty laundry piled on the floor.

"And look at you. Man, you used to be sharp and on point. Why did you run Regine off?"

Guy looked at Alex in disbelief. "What do you care?! You acted like you never liked her anyway. You only liked her when she cooked and cleaned up after you."

Alex briefly held his head down, before he looked up at Guy. "You know it wasn't like that. I like her, but I realized she was wasting her time trying to please you," he sadly acknowledged. "Every time you'd asked her to do anything for you, she was at your beck and call. You knew she loved you, but you made it obvious that you didn't love her back."

Guy was crushed. He knew Alex was telling the truth.

"We miss her," Dana interjected, while Cassandra nodded in agreement.

Alex was exasperated. "It's Justina, isn't it?!" he sharply concluded. "You were always stuck on stupid when it came to her. You blew it over someone who could care less about you, or us. You're such an idiot!" he shouted, before he turned his back on Guy and quickly walked away.

"Watch your mouth," Guy weakly replied. He turned toward the twins and noticed their questioning gazes. "I'll try calling Regine, again," he assured them. "I promise."

They appeared satisfied and retreated to their bedroom. Guy could not believe the backlashing he had just received. *Can't they understand that I'm going through hell too? Regine was my best friend. Justina, well Justina...made me look like a straight up fool.*

Guy grabbed his car keys, ran out the door, and drove to Regine's apartment to beg for forgiveness. "Where in the hell is she?!" he asked aloud, as he stood outside her door. Regine's neighbor overheard him, and told him she had been gone for two weeks. Guy put his head down as it dawned on him that he may never see Regine again.

Over the next four months, Guy tried getting on with his life by dating other women. Every time he went on a date, he looked for Regine's qualities. He quickly learned that the women he dated had far too many issues; they did not like children, they did not know how to cook, or they were more interested in what Guy could do for them.

Shortly afterward, Alex walked into Guy's office and caught him holding a picture of Regine. Alex shook his head. "Man, there will never be another Regine. When are you going to realize that?"

"I know...," Guy mumbled, as he returned the framed picture to the "Wall of Fame," which was Regine's idea. She had everyone's picture personally framed, and tacked a gold star underneath each one. He suddenly noticed how she had put her personal touches on everything in the house.

"You need to find her," Alex insisted.

"I know, Alex!" Guy said, clearly frustrated. "I've been trying. I've been calling her apartment and cell numbers. I also called her godparents and they're not telling me anything. Her godfather even warned me to leave her alone. Can you believe he told me it would be in my best interest to stay away from Regine?"

"Try harder!" Alex persisted, as he walked out of Guy's office.

Guy had been beating himself up over the past four months. *I messed up. Dana and Cassandra barely talk to me. And Alex is upset with me too. I did not realize how much Regine helped me, until recently. We took her for granted. How can I regain her trust?*

Guy rested his elbows on his desk, and covered his face with his hands in agony. Suddenly, he perked up at the thought of calling his best friend, Mike Solomon, who also happens to be a private investigator. They met in junior college, and later attended the University of South Florida where they graduated together.

Mike, also known as Big Mike, was not big in size; he was only 5'8, 165 pounds. Big Mike was a childhood nickname given to him by his family, and had stuck throughout the years. He and his girlfriend met Regine twice, and instantly liked her. They tried to convince Guy that Regine was perfect for him, but Guy told them he was not in love with her.

Guy dialed Big Mike's number, and explained his dilemma.

After hearing Guy's spiel, Big Mike refrained from telling Guy he was a fool.

"I need to find her," Guy said out of desperation.

"Regine's a good woman," Big Mike frankly said. "How did you let her get away?"

"I've been beating myself up ever since she left," Guy sadly admitted. "Just find her."

"I'll do my best," Big Mike confidently replied. "But if she gives you a second chance, don't blow it."

Chapter 13

Movin' On

*A*fter arriving in Manassas, Virginia, Regine realized being away from Guy, and all the drama associated with him, was the right decision. She was busy fussing with her hair in front of the mirror, when Grandmother Bessie walked into her bedroom and sat on the bed.

"Regine baby, come over here and sit down next to me," Bessie insisted. "We need to talk about the move you made to drive all through the night to visit me - not that I mind. I know something is troubling you. You're not running from the law, are you?" she joked with a hearty chuckle.

Regine sat on the bed next to Bessie. "Of course not, Grandma. You're right, though...about something troubling me. It's Guy. I've been in love with him for a long time, and I have done everything possible to prove it to him."

"But what has he done to prove that he loves you?"

Regine briefly looked down as she thought about her grand-mother's question. "He made me feel like I was a part of his family when my own mother didn't want me. Grandma, you were always there for me, but it still hurts that Sue abandoned me."

"Baby, she didn't abandon you. She was ashamed to let you see her like that."

"Grandma, don't do this! Don't make any more excuses for her. What about now?! What is her excuse now?! I'm a grown woman and she doesn't visit or call me."

"Baby, look at her life. She dropped out of college only to wind up on drugs. She's in rehab trying to get her life back on track, so give her a chance."

Regine had always wanted a relationship with her mother, but Sue was like a stranger to her. Though, she was happy to know that her mother was getting help for her addiction.

"Grandma, I wanted things to work out so badly with Guy. I did everything to make it work."

"Regine, you've always been a giver. I was hoping you would've bypassed my trait. When I courted your granddaddy, I did the same thing. I told him when we were going to get married, where we were going to live, and how we were going to prosper. That was the problem – I gave all of me. And the more I gave, the more he took. I didn't realize I wore myself out trying to please that man, until the day he died. I never knew if he appreciated me. So when the Deacon offers to buy me lunch and take me to and from, I accept. You get my drift?"

Regine nodded, then smiled at the thought of her grandmother dating Deacon Alfred Franklin. She had gotten up in the middle of night and caught her grandmother hugged up with the Deacon on the sofa, watching TV. She thought it was sweet.

Bessie continued, "All I'm saying is - if you find yourself giving all the time, it's time for a change."

Regine smiled. "Grandma, can I live with you until I'm able to find a place of my own in Virginia?"

Bessie laughed at Regine's question. "Child, you never have to ask. I'd love for you to stay with me, and you don't need to go out and get your own place either."

"Thank you, Grandma," Regine said, as she embraced Bessie. She conceded she has the best grandmother in the world.

Four months later, Regine decided to call Earl Banks, her classmate from the St. Petersburg Culinary Art School. They had been friends since the first day of school. Whenever she was down and out over Guy, she could always turn to Earl for manly advice.

"Hi Earl. I'm calling to let you know I've decided to permanently relocate to Virginia."

"Are you serious?!" Earl shockingly asked.

"Yes," Regine sadly admitted. "Guy hurt me for the last time. I need a fresh start."

"You don't have to do this," Earl explained. "Guy shouldn't be the deciding factor. You fail to realize that a lot of people care about you. I care about you. I love you," he softly admitted.

Regine was speechless and stunned by Earl's confession. She never realized he was attracted to her. She had always considered him the quintessential pretty boy: light complexioned, wavy hair, tall, slender, and debonair. She also thought he was the type of man who spent excessive time and money on his appearance.

"Regine, did you hear me?!"

"Yes, but…we're just friends," Regine stammered. His confession threw her for a loop. She was not attracted to Earl, and never thought of him as more than a friend.

"Just give me the opportunity to show you how special you are to me. I'd like to come and visit you, if you don't mind."

"Earl, I don't know. My emotions are all over the place right now. Besides, what happened between you and Sara? I thought you two were dating."

"Sara and I are just friends."

"But I thought you and Sara were more than just friends."

Earl sighed. "Regine, I only talked about her because you always talked about Guy. We went out a couple of times, but I realized a long time ago that we could never be more than friends. Besides, Sara and I are too much alike. Everything I want in a woman, I found in you."

Regine did not know what to say. She thought Earl and Sara seemed like the perfect couple. To her, Sara looked like a real life Barbie doll. Her hair was long and always professionally styled, and she had impeccable taste in clothes and shoes. Regine knew Earl was just as vain about his appearance.

"Earl, I don't know," Regine softly said. "You really don't know me well enough to say you love me."

"But you're wrong. I've gathered information about you from every conversation we've ever had. I know you put others' needs before yours. That will change if you give me the opportunity to take care of you. I know Justina and Guy betrayed you. I want to show you that I will never betray you, but shower you with love and attention. I know your mom abandoned you when you were a little girl. Let me be the man that will protect you and never leave you. You told me Guy never told you he loved you. I'm not afraid to admit it. Let me show you how much."

Regine began to cry. "Earl, this is too much to digest," she sobbed. "Let me call you back."

"Just know I won't stop until you're in my life for good. Goodbye for now, my love."

Regine hung up the phone in a daze. Then she went and sought advice about her conversation with Earl. She found Bessie on the back patio reading her Bible. "Hi Grandma, can I talk to you?"

Bessie looked up and smiled. "Sure, baby. Have a seat."

Regine sat down and told Bessie about her dilemma with Earl. Then she looked into Bessie's eyes and asked, "What do you think I should do?"

Bessie's forehead wrinkled from worry. "How well do you know him?"

"Well enough to know that his confession doesn't make any sense."

"Well, that's your answer. Follow your instincts, baby."

"Thanks, Grandma, for always being here for me."

"I wouldn't have it any other way, suga'," Bessie said, as she excused herself to make a phone call.

One month later, Regine returned to St. Petersburg to break her apartment lease and pack up the rest of her belongings. When she pulled into her parking space in front of her apartment complex, her neighbors bombarded her with questions of her whereabouts.

"Regine, your good-looking friend, Guy, came over here several times looking for you," one neighbor explained. "He seemed desperate."

"Yeah, he said it was an emergency," another neighbor chimed in. And another neighbor whispered to another about Guy having it bad for Regine, then added, "Yeah girl, she must've put it on him."

Regine blushed in response, then thanked her neighbors for relaying her messages. Next, she checked her mailbox, then walked into her apartment and immediately turned on her answering machine. She clicked the play button and plopped down on her sofa to listen to her messages.

Beep! "Regine, I know you're there, sweetheart," Guy said. "Please pick up the phone. We need to talk. Regine…I know I hurt you." After a short delay, his voice came back on. "You were right about Justina," he added, before hanging up.

Regine whispered to herself, "I told you so."

Beep! "Regine, I know I haven't been nice to you, but I really do miss you. If you're staying away because of me, I'm sorry. Guy is depressed and you have everyone around here worried about you. Please give us another chance to make it up to you."

Regine immediately sat up on the edge of the sofa, finding it hard to believe that Alex called to apologize. He had always acted like he detested her.

Beep! "Regine, I care about you. I'm sorry. Please Regine…where are you?" Guy probed.

Beep! "Please call me back." Another plea from Guy. The remaining messages were also from Guy.

Regine thought, *Not once did he say he loved me. No Guy, I refuse to return your calls. I need to get on with my life. I deserve someone that truly loves me. And you really need someone you can profess your love to, because it's definitely not me.*

Regine took her phone off the hook, and sat at her computer to type a letter of withdrawal from the Culinary Arts School. Next, she called the moving company. In the end, she decided calling Guy and his siblings was out of the question. She knew her strengths, and they were not one of them.

The next day, Regine went to her landlord's office to break her lease. Initially, she thought someone had died. Approximately one dozen rose arrangements were scattered along the front desk and other surrounding areas. They were strange looking because some were fresher than others.

"Mr. Burger, what's up with the roses?" Regine curiously inquired.

The landlord was startled by Regine's voice, but smiled when he looked up and saw her. "Regine, it's so good to see you!" Mr. Burger exclaimed. "I didn't know how to contact you. These roses are for you. There were specific orders that they not be returned to the florist unless you sign for them. I had to get rid of some of them."

"Are you serious?" Regine rhetorically asked, before she threw her purse on the countertop and read the cards attached to the bouquets. It quickly became apparent that Guy sent all the arrangements. *Regine, you are very special to me. Regine, I care about you. Regine, please call me. Regine, I miss you. Etcetera, etcetera, etcetera.* Not one single note mentioned that Guy loved her, only that he was sorry for causing her grief. She accepted his apology, but was not ready to confront him.

After completing the task of breaking her lease, Regine called Earl and asked him to meet her at their favorite fast-food restaurant. In her eyes, Earl and Sara seemed happy and in love. They always doted on each other, which is why she questioned Earl's admission of his love for her. Regine had already made up her mind about him, and thought it best to talk to him in person.

Earl walked into Miami Subs looking like he just left a photo shoot. He removed his shades when he spotted Regine sitting at a booth in the back of the restaurant. "It's so good to see you!" Earl said with vigor, as he embraced her and gave her a peck on the cheek.

"Same here!" Regine happily replied. "I took the liberty of ordering for us. I hope you don't mind."

Earl looked at the curly fries and hot wings, and dived in. Half-way through their meal, Regine asked, "What's going on between you and Sara?"

"We're just friends."

"I thought about it and I'm telling you, based on my past observations, you were more than just friends. So talk to me."

"It's not important. Have you thought about what I told you?" Earl questioned, before taking a sip of soda.

"Yes," Regine reluctantly admitted.

Earl looked into her eyes for an answer. "Well...?"

"I don't know what to believe," Regine finally said. "I like you, but I never looked at you as more than a friend."

Earl grimaced. "You're still in love with Guy, aren't you?"

"Yes," Regine painfully admitted, "but it doesn't matter. I have to get on with my life."

Earl was getting ready to respond, but heard commotion coming from the front entrance of the restaurant. He became alarmed when a woman frantically headed toward their table. It was Sara, his girlfriend.

"You dog! I knew it!" Sara yelled, before she slapped Earl across the face.

Regine was startled. She had never seen Sara so violent and distressed.

"You claimed you and Regine were just friends!" Sara angrily said, while briefly directing her gaze toward Regine. "So why didn't I know about this little reunion?!"

"But baby, let me explain...," Earl stammered, as he put his hands up to block his face. He feared Sara would slap him again.

"Sara," Regine interjected, "you must believe me when I tell you there's nothing going on between me and Earl."

"Yeah baby," Earl weakly added, "I love you. I would never do anything to hurt you."

"Oh yeah," Sara shrewdly replied, "so why didn't you tell me you were calling off our date to meet with Regine?"

Earl was speechless. He did not know what to say.

"Just what I thought," Sara said, before she turned to Regine. "You can have him! I've taken him back too many times, only to realize he isn't worth it!"

"But baby, wait!" Earl strongly begged, while grabbing Sara's arm.

Sara yanked her arm from his grip. "No! It's over! This is something I should've done a long time ago." Then she turned to Regine.

"He's all yours." On that note, she walked away and never looked back.

Earl sat there, stunned. He looked at Regine for sympathy, but she was seething.

Regine stared at Earl with contempt. "Don't you dare say anything, because there's nothing you can say. You're so selfish! Lose my number. Our friendship is over!" As Regine got up and left the table, she knew she never wanted to see Earl again.

Earl was dumbfounded by what just transpired. He knew he had just ruined his three-year relationship with Sara, and his friendship with Regine. He tried to make sense of why he pursued Regine in the first place. Maybe it was because, deep down, he knew his parents did not like Sara, but knew they would love Regine.

When Regine returned to Virginia, she told her grandmother what happened. In response, Bessie quizzed her about Earl, requesting his address, his place of work, and other information.

"Grandma, what's up with all the questions?" Regine asked with puckered brows.

Bessie shifted her eyes downward. "Nothing, baby. I just want to make sure you're all right, that's all."

Regine shook her head. "Grandma, you are too much. Trust me, Earl is the last person I want to see again," she confidently admitted. She smiled before she kissed Bessie on the cheek and went to her bedroom.

Three days later, Earl was involved in a fatal car accident. The brakes went out on his car while he was driving. He lost control and slammed his car into a tree, avoiding an oncoming collision. Tragically, he died at the scene. Foul play was not suspected, nor was Regine notified of his death.

Chapter 14

Success by Design

The big day finally arrived when Justina walked across the stage to receive her juris doctorate degree. A short time later, she passed the bar exam on her first attempt. Her dream of becoming a big-time attorney was quickly becoming a reality.

Justina decided to intern for Johnson and Johnson Associates, a prestigious law firm in Atlanta that specializes in criminal and civil law. She not only performed well, but also exceeded the firm's expectations. She was a *"fire cracker"* in the courtroom, cutting down anyone who came into her path. There were several occasions in which she made the plaintiffs squirm in their seats.

Her line of questioning was routinely laced with sarcasm and contempt. Justina rightfully earned a reputation for being shrewd and fierce. She had won all but one case, and blamed the loss on her client, who had a sudden case of morality. After drilling him thoroughly, telling him 'what to say' and 'how to say it', she discovered he was a religious fanatic who could not lie on the Bible. From that point on, she made it her business to investigate her clients' personal backgrounds, beliefs, and morals, using the information to devise an effective line of defense.

Johnson and Johnson Associates offered Justina a job after her internship ended, but she turned them down, opting to be her own boss and have control over her own destiny. Grateful to her parents for their monetary gift of $100,000, she had just enough money to start her own law firm in the hustle and bustle of downtown Atlanta.

In preparation for the grand opening, she had her office beautifully decorated with top-of-the-line redwood furniture, and expensive pictures. Flowers and congratulatory cards also adorned her new law office, which was situated on the third floor of a corporate office building. She signed a three-year lease, and paid the rent one year in advance.

One of her classmates from law school, Roger McCarthy, celebrated with her. She had convinced him to join her law firm as a partner. Roger was fine with the idea, but had reservations about making Atlanta his permanent home. He also began second-guessing his decision of becoming Justina's partner when he found out about her out-of-control spending habits. Justina justified her spending pattern by stating that the beautification of the office and its location, were vital to the success of their law firm. This was just one of the many things they disagreed on. In the end, he had succumbed to her wishes.

After Roger earned his law degree, he had several offers to work for well-established, reputable law firms. He chose to work for Justina because she offered him partnership, which typically came years later. He recognized this opportunity was too good to pass up, even though his family was extremely wealthy. They owned the Sierra bread food chains around the world.

Since Roger wanted to make sure no one discovered his connection to their family business, he made a conscientious decision to use his mother's maiden name in lieu of his birth name: *Roger Salvador*. Justina never knew about his name change or his family's wealth, and he wanted to keep it that way.

Roger was busy unpacking boxes when the florist walked into the office. After signing for the floral arrangement, he delivered them to Justina's corner office.

"Justina, this bunch of roses just came in for you. Where do you want them?"

Justina looked up from the file cabinet, and off-handedly yelled, "Put them anywhere! By the way, who are they from?"

Roger read the attached card as he stood near her door entrance. "This is strange. They're from someone named Guy. Go figure."

Justina frowned. "Is his last name Simmons?"

"Yeah. Do you know him?"

"Yes," Justina reluctantly admitted. Her heart still yearned for Guy, especially since he was the only man she had ever made love to.

Before Roger could probe any further, Justina hastily retrieved the roses from him and closed the door in his face. She sat behind her desk and read the attached card. *Congrats Justina. I wish you nothing but joy, happiness, and success.* She rolled her eyes and threw the roses into her office wastebasket. Justina decided she was not going to allow Guy to become a distraction.

During their first month of business, Justina and Roger had few clients. After attending numerous charity events and hobnobbing with Atlanta's elite, they seemed to make leeway. They also received numerous referrals via recommendations from the City Commissioner and the Mayor.

One month later, they hired a full-time secretary at Roger's insistence and personal recommendation. Roger thought Kathy Little was the perfect candidate for the position. He was especially impressed with her credentials.

Two weeks into the job, Kathy had her first run-in with Justina when she was packing up her belongings to go home for the day. She was brain-dead after revising a memo a dozen times, trying to satisfy Justina. She thought, *This woman has worked my last nerve!*

Justina came out of her office and stood by Kathy's desk with an attitude and a box of unsharpened pencils. "And exactly where are you going?!"

"Home!" Kathy strongly declared, as she grabbed her purse and threw it over her shoulder. "I should have been off work an hour ago."

"Oh no you're not!" Justina snapped. "I need this box of pencils sharpened before you leave." Then she quickly returned to her office, slamming her door shut.

Kathy knew Justina was being spiteful. In the short time she worked for her, she had never seen Justina use a pencil. Tired and fed up with Justina's crap, Kathy immediately began throwing all of her personal things into an empty box.

Roger walked out of his office after hearing the commotion from the front office. He looked at Kathy's frazzled appearance, and asked, "What are you doing?"

Kathy grumbled, "There's not enough money in the world to make me stay here and work for that devil in a suit!"

Roger knew she was talking about Justina. "Wait! Let me talk to Ms. Reyes," he insisted, as he quickly walked over to her desk. "I'm sure it was just a misunderstanding. Please Kathy," he pleaded, covering the box with his hands to stop her from packing.

Kathy thought about it, and agreed to wait. "Okay, Roger, but I will not allow her to continue disrespecting me! I'm afraid I'm going to hurt that heifer if she snaps at me one more time! I do my job and I work hard, but I'll be damned if that hussy is going to continue treating me as if I'm her personal slave!"

"I know, I promise…it won't happen again," Roger assured her. "Go ahead and leave. I'll take care of Ms. Reyes."

After Kathy left, Roger walked into Justina's office. "I need you to stop harassing Kathy. If you don't, she can and will sue us."

"Oh no she can't!" Justina spouted. "I want her out of here! She's incompetent!"

Roger begged to differ. He knew he could not reason with Justina when she was riled up. "Okay fine," he conceded. "But do know she has threatened to file a complaint with the Equal Employment Opportunity Commission," he lied.

"But, she can't," Justina cautiously replied.

"She can and she will if you fire her," Roger threatened. "Just because you're both black, it does not preclude Kathy from taking civil actions against you."

Justina lowered her head as she pondered what Roger was saying. "Okay," she finally said, "but make sure she stays out of my way. From now on, Kathy's your responsibility, not mine!" she sharply added, before she swiveled around in her chair, turning her back to him.

Roger was relieved. He simply said, "Deal."

From that day forward, Justina ignored Kathy. Anytime Justina wanted Kathy to do something, she put instructions on a sticky note and left it on her desk. Kathy was also relieved, since she no longer had to deal with Justina's verbal assaults.

Chapter 15

The Good and the Ugly

Regine was slowly getting over Guy. That is, until he started calling her grandmother's home. No one knew where she was except her godparents, and they would never give Guy her grandmother's unlisted phone number.

Bessie was in the kitchen when Guy called again. She heard Regine pick up the phone, say "hello," and seconds later, slam the phone into its cradle. She walked into the living room, and noticed Regine sitting on the sofa, pouting.

"When are you going to talk to that boy?" Bessie anxiously inquired. "He's been calling every day for the past month."

Regine frowned. "Grandma, I can't see myself going back to him. I refuse to become anyone's sloppy seconds," she replied, as she picked up the remote control to turn on the TV.

Bessie sat next to Regine on the sofa. "Maybe it won't be like that with you. Maybe he regrets his decision and wants to do right by you." Then she realized Regine was surfing the channels with the remote control. "Turn off the TV," she said, as she lightly touched Regine's leg. "I have something to tell you. I should've told you this a long time ago."

Regine complied with Bessie's request and turned to face her.

"Your Granddaddy, Kenneth, was no prince," Bessie sadly acknowledged. "He was cheating on me. He told me he broke it off with this woman, but I suspected he went right back to her. Well, anyway, that woman was married, and her crazy husband found them at a hotel together. He shot and killed Kenneth on the spot."

Regine opened her mouth and gasped. "I didn't know Granddaddy died like that."

"That's because I was too ashamed to admit it," Bessie whispered.

"So you think I should forgive Guy?"

"Not only should you forgive him, but you should also give him another chance. First, let him show you he's changed."

94

Dumbfounded, Regine admitted, "I don't understand."

Bessie sighed. "Baby, nobody's perfect; not even me. Guy is young. He's going to make mistakes. Everybody makes mistakes. It's how you deal with them, is what counts."

Regine sighed after realizing she missed the message her grandmother was trying to convey. "Thanks for sharing your story, but it's going to take some time before I can forgive Guy."

"I know. But when you do, don't ever bring this issue up again. It'll eat you up inside. I was mad at your granddaddy long after he died. You are a strong woman." Then Bessie pretended to flex her muscles, before adding, "You were named after me, so that makes you a superwoman."

Regine laughed. "Grandma, you're something else. I love you."

Bessie smile. "I love you too, baby." Bessie stopped short of telling Regine about her relationship with Lucy.

One month later, Regine started dating a young man she met in church. Sam White was six years older than Regine, average looking, and seemed nice. He took chivalry to the next level, by overwhelming her with gifts, flowers, and attention. For the first time in her life, Regine felt like a queen.

Bessie, however, was leery of Sam's intentions and began asking pointed questions. "Regine, what do you know about him?"

"Grandma, it's not serious. We just started dating."

"Baby, you can't be that naïve. Have you ever been to his house?"

"No, not yet. Sam said he's too embarrassed to show me his place, because it's always messy."

"Did you volunteer to help him clean it up?" Bessie probed.

"Grandma…what's up with the questions?"

"Baby, just be careful. Something isn't right about him. You sure you're not dating the first man that asked you out, just to get even with Guy?"

"No, that's not it. I have to get on with my life. How long do you want me to wait?"

"As long as it takes. Always put God first. If you don't, you will fail. Mark my words," Bessie said, before she left Regine to ponder her questions.

Everything Bessie told Regine about Sam resonated as she prepared for a date with him that evening. When he pulled up in the driveway, Regine rushed outside to greet him. "Hi Sam. Why don't we go over to your place tonight?" she eagerly asked, as she stood next to his truck.

Sam held the door open for her to get inside. "Baby, I told you, my place is a mess."

Regine buckled up and waited until Sam was in the driver's seat before responding. "I'll help you clean up."

Sam ignored her as he backed out of the driveway and pulled onto the highway. "Babe, I was thinking, maybe we could drive to the beach tonight and get a couple of drinks."

It did not escape Regine that Sam dismissed her request. Twenty minutes later, she decided to probe further. "Sam, why can't I ever reach you on your home phone?"

"Oh, sometimes my kids are on the internet. We have a dial-up internet connection," Sam casually explained. "You know how it is."

"Kids?! Regine yelled. You never told me you had kids!"

"You never asked!" Sam shouted back.

"Well…let me ask you another question," Regine said with an attitude. "Are you married?" When Sam remained quiet, Regine asked again, but louder, "Are you married?!"

Sam kept his attention focused on the road. "Yeah…but I'm getting a divorce," he finally said.

"Where does she live?" Regine asked, knowing at this point that it did not matter.

Five seconds went by before Sam finally said, "With me. But I sleep on the couch," he quickly added.

"And you're generous enough to give her the bed?" Regine sarcastically inquired.

Sam briefly glanced in her direction. "Yeah," he said with an attitude.

Regine shook her head in disgust. "Just take me home!"

Sam glanced over at Regine and grimaced. "Why are you tripping?!"

Regine had enough of his deception. "Just take me home," she repeated.

Sam quickly pulled over to the side of the road, and threw his gear in park. "Get out!" he demanded, as he turned to Regine with fire in his eyes.

"What?!!" Regine exclaimed, looking at Sam as if he lost his mind. "You're not going to leave me on the highway like this! Just take me home!" she said with force.

Sam grimaced. "You know, you're such a cunt! I don't know why I wasted my money, or my time on you! Get the hell out of my truck!" He abruptly reached over and opened the door after Regine did would not budge.

Regine looked at him in disbelief before getting out of his truck. Sam pulled away and did not look back. It was dark outside and the highway was practically void of cars. She could have called her grandmother, but she did not want Bessie to worry. Instead, she walked two blocks to the nearest convenience store and flagged down a cab.

Regine made it home safely. As she walked through the front door, she noticed her grandmother sitting in the recliner reading her Bible. "I love you, Grandma," she said with a somber attitude.

"I love you too, baby" Bessie genuinely replied without looking up.

Regine walked upstairs to her bedroom and whispered to no one in particular, "Thank you Grandmother, for your wisdom. And thank you God, for protecting me."

The next morning, Regine and Bessie were sitting at the kitchen table, drinking coffee and listening to the morning news. The news reporter suddenly announced that a young black male drove off the Chesapeake Bay Bridge a little after midnight. He was driving a red Range Rover.

Regine gasped as she paid closer attention to the news reporter.

The reporter continued, "The man has been identified, but the police are in the process of notifying family members. More news to follow…."

"What's the matter, suga'?" Bessie knowingly asked.

"I think they were talking about Sam. They described his truck," Regine hesitantly admitted. Then she said in a soft voice, "I didn't tell you this, but Sam put me out of his truck last night. We were near that bridge. I need more information to be sure."

Regine stood up and rushed to the phone, but Bessie jumped up from her chair and quickly grabbed it from her. "What?" Regine asked with a bewildered gaze.

"Baby, don't involve yourself in this," Bessie said, as she put the phone on its cradle. "Let the police do their job. Do you think Sam's wife and kids would appreciate it if you called to report that he was out on a date with you?"

"I suppose you're right," Regine sadly acknowledged. "I'm going to go lie down." She pondered her grandmother's last statement, and realized she did not recall telling her that Sam was married and had children. *Maybe she overheard my prayer last night,* she guessed.

When the doorbell rang thirty minutes later, Bessie answered the door and was pleasantly surprised. "Regine!" Bessie called out.

Regine responded from upstairs. "Yes, Grandma?"

"Somebody sent you flowers," Bessie said, admiring the bouquet. "They sure are beautiful."

Regine ran downstairs and was overwhelmed by the biggest bouquet of multi-colored roses she had ever seen. "That, they are," she cautiously said, as she opened the card. *Regine, please give me a second chance. I miss you.* She frowned when she discovered they were from none other than Guy. Again, she noticed that there was no mention of love.

"Who are they from, Guy?" Bessie asked.

"Yes," Regine softly replied, still wanting to be a part of his life.

"I figured as much. That boy is not giving up on you," Bessie said, while putting on her coat. "Well, I'm going out tonight. My friend is taking me to dinner. Do you want me to bring you something back?"

"No, I'm okay. You go out and enjoy yourself. I have a lot of reading to catch up on. Tell Deacon Franklin 'hello' for me," Regine mischievously added with a smile.

Bessie paused, then pretended not to hear Regine's comment. "Don't stay up for me. I'll get home when I get home." She winked at her granddaughter before she walked out the door.

Bessie wondered how Regine figured out she was going on a date with the Deacon. She thought she made it clear to Regine that they were just friends. Truth was, Bessie and the Deacon had been secretly seeing each other and she preferred to keep it that way.

All of Bessie's thoughts evaporated when she saw her tall, dark, big and handsome boyfriend. Deacon Alfred Franklin was waiting for her by his car. Just the thought of his muscular arms wrapped around her body brought a smile to Bessie's face. She was glad he was a part of her life. Early on, she had pegged him as an attentive listener, who was always been concerned about what was going on in her life.

Sixty-eight-year-old, Alfred Franklin, was also smitten with Bessie. He rushed over to open the passenger door for her. "Hey, sweetie pie. How are you?" he genuinely asked with a smile that lit up a stadium.

Bessie blushed. "I'm fine," she replied with a giggle.

"I hope you don't mind going to get some fried fish. Maybe later, we could sit out by the lake."

Bessie smiled. "Sounds good to me."

Chapter 16

Knowledge is Power

Regine's parents, Sue Croswell and Kevin Graham, met at a frat party while Sue was attending Howard University in Washington, DC. Kevin was a local drug dealer at the time, but Sue did not care. She was enamored with his rugged look and hardened disposition, and she especially loved the way he protected and spoiled her. She fell in love with him at first sight.

Kevin was also in awe of Sue. He loved her big beautiful brown eyes and shapely body. He pursued her, and soon realized she was not serious about her education. Nonetheless, he had encouraged her to stay in school and get a degree. Kevin knew all too well about the hard knocks of life, as he had spent most of his life in and out of jail on various charges, ranging from strong-armed robbery to drug trafficking.

Unfortunately, Sue did not heed Kevin's advice. She preferred hanging out and partying, and was determined to do it with or without him. The last time she showed up at his apartment, he blocked her from entering.

"Why can't I come in?" Sue whined.

Kevin ignored her question and grumbled, "Are you still in school?!"

"They...put me on...academic probation," Sue replied with trembling lips, while averting her eyes downward.

"You never answered my question," Kevin acknowledged.

Sue was speechless.

Kevin knew Sue was getting high and wondered if he had anything to do with it. "I can't tell you what to do," he finally said, "because I'm not a good example." He sighed, before asking, "What happened to the young lady I fell in love with? Now you're 'round here getting high all the time, and you're not going to school like you're supposed to. Do me a favor and drop back in college, full time."

"But baby, school isn't for me," Sue softly admitted. "I just want to be with you."

Kevin grimaced. "I'm a nobody! Don't you get it?!"

"No! You don't get it! I'm pregnant," Sue belatedly admitted. She had kept her pregnancy a secret for two months. Then she quickly added, "And yes, it's yours."

"You can't have it!" Kevin barked. "Get rid of the baby! I have nothing to offer you, or the baby."

"But Kevin...."

"Just do it!" Kevin exclaimed, as he hastily removed a wad of cash from his front pocket and peeled off five $100 bills. "This should be more than enough." Kevin handed her the money, then slammed the door in her face.

Sue cried all the way back to the dorm.

Kevin avoided Sue for the next four months. When he finally saw her, Sue was still pregnant and on drugs. His heart sank when he realized she was also prostituting. He contacted her mother, Bessie, and made arrangements through one of his cronies to have Sue show up at a hotel under false pretenses.

When Sue arrived at the hotel, two deputies took her into custody. Bessie used the Florida Baker Act law to put her into a mental facility up to seventy-two hours, against her will. Bessie had also convinced Sue to go to a private drug rehab center for the remainder of her pregnancy.

Three months later, Sue had a beautiful baby girl. She named her Regine, after her mother, Bessie Regine. She had stayed clean for a year before she became strung out on drugs again. Subsequently, Regine was placed in Bessie's custody.

Sue stopped by one day to visit Regine under Bessie's close supervision. When Bessie briefly left them alone in the living room, Sue took her baby and ran out of the house. Bessie panicked and called Kevin, telling him what happened. He searched high and low until he found Regine alone, wrapped in a blanket, and in a vacant room of a condemned building. It looked like Regine had cried herself to sleep. Sue was nowhere to be found.

Fearing Sue would try to take Regine again, Kevin arranged for Regine to be placed in her godparents' custody in St. Petersburg, Florida, his hometown. He figured if he sent Regine far away from her mother, Sue would not go looking for her.

It did not take Sue long to discover Regine's whereabouts. While visiting her mother one day, Sue discreetly rummaged through Bessie's mail and found a letter from the O'Neal's with a return address. Curious to see for herself that her daughter was being raised by good people, Sue appeared on the O'Neal's doorstep three years later.

Cecilia O'Neal answered the door and threatened to call the police, but changed her mind when Sue broke down crying. Cecilia assured Sue that Regine was being well cared for. She also promised to send pictures and keep her up-to-date on Regine's activities. Regine never knew about Sue's visit, nor did she know Cecilia stayed in touch with her mother.

Six months later, the paramedics found Sue in a crack house, badly bruised, after getting beat up by one of her johns. While in the hospital recovering from her wounds, she committed to becoming drug-free. Shortly afterward, she admitted herself in a State-funded rehabilitation center in Tallahassee, Florida.

Three months later, she looked at her reflection in the mirror and noticed she had gained a little weight, and her hair was growing again. Even better, her confidence had been restored. That is, until she found out she was HIV positive during a routine physical. After receiving her diagnosis, she wanted to give up. The thought of reuniting with Regine was her only glimmer of hope. Sue desired to make amends with her daughter some day.

In rehab, Sue met and befriended Rowena Smallwood. The rehab patients and staff often commented on how much they looked alike. Rowena was forty-four but looked ten years younger. Sue was forty-two but looked older. Although Rowena's complexion was lighter, they were both very beautiful and possessed similar features, including their big, beautiful brown eyes.

Sue felt comfortable telling Rowena how she got hooked on drugs and lost custody of Regine. She also told her she hoped things would be different this time, because she desperately wanted to be a part of her daughter's life. Rowena shared with Sue how she had fallen on hard times as well. They were alone in the confines of their room when Rowena shared her story.

"I was messing around with a drug dealer who gave me access to all the drugs I wanted," Rowena lamented. "I was high twenty-four-seven, but things changed when my boyfriend got locked up for drug trafficking. He was given a sentence of twenty-five years to life.

After he went to jail, I couldn't afford to buy drugs, so I decided to get my life back on track and get clean. A year later, I met my husband, who was a lot older. He promised to love my children as if they were his own. He even adopted them when we married. Their biological fathers never signed their birth certificates so the process was easy."

"So what happened?" Sue curiously asked. "Your husband seemed like a good man."

Regine heavily exhaled. "Well, I ran into an old friend I used to snort cocaine with. That one hit did it. I stopped caring about life, and I stopped taking care of my kids. I started stealing and doing whatever it took to support my habit. The final straw was when I almost gave my baby away for drugs. Fortunately, my husband found out about it and intervened. He went to court and won custody of all my children. He divorced me. So now I don't have a husband, or my children."

"At least you know your kids are being well cared for," Sue said without passing judgment.

"I love my children, but I know they're better off with him."

Sue and Rowena graduated from rehab one month later. They were the only patients who did not invite guests to the ceremony. After they were discharged, Rowena convinced Sue to move into a two-bedroom apartment together.

Within one week, Sue got a job at McDonalds, which was within walking distance of their apartment. Sometimes Rowena drove her to and from work in her brand-new Pathfinder. Sue often wondered how Rowena was able to afford a luxury vehicle, especially since she did not have a job.

When Rowena noticed Sue reading anything she could get her hands on, she asked, "Have you thought about returning to college to get your degree?"

"I have, but I figure I'm too old to start over," Sue replied without looking up from her book.

"You're never too old. You should think about it," Rowena said, as she looked over Sue's conservative appearance. She wanted to do something special for her. "Sue, let's go shopping," Rowena happily suggested.

Sue looked at Rowena like she was crazy. "Girl, you know I don't have extra money to splurge like that."

"Don't worry about money; I got you," Rowena said, as she opened her compact mirror and glided bright red lipstick across her full lips.

"But how?"

"Don't worry about how. My money is legit."

Sue put her book down and gazed at Rowena. "Okay," she skeptically replied.

"Great! Go freshen up."

Rowena took Sue to Macys and Bloomingdales, and purchased several outfits for day and eveningwear. Afterward, they went to the spa where they received a full treatment, including new hairdos, eyebrow waxing, massages, manicures and pedicures.

Rowena also took Sue to the Clinique station in Macys for a makeover. She looked at the young makeup artist's nametag. "Listen Keirra, you have to hook my sister up, a'ight?"

Keirra laughed softly when Rowena used slang language to get her point her cross. "We straight. I got you," she responded in kind, with a genuine smile. Twenty minutes later, Keirra gave Sue a mirror. Sue opened her mouth from shock. She could not believe the transition; she looked ten years younger. She smiled, then instantly covered her mouth with her hand.

Rowena noticed and whispered in her ear, "I made a dental appointment for you today, to get your teeth fixed."

Sue was grateful, but felt overwhelmed by Rowena's generosity. "Why are you doing all of this for me?"

"Because I feel as though I've known you all my life. I care about you," Rowena explained, as she embraced Sue. "You're the sister I've always wanted."

Sue cried in response. Rowena hugged her again, and told her not to worry about repaying her.

When they returned home from the Dental office, Sue checked the mailbox and found a letter from Cecilia, Regine's godmother. It was a congratulatory card with a check for $5,000. Sue was overwhelmed by Cecilia's generosity, and immediately picked up the phone to call her.

"Hi, Cecilia, this is Sue. I just received your card, along with a big check. You didn't have to do this. You've done enough already."

"Sue, I'm proud that you sought help for your addiction. Besides, it was the least I could do. Regine has been a blessing to us."

"Thank you, but I couldn't have done it without knowing you were looking after her. Your guidance has made her into the wonderful woman she is today, and I appreciate it. By the way, have you heard from her?"

"Well….she's better now," Cecilia cautiously said. "She had her heart broken by Guy, a young man she used to be close friends with. To make a long story short, he took an interest in her best friend,

Justina. Regine has since relocated to Virginia to live with your mother. Your mom is up in age and could use some help around the house."

Sue began crying. "My baby…was hurt," she sobbed.

"Yeah, but don't worry. She's fine. She's probably dating someone else by now. That happened a while ago," Cecilia added on a lighter note.

"Where can I find this Justina girl?" Sue asked, still choked up.

"Don't worry about her. She's not even with Guy anymore. Her mom told me she graduated from law school, and has since permanently relocated to Atlanta to open her own law firm."

This revelation did not make Sue feel better about what Justina did to Regine. "Oh…okay," Sue muttered. "I'm going to call my mother to check on her. Uh…Mrs. O'Neal?"

"What is it honey?"

"Thank you for everything. Please tell your husband I said 'thank you' as well. I really appreciate all you and your husband have done for Regine."

Cecilia smiled. "We know you do. We just want you to be okay. You've always been Regine's mother, and we appreciate the opportunity to be a part of her life."

"Thank you. I needed to hear that," Sue sincerely admitted.

"Good luck and keep in touch."

Sue hung up the phone and contemplated her next move. She wanted to hurt Justina, just like Justina hurt Regine. She knew she was not thinking rationally when she asked Rowena how she felt about relocating to Atlanta.

Rowena frowned. "As in Georgia?"

"Yes, just temporarily," Sue timidly replied. She knew she was pushing the envelope by asking Rowena to come along.

"Well, I've never thought about it. What's in Atlanta?"

"My baby," Sue weakly said, as tears flowed down her face.

Rowena quickly sat up on the edge of the sofa. "What's wrong with Regine?"

"She hurt my baby," Sue numbly replied.

"Who?" Rowena asked, as she walked over to console her.

"Justina," Sue answered, still crying uncontrollably.

Rowena grew concerned. "You need to calm down and explain what you're talking about."

After Sue recited what Mrs. O'Neal told her, Rowena understood her quest. She thought about it for a few seconds, then asked, "When do we leave?"

"Are you serious?!" Sue incredulously asked, as she gazed into Rowena's eyes.

"You're my girl. We have to look out for each other."

Sue used the money she received from Mrs. O'Neal to cover their relocation expenses. Rowena offered to drive her SUV and assist with any other expenses they incur on the trip. Sue wondered again, how Rowena had what seemed like unlimited access to money.

Upon arriving in Atlanta two weeks later, Rowena and Sue located Justina's office. Rowena scoped out the office and spotted a tall, thin white man walking out of the building and up the street to the local pub. She rushed back to the SUV and told Sue about the man.

"Do you think he works for the same law firm?" Sue curiously asked.

"I don't know. There's only one way to find out," Rowena suggested, while getting into the backseat to change.

Sue frowned. "What are you doing?"

"Just stay put. He's going to take one look at me and sing like a canary," Rowena said with a chuckle.

"But why did you change into that outfit?" Sue asked, checking out Rowena's purple, tight-fitting mini dress. "What are you trying to prove? You look like you're auditioning to become a professional stripper."

"Trust me, I got this," Rowena said, as she brushed on facial powder and applied more red lipstick. She stepped out of the SUV to put on her purple three-inch heels, then removed the rubber band to let her long black, freshly styled hair flow down her back.

Rowena walked into the pub with an air of confidence. Her walk was slow and deliberate, and her barely there outfit grabbed the attention of every man in sight. They could not take their eyes off her.

Rowena spotted a vacant seat next to Roger. "Hi, is this seat taken?" she asked with a wide grin.

Roger looked up from his beer and his eyes instantly went to her chest. "No, it isn't."

"How are you?" Rowena asked, as she sat on the stool next to his.

Roger looked up and murmured, "I'm fine."

Rowena smiled and batted her eyes. She knew men were crazy about her eyes, as well as her other assets. "I hope you don't mind me sitting here."

Roger stuttered, "No...um...not at all." He was overcome by her beauty.

"Are you new to this area?" Rowena cautiously asked, noticing how Roger closely resembled the skinny version of John Travolta.

"Not really. I'm a partner at the law firm down the street. I started a practice with my partner after getting my law degree from the University of Georgia." *Gosh, why am I rambling?! This woman isn't interested in me.*

"Friend?"

"No, it's nothing like that. We were classmates, that's all." Roger realized he was rambling again, so he handed Rowena his business card.

Rowena looked at the card. "Are you Reyes?"

"No, I'm sorry. I forgot to introduce myself. I'm Roger McCarthy. My partner is Justina Reyes."

"Is she from here?" Rowena casually asked, waving to the bartender.

"Yes...I mean no. She's from Florida."

Rowena waited until the bartender filled her drink order before responding. "Oh, is that right?" she asked, seductively drinking her tonic on the rocks. Then she suddenly put her hand on her chest and feigned embarrassment. "Oh, forgive me! You gave me your card, and you don't even know my name," she said, as she put her drink down and extended her hand. "I'm Rowena Smallwood."

As Rowena shook Roger's hand, she invaded his space. "Can I give you my number?" she purred in an enticing and seductive tone. "I'd like to get to know you better."

Roger was surprised with her boldness. "Oh, okay....sure."

Rowena wrote her number on a napkin with a pen she borrowed from the bartender. "Promise...you'll call me," she pleaded in a soft voice, as she handed him the napkin with her number.

"Okay, I'll do that," Roger hesitantly said.

The bartender witnessed Rowena and Roger's exchange, and did not think Roger was her type. He had a bad feeling about her.

Rowena stood up and slowly strutted out of the pub. She walked slow enough for Roger to get a good look at her apple-bottom. It worked. He could not take his eyes off her.

Rowena returned to the SUV with a look of satisfaction.

"Well?" Sue asked.

"The man I followed inside the pub was Roger McCarthy. He's Justina Reyes' partner at their law firm."

"Are you serious?!" Sue asked with amazement.

"I'm for real. Leave it up to me. That man's nose is wide open. I wouldn't be surprised if he tells me his whole life story."

They laughed in response, then gave each other a high five.

"Let's go home and plan our next move," Rowena suggested.

Roger had been dateless for months when he met Rowena. He eventually called her and asked her out. The outfit she wore on their first date was more revealing than the one she had on when he first met her in the pub. She had on a red mini dress with matching net-stockings.

Throughout dinner, they decided not to ask personal questions, keeping the conversation light. Roger stared at Rowena with a big smile on his face.

Rowena suddenly became uncomfortable under his gaze. "What is it?"

"It's obvious that you could get any man of your choosing. Why me?" Roger asked, as he observed the way men undressed her.

Rowena smiled. "You were the only one at the pub who seemed approachable. I knew you would be the perfect gentleman."

"Is that so?" Roger coyly asked.

"Yeah. Are you attracted to me?" Rowena casually asked. She already knew he was, but felt compelled to ask anyway.

"To be honest, I haven't been able to get you out of my mind since the day we met. I'm hoping this is the beginning of a long friendship. You never know where it might lead."

"I'm willing to take that chance," Rowena said, as she batted her eyes.

Roger clicked his glass of wine with hers. "Here's to possibilities."

Rowena smiled, as she thought, *This is the type of man I could see myself with if I were seriously dating.*

Roger was so excited about his relationship with Rowena, he even told Justina the little he knew about her. In response, Justina told him he could do better. Roger was used to Justina's snide remarks and chose to ignore her assertion.

One week later, Rowena walked into the office to meet Roger for lunch. Justina scrunched up her nose as she looked at Rowena from head to toe. She instantly disliked Rowena, but the feeling was mutual.

"I'm here to see Roger," Rowena sharply announced, unfazed by Justina's funky attitude.

"I see!" Justina cruelly said, before she turned on her heels and walked into Roger's office. "That *thing* is here to see you!" she rudely announced. She briskly headed to her office without waiting for Roger's response.

Roger was puzzled by what Justina meant. He walked out of his office and smiled when he saw Rowena. "Hi Rowena. Before we go to lunch, I need to talk to Justina for a few minutes. Do you mind?"

Rowena smiled. "Of course not."

Roger walked into Justina's office, slamming the door behind him. "Justina! Your reference to Rowena was uncalled for!"

"Well, I call it like I see it!" Justina snapped.

Roger frowned. "What's your problem?!"

"I can't help who you choose to affiliate with, but don't expect me to like it!" Justina sharply retorted. Then she redirected her gaze to her computer monitor and yelled, *"Loser!"* under her breath.

Roger gave up on trying to reason with Justina, and stormed out of her office.

Chapter 17
Trouble in Paradise

*O*ver the past several months, Roger and Justina's business relationship became even more strained and intense. He once suggested she go see a therapist for her mood swings. After Justina cursed him out from *A to Z*, Roger never broached the subject again. He learned to stay out of her way whenever she was riled up.

Even though there was dissension within the office, Justina needed someone to talk to after learning one of her client's jumped bail. And talking to her secretary, Kathy, was out of the question. She walked into Roger's office and welcomed the change in focus. "Hi Roger, do you have any plans this weekend?"

Roger did not see or hear her. He was busy leafing through a file.

"Roger?!"

Suddenly alarmed by her voice, Roger looked up and stammered, "Uh...oh. I'm sorry, Justina. I didn't hear you. I'm busy prepping this case for a preliminary hearing first thing Monday morning."

"I was just asking about your plans this weekend."

Roger was surprised she cared. "Well, my girlfriend and I are going out on the town tonight," he proudly professed.

Justina raised a brow. "Girlfriend?" she curiously asked, as she invited herself into his office and sat in a chair across from his desk.

Roger placed the file on his desk, and snidely commented, "Unlike you, I have a life. Rowena and I have been dating for quite some time."

"Rowena?! The black girl?!" Justina quizzed, as her eyes grew bigger.

"Why are you acting so surprised? What are you saying? I hope you're not shallow. After all, it's the millennium, not the fifties."

"No, it's not that...it's...."

Roger held up his hand, interrupting her thoughts. "You really need to get out more often," he suggested, as he put his hand down. "If you hadn't acted so distant, I would've asked you out a long time ago." *Now that I've gotten to know you, the chance of that happening is highly unlikely.*

Justina was surprised by Roger's admission. She never saw him as a potential mate. To her, he looked like the white version of Steve Urkel from Family Matters; she could not even imagine herself with the black version. However, she acknowledged that Roger was a brilliant attorney.

Even though their professional relationship was not perfect, Roger felt sorry for Justina. He knew she went home alone every night. After deep thought, he asked, "Why don't you tag along with me and Rowena tonight? You never know, you might meet your soulmate," he teased.

Justina frowned. "Roger, I'm flattered, but business comes first. Enjoy your night out," she said, as she stood up to leave. "I'm going back to my office to read some briefs."

Roger was prepared to leave, but felt compelled to get Justina out of the funk she appeared to live and breathe in. He smiled as he conjured up a plan to make sure she had a good time tonight. After making a quick phone call, he went to her office and found her behind her desk.

"Justina, let's go out; just you and me. I'll call Rowena to break our date."

Justina looked at Roger with grave apprehension.

"Come on Justina. We're just friends hanging out in Hot-Lanta. Okay?" he persisted. Roger wanted her to loosen up for a change.

Justina mulled over his suggestion, and decided that it might be a great break in her monotonous life. "Okay Roger. Pick me up from my condo around eight o'clock with your girlfriend. I don't want Rowena to get the wrong idea about us," she explained with a light chuckle.

Roger laughed and nodded in agreement.

Roger promptly arrived at Justina's condo at eight. As soon as she buckled up, he told her they were going to Club Dominoes for the evening. Justina and Rowena reacquainted themselves. In each other's presence, Justina was snobbish and arrogant, while Rowena was passive and aloof.

Justina thought Rowena looked like a hooker in her hot pink, tight fitting mini dress with matching hoop earrings, lipstick, and eyeshadow. She was also sporting an afro-puff wig and hot pink four-inch pumps. Justina's own attire was conservative. She wore a black slip dress and black pumps, and her makeup was subtle.

An hour later, they entered the club where hip-hop music was blaring, and a silver ball hung from the ceiling, reflecting multiple colors and bouncing off the walls like sparkles. The club was dimly lit and elegantly decorated with purple velvety chairs and pristine white tablecloths. Small vibrant tea candles in silver decorative bowls were placed in the center of each table. The club was filled with Atlanta's elite.

Roger reserved a corner table for them, which was in clear view of the dance floor. Shortly after receiving their drinks, the waitress brought Justina an identical drink.

Justina was puzzled. "Wait! This is a mistake. I didn't order this second drink."

"I know," the waitress said. "The gentleman across the room ordered it," she said, pointing in his direction. "He told me he'll be picking up the tab for this table tonight, so you and your friends are free to order whatever you like."

"You've got to be kidding," Roger said.

"This is so cool," Rowena chimed in.

Justina looked over at the man in question, and discovered the most beautiful sight she had ever seen. She saw that he was tall, dark, muscular, and fine in every sense. *Wow! That man is a tall glass of water. Look at those dark eyes and that beautiful smile.*

Seconds later, the mystery man approached their table with a big cheesy smile. "Hello," he said to Justina with bass in his voice. "I noticed you as soon as you walked through the door. I must admit, you look heavenly," he heartily added.

Justina blushed in response. She instinctively thought of Barry White after hearing his voice.

He looked at the vacant seat next to Justina's. "May I sit here and chat with you for a little bit? That is, if this seat isn't already taken."

"Sure," Justina quickly replied, as she waved her hand toward the vacant seat. She was unusually jittery. She neglected to ask this man for his name.

Roger extended his hand. "Hi, I'm Roger, and this here is my lady, Rowena," he said, protectively putting his arm around Rowena's shoulder. "The young lady you're trying to lure from us is Justina."

He reached over and shook Roger's hand, then Rowena's. "It's a pleasure making your acquaintance. My name is Calvin Calloway."

"We really appreciate you picking up the tab," Roger said with vigor and humor, "but I can handle this."

"Sure, but let me take care of the tab this time," Calvin warmly said. "The next time all of us go out, you can treat. Deal?"

Justina thought Calvin was being rather presumptuous. However, she was immediately attracted to him, and liked his *'take charge'* attitude.

Roger noted Justina's unusual giddiness, and did not hesitate to take Calvin up on his offer. He and Rowena headed onto the dance floor to give them some privacy.

Calvin turned to Justina and smiled. "Anyone ever tell you that look like....?"

"I know, Halle Berry," Justina consciously replied with a bright smile.

"But you're prettier and younger," Calvin added.

Justina blushed, covering her smile with her right hand.

Calvin smiled. "How old are you?"

"I'm 25, and you?"

"I'm 31. How do you feel about dating an older man?" he asked with a sly grin.

"Come on now, you're not that much older. And why do you assume I'd be interested in dating the likes of you?" Justina teased.

Calvin laughed in response. "Okay, you got me. So tell me Justina, why are you here without a date tonight?"

"I'm just taking a break from work. I own a law firm here in Atlanta," Justina professed, handing Calvin her business card. "Reyes and McCarthy. My partner, Roger McCarthy, is the one you just met. We primarily specialize in criminal and civil complaints."

"Impressive," Calvin acknowledged, as he looked at her business card.

Justina did not agree. Instead, she cringed at the thought of some of her clients and their heinous crimes. Many of her clients defaulted on their payment agreements, costing her more money to sue them to get her money back.

"So what brings you here alone?" Justina asked, eager to change the subject. "Are you a regular?"

"Like you, I needed a break from work. And it helps that my friend is part owner of this joint," Calvin proudly announced.

"How convenient," Justina replied, as she briefly looked out on the dance floor to check out Roger's dancing skills. She was surprised he moved so well. Then she looked at Rowena and suddenly felt nauseous. She thought, *I do not understand what Roger sees in her. She's so ghetto and loud. Oh, and let's not forget her clothes*

that scream 'I'm too little for you'. On top of that, she is an unem-
ployed moocher. What in the heck is Roger thinking?!

Justina rolled her eyes and shook her head before she refocused her attention to Calvin. "So, tell me about yourself."

"I'm an attorney at a law firm in Stone Mountain," Calvin proudly admitted. "We primarily deal with corporate law, but dabble in civil cases as well. We represent several organizations throughout Georgia."

"Would that firm happen to be Saunders and Associates?" Justina curiously asked.

Roger smiled. "Yes, that's it! I see my firm's reputation precedes itself."

"I couldn't agree with you more. Your firm deals with several high-profile cases."

"But your specialty in criminal law sounds really interesting. Maybe we could go out sometime and share stories."

"It sounds like a plan." Justina knew she did not want to talk about work. In her mind, she was toiling over the idea of introducing Calvin to her family in the very near future.

Calvin noticed Justina had been bubbly ever since he sat down. He knew he could stay at the table the rest of the evening without any objections from her.

From the dance floor, Roger looked over to the table and witnessed an unusually happy Justina and a persuasive Calvin engaging in an animated but friendly conversation. Roger could not help but feel a tinge of guilt over leaving Justina alone with this stranger. At the same time, he did not realize she would be so easily wooed by Calvin.

After dinner and a couple of dances, Roger decided to call it a night. He turned to Calvin and said, "I really appreciate you picking up the bill this time, but the next time it's on me."

"Maybe next weekend?" Calvin cautiously asked, while looking in Justina's direction for confirmation. "Or whenever Justina's available."

Justina ignored Calvin and turned to Roger. "Umm…can I speak to you in private?"

"Sure," Roger said, as they walked a short distance from the table. Justina whispered to Roger, "I can't believe we're leaving so soon. Can I persuade you and Rowena to stay longer?"

"Rowena and I are getting up early tomorrow to run some errands."

Justina sighed in response.

"Justina, Calvin seems nice. Maybe you can get him to take you home."

Justina frowned. "Are you crazy? I don't know him like that."

"Trust me," Roger replied, as they walked back toward their table. Then he looked at Calvin with knowing eyes. "Do you mind escorting Justina home?"

"I'd be honored," Calvin smoothly replied.

Justina was not sure she wanted this stranger to know where she lived. She knew where he worked, but Roger did not. "Roger, if you don't mind, I'd like to walk you and Rowena to the front entrance. I have something to tell you."

"Sure Justina." Roger said, before he turned to Calvin and shook his hand. "It was nice meeting you."

"Same here," Calvin replied.

Upon reaching the front entrance, Justina stared at Rowena with contempt. Sensing Justina did not want her listening to their conversation, Rowena stepped aside to give them some privacy.

Justina eyed Rowena until she put enough distance between them. Then she turned to Roger. "Calvin seems nice enough, but just in case I turn up missing, he works for...."

Roger interrupted her. "Justina, I care about you. I would never put you in harm's way. I am very familiar with Calvin Calloway. He's a partner at Saunders and Associates. He received his law degree from Emory, a bachelor's and a master's degree from Howard. He lives in Stone Mountain, and drives a Mercedes, tag number: CALWAY. And Justina, he's not married."

Justina was pleasantly surprised and delighted to hear Calvin's short bio. "Okay, I get it, but how did you gather so much information so quickly? And why is it that I wasn't privy to these facts beforehand?"

"To be honest, I wasn't sure if you'd be interested in him. Besides, did you forget that we hired a private investigator, Christopher Townsend, a week ago? I had him do a quick background check." Roger kissed Justina on the forehead, and said, "You'll be fine. Have a good time."

Justina returned to the table where Calvin happily awaited her presence. For the next hour or so, she discovered she had a lot in common with him.

"Calvin, you're a male version of me," she joked.

Calvin took a sip of wine and smiled. "Well Justina, we may very well be on the right path to happiness. I think we should call it a night," he said, as he looked at his watch. "It's getting late. Besides, I don't know how your overprotective friend, Roger, would feel about me getting you home in the wee hours of the morning."

"I suppose you're right," Justina replied with a light chuckle.

The valet attendant drove up in a Toyota Camry and handed the keys to Calvin. Justina frowned, as she turned to Calvin. "I thought you drove a...."

"My Mercedes is in the shop," Calvin quickly answered, as he opened the passenger door for her.

"Oh, okay."

An hour later, Calvin pulled up in front of Justina's condo, turned off his ignition, and placed his hand on top of hers. Looking into her eyes without saying a word, he leaned over and kissed her gently on the lips.

Justina was receptive to his kiss. Then, in a raspy voice, she asked, "Would you like to come inside for coffee?"

Calvin wasn't expecting this reaction. "I'm afraid I wouldn't be able to control what I feel for you right now," he lied.

"It's okay. I feel the same way," she acknowledged. *Hell, I've been celibate for a long time. We're both grown. I consent!*

"Do you?!" Calvin sharply asked. "Baby, I'm not looking for one night of pleasure. I'm looking for a lifetime of passion with a very special lady. I believe I found my future tonight. Please give me the opportunity to court you."

Justina thought about his request. "I'm not good at committing to anyone, not even to the man who took my virginity," she confessed with regret. *Ouch! That's too much information. Why is Guy Simmons all up in my head tonight?!*

"That's because you never met me," Calvin smoothly replied. "Baby, I want to wine and dine you. I want you to be my princess. Let me take care of you and buy you the world."

Justina's antenna went up when he recited her own personal mantra: *Buy me the world.* "I have everything I need," she finally said.

"But, do you have everything you want? What is life with things and money when you don't have someone to share them with?"

Justina was touched by his words. She had never met anyone who wanted to commit in such uncomplicated terms. At that moment, she realized she may have found her soulmate.

Calvin eagerly asked, "Are you available tomorrow? Maybe we can catch a movie."

"I don't know. Can I call you instead?"

"Sure, here's my business card," Calvin said, as he handed it to her.

Justina took the card and viewed its contents. "No home number or address?"

"I just relocated to Atlanta. I haven't turned on my phone just yet, but my office and cell numbers are on the card."

Justina remembered she was in the same situation when she first relocated to Atlanta. She smiled and told Calvin she would be in touch.

In the comfort of her bed, she reminisced over meeting Calvin. She was lovestruck, but did not think it was possible, so soon. *Calvin Calloway, you are blowing my mind.*

Calvin could not wait to update his co-conspirator. All he had to do was pique Justina's interest in him. He looked forward to reporting the evening's events, so he could get his first installment. Calvin readily picked up his cell phone and dialed his co-conspirator's number.

"It's a done deal," Calvin said. "How soon can I get my money?"

"As soon as Justina's life is filled with misery," the mystery person responded.

"I don't get it. She seems like a cool person. What's your beef with this chic?"

"Let's just say, she has ruffled a lot of feathers. That law degree only added insult to injury. I hope you're not spell-bound because she's a conniving, two-timing, selfish b-tch!"

"Hold up! This is too much drama! As long as I get my money, as agreed, that's all that matters."

"That's fair. The less you know, the better off you are. If you play your cards right, I might throw in a bonus."

Before Calvin could respond, the caller hung up. He was perplexed over the sketchy details of his role, but it was mute issue at this point. He knew if he did not fulfill his mission, his life would be in danger.

Chapter 18

Stolen Promises

Rowena instantly liked Calvin when she met him that night at the club. She had a sidebar conversation with him when Justina and Roger briefly stepped away from the table.

"You know," Rowena said, "if I were you, I wouldn't talk to Justina. She is psycho!" Calvin laughed heartily when Rowena mocked Justina by twirling her finger around and acting like a crazy woman.

Rowena smiled as she moved closer to Calvin. "How would you like to meet a real woman? She'd be perfect for you."

Calvin raised a brow. "But I thought Justina was your friend."

Rowena frowned. "That woman is no friend of mine!" she sharply replied. "If you know what's good for you, you'll never see her again."

"It's business, not personal," he replied with a sly grin.

Rowena smiled as she read into what Calvin was saying. She concluded that they might have something in common.

Calvin thought Roger was too nerdy for a woman like Rowena, so he asked, "What's up with you and your boy?"

"Like you, it's business, not personal," Rowena cunningly said. "Is there any way I can contact you after tonight?"

"Only if I have a way of contacting you?" Calvin boldly asked.

Calvin and Rowena slipped each other their contact information right before Justina and Roger returned to the table.

The next day, Calvin allowed his curiosity to get the best of him and called Rowena.

"I'm glad you called!" Rowena said with excitement. "When and where can we meet?"

Calvin was taken aback. "We?" he coyly asked.

"Yeah, you, me, Roger, and my girlfriend. You know, the one I told you about."

"Is Roger okay with this?"

"He's cool. Trust me."

"Okay, let's meet at Tony Romas off exit 21, around six."

"I'll see you then!" Rowena cheerfully replied.

Calvin hung up the phone in a daze. He wondered if Roger was really okay with this arrangement.

As soon as Rowena hung up the phone, she asked Roger to go with her and Sue to meet with Calvin. However, Roger was furious. He asked, "Are you sure this is a good idea? Calvin seems to be smitten with Justina."

Rowena rolled her eyes skyward. "Calvin is a grown man!" she said with an attitude. "Let him decide who he wants. It's not like he's married to Justina." After Roger did not respond, she softly asked, "Are we cool?"

"Yeah whatever, cool," Roger said with skepticism. He was nervous about Rowena finding out about the arrangement he had made with Calvin. Roger wanted to maintain a clean image in Rowena's presence, and was not sure how she would react to him being a part of a scheme to ruin Justina.

Calvin approached Roger when he was in the pub one day ranting about Justina. Roger was upset because Justina had just embarrassed him in front of one of his clients, again. This time, Justina had crossed the line by calling him a *"loser"*, when he did not accept the State's plea bargain. The State wanted his client to plead guilty in exchange for a lesser sentence, but Roger knew his client was innocent and had a strong alibi. Roger won the case, had the charges dropped against his client, and successfully sued the State for pain and suffering. He never got over Justina's insult, or the fact that she never apologized to him.

After Calvin overheard Roger's spiel about Justina, he approached Roger with an offer he could not refuse. Calvin explained his plans to sabotage Justina's business, and asked for Roger's assistance.

"Count me in!" Roger eagerly replied. He was gung-ho on seeking revenge, and was more than a willing participant.

"If you're that miserable," Calvin said, "why don't you just quit and open your own law firm, or go work for another firm?"

Roger sighed. "I wish it were that simple. For one thing, I don't have enough capital or resources to open my own law firm. And secondly, it's impossible to get partnership when you're a fairly new attorney."

"What if I gave you the capital to open your own law firm?"

Roger gazed at Calvin in disbelief, before asking, "Are you serious?! That would be perfect."

"Tell me what you know about Justina," Calvin insisted.

"Well, for one, I think you're her type. I've observed the way she looks at tall, dark, handsome guys."

For the next thirty minutes, Calvin learned a lot about Justina, including her likes and dislikes. Roger and Calvin devised a plan and set it in motion. The night Calvin coincidentally met Justina at the nightclub was only the beginning.

Calvin was already seated at a table when Sue, Roger, and Rowena walked in. He was blown away by Sue's beauty. She was thinner than Rowena, but just as shapely. He stood up and shook her hand.

"It's a pleasure to meet you," Calvin said, as he kissed the back of her hand.

"The pleasure is all mine," Sue shyly replied.

Calvin pulled out Sue's chair. "Please, have a seat." Then he acknowledged Roger with a handshake, and kissed Rowena on the cheek. "We meet again."

Roger mumbled, "Awkwardly."

The clan spent the remainder of the evening talking about frivolous things. They were afraid to reveal too much about themselves; everyone at the table had secrets.

Sue liked Calvin because he reminded her of Kevin, Regine's father. To her, he was charming, slick, and kind of rugged. She detected a street thug mentality behind Calvin's façade. After dinner, they made plans to see each other again.

Calvin quickly learned that Sue was book-smart and street-smart, and could easily transition when necessary. Also, unlike Justina, she gave him space to breathe and conduct business without asking questions. Even though he did not know the specifics of Sue's past, he believed they had a lot in common.

On their third date, Calvin kissed Sue and was instantly bitten by the *lovebug*. Sue was also in daze, desiring Calvin with her heart and soul. She wanted to tell him about her HIV status, but he shushed her. She also tried to tell him about her past, but he told her he had a rough past too.

"Baby, you don't owe me any explanation," Calvin finally said.

"But I feel I do. You don't understand...," Sue tried to explain.

Calvin put his finger to her lips and shushed her, again. "Let's make tonight special. Everybody has skeletons in their closet. Whatever it is, I'm sure you're sorry." Then he passionately kissed her and laid her across the bed. Before they went any further, Sue insisted that they use a condom. He obliged her request.

After they made love, Calvin looked into Sue's eyes and confessed. "You know I'm seeing Justina, but it's just business," he softly admitted.

Sue gazed into his eyes. "What kind of business?"

"Let's just say, I'm going to make a lot of money."

Sue grinned. "Oh, I get it. Justina's part of a scam," she casually replied.

"Yeah, something like that."

"Cool."

Calvin was surprised when she did not probe further. "For real?!"

"Yeah, I'm down with whatever. Just be careful," Sue cautioned, as she leaned over and kissed him on the lips.

Calvin decided Sue was the type of woman he needed in his life. "I'm glad you feel that way," he said with relief. "I may need you to handle some transactions for me later on."

"Okay. Let me know what I can do to help," Sue offered with a smile.

Calvin smiled back. "Listen, I gotta go out of town for a while. You cool with that?"

"Yeah baby. Go handle your business."

Calvin smiled as he thought Sue Croswell was unlike any woman he had in the past. He felt he could trust her with his life. Even better, he could confide in her about his dealings with Justina, and was surprised when she took it in stride. *Yeah, she's a keeper,* he concluded.

After Calvin dropped Sue off at the hotel, she began to worry her plan was off track. Sue felt that she not supposed to fall in love, and was trying to fight it. She walked into the hotel room and found Rowena standing in front of the mirror, hot curling her hair.

Sue sat on the bed and gazed at Rowena.

"What's wrong?" Rowena asked, as she briefly glanced back at Sue.

"We've been here for a month," Sue thoughtfully acknowledged. "A lot longer than I anticipated. We had a plan, remember. We were supposed to come here, get payback on Justina and leave."

Rowena glared at Sue in the mirror. "I thought you liked Calvin. What's up? You're not feeling him?"

Sue sighed. "Yeah, that's the problem."

Rowena turned and faced Sue. "Well, what's the problem?"

"You know...I'm HIV positive. I haven't told him yet," Sue weakly admitted, while averting her eyes downward.

"Why are you fretting?! Whenever you have sex, use a condom," Rowena frankly replied.

"You don't understand...," Sue tried to explain.

Rowena turned off the curling iron, then sat on the bed next to Sue. "No, you don't understand. Just because you're HIV positive, you don't shut down on life. You've been drug-free for eight months. You know what that means; it means you made a decision to live."

"I know what you're saying," Sue softly admitted, "but I'm scared."

Rowena hugged Sue, as she said, "I know. I'm scared for you, but you have so much to live for. Soon, you will make amends with Regine and finally be a part of her life. Your desire to come to Atlanta to seek vengeance on her behalf is admirable, but someone else beat you to it. Just make sure you remain Calvin Calloway's confidant so he will continue to keep you in the loop. Trust me, he'll tell you precisely what he plans on doing to Justina."

"I suppose you're right. I like him a lot, though," Sue humbly replied, realizing her feelings were much stronger. She was in love with him.

"I know, but we have to keep our game face on. You with me?" Rowena questioned, playfully pushing Sue with her shoulder.

"Yes," Sue said, giggling, and lightly pushing Rowena back.

"Oh before I forget, we're moving out of this hotel into a fully furnished two-bedroom apartment in Buckhead, Georgia. It's about thirty minutes from here."

Sue was perplexed with the change in plans, but figured the goal remained the same. "Rowena, I want to ask you something, and please don't be offended."

Rowena tensed up, not sure where this conversation was headed. "What is it?" she finally asked.

"Where are you getting all this money from?"

Rowena thought about Sue's inquiry before responding. "You see, I didn't tell you because I don't want you to worry," she thoughtfully said. "Well…my ex-boyfriend hooked me up before he went to jail. Let's just say, we never have to worry about money. Cool?"

"Yeah, I appreciate this, but...."

"But nothing," Rowena interjected. "I love you girl," she affectionately admitted, before she kissed Sue on her cheek. "I'll be back tomorrow." Rowena got up to leave and took her overnight bag with her. She was going to spend the night with Roger.

Sue accepted Rowena's excuse but thought her story sounded lame, especially since Rowena had already told her she got clean because she could not afford to buy drugs. She decided to keep her suspicions about Rowena to herself.

Roger fell hard for Rowena after they had sex the first time. He was nervous because he never had sex with a black woman. Rowena was also nervous. She did not think she could go through with it. But with the lights off, she did not see the difference between Roger and the two black men she slept with in her lifetime.

After a full night of passion, Roger held on to Rowena for dear life. He did not want the night to end. He wondered about how his family would react if he took her home to meet them. Thinking about this, suddenly made Roger uneasy with the idea. He knew most of his family members would not readily accept Rowena based on comments they made about minorities in the past.

Roger lightly touched Rowena's shoulder. "Hon', are you awake?"

"Yes, Roger," Rowena said with a twinkle in her eyes.

"I'm thinking about quitting the law firm."

Rowena turned to face him. "Roger, you deserve that partnership. Can you go anywhere else and become a partner right away?"

"No, but I don't know how much longer I can tolerate Justina's abuse. I especially hate the way she treats you."

"Baby, don't worry about me. I'm a big girl," she softly said, cuddling next to him.

Roger was deep in thought as he wrapped his arms around her. "Rowena?"

Rowena looked into his eyes and asked, "What's wrong?"

"I think I'm falling in love with you," he finally admitted. "Truth be told, I fell in love with you on our first date."

Rowena smiled. "Roger, I don't think that's possible. We really don't know each other very well."

"So fill in the gaps," he requested, believing there was nothing Rowena could tell him about her that would trump his love for her.

"Well, for starters, I don't have a job yet."

"Okay."

"I'm not close to my family."

"I'm not either. Go on...."

Then Rowena found it hard to admit, "I don't think I'm good enough for you."

Roger laughed in response. "That should be the least of your worries. You are perfect in every way. I love you."

"Are you sure?"

"Yes, I'm sure. I haven't been with many women in my lifetime, but it feels right when I'm with you," Roger said, as he lightly touched her cheek.

Rowena sat up in bed and turned on the lamp. "Are you sure you're not feeling this way because I'm the first black woman you've ever been with?"

Roger chuckled. "I'm sure it's not just your skin color. I know my feelings are true, because I want to be with you all the time. Not a day that goes by that I don't think about you," he softly admitted, while gazing into her eyes.

"I think the feeling is mutual," Rowena reluctantly admitted, "but let's take it slow." She kissed him good night and turned off the lamp. She tried to convince herself that this fling with Roger was just a part of the plan.

They snuggled up next to each other and fell asleep minutes later.

A month later, Roger was convinced Rowena was the woman for him. He picked out an engagement ring from a local jewelry store, and made reservations at the French Cuisine. When they arrived at the restaurant, Rowena turned to Roger and asked, "What's the occasion?"

Roger smiled and gave her a peck on her lips. "You're special to me, and you deserve to be treated well."

"You're special to me too," Rowena half-heartedly replied. She was not sure where this conversation was headed, or what she was supposed to say.

After they ate dinner, Roger ordered a bottle of champagne for their table. Then he smiled as the waiter filled their flutes.

"What's going on?" Rowena anxiously asked.

When Roger reached for her hands across the table, Rowena intuitively placed her hand in his. "I've been thinking," he thoughtfully said, "I know it's only been a month, but we know what we want at our age." He assumed they were the same age.

Rowena's voice trembled. "What are you saying?" *I just know this man is not about to propose to me.*

"I'm saying that I don't have to wait another hour, another month, or even another year to know I love you. I want you to be my wife," Roger happily admitted.

Rowena raised her brows. "Are you sure?" she cautiously asked. She was truly in love with him, but thought Roger was only in love with the image she portrayed.

Roger smiled before he admitted, "I have never been surer of anything." He let go of her hands and reached into his pocket, grinning from ear to ear. Then he pulled out a small box and opened it to display a two-karat diamond engagement ring. "Will you marry me?"

Before Rowena answered, a violinist came to their table on cue and began playing a sweet melody. Rowena was so caught up in the moment, she jubilantly shouted, "Yes, yes, yes!" She beamed as she cried real tears of joy. *God, why couldn't this be the real thing?*

Roger stood up from his chair and went to her. "You just made me the happiest man in the world." He hugged and kissed her passionately.

"Can I ask one thing?" Rowena nervously asked.

"Sure."

"Can we hold off on setting a date for the wedding?"

Roger laughed softly. "Sure, but don't leave me waiting too long."

The next day Roger told Justina about his engagement to Rowena. Justina was shocked, and could not believe he was going to marry someone like her.

"Roger, are you sure? You've only known her for one month."

"Don't start, Justina! I don't need your approval!" Roger sharply said. "I just thought I should let you know."

"Well, congratulations are in order," Justina sarcastically replied.

Roger frowned. "You don't have to like her; just show her some respect. No more name-calling. Understood?"

"Now Roger...."

"No more insults! I mean it! The next time you insult my fiancé, I walk!" he firmly stated.

Justina thought of a response but held her tongue. She needed Roger more than he would ever know, especially since their business account was still in the red. Even more, she hated to admit that she was jealous of Rowena. She wondered when someone was going to propose to her, and was hoping that that someone would be Calvin Calloway. She smiled at the possibility.

Chapter 19

Surviving the Storm

Guy finally gathered the nerves to call Regine again. He had repeatedly left messages, but she never returned his calls. It had seemed like a lost cause, until she finally answered.

"Hello Regine," he said with caution.

Regine did not respond, but he knew it was her. Guy clutched the phone tightly to his ear. "Please don't hang up."

Regine closed her eyes and took two deep breaths to calm down. "Why do you insist on calling me?" she asked in a measured tone. "And how did you get this number in the first place?"

Guy continued to hold on to the phone tightly, hoping she would not hang up on him. "A friend told me you relocated to Virginia. Are you ever coming back to Florida? I miss you."

Regine stood erect and cocked her head to one side. "Why should I?!" she snapped. "You made up your mind when you screwed me for Justina!" She thought she was over him, but her heart said otherwise.

Guy knew he could not rationalize his mistake. He began sweating profusely, while pacing back and forth. "Baby, please. I made a mistake. I...I didn't appreciate you. Please...give me a chance to make it up to you. The girls miss you like crazy. And Alex, he asks about you all the time." His shirt was drenched with perspiration as he held his breath, awaiting her response.

Regine tightened her lips and rolled her eyes skyward. "Name one good reason why I should give you a chance. What makes you think things will work if you can't even say three words?"

Guy was speechless because he did not understand what she meant.

Regine waited two seconds for his response before slamming the phone onto its cradle. Then she went into her bedroom to lie down. Guy's phone call unnerved her, but her recent visit to the doctor's office dampened her spirits even more.

The doctor told her there were some irregularities with her ovaries; a result from the abortion she had during her first year of college. Regine knew she was reckless when she went off with PJ, the first man who claimed to love her. It was apparent that something was wrong when she began experiencing significant abdominal pains. Her grandmother had convinced her to go to the doctor.

"I'm sorry to be the bearer of bad news," the doctor said, as he closed his notepad, "but we must remove the growing infection. It could be potentially fatal if left untreated. I would recommend that you have a hysterectomy, but there are other alternatives such as...."

Regine stopped listening to the doctor's spiel after she understood what he was saying. She held her head down, crying uncontrollably. *God, look at my life! It seems I have always suffered. I have no man, no parents, and now I will never give birth to my own child. This is too much to bear.*

The doctor gave Regine tissue to dry her eyes. She thanked him and told him she would schedule an appointment for the surgery.

After crying for what seemed like an eternity, Regine no longer felt self-pity or depressed over the bad cards life dealt her. Instead, she silently prayed, asking God to forgive her for the bad choices she had made in her life.

After Regine hung up on Guy, he went into the living room and sat on the sofa next to Alex, who was watching a basketball game on TV. Guy was unfazed by the game. He was in deep thought over the phone call he just had with Regine. Several minutes later, Dana and Cassandra entered the living room and stood in front of Guy.

"Did you reach her yet?" Dana boldly asked with her hands on her hips.

Guy knew Dana was referring to Regine. He also knew the girls missed her terribly. It hurt him to see the sadness in their eyes. He sighed, then regretfully said, "I tried, but she keeps hanging up on me."

Dana swirled her neck and crossed her arms. "There's only one thing to do," she said with conviction, "and we already packed our bags."

Guy sat up on the edge of the sofa and looked at Dana, who retained her sassiness. "What are you talking about?" he incredulously asked, looking back at Alex with a questioning gaze. His little brother shrugged his shoulders and pretended to be engrossed in the game.

Cassandra stood next to Dana, and shyly said, "We decided we should go to Virginia to get her."

Guy sighed as he put his hand on his chin, mulling over their idea. He looked at the girls and saw determination in their eyes. "You girls can't be serious," he finally said.

Dana purposely fragmented her response when she said, "Oh…yes…we…are! We have $26.00 saved from our allowance for gas money and snacks. We're ready."

Guy thought about it, then said to no one in particular, "It's a long way, but Regine is worth it." He turned to Alex and asked, "Are you going?"

Alex blinked and looked at Guy as if he lost his mind. "For homemade cake, cornbread, collard greens, etcetera, etcetera. You're darn right I'm going! We need her. I miss her," he firmly said, as he slumped back in the sofa.

Guy frowned. "Regine means more to me than her cooking," he sternly replied.

Alex's eyes hardened as he sat up on the sofa. "I didn't mean it like that. It's just that things haven't been the same without Regine. She was the backbone that held this family together. If she comes back, I'll pitch in and make sure she doesn't have to do everything for us."

"So, it's settled," Guy said with finality, as he brushed his hands across his pants leg. "We'll leave early in the morning."

Dana and Cassandra cheerfully embraced each other, then rushed to their rooms to double-check their pre-packed suitcases.

"Guy, we're already packed," Alex replied without taking his eyes off the basketball game. "You go pack. We knew you would go along with our plan," he added with a smug grin.

Guy laughed as he walked into his room to gather his belongings. *I do love you, Regine. The next time I see you, I'm going to say it and show it. I was such a fool for letting you go.*

The next morning, they woke up early for the drive to Virginia. "Okay girls, are you ready?!" Guy anxiously asked. Cassandra and Dana nodded, while Alex stood by the front door waiting patiently. Luckily, Alex had his driver's license and was able to help with the fifteen-hour drive.

As Guy turned off the exit leading to the address Big Mike gave him, his hands began sweating and his heart was beating rapidly. He kept praying and hoping Regine would give him another chance.

Alex looked over at Guy and noticed he looked stiff. "You know what to say, right?"

"Of course I do," Guy said with uncertainty, as he parked his car. His heart was heavy when he knocked on the door. He did not know how Regine would react to their surprise visit. When Bessie answered the door, he was positive they had the wrong address.

Guy cautiously said, "Hello, we're looking for Regine."

"And who are you?" Bessie asked with a welcoming smile. She already knew who they were, especially when she saw the twins. Regine kept a picture of them on the nightstand in her bedroom.

"I'm Guy. This is Dana and Cassandra, my sisters," he said, while pointing to each sibling. "And this is my little brother, Alex."

Bessie smiled and opened the door wider for them to come inside. "Well it's about time!" she joyfully said.

Guy froze in place. "What…I mean, I beg your pardon?"

"Come on in," Bessie insisted. "I don't know what took you all so long to get here. Oh never mind. It always takes a man a long time to discover what he had when it's gone."

When they walked through the front door, Bessie said, "Go on in the living room and have a seat. I'll let Regine know you're here."

Guy turned back to Bessie after walking through the front door. "Ma'am, I'm sorry. I didn't get your name."

"Just call me Grandma Bessie. You all hungry? Regine cooked enough food to feed an army, and you all know she can burn. Regine made me a butter lemon cake last night," she said, as she pointed to the cake on the dining room table. "It's absolutely delicious. You all are welcome to a slice."

Alex eagerly jumped up from the sofa and spoke up. "Grandma Bessie, may I please have a slice of cake and whatever else you have on the stove? I'd love to stay for dinner, if that's okay with you."

Bessie laughed so hard she started coughing. "Well baby, you came to the right place. Go on and help yourself. I'm going up stairs to get Regine. She's been talking about all of you since she's been here."

Bessie went upstairs and knocked on Regine's bedroom door. "Regine, baby. You have company. Get dressed and come on downstairs."

"Who is it?" Regine groggily asked. She was in a deep sleep dreaming about Guy and his siblings.

"Just come downstairs and find out for yourself," Bessie replied. She was looking forward to seeing Regine's surprised reaction.

Halfway down stairs, Regine froze in place as her mouth flew open. She thought she was still dreaming. Hesitantly, she continued walking downstairs, while gazing at Guy and his siblings.

When Dana and Cassandra saw Regine, they jumped up from the sofa and ran into her arms. "I missed my girls!" Regine excited professed, while embracing and kissing them.

"We missed you too!" Dana and Cassandra cheerfully said in unison.

Alex stopped eating his slice of cake long enough to tell her he missed her. Regine smiled in response, then cautiously directed her gaze to Guy. "Hello," she said to him in a leveled, emotionless tone.

Guy was pleasantly surprised by Regine's appearance. He noticed that she had lost weight and her hair had grown longer. He slowly approached her and reached for her hands. "Hello Regine, we've missed you. We didn't realize how much until you left. We need you. I need you." Then without hesitation, he finally said, "I love you."

Regine opened her mouth to respond but closed it. She did not expect to hear these words from Guy.

"Please Regine," Guy pleaded, "give me a second chance to prove to you that I'm a changed man."

Regine glanced down before responding. "I don't know…I think it's too late."

Guy's eyes grew bigger. "Is there someone else?"

"No," Regine softly said, as she pulled Guy aside, out of earshot of his siblings and Bessie. "I don't want to end up like your mother," she fearfully admitted. "I need to know if you're still dealing with Justina. And if not, explain how this time would be different."

Guy gazed into her eyes with sincerity. "Regine, Justina made it clear to me that I could never be a part of her life. You were right about everything. I know I don't love her, because love hurts. When she walked out of my life, I was heartbroken, but it was nothing like the pain I felt when you left me." Guy got down on one knee and held her hand. "I promise, if you will give me a chance, you won't regret it." He hesitated before adding, "I've always loved you, but I let my ego get in the way. I'm sorry for everything I put you through."

Regine cried, releasing all her pent up emotions. "I love you too," she whispered. Guy stood up and embraced her, then gave her a long, passionate kiss.

Bessie witnessed their exchange and jokingly said, "That settles it, let's discuss the wedding plans." Regine was shocked at Bessie's suggestion. However, Guy liked the idea.

Regine held up her hand. "Hold on, Grandma. I need to talk to Guy about some things." She looked into Guy's eyes and softly added, "Things that might make him change his mind about me."

Bessie raised her hand and playfully swatted at the air. "Ah child, hush that nonsense. You love him and he loves you. What is there to talk about?"

"Grandma, if you don't mind, I need some privacy with Guy," Regine stated, as she took Guy's hand and guided him outside.

They went for a short walk. The weather was nice and cool. Guy felt as though he had conquered a queen, but feared it might be too late. Regine, on the other hand, realized her dreams partially came true with Guy's admission of his love for her. Not giving Regine the opportunity to explain why they shouldn't be together, Guy spoke first.

"Regine, I acted like a jackass. I took you for granted. You've always been there for us. I'm sorry I hurt you. If you give me a chance, I'll make it up to you. I cannot go on without you."

Regine was humbled by his confession. "Guy, there's something I must tell you," she nervously said, as she averted her eyes downward. "I can never have children of my own."

For a few seconds, Guy was quiet, expecting to hear the worst. "Baby, is that it?! Regine, if you want a baby, we can always adopt. I, for one, have other goals to pursue. Since my parents died, I've been taking care of my siblings, and you know it hasn't been easy. In fact, I'm already looking forward to attending Dana and Cassandra's high school graduation," he lightheartedly replied with a chuckle.

Regine looked surprised. "So you really don't mind that I can't have children?"

"Heck no!"

Regine was overwhelmed by his thoughtfulness. "Oh Guy, I love you," she softly admitted.

Guy grabbed her hand and kissed her lips with passion and vigor. His heart was fluttering the whole time. He knew he was in love with her and could not wait to prove it. "Please come back to Florida with us," he pleaded.

Regine shook her head. "I don't know, Guy. Let's take things slow."

Guy held her hand as he closed the space between them. "I want to show you things are going to be different between us."

Regine frowned. "By shacking?"

"No, baby. I want you to be my wife."

Regine was very surprised and elated to hear his admission, but realized she was nervous about moving in with him, so quickly. "Guy, so much time has passed between us. I'm not the same person you knew over a year ago."

"I know," Guy grimly responded. "Would you at least consider staying in the guest room as our visitor? That way, we can rekindle our friendship. Let me prove to you that I'm a changed man."

Regine thought about his request and finally said, "Okay, but there will be no sex. Deal?"

Guy did not know if he could handle not making love to her, especially in the same house. "Deal," he said to appease her.

Guy and his siblings spent the rest of the weekend with Regine and Bessie. They made arrangements to return the following weekend with a U-Haul, to pack up Regine's belongings. Dana and Cassandra fell in love with Grandma Bessie, and convinced her to visit them.

One week later, Guy and his siblings returned to Virginia to pick Regine up. They were surprised and elated when Bessie agreed to come with them to visit for a couple of days. Upon returning to St. Petersburg, Regine and Bessie settled into the guest room, while Guy and Alex unloaded the U-Haul.

When Guy entered the house with the last box, he spotted Regine in the kitchen. "Regine, what are you doing? I want to cook dinner for you."

Regine cringed when she thought about the last meal Guy burnt. "Guy, don't take this the wrong way, but I love my life too much to allow you to cook for me. I'll cook for us; I don't mind."

Guy laughed. "Okay, you got me. But afterward, I want you to relax."

Regine smiled. "Deal. Besides, Grandma Bessie will be leaving the day after tomorrow, and I don't want her going home with an upset stomach."

During the next month, Regine re-enrolled in Culinary Arts School and settled into Guy's home. She instantly noticed how Guy, Alex, Dana, and Cassandra did not allow her to clean up after them, nor did they depend on her for everything. Even Alex caught her off guard when he asked her, "Is it okay if I go hang out with my dawgs?" He never asked before. He did not have to ask now that he was practically a grown man.

Regine was over the stove cooking when she briefly looked up and joked, "Your dawgs? Do they bark?"

Alex laughed.

"Can you be home in time for dinner?" Regine asked, as she turned the temperature down on the stove.

"Okay." Alex turned to leave but turned back around.

Regine looked at him with a questioning gaze. "What is it?"

Alex smiled as he held his basketball under his arm. "It's good having you home," he softly admitted. "I love you. You've always been nice to me."

Regine smiled. "I'm glad to be back. I love you too," she sincerely replied.

Alex blushed as he headed outside. He knew he did not have to worry about being home in time for dinner, especially since Guy forewarned him of his plans with Regine for the evening.

As soon as Alex walked out the house, Regine removed the casserole out of the oven, then looked at the clock hanging above the stove. "Dana! Cassandra!" she yelled from the kitchen. "Did you girls finish your homework?"

The twins were in the living room when Regine called for them. They rushed into the kitchen and responded in unison, "Yes! We're finish."

Dana breathlessly asked, "Now, can we go with Grandma Bessie to the play."

"Only if I can tag along," Regine said with a smile.

Guy overheard Regine as he discreetly entered the kitchen. "I don't think that's a good idea."

Regine was surprised to see Guy in the middle of the afternoon. "Where did you come from? And why are you home from work so early?"

Guy looked at her and smiled. Then he put his briefcase down on the bar stool and leaned against the counter. "I have good news, which requires a celebration," he slyly admitted, as Bessie walked into the kitchen behind him.

When Regine looked at the girls and Bessie, Guy firmly stated, "Just the two of us."

Regine looked at the stove, then turned back to him. "What about dinner?"

Bessie playfully pushed Regine away from the stove. "Child, I taught you how to cook. Go get dressed. I want you and Guy to have a good ole' time," she said with joy in her voice.

Regine suspected Bessie and Guy were up to something. She suspiciously eyed them as she removed her apron. "Give me an hour to change," she finally said with a wide grin. Then she quickly bolted upstairs to get dressed.

Guy smiled. "Baby, take your time."

Bessie turned to Guy and whispered, "You have the ring?"

Guy pulled the ring box out of his pocket and showed it to Bessie. "I hope she likes it."

Bessie held it up and admired its beauty. She was beaming as she returned the ring to Guy.

Guy asked, "Did I ever tell you that I'm glad you're here?"

"No, but I assumed so. I can only stay a few more weeks. But don't worry; I'll return soon," she said with a genuine smile.

Guy smiled in response. "Regine enjoys having you around, and I want to do whatever it takes to make her happy. I love her. I promise, I'll never hurt her again."

Bessie hugged him. "Don't let me down. I know you and the kids love her, but I was there when she cried a long time. Love hurts, so be sure this is for real."

"I'm sure. You have my word," Guy confidently replied.

Guy and Regine drove thirty miles north of St. Petersburg before turning off at the Clearwater exit onto I-19. Twenty minutes later, she looked around at the desolate area with no homes or landmarks in sight. "Where are we going?" Regine asked, as she looked at Guy for an answer.

"It's a surprise," Guy mischievously replied.

"I can't take it anymore," Regine exclaimed. "If you don't tell me where we're going, I'm going to scream," she teased, as she continued looking at the scenery.

Guy remained mum.

Suddenly, Regine let out a screeching noise. *"Ahhhhh...!"*

Guy laughed. "Okay, okay. I give up. Can I at least pull off the road?" he asked, looking in his rearview mirror.

"You better hurry up and tell me before I start again," Regine teased.

"Girl, you crack me up." Guy laughed as he pulled over to the side of the road. He got out of his car and went to the trunk.

Without prompting from Guy, Regine got out the car and walked over to him. "What are you doing?"

Guy smiled as he opened the trunk. "I have something to give you. It's just a small token of my appreciation." He retrieved a red box with a big white bow on top and handed it to her. Regine quickly tore off the ribbon and opened the box. She was surprised and speechless by what she saw.

Guy instantly noticed the sadness in her eyes. "Baby, this is not the reaction I expected."

"Oh Guy, you don't understand. I love it," she said, as she removed the diamond necklace from the box, admiring its beauty.

"Are you disappointed?"

"No," Regine softly replied, still casting her eyes on the necklace. She was, in fact, disappointed but tried to hide it.

Guy held up his pinky finger. "Regine, were you expecting something else?"

"No," she solemnly replied, but perked up when she saw a glimpse of something sparkling on Guy's finger. "Oh Guy! Is that what I think it is?!" she asked, beaming with excitement.

"Oh, you're asking about this little cruddy thing on my finger."

"May I have it?!" Regine excitedly asked, as she quickly removed it from his finger and slid it on hers.

Guy chuckled. "Can I at least ask you to marry me?"

"The answer is yes!" Regine eagerly announced, without taking her eyes off the three-karat, pear-shaped diamond engagement ring.

Guy smiled as if he had won the lottery.

Regine looked around, observing the scenery. "But why did we travel so far out?"

"Before you distracted me, we were driving to the site of our new home."

Regine became alarmed. "Can we afford a new home? The girls will be in college in a few years. We have so many plans and not enough money, just yet."

Guy smiled, realizing she was always putting others first. "We don't have to worry about money for a while. You're looking at the new Vice CEO of this state's largest technology firm."

"Really?!" Regine said, jumping up and down with glee, before hugging and congratulating him.

"Yes, I'm for real. Baby, I make enough to build a beautiful home for us, and go on lavish vacations every summer and holiday."

"Guy, this is wonderful news!"

Guy cupped her face and kissed her. "Baby, you make my life complete. Start making wedding plans, because I don't know how much longer I can wait to make love to you."

"Thank you for being patient," she softly said.

"It'll just make our love-making that much sweeter," he charmingly replied.

They returned to the car and drove to the vacant spot of their new home. When Regine got out of the car and looked around, she realized their house would be overlooking the Gulf Coast. "Guy, it's beautiful here."

"Baby, get used to it. Construction starts next week," he said, as he found a place for them to sit comfortably and watch the sunset.

Regine was elated, as her dream of marrying Guy was coming true. She had known he would be successful one day, but never imagined the magnitude of his success.

Guy did not tell her his success had not come without a price. He has always experienced dissension from his peers, but his new position only worsened matters. His colleagues were surprised when he moved up the ranks so quickly. Some even accused him of brown-nosing and personally knowing the owner. Guy knew he was fortunate, but had to admit that there were other qualified and experienced employees more fitting for the position.

Jeanine was delighted to hear about Regine and Guy's reunion. She clasped her hands and rejoiced when her private investigator, Tim Carter, told her about the land Guy had just purchased for the mansion.

"I'm glad he has finally come to his senses," Jeanine cheerfully said. "Any word on Justina yet?"

Tim sat up in his chair. "Don't worry about her. She seems totally smitten with Calvin Calloway."

Jeanine sighed and grimaced. "Well, I won't be satisfied until she's married." Then she frowned and asked, "Any word on that?"

"I'm expecting an update any day now," Tim confidently replied.

"Good. Stay on top of it," Jeanine ordered, as she stood up and walked toward the door.

Tim stood up and followed her. At the entrance, he turned to Jeanine and asked, "What if Calvin marries Justina beforehand?"

Jeanine smiled at the thought. "That'll be great! But, until that time comes about, make sure Calvin completes his mission. I'm still concerned about Guy's safety. I don't trust Regine's father."

"Don't worry about that. I can assure you that Guy isn't on anyone's hit list."

"That's what I needed to hear," Jeanine said, as she opened the door for Tim to leave. She relaxed in her chair after hearing the good news. Jeanine wanted to make sure her stepsons were stable before the inevitable. This time her chemotherapy session went a little easier. She was now at peace.

Chapter 20

Bittersweet

During their first two months of dating, Justina enjoyed Calvin's company. He wined and dined her, making her feel special. Unfortunately, their relationship took a downward turn when she suddenly found it difficult to reach him. Calvin rarely answered his cell phone, and his office number was repeatedly intercepted by his answering service.

When Justina finally reached him, a week later, she complained nonstop. "Calvin, why don't you answer your cell phone anymore?!"

"Baby, I told you, I keep my cell phone turned off during meetings, and at night, while I'm sleeping."

Justina thought Calvin was hiding something, so she probed further. "You could at least get a landline for your home," she stated, as it dawned on her that she had never been to his home. "I think you're hiding something, and I have a feeling it involves another woman." She hung up on him, deciding to cut her losses.

After Calvin heard the dial tone, he started chiding himself for being so careless. He had been spending most of his free time with the new love of his life, Sue Croswell. It was very difficult juggling two women at the same time, but he realized early on that Sue had his heart.

Calvin kept trying to call Justina, but she never answered or returned his calls. On his last attempt, she answered with an attitude.

"Hello Justina," he cautiously said, certain that she was still angry with him. "Is everything okay between us?"

"Are you serious?!" Justina rhetorically asked. "Calvin, you're trying to play me for a fool! I've moved on with my life and I suggest you do the same."

"But let me explain…."

"There's nothing to explain!" Justina firmly stated. She paused for a few seconds, before asking, "What's your home address?"

"Why?" Calvin nervously inquired.

"I'm calling the phone company to hook up a line for you." Justina lied to see how he would react.

Calvin was speechless.

"What is it?!" Justina was dying to know. "Are you married? Be straight with me for a change." When Calvin did not respond, she sighed and shook her head. "You know, it was nice knowing you."

Within a millisecond, Calvin heard the dial tone. He became frustrated with himself as he closed his cell phone. *Damn! How am I going to rectify this mess?! I need another strategy.*

Ever since they met, Calvin had been acting like Justina's little puppet. It worked up to this point, but now he had to make some changes. He picked up the phone and called a local realty company. "Yes, I'm looking for a fully furnished home to rent," he told the leasing agent.

"How long will you be staying, Mr...?"

"Calloway. I'm going to need the place for at least six months, maybe longer."

"Does it matter how many bedrooms?" the agent probed.

"No it doesn't. My wife and I are looking for something in Stone Mountain, Georgia."

"We have a few, but you'll have to sign a twelve month lease. How soon would you like to see them?"

"Today. I'll be there in thirty minutes."

Calvin moved into a rental property the following week. He paid with cash, and threw in an extra thousand to circumvent a background check.

☼

After Justina hung up the phone, she walked past Roger on her way to get a cup of coffee. She failed to acknowledge him, because she was still thinking about the conversation she just had with Calvin.

"What's wrong, Justina?" Roger asked, as he watched her pour herself a cup of coffee.

"I'm not in the mood to talk about it!" Justina snapped. "Are you still working on the Thurman brief?

"I took care of it last week."

"Good. How soon are we going to trial?"

"It is scheduled in two weeks."

"Okay," Justina curtly responded, before returning to her office.

After a few seconds, Roger followed Justina to her office, detecting something serious was going on. "It's Calvin, isn't it?"

Justina frowned as she looked up from the file she was reviewing. "Roger, I don't want to talk about it! Calvin is such a jerk! I have a feeling he's playing games and I don't have time for his BS."

"Justina, I think you're being paranoid. Do your suspicions have anything to do with the fact you're in love with him?"

Justina did not reply. She knew she was in love, and still yearned to be with Calvin.

Roger interrupted her thoughts. "You know how guys are," he explained. "You have to tell us what you want and how you want to be treated."

Justina grinned. "I know. Men are from Mars, women are from Venus."

Roger chuckled. "You need to talk to Calvin to resolve any insecurities you have about him. In the meantime, call our investigator to see if he can find out any more information. If Chris discovers Calvin is seeing someone else, as you probably suspect, then you walk away from the relationship. If he doesn't, you should consider giving him another chance," Roger suggested, before returning to his office.

That's a good idea, Justina thought as she looked up Chris's number in her phone book. "Hi Chris, this is Justina. I need a follow-up investigation on someone. His name is Calvin Calloway. You conducted a preliminary investigation on him a few months ago. He claims he lives in Stone Mountain. I need his home address and anything else you can find out about him."

"No problem. Give me three days."

Justina hung up the phone with a sense of relief, knowing her curiosity about Calvin would be resolved soon.

Calvin looked at the caller ID and picked up phone on the first ring. "Wassup?"

Chris's voice trembled. "Ms. Reyes just called. She requested a follow-up investigation."

Calvin smiled. "I told you she would, but I thought it would have been sooner."

"You got my money?" Chris nervously asked.

"Yeah. You'll get it as soon as you convince her I'm legit."

"It's still two grand, right?"

"Man, just make sure I look squeaky clean," Calvin harshly replied. "You'll get your damn money!" he yelled, before he hung up on Chris. He had never given Chris a reason to doubt him, and wondered what prompted Chris's inquiry.

Chris was desperate. He needed the extra money to catch up on his overdue mortgage. He was working as a security guard at a nursing home when Calvin first approached him out of the blue. Calvin asked Chris if they could meet after work, and offered to pay him $100 for his time. They agreed to meet at a local pub.

"What can I do for you?" Chris asked, as he took a seat next to Calvin.

Calvin handed Chris a business card from the Reyes and McCarthy law firm, and asked, "How do you feel about working for this law firm? They are located in a corporate office in downtown Atlanta."

Chris eyed Calvin suspiciously, then looked at the business card. "What will I be doing?"

"Conducting investigations and running a few errands. You'll never have to physically be in the office."

"How much?"

"How much do you make now?"

"I take home $400 a week."

"We'll pay you $700 a week. How soon can you start?"

Chris was elated, but he had doubts.

Calvin noticed his reluctance. "I tell you what – after one week, if you don't like it, you quit. Plus, I'll pay you one week in advance. All you have to do is be available when we need you."

"We?"

"You will primarily be dealing with me and Roger McCarthy."

Chris conjured up several questions in his mind about this offer. He could not understand why Calvin did not go directly to a private detective agency. Why was he approached at a nursing home of all places? And why did he have a feeling there was something underhanded about this offer? Chris's common sense told him to walk away, but he thought about his overdue mortgage and threw common sense out the window.

"I need $1500 up front," Chris countered, "and I want a $1000 a week."

"Whoa! You drive a hard bargain," Calvin dramatically explained. After briefly thinking about Chris's counter-offer, he said, "Deal. Report to the law office first thing in the morning, and ask for Roger McCarthy. He'll be expecting you."

For most of Chris's adult life, he had a hard time finding and keeping jobs. He was excited about this opportunity, and thought his luck had changed for the better, especially when he began receiving offers from other law firms and organizations with impressive recommendations from Roger. Unfortunately, Chris was now having regrets. Even though he was able to catch up on his mortgage, as a result of his arrangement with Calvin, he had a feeling things would end disastrously. He wondered if he should have allowed the bank to foreclose on his house, instead.

Chapter 21

Blind Ambition

One week after the break up, a local florist delivered a bouquet of red roses to Justina's office. Justina eagerly opened the card, which read: *Please give me another chance. Love, Calvin.* Although she was pleased with Calvin's gesture, she was still uneasy about his intentions.

Seconds later, Chris walked into the office with a look of confidence. He eagerly approached Kathy's desk and announced, "I'm here to see Attorney Reyes."

"One moment, please." Kathy pressed the intercom to alert Justina. Two seconds later, she turned to Chris and said, "You may go in now. She's expecting you."

"It took you long enough!" Justina snapped, as Chris walked into her office. "What did you find out?!"

"Ms. Reyes, I have confirmed that this guy is well-rounded. He lives in a five-bedroom house in Stone Mountain, has never been married, does not have any kids, and his credit history is excellent. In addition, his resources and assets well-exceed his liabilities," Chris added, as he handed her the report.

Justina smiled as she reviewed the file.

"Oh, by the way, he's a workaholic," Chris explained. "He goes on a lot of business trips."

"I see. What about his criminal record?"

"Not even a traffic ticket. If I was a woman, I'd marry him," Chris joked. "I'll have to make sure my wife never meets him." He laughed heartily at his own comment.

Justina looked at him with a scowl on her face.

Chris got the message and stopped clowning around. "He lives about an hour from here," Chris indicated. "Do you want me to continue following him?"

Justina was satisfied with the investigative report. "No, that's not necessary."

"Ms. Reyes, can I ask you a personal question?"

Justina nodded as she sat back in her chair.

"Are you interested in this guy?"

"That's none of your business!" Justina sharply replied, then stood up as a gesture to let Chris know their meeting was over.

"That'll be all Chris. Here's your check," she said, as she hastily handed it to him.

"Thank you," Chris hesitantly said, before he took the check and walked out of her office. Although he felt bad about giving Justina the bogus report, her nasty attitude lessened his guilt.

Justina perused through the report and was truly impressed with Calvin Calloway. *Wow, maybe he's not so bad after all. Just a little inconsiderate. If I play my cards right, I could end up Mrs. Calvin Calloway.*

Then she said aloud, "All my life, I've waited for the right man, toying with little men until Mr. Right came along. The sound of Mrs. Calvin Calloway sounds good to me."

Kathy overheard Justina's proclamation through her office door, and she shook her head in disgust.

As soon as Chris walked out of Justina's office, he pulled out his cell phone and called Calvin. "She bought it," Chris confidently stated. "When can I get my money?"

"Wait a minute!" Calvin exclaimed. "How do you know she bought it?"

"The expression on her face spoke for itself. She was highly impressed with you. So when can I get my money?"

"When I'm fully convinced. In one week, if all goes well, I'll pay you the two grand I promised, plus an additional five hundred for your troubles." Calvin disconnected the call, fully satisfied with the status of his plan. Next, he phoned his co-conspirator.

"Hey, Calvin. Wassup?" his co-conspirator inquired.

"All is going well," Calvin confidently admitted. "Soon, your wishes will be fulfilled."

"I'll send you the money we owe you, but we need you to do one more thing."

"What is it?"

"Pressure Justina into marrying you."

Calvin became frustrated with the change in plans, but then he thought about the mighty dollar. "If that's the case, I'm going to need an additional twenty-five grand."

"No problem, I'll wire transfer the money today."

When Calvin hung up, he called the florist and sent Justina six more flower bouquets. An hour later, he received a phone call from none other than Justina Reyes.

"Do you like the roses?" Calvin asked, before giving her the opportunity to greet him.

"One bouquet would've been enough. My office looks like a funeral parlor!" Justina elatedly noted.

Calvin chuckled before saying, "Nothing but the best for a very special lady. Now will you please give me another chance? I realize I acted like a jerk. Let's start over. Oh, before I forget - do you have a pen and paper handy?"

"Yes, why?"

"Because I have seven lucky numbers for you."

Justina smiled as Calvin recited his home phone number.

"You know you have a sexy business voice," Calvin cooed.

Justina blushed. "Is that how you talk to all your clients?"

"Only the ones I want to make permanent in my life," Calvin smoothly replied.

"You're something else," Justina teased, laughing softly.

Calvin smiled. "Only because I'm hot for you."

Justina giggled before turning the conversation to a serious note. "Calvin, let's be frank. You're an attractive man. That's a given. You're intelligent, and like me, you want to be in control. That's the problem. Let's skip this charade and admit what we both want."

Calvin was amused by her boldness, and decided to take her up on her offer. "Okay, my cards are on the table. I want to make love to you. Can you meet me at the Shalamar hotel at five o'clock this evening?"

"No, three o'clock sounds more reasonable," Justina countered, sounding hard and in control. "Fresh strawberries dipped in chocolate are a must, and a bottle of wine would be a plus. If you're more than a minute late, I'll gather that you've reconsidered, and there will be no hard feelings."

Grinning from ear to ear, Calvin asked, "No strings?"

"No strings," Justina boldly replied.

Calvin promptly arrived at the hotel, and waited in the room for Justina. He brought along a bottle of wine and put it on ice. After arranging the bowl of strawberries and hot chocolate dip on a tray, he looked at his watch, realizing Justina was an hour late. Just as Calvin started second-guessing himself, he heard a keycard opening the door.

"You're late," he said, as Justina walked through the door.

"You noticed," she mischievously replied.

"Do you have a reason? You ranted about the importance of being on time and look at you."

"Do you want to pout or do you want to do something else?" Justina seductively asked, while opening her London Fog windbreaker to expose her black lace lingerie.

Calvin stood up and whistled. Not a moment was wasted helping Justina remove her windbreaker. He used his teeth to take off her lingerie, then picked her up and laid her across the bed. When he attempted to get on top of her, Justina pushed him off. Instead, she took over and straddled him, remaining on top throughout their afternoon of passion.

While they made love, Justina controlled everything. She even inspected his goods before she put the condom on for him. Calvin allowed her to have the impression that he was powerless. Their first sexual encounter was mind-blowing. They were exhausted but satisfied.

Calvin woke up a couple hours later to find Justina gone. He looked at the nightstand and noticed two one-hundred dollar bills with a note that read: *Thank you for an unforgettable afternoon. Here's a little something for your troubles.* He chuckled as the scene from Eddie Murphy's movie, "Boomerang," instantly came to mind. Robin Givens pulled the same stunt on Eddie Murphy. Calvin saw this as a sign of better things to come.

For the next month, Calvin and Justina were together practically every day. They went out to dinner, movies, parks, and museums. Eventually, all of Justina's insecurities about Calvin vanished.

"I'm glad we're together again," Calvin professed.

Justina grinned. "I am too. What prompted you to finally get a phone?"

"I realized I was about to lose the woman of my dreams." Looking into her eyes, Calvin continued, "I don't want you to misconstrue my intentions. I plan on making you my wife one day."

Justina smiled. "This new revelation is very presumptuous of you. Be careful what you ask for."

"Darling, I only have eyes for you. You belong in my future." *Damn, I sound corny as hell. But it's working. She's all dreamy-eyed, envisioning little hearts in her head.*

"Calvin, how do you know we're compatible? We haven't known each other that long."

"However long it takes, I will prove to you that we belong to-gether. Maybe we can start by going on a cruise to the Bahamas next weekend." After noticing her reluctance, Calvin held her hands and looked into her eyes. "Please don't say no. I already purchased the tickets." Actually, the tickets were courtesy of his co-conspirator.

Justina decided Calvin's spontaneity was his downfall. "I'd love to," she admitted with reservations. "You've been so good to me. At least let me pay my share."

"No, you keep your money. This treat is on me," Calvin insisted.

"What about sealing this deal with a kiss?" Justina asked, as she placed her right hand on his cheek and gave him a small peck on his lips.

"Now that, I can handle," Calvin happily replied.

Justina smiled as she lightly placing her hand on his chest. "Would you like to spend the night?"

"Yes, but I'm afraid you'd make me leave in the middle of the morning," Calvin teased.

Justina lightly chuckled. "You're too much." She knew his an-swer, and looked forward to a night of passion with her prince.

When Calvin told Sue about the cruise, she did not take it as well as he thought she would. "Baby, what's wrong? I told you it was just business."

"That's not it," Sue whined.

"Baby, I'm going to miss you too. Justina doesn't mean any-thing to me."

"I know…but sometimes I feel I can't compete with her. She's beautiful," Sue admitted, as she looked downward.

Calvin chuckled. "Baby, when was the last time you looked in the mirror? You are so sexy and beautiful," he said, as he cupped her face. "I'm in love with you, not her. Don't ever doubt my love for you."

Sue looked into his eyes and instinctively believed him.

"I will never do anything to hurt you," Calvin sincerely con-fessed. "You are my heart."

Sue's heart fluttered in response. She felt loved and in love; and so did Calvin.

Chapter 22

Homecoming

Justina and Calvin had a blast on the cruise. Calvin made sure Justina felt like she was the only one that mattered to him. It worked because she was "*head over heels*" in love. On the way home, Justina told him she was getting homesick, and would be driving home next weekend to spend time with her family. She asked if he would like to go. Calvin eagerly agreed, especially since his co-conspirator told him not to let Justina out of his sight.

During this trip, Justina wanted to accomplish two things. First, she wanted Calvin to impress her parents, particularly her father. She was tired of hearing her father talk about how Guy Simmons was the 'good catch' that got away. Next, she wanted to see whether Regine and Guy were truly happy.

When they walked into the house, Justina's parents merrily greeted them. However, within a millisecond, Mr. Reyes' smile turned into a frown. He immediately picked up bad vibes from Calvin. Mrs. Reyes, on the other hand, thought he was an excellent choice for their daughter.

"Justina, Regine is expecting you," Mrs. Reyes explained. "Why don't you go on over and visit her? It'll give us some time to get to know Calvin."

"I agree," Mr. Reyes quickly chimed in. "You go ahead and visit Regine. Make sure you tell Guy and Regine 'hello' for us," he added.

Justina kissed Calvin, and told him she would be back soon. She dressed up for the visit because a small part of her wanted Guy to miss her. Her flashy attire did not go unnoticed by her parents, or Calvin.

As soon as Justina walked out the front door, the question and answer session began. "So Calvin, tell us about yourself," Mrs. Reyes insisted.

"What is there to tell?" Calvin laughed but cut it short when he looked at Mr. Reyes' grim expression. "I live a simple life," he finally said. "I'm sure Justina filled you in already."

"You can start by telling us your intentions with our daughter," Mr. Reyes sharply stated.

"I like her a lot. She's a sweet girl. She's spoiled, but I suppose you already know that," Calvin added with a light chuckle. Mrs. Reyes softly laughed in response; Mr. Reyes did not.

"Tell me how you met our daughter," Mr. Reyes prodded.

"We met through a mutual acquaintance. You know...her partner, Roger."

"That's strange," Mr. Reyes countered. "Justina didn't mention that. She told us she met you at a club."

Calvin remained quiet. *Okay, he got me. If he already knew, why did he bother asking?*

"So Calvin, where are you from?" Mrs. Reyes asked.

The question and answer session went on for the next hour, nonstop. Calvin was under intense scrutiny; he could not wait for Justina to return.

When Regine learned of Justina's impending arrival, she was looking forward to rekindling their friendship. It was time to let by-gones be by-gones. She went outside just as Justina pulled into the driveway.

"I'm so glad you came," Regine said, as she warmly embraced Justina. "How was your trip?"

"Long, but exciting," Justina elatedly replied. Then she proceeded to tell Regine all about Calvin and her life in Atlanta.

Regine smiled in response. She was genuinely happy for Justina.

Justina followed Regine inside their house and gasped at the sight of beautiful expensive furniture and pictures. "Wow! Look at this place!"

Regine genuinely asked, "Would you like a tour?"

"No, that's not necessary," Justina said with an air of superiority. "Once you've lived in a house this size most of your life, they're pretty much the same," she added with a wide grin.

Regine detected sarcasm in Justina response, but chose to ignore it. She was still trying to figure out why Justina was dressed like a runway model. Her halter-top dress, three-inch heels, heavy makeup, and expensive gaudy jewelry, including the diamond earrings, were excessive for a casual visit. She did not know what Justina was trying to prove.

They went on the front porch to talk. Regine told Justina about her engagement, and explained how Guy proposed to her. She also discussed their upcoming nuptials. Then she chuckled when she told Justina that her grandmother had taken over as the wedding coordinator.

Justina countered Regine's news by telling her she believed Calvin was going to propose to her when they return to Atlanta. At least, that was her wish.

"That'll be great!" Regine blissfully said with a big wide grin. "Then we'll be two married women!"

Before Justina could respond, Dana came outside and asked Regine if she could help her with a homework problem. Regine turned to Justina and asked, "Would you like to come inside with me?"

Justina waved her hand. "No, it's okay. I'll wait for you to return."

As soon as Regine went inside, Guy drove up the driveway, and was extremely surprised to see Justina sitting on the front porch. He wondered why she was there. He retrieved his briefcase from the trunk of his car, then walked up the walkway to greet her.

"Justina, what a surprise!" Guy said, as he gave her a welcome hug. "It appears life is treating you well," he added, after noticing her dressy appearance. He thought she looked like a million bucks, and wondered what the occasion was.

"Thank you," Justina bashfully replied, then held out her hand to show him she still had the engagement ring he gave her over a year ago. After Guy pretended to look at his watch, Justina put her hand down, and said, "I'm just following my dreams. What about you?" she seductively asked, sticking out her chest and batting her eyes.

Guy was unfazed by the ring, and her assets. "God has blessed me too. I was promoted to Vice CEO of Lucent Technology, formerly Calvent Lucent Technology. You remember; it's the same organization I've been with since high school."

"Good for you!" Justina replied with amazement.

"Yep, you weren't the only one with dreams. One of them has already come true. The other is making Regine my wife. If it wasn't for her, I don't know if I could've managed," Guy proudly professed.

"I see," Justina awkwardly said. She suddenly had a loss for words, and began fidgeting with her car keys.

"By the way, have you seen the love of my life?"

"Oh yeah…um…she stepped inside to check on your sister."

"I had a rough day, so I'm going inside for the evening."

In that instant, Guy silently forgave Justina for all the heartache and pain he suffered while attempting to be a part of her life. He walked to the door, then briefly turned around. "Take care of yourself."

"You too," Justina said with a tight smile. A part of her wished he was still interested in her.

Guy went inside and found Regine in the kitchen preparing two drinks; one for Justina and the other for herself. He went over and passionately kissed her. "I love you, baby."

"I love you too," Regine said with soft laughter, as she looked into his eyes. "You seem so happy to see me."

Guy gloated. "I'm always happy to see you. You're my queen." He gave her a peck on the lips before heading to his bedroom.

At that very moment, all remaining insecurities and doubts Regine had about Guy vanished. It helped that he had not mentioned Justina's name since arriving home.

No one seemed to notice the car with heavily tinted windows parked a couple of houses away. The driver witnessed Justina and Guy's exchange, and registered Justina's disappointment when Guy walked into his house. The driver was given instructions to intervene if Justina tried to cause a rift between Guy and Regine. Happily, he was able to report – INTERVENTION NOT NECESSARY.

Justina returned to her family's home where she found Calvin entertaining her mother. She saw the scowl on her father's face as he eyed Calvin, and knew he was not impressed with him.

Calvin was relieved to see Justina. He stood up when she entered the living room. "Hello baby, how was your visit?"

"It was fine. Regine and Guy seem very compatible and very much in love."

"So are we," Calvin pretentiously said, "and one day you will be a permanent fixture in my future." He kissed Justina on the lips while gazing into her eyes.

Justina blushed in response. Her mother was ecstatic with the idea of Calvin and Justina getting married, but her father was suspicious of Calvin's motives.

Calvin was hoping he had not laid it on too thick for Justina's parents. He glanced in Mr. Reyes direction and read his vibes. "Well, we must be leaving now," he quickly said, without conferring with Justina. "We have a long drive ahead of us." Then he limply shook Mr. Reyes' hand, and lightly embraced Mrs. Reyes before thanking them for their hospitality.

"It was nice meeting you too, Calvin," Mrs. Reyes said. "Make sure you take care of our baby."

Calvin bore a fake smile. "She makes it easy for me to care for her. I'll make sure she calls when we return to Atlanta."

Mr. and Mrs. Reyes walked them to the car, then warmly embraced Justina. Mr. Reyes followed Justina to the passenger's side and told her if she ever needed to talk, he would always be there for her. He frowned as he watched Calvin back out of the driveway and leave with his daughter.

Once they were on the road, Calvin briefly glanced in Justina's direction, and asked, "Is it okay with you if we make a brief stop in Clearwater, Florida? I've never been there, and would love to visit the city everyone is always raving about." Calvin was lying, and was hoping she would go along with his plans.

"That's fine with me. I haven't been to Clearwater in years," Justina acknowledged. "Besides, Regine told me Guy is building a house for them in a new development, off Highway 64. I'd love to see the exact location."

During the drive to Clearwater, Justina thought about the conversation she had with Regine. She still could not believe her and Guy were engaged, and seemed so happy. She thought it was amazing how Guy was able to get over her so easily.

Regine had apologized to Justina for everything that transpired in the past, and had asked her for forgiveness. Justina readily accepted Regine's apology, but did not apologize for her own actions. They had spent the remaining time discussing wedding plans. Regine was so excited, she did not notice Justina's gloomy mood.

"Calvin, before I forget, Regine invited me to their wedding. I don't want to go alone. I was hoping...."

"No need to ask. When is it?" Calvin asked, knowing this bit of news will motivate Justina to think about marriage, hopefully to him.

Justina was surprised he readily agreed, but then she remembered Calvin's impulsive tendencies. "The wedding is next month."

Calvin smiled. "Great. We can make the trip a mini-vacation."

Justina giggled. "If you don't stop being so good to me, I'm afraid I'll fall in love with you."

That was Calvin's goal. He was relieved his plan was back on track. The new mission was simple: *Don't kill her; just make sure she's left financially crippled and emotionally broken.*

As promised, Calvin drove Justina to the location of Guy and Regine's new home. When Justina realized the house was already under construction, she felt a pang of jealousy. The structure was actually the size of a mansion. She was angry with Regine for not being entirely honest with her.

Calvin noticed Justina pouting, but he had too many other things on his mind. He told her he had to make a quick stop at a particular ATM machine. He left her in the car and walked around the corner. His co-conspirator gave Calvin his second package of money, while

Calvin brought him up to speed on the visit with Justina's family, and the wedding they would be attending next month.

When Calvin pulled in front of Justina's condo, she asked him to come inside. Calvin told her he had to head to the office, to prepare for a meeting. Justina did not believe him. She pouted as she slammed his car door shut.

Justina panicked after stepping inside her condo, and discovering several missed messages on her voicemail from her father.

"Hello?" her father answered.

"Hi, Dad. Are you okay?" Justina nervously asked.

"Yes, I'm fine. I just wanted to know if you made it home safely."

Justina rolled her eyes and became annoyed. "Dad, this is not the first time I've traveled. Why were you worried?"

"Justina, I don't trust that man you're with. There's something about him that troubles me. What do you know about him?"

"Dad, don't worry. My investigator checked him out."

"Justina...."

"Listen, Dad! I'm a grown woman! This is my life! Calvin is not Guy Simmons, and I'm glad he isn't! He's better than Guy!"

"But Justina...."

"But nothing! Dad, for once, can you be happy for me?! I can't deal with this right now! I'll call you later!" Justina said with fire in her eyes. She hung up, feeling very frustrated with her father. She wanted Calvin to feel welcomed and her father had disappointed her. Right now, she was not sure if she could ever forgive him.

Justina did not know her mother was on the speakerphone.

"Did you hear her?" Mr. Reyes asked his wife.

"Yes," Mrs. Reyes replied. "I tend to agree with Justina. Calvin seems like a nice young man, and Justina told me he's very wealthy. What more can we ask for?"

"I just don't want her to make a hasty decision, especially since she knows Guy and Regine are getting married next month. She's too impulsive."

"Honey, give her a break. Trust that she'll make the right decision."

Mr. Reyes thought about the conversation he had with Calvin, and knew he could not be trusted. Calvin told Mr. and Mrs. Reyes he was 35, attended Morehouse, and had a daughter. However, Justina told her parents Calvin was 31, attended Emory and Howard, and did not have any kids.

Mr. Reyes also noticed the way Calvin squirmed in his chair whenever they asked him a question. *No,* Mr. Reyes concluded, *something about this character is not right. He's lying about frivolous facts, so I can only imagine what he's hiding.*

As soon as Calvin left Justina's condo, he called Sue and told her about his plans to accompany Justina to her friend's wedding. "Is it okay with you if I go?"

"Sure. Who's getting married?"

"I think Justina said her name was Regine. Why do you ask?"

Sue stifled her shock. "Oh, no reason…um…I was just curious, that's all.

"Good. I'll see you tomorrow."

Sue hung up the phone and sat down on the sofa, mulling over her decision to go to her daughter's wedding.

When Rowena walked into their apartment, she asked, "What's up with the gloomy face?" She sat next to Sue, awaiting her response.

"Calvin told me he plans to attend Regine's wedding next month. I thought about it, and I can't fathom not attending my only child's wedding. I'm going," Sue said with conviction.

Rowena frowned. "Do you think it's a good idea for you to show up, knowing Calvin will be there with Justina?"

"My baby is getting married. I wouldn't miss it for anything in the world," Sue firmly stated.

Rowena chose her words wisely. "I know…she's going to be beautiful. But how are you going to blend in without Calvin noticing you?"

"I'll find a way. Besides, I'm not sure if I'm ready for Regine to see me yet. I need time to talk to her in private, first."

Rowena had her own opinion but kept it to herself. "I feel you," she simply said, realizing there was nothing she could say to convince Sue that it was a bad decision. "Go handle your business, and make sure you take a picture of my niece."

"Niece?" Sue asked with a quizzical gaze.

"Girl, I'm just tripping," Rowena teased, realizing she almost let the cat out of the bag. "We're good friends, so I sort of adopted your daughter as my niece. I hope you don't mind."

"Nah, that's fine. Besides, she doesn't have any aunts and uncles.

Rowena rolled her eyes and thought, *If only you knew.*

Chapter 23

The Wedding

February 2008....

Regine and Guy's wedding took place on the St. Petersburg pier. The wedding party consisted of two bridesmaids, two grooms-men, a maid of honor, and Alex as the best man. Guy's sisters were the junior bridesmaids. The wedding colors were lime green and white. Silver symbolic wedding bells, and lime green and white flower arrangements cascaded throughout the wedding hall. Regine had no idea her biological father made sure she had the fairytale wedding of her dreams.

Regine was in the bridal suite getting dressed for the big event. She was so nervous; she had butterflies in her stomach. "Grandma, what if I forget my vows?"

"Stop fretting," Bessie replied with a chuckle. "You're making me nervous."

"Why did this wedding have to be so big?" Regine asked with amazement. "It seems that you and Guy invited everybody in Virginia and Florida. And why did we have to have the wedding on the St. Petersburg pier? My hair is falling out of place with all this wind. I hope those stupid pelicans don't dive in and take a dump on me. I can't understand why people chose today to go fishing on the pier. Don't they know today is my wedding day?!"

"Child, stop all that rambling," Bessie teased. "The wedding is going to be beautiful. It's not every day people get the opportunity to marry on the pier. And don't worry about your hair. The wind won't blow the little that's there. I still don't know why you had your hair cut the day before your wedding."

"It's not that short. Guy likes my new hairstyle," Regine admitted, while fluffing her tresses in the full-length mirror. "I guess I'm just nervous. Do you think it was a good idea to invite Justina?"

Bessie laughed softly. "You should thank her. If it weren't for that heifer, Guy wouldn't have known what a wonderful person you are. You should've made her your maid of honor."

Regine twisted her mouth and frowned. "I don't know about that. Besides, Justina sounds happy with the new guy she's dating."

"Enough about that *Jezebel!* This is your day, not hers," Bessie firmly stated.

Regine stood in the full-length mirror, admiring her wedding gown, which was designed to fit her curvaceous figure. She looked elegant in the white, strapless, modern a-line gown with a simple detachable train.

"You're so beautiful," Bessie said with tears in her eyes. "You remind me so much of your mother."

"Thanks, Grandma. I'm so glad you're here. I love you so much."

"I love you too, baby. You know…your mother wanted to be here but…."

"Don't! No more excuses! I'm older now, and you no longer have to defend her. Sue made a decision, and chose drugs over me."

"That was so long ago. She's trying to get her life together," Bessie delicately admitted.

"I know, but this is supposed to be a special day for mothers and daughters to share," Regine somberly replied, briefly closing her eyes to hold back the tears.

Bessie embraced Regine and told her not to worry. She promised things would get better. Then she stepped aside so the Aularel makeup representative, Ms. LaVern, could apply Regine's makeup.

As Ms. Lavern added the final touches to Regine's face, Justina bulldozed her way into the bridal suite. "Wow!" Justina exclaimed, as she threw the door open and walked toward Regine. "I didn't know you could look so beautiful. You really need to wear makeup all the time. It goes well with your dark complexion and big eyes. And girl, you lost so much weight. Look at you! With a handsome man like Guy, you needed to lose a few pounds. And why are you wearing white?! You know you're not a virgin," she added with a mischievous grin.

Regine stood still, stunned by Justina's comments. Ms. LaVern was also shocked by Justina's boldness.

"Justina!" Bessie shouted, as she protectively stood in front of Regine. "This bride-to-be can't have any visitors right now!" Then she aggressively pulled Justina by her arm to the door and pushed her out with great satisfaction. "Wait in the wedding hall like all the other guests!" Bessie sternly said, before slamming the door in Justina's face.

Regine could not hold back her tears before Justina left the room. Justina noticed, and felt vindicated. A part of her wanted Regine to call off the wedding.

"The nerve of her!" Regine cried out. "How could I have been so stupid as to invite her to my wedding?!" she asked, sobbing uncontrollably. "I thought she was sincere when we agreed to put aside our past differences."

Bessie embraced Regine. "Baby, no matter how hard you try, people like Justina live with a jealous heart. She'll always be miserable. Remember, misery loves company. This is your day. Don't let anybody steal your joy."

When Justina left the bridal suite, she ran into Guy in the hallway, dressed in a white tuxedo. She thought he looked handsome. She smiled when she approached him. "Hi, Guy. I'm sure today is really special for you. I want to wish you and Regine nothing but love and happiness for the rest of your lives," she sarcastically remarked.

Before Guy could respond, Justina kissed him on the lips and tried to give him some tongue action. He quickly removed her arms and pushed her away from him.

"Justina! This is not appropriate!" Guy grumbled, while trying to conceal his anger. "I'm getting married today, and you're not going to ruin it for us!"

Justina was speechless. After realizing Guy could not be swayed, she returned to the wedding hall and sat among the other guests. She purposely stayed away from her parents, who were seated several rows in front of them. She was still upset with her father for giving Calvin a hard time. The friction between Justina and her father was a relief to Calvin. He had a feeling Mr. Reyes had already figured out he was a fraud.

Bessie used comforting words to calm Regine's nerves. She also asked Ms. LaVern to redo Regine's makeup, but nothing seemed to boost her spirits. Thankfully, Regine smiled broadly when she began walking down the aisle with her godfather, Mr. O'Neal, as Brian McKnight's song, *Back at One,* played in the background.

Guy and his younger brother were standing together, looking dapper. Guy wept as Regine approached the alter. He was totally blown away by her beauty.

Regine had no idea her biological parents were sitting at the rear of the wedding hall, witnessing this joyous event. They were sitting apart; neither recognized or realized the other was there. They were both heavily disguised. Kevin wore a fake mustache and a toupee to cover his baldhead, and Sue wore a reddish-brown wig and sunglasses. They easily blended in with the three hundred invited guests, and the fifty or so who had crashed the wedding.

Justina could not help but feel a tinge of guilt while witnessing the nuptials. Most of all, she was amazed at how beautiful Regine looked. She pouted during the ceremony, wishing she could trade places with Regine. Calvin took note of Justina's behavior and shook his head. He thought Justina was a fool for rejecting Guy in the first place.

After Regine and Guy exchanged vows, they engaged in a passionate and lengthy kiss, which tickled some of the attendees. The pastor even pretended to clear his throat to get their attention. As they exited the wedding hall, doves were released from a cage, signifying their new beginning as husband and wife. Regine's biological parents inconspicuously left following the ceremony, but Justina remained seated.

"Justina, are you okay?" Calvin asked. "The wedding is over and we're still sitting here."

Justina was in a daze. She always thought Guy would be there for her. "Yeah, I was thinking, that's all," she solemnly admitted.

"I suppose you won't tell me what you were thinking," Calvin knowingly remarked.

"It's nothing. Let's go greet the newlyweds," she eagerly suggested.

"There's really no rush. They're going to their new home for the reception."

"Oh yeah, I forgot."

"If you don't want to go, I understand." Calvin knew Justina was envious of Regine, so he wanted to make this as painless as possible for her.

"That's not it. It's just…I thought we might get an early start on our mini vacation, remember?"

"Do you think your friends would appreciate us bailing out so soon? Besides, I was looking forward to going to the wedding reception. I heard from a few guests that Regine and her grandmother prepared the food."

"That was dumb. Why didn't they hire a caterer? They have enough money," Justina stated with envy.

"Baby, don't hate. Be happy for them. To answer your question, I overheard from one of the guests that Regine plans to open a restaurant soon. She thought it would be fun to try out some of the main entrees with the guests."

"You seem to be overhearing a lot. What else did you overhear?" Justina curiously asked.

Calvin smiled. "Just networking and passing out a couple of business cards, that's all."

"You're a piece of work," Justina snidely remarked.

Regine and Guy arrived at their new house two hours later. They took the scenic route to give their guests enough time to arrive in advance, for the reception. As they exited the limo, everyone lined up to personally greet them. Regine had trepidations when she saw Justina standing in the line-up with her male friend. Guy picked up on her vibes and held her hand, tightly. He assured her they were strong as '*one*'.

"Congratulations to both of you!" Justina overly expressed, as she wildly shook Guy's hand and aggressively hugged Regine. It was an awkward gesture because Regine did not hug her back.

Guy thanked Justina and Calvin for coming, but Regine was despondent. She looked away from them.

"We wouldn't have missed it for the world!" Justina pretentiously replied. She looked over at Regine and commented, "Girl, look at you! I almost didn't recognize you! How did you lose so much weight?! Jenny Craig? Weight Watchers?" she mischievously probed.

Regine remained quiet.

"Remember how everyone used to call you *rolley polley* back in high school?" Justina spitefully asked. Regine was disgusted with Justina's remarks. She turned and walked away.

Guy was livid. He stared at Justina as if she had lost of her mind.

Justina turned to Guy with a bewildered expression, and asked, "What is her problem?"

"Go figure!" Guy sharply replied. "Could it be that you just insulted my wife on what's supposed to be the happiest day of our lives." Then Guy cocked his head to one side. "So Justina, you tell me what's going on?"

"What?! I don't know what you mean," Justina answered, looking dumbfounded. Calvin remained speechless. He could not believe she was trying to act innocent.

"Just leave! Both of you!" Guy barked, shifting his eyes from Justina to Calvin.

Calvin grabbed Justina's arm and guided her outside. As soon as they got in their car and buckled up, he asked without looking at her, "Are you still in love with him?"

Justina was not sure. "No, it's just...."

Calvin held up his hand to silence her. "Let's get out of here," he offhandedly replied.

"Are we still going to St. Augustine to have the mini vacation you promised?" Justina timidly asked, trying to lessen the tension between them.

"Yeah, sure, whatever!" Calvin snapped, still upset with her because she made him look like a fool.

After Justina and Calvin left, Guy found Regine alone, crying in their bedroom. He went over to the bed and put his arms around her. "Baby, it's okay. Justina and her friend are no longer here. I asked them to leave."

"Guy, Justina said some really cruel things to me," Regine admitted, as she sobbed on his shoulder.

"Whatever she said, it was out of jealously. It's all right as long as we have each other. That's all that matters," Guy said, as he gave her his handkerchief.

Regine smiled and dried her tears. "You're right," she weakly replied. "Let's go back to our guests and forget about Justina."

They returned to their guests arm and arm. The reception went on as planned. Everyone boasted about the exotic food Regine and Bessie prepared for the reception. And Alex gave a tear-dropping toast.

Regine's godparents thought Guy was perfectly suitable for her. Alex, Dana and Cassandra were happy Regine was finally a part of their lives. And Bessie could not stop smiling. She was proud of Regine, and happy Guy came to his senses.

"Guy, Regine is beautiful," Alex commented, while watching her dance with her godfather.

"Alex, are you sweating my wife?" Guy jokingly asked.

"Of course not. I'm just proud my big brother made the right decision, this time."

Guy blushed. "You think so?"

"Man, you were so blind before. Everyone else could see that Justina wasn't right for you, except you."

Guy turned to him and grinned. "You got me. I made a lot of mistakes in my life, but nothing was as bad as almost losing Regine." He paused, then said, "Enough about me. Have you made up your mind about which graduate school you'll be attending?"

"Yeah, I'm going to stay in Florida. I narrowed my choices to Nova Southeastern in Davie and Florida International University in Miami."

"Good. Don't procrastinate on submitting your applications."

"Point taken. I'll decide by next week."

"I'm very proud of you," Guy said, as he put his arm on Alex's shoulder. "You've always exceeded my expectations. Mom and dad would've been proud of you too."

"I couldn't have done it without you and Regine, always riding my back and bribing me to do well in school," Alex said with a chuckle.

They gave each other a brotherly hug and laughed. Soon after, they were both on the dance floor. Everyone laughed as Guy pretended to gasp for air minutes later.

After their guests left, Regine and Guy were driven to St. Augustine for their honeymoon. They arrived around midnight. Regine woke up from her nap and viewed the scenery. "Guy, St. Augustine is absolutely beautiful. This place reminds me of an isolated island."

Guy smiled. "Like St. Petersburg, right?"

"Come on Guy. You know what I mean. I never imagined St. Augustine could be so beautiful."

"Considering you slept all the way here, I agree," he teased.

Regine smiled. "Why did you choose this place for our honeymoon?"

"My mom and dad used to come here every now and then. I wanted to visit the place they enjoyed so much."

"You rarely talk about them."

Guy sighed. "For a long time, I was angry with them for dying. I even blamed God. Now I know that God has a purpose for all of us. Maybe it was just their time."

"If they were alive today, they would be so proud of you. Because of you, your brother and sisters are well cared for."

Guy leaned over and kissed her. "I couldn't have done it without your help."

Minutes later, they checked into a hotel at the Renaissance Vinoy Resort near the beach. Regine surprised Guy by putting on a sheer white gown with matching string bikini panties and bra. Guy sported black silk boxers.

Guy whistled when Regine walked out of the bathroom. He was instantly aroused by her beauty. "Baby, you are absolutely stunning."

Regine smiled as she looked at his boxers. "You're not bad looking yourself."

Guy walked over and kissed her passionately, gently touching her skin as if she were a delicate flower. After he disrobed her, he dissected her body as if it was a work of art.

Regine laughed softly as Guy picked her up and carried her to the king-sized bed. He gently laid her down on the bed, and removed his boxers. Then he sat down on the edge of the bed, leaned over and kissed Regine, whispering softly in her ear, "Baby, I love you. I need you."

"I need you too," Regine cooed, shivering from the warmth of his touch, while he slowly disrobed her. When Guy got on top of Regine and inserted himself, his body was on fire as he held on to her for dear life.

This time, their lovemaking was noticeably different. The rhythm of their bodies was in sync. Emotionally, Guy was there; his mind, his heart, and his soul needed her. Not only was Regine physically satiated, but she also felt loved and in love. They were exhausted as they fell asleep in each other's arms.

Guy woke up in a good mood. He was happy Regine was in his life on a permanent basis. He sat on the bed admiring her beauty before waking her with a kiss on the cheek. "Good morning, Mrs. Simmons."

"Good morning, Mr. Simmons," Regine groggily replied, rubbing her eyes to wipe away the sleepiness. "What do you have planned for us today?"

"Maybe we could catch a tour or go solo. I can't wait to stop by *Ripley's Believe it or Not* museum."

"Sounds like fun!" Regine happily replied.

"But first," Guy said, as he leaned over to kiss her, "how about a repeat of last night."

Regine smiled as she pulled back the blanket to expose her nakedness. "Is this what you're talking about?" she seductively inquired.

Guy grinned as he climbed on top of her, smothering her with kisses.

Upon arriving at the museum, Guy and Regine looked at the tour times. "It looks like the next tour doesn't start until eleven-thirty," Guy said. "In the meantime, let's go visit the smallest house ever built. I still find it hard to believe people actually lived in a tree stump. It's definitely unique."

"I wonder how they kept termites and bugs out," Regine said, as they walked through the tree house. "Look at that tiny stove and sink over there," she pointed out.

"Regine, I think that's just for show," Guy humorously replied.

Regine playfully folded her arms and twisted her mouth. "Okay. Answer this: how did they stay warm? Surely they couldn't light a fire in this tree house."

"Maybe they went outside," Guy joked.

"I doubt it," Regine said with a light giggle. "You're right about this place being mysterious and all."

"I'm really curious to see what's inside," Guy said, "especially since this is just the beginning of all the bizarre things we'll see. Let's line up for the tour; it starts in ten minutes."

For the next hour, they saw some of the most unusual things. When they walked in the dark section of the museum, Regine scrunched up her nose. "*Ewwww...*," she screeched, "they actually have dead people and animals in here!" Then she looked at Guy and curiously asked, "Why did you say your parents enjoyed visiting this town again?"

Guy laughed as he thought this museum had interesting but strange artifacts. "I didn't," he finally said, "but I aim to find out. Remember, there's more to St. Augustine than this museum."

Toward the end of the tour, they looked on the other side of a see-through mirror and watched people make fools of themselves. Regine laughed until she took a closer look. "Guy, look! That's Justina!"

Guy was stunned as he watched Justina pose and make weird faces in front of the mirror. "You've gotta be kidding," he said under his breath.

Regine frowned. "Look at her! It's as if she knows we're looking at her."

"Let's go Regine," Guy said, as he grabbed her hand and walked out of the museum. "Justina's the last person I want to see."

Coincidentally, Guy and Regine were about to get in their rental car when they spotted Justina and Calvin briskly walking toward them. Actually, Calvin was trying to catch up with Justina, to prevent her from making a fool of herself, again.

"We meet again!" Justina exclaimed, while trying to catch her breath. "Hello Mr. and Mrs. Simmons."

"Hi Justina. What a surprise to see you here," Guy flatly replied.

"My fiancé, Calvin, and I decided to stop in St. Augustine. We enjoyed it so much last month," Justina said, after Calvin breathlessly caught up with her.

"Fiancé? Good for you," Guy flatly replied. This bit of news was a relief to him, but Regine remained tight-lipped.

Tired of the bad vibes emitting from both Regine and Guy, Calvin bid them farewell as he grabbed Justina's arm and headed for his car. He thought, *What is Justina trying to prove?! Since when did I become her fiancé?! And I'm sure we've never visited St. Augustine.*

Justina felt a sting of jealousy at seeing Regine and Guy so happy and in love. She and Calvin returned to their car in silence. After they got in, she asked, "Is it okay if we get a bite to eat before we get on the Interstate?"

"Sure, whatever," Calvin said with a hint of agitation.

"We passed by a seafood restaurant off Interstate-4. Let's stop there," Justina persisted.

Calvin thought, *This girl wants an arm and leg. Fine, it's her money. She actually paid for everything on this trip because she didn't want me to feel obligated to her. I wonder where she got that warped thinking.*

Calvin pulled into a parking space in front of the restaurant, got out of his car and walked inside. Justina was furious because normally he would open the car door for her. She decided to ignore him and make the best of the evening.

"This is a nice restaurant Calvin, isn't it?" Justina asked, once the hostess seated them.

"Sure, nice and expensive," Calvin frustratingly replied, as he stood up and backed away from the table. "Look Justina, I have to make a phone call. I'll be back."

Justina stuck out her tongue and frowned when Calvin walked away from the table. In that instance, she decided to place their orders without waiting for him.

Calvin flipped open his cell phone and called his co-conspirator. "I just called to let you know we're in St. Augustine, and we'll be heading back to Atlanta after we eat dinner."

"How in the hell did you end up in St. Augustine of all places?!"

"I had nothing to do with this! You told me to let Justina think she was in control, and that's what I'm doing?"

"But, St Augustine?!"

Calvin sighed. "Okay, I hear what you're saying. We're out of here as soon as we eat."

"No! Leave now!"

Within a millisecond, Calvin was listening to a dial tone on the other end. He quickly returned to the table and told Justina they must leave immediately.

"At least let us enjoy our meals," Justina insisted.

Calvin continued standing. "We don't have time. I'll get some take out bags. We can eat in the car," he anxiously suggested.

Justina did not budge. She crossed her arms and pouted, sticking out her bottom lip.

"I'm sorry," Calvin softly said, "but I'm working on an important case, which requires that I return tonight."

Justina was unmoved.

Calvin sighed, then smiled after coming up with a better approach. "Baby, I'll be able to fulfill your every dream, which starts with getting something to slip on that beautiful finger of yours," he charmingly noted, eyeing her ring finger.

Justina's eyes spoke volumes. She instantly became cooperative, and took the initiative to ask for takeout bags.

After Regine and Guy left the museum, they drove to the pier in silence. Regine meditated over whether she made the right decision to marry Guy. She could not help but remember the bond he and Justina shared, and the fact that Guy had asked for Justina's hand in marriage almost two years ago. She was suddenly overwhelmed with doubts about him.

Guy parked the car and suggested they walk along the beach. He noticed that Regine was very quiet ever since they ran into Justina. Knowing he was partly to blame for her pain, Guy regretted ever getting involved with Justina.

Their honeymoon ended on a sour note. Guy reluctantly obliged Regine's request to return home two days earlier than planned. It seemed as though her cheerful spirit was sucked out of her.

Chapter 24

Honeymoon's Over

Regine did not think it was a coincidence when Justina showed up in St. Augustine, Florida. She also found it hard to believe Guy's explanation that Justina was jealous of her. She had always believed Justina had everything going for her, including her beauty and intellect.

When they returned home, Regine was pleasantly surprised to see Dana and Cassandra standing outside waiting for them. As soon as the car stopped, Regine greeted them with warm embraces. She left Guy to tend to their luggage, while she walked into the house with the girls. She found Bessie over the stove cooking several of her many famous dishes.

"Hi, Grandma," Regine said, as she walked over and hugged Bessie.

Bessie smiled. "Hi baby. Why did you and Guy decide to return home so soon?"

Regine sighed as she averted her eyes toward the twins. "It's a long story."

Bessie followed Regine's gaze and quickly changed the subject. "How was the honeymoon?"

"Grandma, it was really nice until...well, Justina was there. It was as if she was taunting me. I finally have my prince, but my wicked stepsister is still looming over me."

Bessie turned the temperature down on the greens, then turned to the twins. "Girls, I need to talk to Regine in private. Go see if Guy needs help with the bags."

"Okay," the twins said in unison.

Bessie walked over to Regine and held her hand. "Guy is a good man. He loves you. Besides, Justina will be completely out of your life soon enough."

"What do you mean?"

"I mean just what I said. The way she was schmoozing with that man of hers at your wedding, I have a feeling that girl is going to marry that man. You'll see."

Regine smiled. "I'm so glad you're here. You always know what to say to make me feel better. Thank you."

"You're welcome. I only want the best for you."

"I know you do. I appreciate you coming to Florida to watch the kids for us," Regine said, as she perked up. "How did the kids fare in our absence?"

Bessie smiled. "They're so sweet. They were no trouble at all. But Alex ate all the leftovers. I had to pull him out of the kitchen," she said with a chuckle.

"I'm sure he had a little help from you," Regine teased. "Remember when I was younger? You couldn't wait until I finished my plate before you replenished it with more food."

"Oh child, stop that nonsense," Bessie replied with soft laughter.

"Yeah, but my weight was out of control," Regine acknowledged.

Bessie grinned. "But now look at you! When you made up your mind to lose weight, you did it. Besides, some men like women with a little meat on their bones. Since I know how you feel about food and eating, maybe I should give this sweet potato pie, these buttermilk biscuits, collard greens, pineapple glazed ham, potato salad, fried chicken, and macaroni cheese to the local shelter."

Guy walked in with their luggage and overheard Bessie reciting the menu. "Hi, Grandma," he said, as he hugged and kissed her. Then he eyed the food on the stove and asked, "When do we eat?"

Regine and Bessie burst out laughing in response.

"Grandma, I know what you're trying to do," Regine humorously stated. "I'll let you slide this time."

"We can eat right now," Bessie said to Guy. "Go put your bags upstairs while I prepare the table." As soon as Guy was out of earshot, Bessie asked Regine to sit down while she took a seat next to hers. "Baby, you know I love you more than you will ever know, and I'll never let anyone hurt you."

"I know. I love you too," Regine sincerely replied.

"Just know, some people are willing to do almost anything to bring sunshine in their baby's life."

"Grandma, I'm a big girl now. Besides, I have a wonderful husband who promised to protect me," Regine confidently replied, as she leaned over and kissed Bessie on the cheek. "Don't worry." Then she ran upstairs to get ready for dinner.

Chapter 25
Too Good to Be True

April 2008....
Justina was considering whether she should call her parents. She desperately needed their financial assistance because her law firm was still in the red. Funding the trip to Regine and Guy's wedding, she concluded, was a bad decision. Her thoughts were interrupted when the office phone began ringing. Justina looked at the caller ID, and pensively answered, "Hello, Calvin."

"Hi Justina, how's it going?"

"It's going okay, I guess," Justina said, sorrowfully.

"Talk to me. You sound a little depressed."

"Oh, it's nothing I can't handle."

Her voice lacked its usual liveliness. Calvin knew something was wrong. "If you ever need someone to talk to, I'm all ears."

Justina did not want to talk about her finances, especially with Calvin. Changing the subject was a much better idea. "I'd feel better if you took me out to lunch to celebrate my 26th birthday."

"That sounds like a plan. Where do you want to go?"

"I was just kidding," she laughed softly.

"Listen Justina, you need a break. I know things at your firm haven't gone as anticipated, so I understand."

Justina quickly sat up in her chair. "Did Roger tell you that?!" she assumed. "Well, I'll have you know business couldn't be better," she said matter-of-factly.

"Calm down baby," Calvin softly said, realizing he offended Justina. "I didn't mean anything by it. It's just...Roger and I have sort of formed a bond. We talk from time to time. Now about your birthday, I'll pick you up from your place tonight so we can celebrate."

Justina wondered what else Roger told Calvin. Resting her head on her desk with the phone to her ear, she took a deep breath and exhaled.

"Justina, did you hear me?"

"Yes," she mumbled.

"What if I pick you up around seven? I'll make reservations at DeSalvo's Italian Bistro. How does that sound?"

"It sounds like a plan. I'll be ready," Justina half-heartedly replied.

Calvin found Roger to be quite resourceful, which is how he found out their law firm was in the red. He also became aware of Justina's personal finances during one of his overnight visits. While discreetly rummaging through her bills, Calvin discovered her last bank statement showed a twenty-thousand dollar balance, and her credit card statements revealed an overzealous spending pattern. He knew he was partially to blame for this. Justina was constantly surprising him with random gifts, from exercise equipment to suits.

Additionally, Roger told Calvin he would be bailing out on Justina soon. Roger had recently submitted his resume to a law firm in Cleveland, Ohio, which was an hour away from his hometown.

Calvin was excited that his plan was lining up, and looked forward to adding more pieces of the puzzle. He eagerly picked Justina up from her condo and took a detour. "Justina, if it's okay with you, I'd like to pick up your birthday gift."

Justina was in deep thought, wondering what Roger could have possibly told Calvin about her finances. She did not want to be treated as a charity case. "Don't go spending your money on me."

Calvin smiled. "But I want to. You're worth it. Besides, I want us to be together forever."

Justina suddenly beamed with excitement in response. She wanted what Guy and Regine had: a beautiful fairytale wedding, a huge mansion, and lots of money. "Are you sure this is what you want?" she cautiously asked.

Calvin glanced in Justina's direction. "If you're saying you don't feel the same, maybe we should part and go our separate ways. Don't you realize I love you," he insincerely admitted.

"I love you too…but we just started dating."

"Justina, you're a very strong, independent woman. I need someone like you in my life, so we can prosper together."

"I don't know what to say."

"Say you want to be my wife."

"Yes, I would love to be your wife, some day," she apprehensively replied.

Calvin smiled as he envisioned a victory dance in his head. After he parked his car in the Zale's parking lot, he turned to Justina and looked longingly into her eyes. "Baby, you're so beautiful."

"Thank you. You're not bad looking yourself," Justina said with a blissful smile.

They walked hand-in-hand into the jewelry store. Calvin quickly turned to Justina, and said, "I think we need to seal our commitment with an engagement ring."

Justina frowned. "Are you sure?"

"Let's make this official," Calvin said, ignoring Justina's questioning gaze. "Will you marry me?" He held her hand and watched her squirm for an answer.

Justina rolled her eyes skyward as she pondered her decision. "Yes," she finally said.

In response, Calvin placed his hand on her cheek and kissed her passionately. "Babe, you just made me the happiest man in the world." Then he eagerly guided her over to the ring display, where he selected and placed a two-karat diamond ring on her finger.

"Now, let's pick out wedding bands while we're here," Calvin suggested.

Justina's heart was racing as she concluded things were moving at a faster pace than she anticipated. "Are you sure?"

"Yes, I'm sure," Calvin convincingly said. "We know we're going to get married. We might as well get the rings while we're here."

"Okay," she reluctantly agreed.

They picked out a pair of solid gold wedding bands, then walked over to the cash register. After the cashier told Calvin the price of the rings, he opened his wallet and pretended to panic as he leafed through the contents. "Justina...I seem to have left...my credit cards...at home," he staggered. "We'll come back tomorrow... I promise, okay?"

Justina knew she was not thinking rationally when she said, "I'll put the rings on my credit card. You can repay me tomorrow. Deal?"

Calvin smiled, breathing a sigh of relief. "Thanks babe."

The sales clerk measured their fingers and told them the rings would be available for pickup the following day. Justina was nervous. *Okay, I just depleted over half my savings. I'm sure my future husband will repay me. So why am I worried?*

"I'll pick up the rings," Calvin volunteered.

"Okay," Justina reluctantly agreed.

After purchasing the rings, they drove to the restaurant in silence. Justina had misgivings while thinking about the money she spent on the rings. They ordered their food, and attempted to make small talk.

Calvin noticed that Justina was unusually quiet, and finally asked, "What's the matter?"

"You're still a mystery to me," Justina admitted, after thinking about her father's concerns about Calvin.

"What is it that you want to know? I told you my whole life story. I'm an only child. My parents are deceased. I'm an attorney. My favorite color is blue. I enjoy basketball...."

"Okay, okay. I get it. But, do you want kids?" she curiously asked. Justina knew she did not want children, but was willing to compromise.

"Of course. At least two. We're going to need a bigger house to raise them in, though."

"But your home is huge."

Calvin picked up his glass of wine and sipped it before responding. "Too small. Baby, when I dream, I dream big. You should know me by now. We should start looking for a house this weekend," he eagerly suggested.

Justina frowned. "I think we should take things slow. We just got engaged," she nervously replied.

Calvin gazed into her eyes with sincerity. "Do you trust me to take care of you and make sure you have the finer things in life?"

"Yes, but I want a wedding. I want my father to walk me down the aisle."

"But Justina, we can use that money toward a down payment for our dream home. Why don't we just have a big reception instead?"

"You don't understand...my father...."

Calvin sighed as he sat back in his chair. "Justina, you know your father doesn't like me, which is why I never thought about asking him for your hand in marriage. If you tell him about our plans, he'll do everything to convince you not to marry me."

Justina knew Calvin was right about her father. "Okay," she sadly agreed.

"Good. I'll call my broker tomorrow. Let's get out of here and go to your place. It seems we have more to celebrate than your birthday," Calvin replied with a sly grin.

Justina became alarmed when Calvin pulled out a credit card to pay for their dinner. He had told her he left his credit cards home when they were in the jewelry store. She reasoned that maybe he did not have enough room on this particular card to pay for the rings.

The next day, Justina and Calvin met with a broker. They were pre-approved for two million dollars, providing Justina sold her condo and Calvin sold his house. "How soon can you put your homes on the market?" the broker asked.

While pensively sitting on the edge of her chair, Justina nervously turned to Calvin, and said, "I think we need to wait until we're at least married."

"Okay, let's do this," Calvin firmly replied. "Let's go to the courthouse and apply for the marriage license today, and by tomorrow, we'll be married."

"Just like that?" Justina asked with reservations.

Calvin gave her a peck on the lips, before saying, "Yes babe. I love you." Then he turned to the broker. "We'll bring you the deeds to our homes tomorrow."

"Good," the broker said. "We may already have several potential buyers. When you come back tomorrow, we will go through the necessary paperwork."

"Actually, you'll be meeting with our accountant tomorrow," Calvin said. "He'll take care of these transactions for us." Then he turned to Justina and handed her a pen and a legal document he retrieved from his briefcase. "I need you to sign this Power of Attorney agreement so my accountant can take care of everything for us."

Justina was sure her father would not approve of this arrangement, so she decided not to tell him. He purchased the condo for her when she graduated from law school. She knew he was going to have a fit when he found out; not any time soon if it were up to her.

"When are you meeting with the accountant?" Justina asked, after signing the legal document and returning it to Calvin. "I'd like to go with you."

"Baby, trust me, I got this," Calvin said with charm. "Besides, we have to make arrangements with the movers to pack our belongings. And maybe later, we can go furniture shopping for our new house," he excitedly suggested.

Justina bit her bottom lip as doubt overwhelmed her. "Everything is happening so fast. Maybe we should slow down."

Calvin angrily slammed his hand down on the broker's desk out of frustration. "Justina, what do you want to do?! Tell me if you don't want to marry me! I'm making major sacrifices for us! I need a lady who's not afraid to take chances in life."

Justina sighed as she covered her face with her hands.

"What is it?" Calvin knowingly asked.

Justina removed her hands from her face, then averted her eyes downward while admitting, "My law firm is…."

Calvin interrupted her. "I already know it's not doing well. You can depend on me. I have major investments that are sure to pay off in a big way. You may never have to work again, if you don't want to."

Justina was relieved to hear this, but she was still having a hard time envisioning the plans he had for them. "I want this just as bad as you," she stressed, "but what's wrong with waiting?"

"Do you believe in me...in us?" he asked.

"Calvin, you seem so sure. My God, we're thinking about buying a mansion together. I just don't want you to wake up one morning and have regrets about us."

Calvin reached for his briefcase and pulled out a file that outlined his net worth, including bank accounts, titles to his vehicles and investment funds, then handed it to her.

Justina was floored as she reviewed the file. She noticed this file was similar to the report Chris had given her but with significantly higher assets and resources.

"I told you," Calvin explained, "I'm serious about us becoming one. I had my accountant draw up the necessary paperwork for your signature. Signing these documents will give you immediate access to my resources."

Justina's heart was beating rapidly. "I don't know what to say," she said, while trying to curtail her excitement.

"Say you trust me," Calvin pleaded with puppy-dog eyes. "If you loved me enough to accept my marriage proposal, love me enough to trust me."

Justina gazed into Calvin's eyes and felt his heart-felt words. She smiled as she signed the paperwork without reading it. Unfortunately, she had just given him authorization to her assets, including her bank account balance.

The next day, Calvin picked up the rings as scheduled, then arranged for an acquaintance to marry them the next day. He had given in to Justina's pleas to have a small wedding, but insisted that he take care of the logistics, including the wedding location and decorations.

After Justina picked out her wedding gown and accessories, she called Roger and asked if he could attend the wedding.

"Only if I can bring Rowena," Roger countered.

"Okay...I don't care," Justina lied. Rowena was the last person she wanted to see on her wedding day.

"Good, I'm sure you won't mind if she brings her friend." Roger knew it would be awkward with Sue there, but Rowena assured him that Calvin and Sue were just friends.

"Fine...whatever," Justina flippantly replied. She would have told him she did mind, but she needed someone close to her to be present on her wedding day.

"When are your parents arriving?" Roger asked. "I'd love to see them again."

"Umm...they're not," she regretfully admitted.

"Are you serious?! Roger incredulously asked. "This is supposed to be one of the happiest days of your life, and you're not inviting your parents?"

"Roger, it's a long story, and I'd rather not talk about it."

"I hope you know what you're doing."

Justina was not sure, but decided to take a chance on happiness.

Calvin invited his co-conspirators to participate in the wedding; one to be the best man, and the other to preside as pastor. He rented the back room of a Japanese restaurant, which was often used to celebrate similar momentous occasions. The place was beautifully adorned with purple and white streamers, balloons, and floral arrangements.

The atmosphere was serene and elegant. Justina wore a beautiful white laced gown and Calvin sported a black tuxedo. Calvin and Justina looked like a match made in heaven.

Calvin was surprised when Sue showed up at the wedding. He told Sue about this bogus wedding arrangement, and was surprised she readily went along with his plans. But he did not expect her to be present for the wedding ceremony.

When the pastor pronounced Justina and Calvin as husband and wife, they kissed while their few guests looked on with questioning gazes. Afterward, they ate gourmet food and drank expensive wine. The conversation was light and bland. Calvin and Sue winked and smiled at each other whenever their eyes met.

Justina was unusually reserved. She kept staring at Sue as if she knew her but could not put a name with her face. Then she looked around and suddenly felt cold. She didn't feel the joy she had anticipated.

Calvin noticed Justina's somber expression. He nudged her and asked, "What's the matter, baby?"

"I just wish my parents were here," Justina admitted. She felt guilty for not telling them she was getting married.

"I know, but we agreed this was for the best. Besides, you know how your father feels about me."

"I know, but...."

"But nothing. Let's get out of here and celebrate our marriage."

They bid their guests farewell, then flew to Los Angeles for three days and two nights. Their honeymoon was spent in a resort hotel on beachfront property. This lavish expense was courtesy of Calvin's co-conspirator.

Justina felt special on their honeymoon. Eventually, she concluded that she made the right decision by marrying Calvin. But Calvin felt sorry for her; he could not wait for his mission to end.

When Calvin and Justina returned from California, they went in search of their new home. The first place they visited was a beautiful mansion. The lawn was beautifully manicured, and there were waterfalls displayed on each side of the driveway.

Justina walked through the foyer, and it seemed like heaven opened up. She was in awe of the ten-bedroom, six-bath mansion with a Jacuzzi and swimming pool. She also fell in love with the 20 X 30 foot kitchen, complete with sterling steel appliances.

On the way out, Calvin submitted a bid to the real estate agent, while Justina stood in the background. A cloud of doubt filled Justina's consciousness as she observed the way Calvin wheeled and dealed. She had a bad feeling about this transaction.

When Calvin pulled out of the driveway, he briefly glanced at Justina and noted she was awfully quiet. "Justina, you haven't said two words since we left our future home. What's wrong?"

Justina was leaning against the passenger door in deep thought. "I don't know. It's beautiful, but can we afford it?"

"Of course. With my assets and few you have, we can live like royalty."

"Are you rich?" Justina asked, even though the file showed that Calvin's net worth was valued at five million dollars.

Calvin chuckled. "Not yet, but I'm well on my way. While we were looking at the house, the broker called and told me he has prospective clients who are interested in buying our homes. With the proceeds, we can move into our new home within four weeks, tops."

The next day, the movers removed all of the boxes from Calvin's home, then went to Justina's condo to pack up and store her belongings in a local storage facility. In the interim, Calvin had arranged for them to move into a hotel suite, courtesy of his co-conspirator.

Chapter 26

Unexpected Guests

For the next two months, Guy and Regine lived in marital bliss. Guy loved Regine, immensely. He looked forward to coming home each night to shower her with gifts and flowers, making her feel like a queen. In return, Regine looked forward to Guy's love and attention, spoiling him daily with her home-cooked meals.

One morning, Guy decided to surprise Regine by cooking and serving her breakfast in bed. Regine became nauseous as soon as he entered the room with the tray of food. She quickly got out of bed and rushed to the bathroom, almost knocking over the tray in the process.

Guy attempted to follow her, but she closed the door behind her. He became alarmed when he heard her vomiting. He lightly tapped on the door. "Baby, are you okay?"

"Yes, I'm fine," Regine weakly said, as she walked out of the bathroom minutes later and sprawled across bed. "After an hour or so, I'll feel better," she assured him. For the past few days, Regine could not keep anything in her stomach. She thought she was coming down with the flu.

Guy sat down on the bed and put his arm around her. "I'm worried about you."

"I'm okay. I probably overate."

Guy did not want to tell her he thought she was pregnant, especially since she had convinced him she could not have children. He was happy she did not follow through with the hysterectomy her doctor recommended. Though, he was still concerned. "I'll take this morning off to take you to the doctor," he insisted.

"Don't be silly. I'll be fine. Besides, I don't want you catching what I have," she weakly replied.

"That's not possible," Guy mumbled.

"What did you say, honey?"

"I said, if after a couple of days and you still feel nauseous, promise you'll go to the doctor."

"I promise," Regine softly said, as she rolled over and closed her eyes.

Guy kissed her on the cheek and left their bedroom. He went into the kitchen where he found Bessie washing dishes. "Good morning, Grandma Bessie."

"Good morning. How's my granddaughter?"

Guy looked up and placed his hand on the back of his neck to relieve some tension. "She's not feeling well, and she won't go to the doctor."

"Don't worry about her. The only thing the doctor is going to prescribe is some vitamins," Bessie said with a smirk.

Guy gazed at Bessie as a smile crept on his face. "How did you know?"

Bessie softly laughed. "Child, when you've lived as long as I have, you just know."

Guy was glad Bessie confirmed his suspicion. "You know she doesn't believe she's pregnant. I wanted to tell her, but she told me the doctor said she can't get pregnant."

"I know, but this is God's will. I'm going upstairs to check on her."

After Guy left their bedroom, Regine knelt down next to her bed and prayed aloud, while a river of tears flowed down her face. "Oh God, please let me be pregnant. I won't ask for anything else. Guy is the man I love. I just want to be able to give this gift of love to him, to us."

Bessie heard Regine praying, so she stopped near the door entrance. When Regine looked up, she was startled to see Bessie. "Grandma...."

Bessie entered the bedroom, as she asked, "Why are you praying for something God has already blessed you with?"

Regine dried her eyes with the back of her hand. "Grandma, you heard me?"

"Yes, but I didn't mean to. I just came up here to see if you needed anything."

"But you don't understand...."

Bessie knelt beside Regine. "Child, everyone has figured out you were pregnant, except you."

"But Grandma, the doctor said...."

"Forget what the doctor told you. He's not God. You had better realize God's blessing is bigger than any doctor. Now, let's pray for a healthy baby, so you can get off those ashy knees and get dressed. We have to pay a visit to the doctor's office."

Bessie prayed, fervently, for Regine to have a healthy baby. She ended the prayer by saying, "Let Your will be done. Amen."

At the doctor's office, Regine left a urine sample, then sat in the waiting room with Bessie to wait for the results. Minutes later, the nurse guided her into another room to wait for the doctor.

The doctor entered the room with a big smile. "We got your test results back, and they show you are positively pregnant."

Regine's face beamed with excitement. "But you told me it wasn't possible."

The doctor looked down at the file and shook his head. "I don't know how this happened, but these results don't lie. I'll prescribe some vitamins for now, but in three months, I want you off your feet as much as possible."

"So you want to see me in three months?"

"No, in three weeks. This is a high-risk pregnancy. I want to make sure everything is coming along as expected."

Regine was stunned, excited, and worried, all at the same time. Bessie warmly hugged Regine after receiving confirmation of her pregnancy, and told her everything was going to be all right.

Guy left work early to receive the news of Regine's pregnancy. First, he stopped by the florist to purchase a dozen roses and a card, thanking Regine for giving him this special gift.

Guy, Cassandra, and Dana waited in the living room for Regine's return from the doctor's office. Dana and Cassandra were trying to guess the sex of the baby, while Guy patiently waited on pins and needles.

When Bessie and Regine walked through the front door, Guy stood up and seemingly held his breath until he heard the news. Bessie said "hello" to everyone and went into the kitchen to start dinner. She did not want to spoil Regine's surprise announcement.

Regine acted nonchalant. She purposely kept them in suspense as she slowly placed her purse on the cocktail table before sitting down in the recliner. She adjusted the chair, laid back, and pretended to fall asleep.

"What did the doctor say?!" Dana curiously asked.

"Please Regine," Guy said, "don't keep us in suspense. What did the doctor say?"

"What do you think?" Regine asked with a sly grin. Then she noticed the vase of yellow long-stemmed roses on the table next to the recliner. "Those are beautiful. Who are they for?" she asked, reading the place card.

Regine,
This is one of the happiest days of my life. Over the next eight months, it will be my honor to wait on you, hand and foot. Whatever you need, you can count on me.
With all my LOVE, Your Baby Daddy

Regine smiled as she turned to Guy. "You knew. When?"

"We all knew!" Dana blurted out.

"This is a high-risk pregnancy," Regine explained. "The doctor isn't sure if I'll be able to carry this baby full-term. He told me I should be in a stress-free environment and off my feet as much as possible...for the next seven months."

"Seven months?" Guy inquired, realizing the baby was possibly conceived on the night of their honeymoon.

Regine nodded.

Guy kissed her, then wrapped his arms around her. "Baby, don't worry. This is God's gift to us. Everything's going to be okay."

Shortly after receiving the news, Bessie and Guy cooked, cleaned, and took care of Regine. Even the girls took on most of the household chores without complaining. Everyone seemed at peace, believing the baby would be fine.

Bessie was also busy planning Regine's surprise baby shower. She invited her best friend, Lucy, and all of Regine's childhood friends. Bessie was so caught up in the moment, she even invited Justina's mother. She figured Mrs. Reyes was not responsible for her daughter's vindictive ways.

Distressed by the change in plans, Justina perked up when she heard her mother's voice on her cellular's voicemail. *"Justina baby. We tried calling you at your home number but it was disconnected. We hope you're okay. We are worried about you. Oh...by the way, Regine is expecting, and you're invited to the baby shower. I hope you can make it. We love you. Call us when you get a chance."*

Justina had mixed feelings after listening to her mother's message. Even though she was still upset with her parents, she wished she could talk to them about Calvin. She never told them she got

married, sold her condominium, and was temporarily living in a hotel. If only she were on speaking terms with her father, things would
have turned out differently.

She was looking forward to moving into their new home. The
new furniture was all picked out and ready for delivery on closing
day. When the broker told her the closing date was being pushed
back due to unforeseen circumstances, she had the new furniture put
in the storage unit with her other furniture.

In light of her current circumstances, Justina was having misgivings about going to the baby shower. She reluctantly picked up the
phone and dialed her mother's number. "Hello, Mom."

"Justina, it's so good to hear from you!" Mrs. Reyes said with a
burst of joy. "Did you get my message about Regine?" she asked,
assuming Bessie made a mistake when she failed to invite Justina.

"Yes, Mom," Justina replied with indifference. "When is the
baby shower?"

"It's next month at Regine and Guy's house, but Regine doesn't
know about it. It's supposed to be a surprise."

"Fine, I'll be there," Justina flatly replied.

"Good, we look forward to seeing you. Your daddy misses you."

"Mom, I'm not ready to see Dad. Just tell him I'm okay."

Mrs. Reyes paused. "But Justina…he's your father."

"Mom, thanks for stating the obvious, but I'm not ready to talk
to him. I'll meet you at Regine's," Justina said, before abruptly dis-
connecting the call.

While still holding the phone, Justina thought about Regine's
pregnancy and felt a pang of jealously. Begrudgingly, she dialed
Regine's number.

Alex answered on the first ring.

"Hi, may I speak with Regine?"

"Who's calling?"

"It's Justina. I was calling to congratulate the mother-to-be," she
unenthusiastically stated.

Alex cringed as he thought about the havoc Justina caused between Regine and Guy. "Regine is asleep," he lied. "I'll tell her you
called." Alex abruptly hung up on her.

Guy walked into the kitchen and noticed Alex's hand on the
phone. "Who was that on the phone?"

"Nobody. Tell Regine I'll call her later." Alex grabbed his car
keys and picked up his suitcase.

Guy asked, "Do you have everything you need?"

"Yeah. I'll be meeting up with my roommate later on."

Guy followed Alex to his car. "Alex, Regine and I are so proud of you. Remember, you have a job at Lucent Technology when you complete your Master's program."

"Thanks, but I'm not sure I want to come back to St. Petersburg on a permanent basis."

"Whatever you decide, we're behind you one-hundred-percent."

"Thanks man."

They embraced before Alex left in his brand new Toyota Scion, a graduation gift from Guy and Regine upon receiving his bachelor's degree. Alex was supposed to be heading to Florida International University in Miami, Florida, but he headed north instead. Justina's phone call had unnerved him. The more he thought about it, the angrier he became.

June 2008....

Regine was four-and-a-half months pregnant when her grandmother gave her a surprise baby shower. The house was filled with friends and family members, and was beautifully decorated with colorful balloons and streamers. Bessie was speechless when Justina arrived with her mother. Then she decided there was nothing to worry about; she believed Mrs. Reyes would keep Justina in check. After all the guests arrived, Bessie told everyone to gather on the back patio.

Guy was in on the surprise and took Regine to the movies, to give the guests enough time to arrive at their house. When he pulled into the driveway, Regine became suspicious. "Guy, why are all these cars here?"

Guy bore a poker face. "I don't know. Let's go inside to find out."

"I have a bad feeling about this," Regine cautiously said.

Guy held her hand and guided her inside. With the exception of balloons and streamers, no one was in sight. Regine looked around, then turned to Guy and asked, "What's going on?"

"We wanted to do something special for you," Guy admitted, nudging her closer to the patio door.

"We who?!"

"Everyone!" Guy merrily shouted, as he opened the patio door and everyone yelled surprise in unison. He kissed her and told her to have a good time.

The guests, including Justina, took turns hugging the mother-to-be. Regine was surprised to see Justina, especially since their last conversation ended on a sour note.

After everyone ate, Regine was escorted to a chair, which was decorated in colorful streamers and balloons. Then her grandmother placed a beautiful paper-mache hat on top of her head. After each gift was opened, the ribbon and bows from the gifts were pinned onto the hat.

Thus far, Regine had received wonderful gifts from her guests. The next one she opened was from Justina, who stood in the background waiting for everyone's reaction. Regine removed the wrapping to unveil a caricature picture of herself, pregnant with flabby arms and legs, a big squishy head, and huge swollen feet. She was speechless, and so were her guests.

No one laughed, except Justina.

Bessie wanted to strangle Justina, but she was busy trying to constrain Lucy. "Let me at her!" Lucy yelled. "I just need one shot at that hussy!"

"Lucy, calm down," Bessie said in a whisper. "You know Regine doesn't know about you. Don't worry; Justina will get hers," she added, while staring at Justina in disgust.

Mrs. Reyes was embarrassed. She quickly grabbed the picture and handed if off to another guest with instructions to get rid of it. Then she encouraged Regine to open the gift from her, which was a beautiful quilted baby blanket.

"I made it myself," Mrs. Reyes proudly professed.

Regine's voice lacked luster. "This is very nice. Thank you." She could not get the picture Justina gave her out of her mind.

Shortly afterward, Regine and her guests sat around discussing baby names and the do's and don'ts of parenthood. That is, until Justina mentioned the abortion Regine had in college. Regine abruptly excused herself and told everyone she was going to lie down.

All the guests directed their gazes and harsh stances toward Justina. Sensing the line of fire, Mrs. Reyes grabbed Justina's arm and rushed her out of the house. She was furious as she walked with Justina to her car.

Upon arriving at Justina's car, Mrs. Reyes faced her and angrily asked, "What has gotten into you?!" First, you're not talking to your father. Then you show up at Regine's baby-shower to embarrass her, embarrassing me in the process."

"Listen, Mom, I don't have time for this."

"No! You will stand there and listen to me! Your father and I made a lot of sacrifices to put you through college. We bought you your very first house, and we gave you money to open your own law firm. We did it because we love you, but now you're being ungrateful! It's time you start showing your gratitude!"

Justina sighed. "Mom, I'm stressed out. I'm going through a lot right now."

"Do you want to talk about it?" Mrs. Reyes sincerely asked.

"No, not just yet. I'll call you later," Justina solemnly replied, before she got into her car and drove off.

Mrs. Reyes went straight home and told her husband what transpired at the baby shower. Then she asked him, "Do you think this Calvin person has brainwashed her? This is not like Justina. Not calling for months, then showing up at Regine's shower and pulling a stunt like that."

"We can't speculate," Mr. Reyes calmly replied. "We just have to hope she comes to her senses and talk to us about what's troubling her."

In the middle of the night, Guy rushed Regine to the hospital. The doctor told him Regine and the baby were fine, but she would have to stay overnight to get her blood pressure down.

Chapter 27

Rude Awakening

*J*ustina was frustrated when she left the baby-shower. She did not understand why her mother was so bent out of shape, especially since Regine seemingly had the dream man and the dream house. She was looking forward to hearing good news about her dream house, from her dream man, when she returned to their temporary residence at the hotel.

"Sorry, babe," Calvin said, as soon as Justina walked through the door, "they changed the closing date, again."

Hastily, Justina threw her suitcase on the floor, and stood eye to eye with Calvin. "I'm tired of living in this hotel! And I'm tired of living out of a suitcase! Maybe my dad was right about you!" she sharply admitted.

Calvin's nostrils flared as his blood pressure shot up. "What did you say?!" he barked, while looking at her in a threatening manner.

Justina slowly backed up. "I...well maybe....we should've waited," she fearfully said, as she quickly walked over to the bed and sat down.

Calvin exhaled and briefly closed his eyes. "Baby, what happened to the trust?" he asked in a much softer tone. "If you want a different house, just say the word. I can make it happen."

"It's going on four months," Justina carefully stated. "I have a feeling something isn't right. Did you call the broker again?"

Calvin sat on the bed next to her and looked into her eyes. "Baby, I told you, things like this take time. The broker didn't know about the lien on the property before it was put on the market."

Justina shook her head back and forth. "It still doesn't make any sense. Why can't we get our down-payment back?" she thoughtfully asked.

"Because we signed a contract," Calvin replied, wondering why she was questioning him.

Justina reached for the phone. "I'll call the broker myself."

Calvin quickly grabbed her hand. "That's not necessary," he nervously explained. "Tell you what, I'll have my firm look into this to see what they can do." He continued holding her hand, but loosened his grip. "Don't worry; things are going to work out just fine," he added, before he kissed her softly on the lips.

Justina suddenly noticed that Calvin was dressed in his business attire. "Where are you going?"

"I have to go to the office to meet a client. Don't wait up for me."

"Oh, okay," Justina suspiciously replied, after looking at her watch. She thought it was strange that he was going to the office so late in the evening, but reasoned that she had done the same thing in the past.

An hour later, Calvin called and left a message on Justina's voicemail, stating that he had to go out of town for an impromptu business trip. She called him back on his cell phone, but he did not answer or return her message. For the remainder of the weekend, she tried calling several times, to no avail. She even tried calling Calvin at his office, but did not get an answer.

When Justina got to her office on Monday morning, Calvin's answering service repeatedly intercepted her calls. She sat back in her office chair, worried about him. Then she intuitively looked up Calvin's office number on the internet. She discovered it was different from the number listed on his business card. Calvin had convinced her early on that his partners agreed to keep spouses and girlfriends out of the office, so she never paid him a visit. At the time, she did not care; she was too busy operating her own law firm. In hindsight, his explanation seemed irrational.

As a last resort, Justina dialed the number listed on the internet. "Hello, may I speak to Calvin Calloway?"

"May I ask who's calling?" the secretary inquired.

"Mrs. Calloway, his wife."

The secretary gasped, then cleared her throat before asking Justina to clarify that she was, indeed, Calvin's wife.

"Put Calvin on the phone!" Justina demanded.

Seconds later, Attorney Calloway came on the line. "Hi Babydoll," he happily said. "How's my lovely wife?"

"Calvin, is this you?" Justina cautiously asked, after determining this voice did not belong to her Calvin.

Realizing he made a mistake, Attorney Calloway sat up in his chair and changed his tone of voice. "This is he. How may I help you?"

"This is Justina, your wife," Justina stated with uncertainty.

The attorney frowned. "I don't think so. My wife's name is Nancy. We just returned from our honeymoon. I'm sure you have the wrong Calloway."

Justina angrily slammed the phone down on its cradle, then dropped back in her chair. After a short pause, she exploded. "Roger! Come in here! I need to talk to you!"

Detecting the urgency in her voice, Roger hurried into her office. "What's wrong?!"

"You can start by telling me what kind of sick game you and Calvin are playing," she said in an accusatory manner.

"What in the hell are you talking about?!" Roger frustratingly asked.

Justina tried to calm down, but she was slowly losing control. "What do you know about Calvin Calloway, or this guy claiming to be him?"

"Only what I told you. You saw the investigative report. We used our own investigator, remember?"

After putting her elbows on the desk, Justina held her head down, clasped her hands, and began to cry. Roger walked around her desk and touched her lightly on her shoulder. "Justina, what's going on? Talk to me," he insisted, when she failed to respond.

Justina lifted her head and in between sniffles, she stammered, "I believe...Calvin is a fraud. I just called...Saunders and Associates. A different Calvin Calloway...answered the phone. And the phone number he gave me isn't listed on the internet."

"Are you serious?!" Roger hysterically asked.

Her voice trembled. "Roger, I need...to see for myself. I need...to go to that office and talk to Attorney Calvin Calloway in person."

"I'll drive you there," Roger insisted, as he returned to his office to retrieve his car keys.

An hour later, Roger and Justina arrived at the attorney's office and approached the receptionist desk. "Hi, we're here to see Attorney Calloway," Roger told the secretary.

"I'm sorry, but he's with a client right now."

"Can you tell him it's urgent?" Roger persisted. "Tell him Roger McCarthy and Justina Calloway is here to see him." Justina winced at the mention of her new name. She had a feeling her new name was not valid.

The secretary paused and gazed at Justina before relaying the message over the intercom. Attorney Calloway appeared at the secretary's desk within seconds. Justina was shocked by his resemblance to the man she married.

Attorney Calloway approached Justina first. "I believe you called me earlier."

Before Justina could respond, Roger extended his hand. "Hello, I'm Roger McCarthy, and this is my partner, Justina Calloway. We'd like to show you something. Is there any way we can go into a private room?"

"Yes, sure," Attorney Calloway said, as he escorted them to a vacant conference room and closed the door behind them.

"We believe you are part of a stolen identity scam," Roger said.

Attorney Calloway was speechless when Roger presented the investigative report. His eyes grew bigger and his hands trembled when he saw all of his resources and assets outlined in the report. "How did you get this information?" he curiously asked, still reviewing the documents in the file.

"Our private investigator researched you by mistake," Roger said. "We have since learned that another person claimed your identity. This person is married to my partner. We have a law firm in Atlanta; Reyes and McCarthy," Roger explained, as he handed the attorney their business card.

Justina looked on with a bewildered expression.

"What the hell kind of joke is this?!" the real Attorney Calloway exploded. "If you don't start talking, I'm going to call the police!"

"Calm down," Roger said. "We've been scammed too. We're on our way to file a police report. You should do the same," he said, as he guided Justina out of the conference room.

As Roger drove to the police station, Justina filled him in on the details relating to her and Calvin's failed house purchase and their temporary residence at the hotel. Justina began crying, uncontrollably. "Oh Roger, what have I done?!"

Roger placed his free hand on top of hers. "It's going to be okay. Calvin won't get away with this," he said, as he pulled into the parking lot.

As soon as they walked into the police station, they signed in and waited to be called. Minutes later, Detective Jones greeted both of them with a handshake, then guided them back to his office to talk privately.

Roger explained Justina's dilemma, while Justina remained quiet. Detective Jones gave Justina some mug shots to browse through, then asked to speak with Roger in private. When Roger and the detective returned fifteen minutes later, Justina explained that she did not have any luck finding Calvin Calloway's imposter from the mug shots.

Detective Jones sympathetically stated, "Your situation is not that uncommon, and it is likely the suspect is long gone. I suggest you put this matter behind you."

Justina remained speechless, while Roger interceded on her behalf. "Thank you for your advice," Roger graciously replied. "We will consider it." In response, the detective smiled and winked at Roger.

☼

Roger drove Justina to the hotel after they left the police station. He also graciously paid the balance of her hotel stay. "You need to get out of this hotel and come and stay with me until we figure out what to do next."

"I can't...," Justina tried to explain. Her pride prevented her from readily accepting his offer.

"You can and you will," Roger insisted.

To appease Roger, Justina said, "I'll think about it."

After Roger left, Justina wanted to find out if Calvin also lied about the lien on the mansion they were supposed to buy. She drove to the broker's office to see if she could get the down payment back, but the office looked as if it had been abandoned for quite some time.

Justina looked down at her engagement and wedding rings and remembered Calvin never repaid her for them. Fearing the worst, she called the credit card companies and discovered all her cards were maxed out.

Short on money, Justina decided to take Roger up on his offer, and moved in with him two days later. It was an easy chore, because most of her things were still in storage. She knew one thing; she would not be at his place long, especially since she could not stand Rowena.

When Justina walked into the living room the very first night, she saw Rowena and Roger hugged up on the sofa. She exhaled loudly, deciding to call it a night.

Rowena ignored the contemptuous way in which Justina looked at her. She turned to Roger and uncaringly asked, "Is she going to be okay?"

"I hope so. I have never seen her so vulnerable," Roger acknowledged, saddened by Justina's predicament and suddenly overcome with guilt.

Rowena whispered in Roger's ear, "I didn't want to say anything, but when are you going to tell her you're leaving the firm? You should tell her as soon as possible. Things can't get any worse than they are now."

"Maybe you're right. I'll tell her in the morning."

Chapter 28

Unfinished Business

Justina woke up with a new attitude. She was not discouraged when Roger told her he was leaving her law firm. She was more determined than ever to find the man who ruined her life. She picked up the phone and called her investigator. "Hi Chris, it's Justina."

Chris paused before responding. "Ugh...Ms. Reyes," he stuttered. "Did someone else jump bail?"

"No, that's not why I'm calling. Remember the guy you investigated several months ago, Calvin Calloway?"

"Yes, I remember. What about him?"

"He's my husband," Justina ashamedly admitted.

Chris' eyes grew bigger. "Oh...um...congratulations. Why didn't you tell me?"

"It was a private wedding." Justina was embarrassed, but thought it was important to disclose this information. "To make a long story short, the Calvin Calloway I married stole someone else's identity, including his background."

"I'm sorry. I didn't know," Chris lied.

"Chris, I believe you may have followed the wrong man."

"How do you figure?" he knowingly asked.

"Everything in your report matches Calvin Calloway, but I need you to go to his office and verify whether it's the same man you followed."

Chris began sweating profusely as his voice trembled. "Give me...a couple of days...and I'll get back to you."

Justina thanked Chris for his assistance. Then she decided to call her parents and relay the bad news, figuring things could not get worse than they already are.

"Hello," her dad answered.

"Hi, Dad, it's Justina."

"I know who this is. How's my baby?!" Mr. Reyes excitedly asked, expecting only good news.

"I don't know how to tell you this," Justina hesitantly admitted, "so I'm going to be straight with you. My finances....are in jeopardy."

"How much do you need to stay afloat?"

Justina sighed. "I wish it were that simple. Roger told me this morning that he took job offer with another law firm. I gave him my blessings."

"Justina, just come home," Mr. Reyes pleaded. "There are plenty of job opportunities in the Tampa Bay/St. Petersburg area."

Justina briefly closed her eyes. "I don't want to come home a complete failure."

"Don't be silly. For the rest of your life, you'll be faced with many setbacks. You only fail if you give up trying. Where's your faith?"

Justina thought, *Oh here we go. Dad is going to start talking to me about God. Where was He when this phony Calvin Calloway character ripped me off?!*

When Justina did not respond, her father asked, "When was the last time you've been to church?"

Justina ignored his question. "Is Mom there?"

"Yes, but I want to tell you to pray and...."

"Dad! Put Mom on the phone!"

Seconds later, Mrs. Reyes got on the phone. "Hi, Justina. How are you?"

Justina heavily sighed. "I have bad news and more bad news," she weakly admitted. "I married Calvin Calloway, the guy you and dad met. But I recently discovered he was an imposter. And, Mom, I no longer own my condo. I sold it under false pretenses. Calvin and I were supposed to buy a new home together with the proceeds, but I found out that was also part of the scam."

Her mother was speechless.

"Mother, did you hear me?"

"Yes, but how...when...?" Mrs. Reyes curiously asked.

"None of that matters. It's a long story and I'd rather talk to you in person. I just ask that you don't pass judgment."

When Mrs. Reyes remained silent, Justina hung up on her. She knew her parents were disappointed. Tears flowed down her face, as she questioned, *"What have I done?!"*

Chris was nervous. He did not think he would still be involved at this point. He hesitantly picked up the phone and dialed Calvin's number.

"Hello," Calvin impatiently answered, on the first ring.

"Hey man, this is Chris."

"Now what?! I told you…you'll get the other half of your money this weekend."

"I'm not calling about that. We have a different matter to discuss. I received a call from Justina today. She wants me to go to the real Calvin Calloway's office to verify whether it was him I followed."

Dumbfounded, Calvin asked, "Why?"

"You should know better than me. It sounds like she's fighting back."

"On the real?"

"Yes. So what do you want me to tell her in my report? I believe she's getting antsy. I need something that's going to stick."

"I'll think of something."

Chris grunted.

Calvin knew Chris was becoming uncomfortable with this change in plans. "For your troubles, I'll throw in an extra grand."

"You don't get it, do you?!" Chris frustratingly replied. "Justina's been good to me. It's true, her attitude stinks, but this is pretty extreme."

"So what are you saying?!" Calvin harshly inquired. "You wanna step?!"

Chris sighed as he put his hand to his forehead. "I'm just way in over my head."

Calvin became furious. "Can I trust you?!"

Chris was afraid to tell the truth. "It's not that, it's just…."

"Just what! You punkin' out?!"

"Nah…but if I get caught, you're going down with me," Chris weakly threatened.

"Are you threatening me?!" Calvin asked with anger in his voice.

Chris knew he misspoke. His voice trembled. "I'm just telling you…Justina's been through hell because of all of us. Roger will soon be working for a big-time law firm soon, but I'm still in this mess."

"Listen punk, you're getting paid to do a job!"

Chris remained silent.

"I know about your beautiful wife and kids," Calvin said in a threatening manner. "I wonder how they'd feel if you just disappeared into thin air one day." He silently laughed, knowing he would not follow through on this threat. He respected the fact that Chris was a family man and a good father.

Chris was suddenly overcome with fear. "Please don't...."

"If your family means that much to you, you had better make sure Justina cannot identify me." Calvin hung up without waiting for Chris's response.

Chris was having a hard time breathing. He could not believe he was caught up in this mess. And things were getting worse.

Two days later, Chris called Justina. "Ms. Reyes, I went to the office the other day, and I can confirm that the attorney is the same Calvin Calloway I investigated."

"Thank you for looking into this," Justina weakly said, as she contemplated her next plan of action.

"Ms. Reyes, are you still there?"

"Yes," Justina softly said. "Chris, what I am about to tell you may dissolve our relationship for good."

Chris suddenly became alarmed as he sat up in his chair, wondering if she had discovered his involvement.

"Chris, I need to close the firm," Justina said with remorse. "I'm afraid I can't even afford to pay you for the information you just provided me."

"I'm sorry this has happened to you. I feel partially to blame," Chris truthfully admitted.

"Don't. You had no way of knowing."

"What about Roger? I thought you two had some type of contractual agreement. You can sue him for bailing out on you."

"I don't want to. Roger has been more than patient with me. I brought all of this on myself," Justina conceded.

Chris thought Justina's response was bittersweet. She did not pay him, but she did not find out about his involvement either. "Well, don't worry about paying me. I appreciate everything you've done for me."

Justina thanked him and wished him luck. She also told him to let her know if he ever needed a reference.

Chris was beginning to like Justina. For the first time, he witnessed her softer side. He felt guilty, wishing he could do or say something that would make her feel better about her predicament.

Chapter 29

The Unraveling

Roger was in the process of packing up his office when Justina told him about her plans to find the fake Calvin Calloway. He tried to tell her that attempting to locate him could be dangerous.

Justina shook her head in disbelief. "Roger, I don't get it. I don't have any enemies. Why would Calvin target me? I never did anything to him or anyone."

Roger seemed apprehensive to respond. "Well Justina, you need to put this behind you, and move on with your life," he finally said. "I'm going back to my office to finish packing." He could not believe Justina thought she did not have any enemies. Behind her back, he personally referred to her as the *witch on wheels,* instead of a broom, because she drove over anyone who got in her way.

Roger reflected on the times Justina had repeatedly yelled at him for not doing something she wanted him to do. He particularly hated it when she put on her *'better than you'* attitude in the presence of his fiancé. So when the opportunity came along to sabotage her professional and personal life, he could not resist. He now realized it was a mistake. If she successfully located Calvin, he knew he could be implicated as well. He had to find a way to dissuade her from seeking the truth.

After packing the last of his personal things, Roger went into her office. "Hey Justina. Have you thought about what I told you?"

Justina was fired up when she pointed out the facts. "This guy made me look like a fool!" she fiercely stated. "There's no way I can face my parents until I know this scumbag is in jail where he belongs!"

"Whatever you decide to do, I'd like to know about your progress, if you don't mind."

"Sure, Roger."

Roger turned to leave but changed his mind. "Justina?"

Justina looked up from the file. "Yes, Roger."

"If you can't find him, I know someone who can help you. He's a friend," Roger hesitantly added.

"Who is he?"

"Let's just say he has a way of finding missing people," Roger answered, as he handed Justina a card with the contact information. "Oh, before I forget. This is for you." He handed her a check.

Justina gasped when she saw the amount. "Are you sure?" she asked, as she looked at him with amazement.

"I know you're short on money. This should be enough to get you through the next month or so. It's the least I can do. I'll be around for at least three weeks, so call me if you need me."

"Thank you. I'll be sure to call you if I find out anything," Justina said, as she continued looking at the check for $25,000.

With Roger's monetary assistance, Justina moved into an apartment in Buckhead, Georgia. Her lease for the law office was paid up for the next six months, so she used the office to conduct her own investigation. Justina reviewed the contents of Calvin Calloway's file again and came up empty. She thought, *Desperate times call for desperate measures. This guy is going to be sorry he ever crossed me.* She took Roger's advice and decided to give his friend a call.

"Hi, is this Thorny Cooke?"

"Yes it is."

"My name is Justina Reyes."

"Oh, Roger told me to expect your call. What can I do for you?"

"I was thinking…maybe we could meet somewhere and talk in private."

Thorny remained silent for a few seconds before responding. "Meet me at my warehouse on Third Avenue in the Hills, at three p.m."

"Okay," Justina reluctantly agreed. An hour later, she found the warehouse and spotted Thorny standing next to an old beat up Ford pickup.

"So what can I do for you?" Thorny asked, as Justina exited her car.

"I have a problem," Justina nervously stated. "There's this guy I want you to locate. He's taken everything from me and I want it back."

"What do I get in return?"

"I'm not sure what you mean," Justina said with a blank stare.

"From what you're telling me, this guy sounds shady. What will I gain by helping you?"

"My gratitude," Justina graciously replied with a nervous smile.

Thorny smiled. "You can make it up to me later. Tell me what you know about this guy."

Justina told Thorny everything he already knew. He was impressed with all the players that put her in this position. Not only did they carry out the plan, but they also left no tables unturned.

Thorny said, after deep thought, "Give me some time. Let me see what I can find out."

As soon as Justina drove away, Thorny pulled out his cell phone to bring Kevin, Regine's father, up to speed. He had notified Kevin in advance of his meeting with Justina.

Chapter 30

Happenstance

*J*ustina needed a friend. She had not befriended anyone since arriving in Atlanta. And the only friend she could trust was married to someone she no longer considered a friend. Justina called Guy at his office, anyway.

"Hello, may I please speak to Guy Simmons?"

"May I ask who's calling?" the secretary asked.

"Umm...Justina Reyes."

The secretary paged Guy over the intercom system. "Mr. Simmons, there's a Justina Reyes on the line for you."

Instinctively, Guy wanted to reject Justina's call, but he was curious to know why she was calling. "Put the call through," he said, after a short pause.

"Hello Justina," Guy flatly stated.

"Hello Guy. It's nice to hear your voice," she said in a friendly manner.

"Save it Justina! I thought I'd never hear from you again, especially after the havoc you caused at Regine's baby-shower." Then he sarcastically added, "We forgot to tell you how much we appreciated your wedding gifts. I'm curious to know why you gave my wife a year's supply of weight-watchers vitamins and food; and me, an 11 x 16 picture of you in a skimpy bathing suit."

Justina chuckled. "I must admit, that was tasteless. Sorry."

"What...hello? Is this Justina Reyes?" Guy asked, as he removed the phone from his ear to see if he heard her apology.

"Come on Guy. I'm not that bad. Can we let by-gones be by-gones? You're the only friend I have," she whined.

"Justina, you know that's not true."

"Yes it is. Everyone else hates me," Justina truthfully conceded.

"If they do, I can't say I blame them. Face it. You owe everyone an apology, including my wife."

Justina sighed.

"For once, put aside your pride and do what's right," Guy insisted.

"Guy, so many things have happened in my life these past few months."

"Talk to me," Guy said, as he sat up in his office chair.

Justina hesitantly asked, "Do you have time? I mean…I can call you later."

"Don't be silly. What's going on?"

Justina was overwhelmed by his thoughtfulness. "Guy, I think I made a mistake by marrying a man I barely knew. After he went missing, I had him investigated and came up empty."

Guy frowned. "Missing?! Justina, what happened?"

"This imposter pretended to be extremely wealthy. I signed a legal document, which gave him access to my assets. I feel so stupid. I even sold my condo so we could buy a house together."

"So you bought a house together. That's great!"

"No, that's the problem. The deal fell through. I went to the broker's office to inquire about the house after Calvin left me, but the broker was nowhere to be found. To add insult to injury, I recently found out the house we were supposed to buy was sold long before we signed a contract."

"Have you checked your credit history lately?"

"No. I don't even get the mail anymore. Calvin had all of our mail redirected to his post office box after we moved into the hotel together."

"Hotel?"

"It was supposed to be temporary. Well, at least that's what he told me."

"What happened to you?" Guy asked with disbelief. "You married a guy after only dating him…."

"Stop it Guy! I heard this already from my parents. I need a friend, not another parent."

"I'm sorry. Listen, as soon as you hang up the phone, call your bank, your broker, and the credit bureau to report your identity as stolen. Also, go by the post office and have your mail redirected to a new post office box. Make sure you tell them not to change your mailing address in the future, without notifying you in advance."

"But I don't think this Calvin imposter is coming back."

"Justina, you're an attorney. Think about it. When you hang up, fax over all the information you have on this guy. I'm going to have a friend look into this matter."

"Guy, that's not necessary. Everything I know about Calvin Calloway is legit, but it has nothing to do with the imposter."

"Fax me what you have anyway. Call me back after you've made those phone calls."

Upon receiving the information from Justina, Guy contacted his friend, Big Mike, and asked him to stop by his office to discuss Justina's dilemma.

"So, do you think you can find the culprit?" Guy asked, as soon as Big Mike showed up at his office.

Big Mike nodded his head in the affirmative. "Give me a copy of the file and I'm on it." Then he looked at Guy with a questioning gaze. "Can I ask you a personal question?"

"Shoot," Guy said, as he handed over the file.

"Why are you doing this? Justina is not your responsibility. Besides, she got what she deserves, after the way she treated Regine."

"Man, no one deserves this. I thought about it, and wondered if I could live with myself if something bad happened to her. Or, what if Dana and Cassandra were in the same situation? I'd want someone to help them. It's true; Justina can be spiteful. But is it worth what she's going through right now?"

"I suppose you're right. Give me a couple of days. I'll be in touch with you soon."

As soon as Big Mike left his office, Guy contacted Justina's father to inform him of her predicament. "Mr. Reyes, I want you to know that I'm doing everything in my power to help her."

"I appreciate you contacting me," Mrs. Reyes sadly replied. "How much is your investigator charging you?"

"Don't worry about it. He's a good friend of mine."

"Guy, I never thought my daughter would be caught up in this type of nonsense. Justina never listens to me and that's the problem. See if you can convince her to come home."

"You know Justina can be stubborn, but I'll do my best."

"Thank you." Mr. Reyes sincerely stated. "I know you didn't have to get involved, but I really do appreciate it."

"No problem."

Mrs. Reyes was on another phone, eavesdropping. After Guy hung up, she hysterically approached her husband with fear in her eyes. "What are we going to do?!"

"Trust Guy to bring our baby home," he weakly said, hanging his head low.

"If you would've tried harder to convince her to stay in St. Petersburg, this wouldn't have happened," she weakly replied, as tears flowed down her face.

Mr. Reyes looked at his wife with a blank stare. "I can't believe you're blaming me. You're the one who didn't think Guy was good enough for Justina. You were fawning all over Calvin when you met him, practically giving our daughter to him on a silver platter."

"I didn't know he'd turn out to be a creep," she said, still sobbing.

"Let's stop blaming ourselves. Justina's a grown woman. Let's just pray for her safety," Mr. Reyes said, as he embraced his wife.

After Justina hung up the phone with Guy, she called her bank. Both accounts showed negative balances. Fearing more bad news, she reluctantly picked up the phone to call her broker.

"Hello John, this is Justina."

"Justina Calloway? Hello, how are you? Are you going to reopen your accounts with us? Your husband was very adamant about closing your accounts and selling your stocks. He cashed out at $100,000. I didn't think it was a smart move. The stock value is steadily rising!" John elatedly proclaimed.

Justina was speechless.

"Hello…hello…Justina?"

Justina slowly breathed in and out before responding. "Yes, I'm still here. I'll call you back."

"Well, all right. You take care and keep in touch."

Justina cried for hours on end. Her entire inheritance went up in smoke. *I'm going to kill Calvin, or whatever his name is! God, help me!* She called Calvin's cell phone again, but this time her call went directly to his voicemail.

A little while later, Justina drove to her office. As she approached the door, she was greeted by a stranger. He was holding a stack of paperwork in his hands.

"Hi, may I help you?" Justina curiously asked.

"Yes, I'm looking for Justina Calloway."

Justina cringed at the sound of her new unlawful name. "Correction! My name is Justina Reyes!" she barked, before she entered her office.

The man looked somewhat relieved and followed her inside. "Your rent has not been paid for three months," the landlord explained. "I have been trying to reach your husband, but I can't find him."

Justina quickly turned to face him. "What are you talking about?"

"Well, your husband rented one of my properties in Stone Mountain. He owes me…."

The landlord's explanation was interrupted when a police officer suddenly entered her office.

"Oh God, what now?" Justina frantically asked, to no one in particular.

The police officer approached her. "Are you Justina Calloway?"

"Yes…well no,…not legally," she stammered.

The officer was not convinced. "You're under arrest. You have the right to remain silent. Anything you say or do, will be….."

Justina panicked. "But what…what for, what did I do?"

"For writing bad checks," the police officer replied.

"But, I didn't do it! It wasn't me! You've got to believe me!" Justina cried out. She looked at her secretary for assistance, but Kathy looked down and pretended to be engrossed in her work.

"Ma'am, you can explain everything at the precinct," the police officer said, as he handcuffed her and continued reciting the Miranda rights. "You have the right to an attorney."

"I know my rights!" Justina yelled, after the officer escorted her to the police car and placed her in the backseat. She held her head down in despair. When she looked up, she saw the landlord.

"Where's my money?!" the landlord asked, loud enough for her to hear him through the bulletproof window.

Justina looked at the man in disbelief and mumbled, "If I get a hold of this Calvin imposter before you do, he won't be around to pay any rent."

Justina found herself in a jail cell after being fingerprinted and stripped of all her personal possessions. Terrified of the other criminals, she held her head down and cried.

One of the inmates approached her. "Hey suga-momma, crying ain't gon get you out from behind these bars."

After wiping away her tears, Justina looked up to find an Amazon-looking woman with enough make-up on her face to paint a building. She also noticed that the woman was missing several teeth.

In response to Justina's questioning gaze, the woman asked, "What?! You've never seen beauty like this before?"

"No, I'm afraid not," Justina cynically replied.

"Is that supposed to be some kind of smart mouthin'?!" the woman asked in a threatening manner.

"No, it's just that you asked me a question," Justina replied with a straight face.

An officer approached her cell and yelled, "Justina Calloway!"

"Yes," Justina said, as she walked to the front of the jail cell and grabbed on to the bars.

"You can have your one phone call now," the officer said, as he opened the cell to release her. He escorted her to a windowless room with one phone and one chair.

Justina did not want to call her parents. And lately, Roger had become strangely incognito. He rarely returned any of her calls, and if he did, the conversation was always cut short. She decided to call her one and only friend on his cell phone.

Guy answered on the first ring. "Hello."

"Hi Guy," Justina said with great sadness.

"Justina, I thought I asked you to call me back," he admonished.

"It's a long story," she sadly admitted. "I'm in jail."

Guy slowly exhaled as he quickly recovered from the shock. "How much is your bail?"

"I don't know yet. I'll know by this afternoon."

"I'm on my way."

"But Guy...."

"Justina, I'm coming to bail you out. Then we'll figure out what to do next," he insisted.

"But Guy, what about Regine?"

"She'll understand. She knows I love her, and will never do anything to hurt her," Guy said with certainty.

Guy's last statement rattled Justina. She wanted to believe he still loved her.

After Guy hung up, he walked into the kitchen and found Regine and Bessie over the stove cooking. "Hey Regine," he said, as he gave her a hug and a kiss.

Regine smiled. "Hello there."

"Hon', can I talk to you in private?" he asked, as he briefly glanced at Bessie.

"About what?"

Bessie witnessed their exchange and intervened. "Go on child. I got the food. Go spend time with your husband," she lightheartedly said.

Regine smiled in response to her grandmother's take-charge attitude. She took her apron off and turned to Guy. "Let's go to the bedroom for some privacy."

Once they were in their bedroom, Guy came clean. "I just got a call from Justina. She's in jail and I need to go bail her out. That is, if it's okay with you." Regine's eyes grew bigger as Guy rehashed the earlier conversation he had with Justina.

"Why did she call you, and not her parents?" Regine curiously asked.

Guy shook his head. "Pride, I guess."

"Figures, but you should tell her parents that she is in jail."

"I already told Justina's father about her earlier predicament. I don't want to alarm him about Justina's incarceration until I find out more information. I just know if Dana or Cassandra were in the same predicament, I'd want someone to help them."

"I know. When will you return?"

"Tomorrow. Would you like to come with me?"

"I feel sorry for her, but I'm not ready to face her right now. Justina's hurt me enough. Go help her. Make sure you call me when you arrive in Atlanta."

When Regine returned to the kitchen to resume cooking, Bessie noticed her worried expression, and asked, "Is everything okay?"

"Not quite," Regine solemnly replied. "Guy's going to Atlanta to help Justina."

Bessie frowned. "You can't be serious. That woman tried to break you. I think about all the things she said and did to you, then you go and let Guy help her. Whatever happened to her, she deserved it!"

"Grandma, no one deserves what she's been through. I wouldn't wish what happened to her on my worst enemy."

Bessie shrewdly said, "Vengeance is mine, says the Lord."

"But Grandma, the Lord didn't have anything to do with this. Someone took matters into their own hands."

"Maybe things were planned that way," Bessie mischievously admitted.

"Grandma, what are you saying?" Regine asked, eyeing her grandmother suspiciously.

"Baby, that girl makes people want to hurt her. What she did to you was wrong. At your wedding and your baby-shower, she showed out. She got what she had coming to her," Bessie said with certainty.

Regine looked into Bessie's eyes and slowly asked, "What did you do?"

"I didn't do anything I will regret," Bessie replied, before turning her back to Regine and walking out of the kitchen.

Regine felt like she was having an out of body experience. She has known her grandmother her entire life, and never knew she could muster such hatred for anyone. Her grandmother had always taught her to leave matters in God's hands.

After Guy posted Justina's bail, he asked Big Mike to pick her up from jail. Two hours later, Justina stood behind a gated door waiting to be released. Big Mike knew it was Justina when he saw her. He understood why Guy was infatuated with her. Even without makeup and fancy clothes, she was beautiful.

Hi, you must be Justina Reyes," Big Mike said. "I am here to escort you to the Hilton Hotel lobby to meet with Guy Simmons."

"Oh…." Justina was surprised Guy did not come himself.

During the ride to the hotel, Justina had mixed feelings about seeing Guy. She wished she had given him an opportunity to make her happy. She thought, *Dad was right about everything. I'm such a fool.*

Guy was immediately blown away by Justina's rugged appearance when she entered the hotel lobby with Big Mike. "Hi Justina. Let's have a seat," he said, as he guided her to a chair, then sat in a chair next to hers. Big Mike took a seat across from them. Guy turned to Justina and asked, "How are you holding up?"

Justina began crying. "Oh Guy," she sobbed, "what have I gotten myself into?"

Guy placed his hand on her shoulder. "Don't beat yourself up. We need that energy to get you out of this mess."

Justina looked up as tears flowed down her face. "Do you know I could spend the next five years in jail for allegedly writing those bad checks?"

"That's not going to happen. We're going to work this out," Guy assured her. "You need a good night's sleep. I paid the landlord, so that's one less thing you have to deal with."

"I didn't know Calvin, or 'whoever he is, rented that house. He told me he owned it. I even watched the movers remove all the boxes after he supposedly sold it."

Guy exhaled loudly. "I need you to lay low a while," he said, as he briefly glanced in Big Mike's direction. "Big Mike is going to stay in Atlanta to find out what happened. You need to be available, just in case he has any questions. Promise you'll stay put until we can get you out of this mess."

"I promise," she lied. Justina knew she could not sit still. Her first priority was finding out how and why this happened to her.

"I'll be returning to St. Petersburg tomorrow," Guy said. "Just stay home and out of sight until Big Mike can probe further. Call him if you need anything."

Instead of taking Guy's advice, Justina went to her office the next day. After she parked her car in the garage, she got out and walked around to the rear passenger door to get her briefcase. Suddenly, someone in a black mask and dark clothes approached her from behind and hit her on the back of the head with a crow bar. She fell to the ground, screaming for help. Justina was silenced after her attacker hit her two more times before jumping into the get-away vehicle and speeding off.

Luckily, when the security guard made his rounds, he discovered Justina's limp body. He felt a light pulse and called 911.

Chapter 31

Troubled Waters

Justina's body seemed lifeless, and her spirit teetered on despair. Her head was wrapped in bandages that covered hints of a small protrusion. Her right arm was not broken but was encased in a temporary sling, and her face was inflamed with bruises.

Enduring enormous pain and grief, Justina could not imagine feeling better. Plus, she was afraid her life may still be in danger. It had been a week since the attack, and no suspects had surfaced. The police investigators assured her that it was a random act of assault and battery.

After a restless night of sleep, Justina woke up to find the two most unlikely people by her bedside. She had called Guy three days after the attack and told him she was in the hospital. Upon seeing Regine, Justina was immediately overcome with remorse, and wished she could do something to 'right her wrongs.' She painstakingly looked into Regine's eyes, and asked, "Can you ever find it in your heart to forgive me?"

Regine calmly replied, "I forgave you a long time ago. For trying to come between me and Guy, and for making me realize that when all is said and done, I matter."

Perplexed, Justina somberly asked, "What? I don't understand. How could you…?"

Regine shushed her, then held Justina's hands in hers while sincerely looking into her eyes. "Justina, I believe all things happen for a reason, and for every action, there's a consequence. Don't get me wrong; the things you said and did to me throughout the years were hurtful. But none of that stops me from wanting to help you." Regine briefly glanced in Guy's direction, and added, "We both want to help you."

Justina's eyes watered as she clasped Regine's hands tighter, and earnestly thanked her for her forgiveness.

Regine cautiously eyed the heart monitor. She wanted to do everything in her power to keep Justina from learning the truth about her attacker's identity. She felt guilty about withholding information that would probably relieve Guy of any guilt he may feel.

Regine reflected on the conversation she had on the phone with her grandmother the day before. She told her grandmother Justina was in the hospital, and her and Guy were planning to visit her.

Bessie was taken aback. "I don't know why you and Guy would go see her!" she exclaimed. "That girl is plain evil! I told you before, she got exactly what she deserves!"

Regine was shocked by Bessie's comments. "Grandma, I need you to be honest with me. Did you have anything to do with Justina getting hurt?"

"If I did anything, I did it for you," Bessie firmly replied.

Regine did not want to assume or guess, so she asked again. "Did you have anything to do with it?"

"Not directly but...."

"But what? If you know something, please tell me," Regine insisted, after Bessie suddenly became speechless.

"Regine, I'm so tired of the way that girl is always treating my baby. I told someone who may have done something about it."

"Who?"

Bessie briefly closed her eyes and sighed. "Remember when I told you that your father was dead?"

"Grandma, are you telling me he's not?! Grandma, is my father alive?!"

"Calm down, baby. Please promise you won't be mad at me. I did it to protect you," Bessie said in her defense. "We love you, baby. We all do."

"Grandma, this is too much. I can't deal with this right now. I'll call you later."

Initially, Regine thought her grandmother was involved in Justina's assault; now she was not sure. She thought about all the years she grew up without a father, and how she had always blamed her mother for not being there for her. Now her father can share in the pain and void she felt all her life.

Regine refocused her attention on Justina. "We have to take care of you. God gives us all chances to make amends." She reflected on this last statement and thought, *even me*. Regine held Justina's hand as she prayed for her speedy recovery.

Guy stood a couple of feet away from Justina's bed and witnessed Regine's effortless act of compassion. He slowly approached her and wrapped his arm around her shoulder. After Regine nodded her approval, Guy moved closer to Justina's bedside and placed his right hand on top of hers. Then he leaned over and looked into her eyes before he spoke.

"Justina, try not to worry about anything except your health," Guy said with compassion. "You have a family who loves you un-conditionally," he said, while briefly glancing at Regine, "and you have us. Regine and I care about your well-being. We would like to invite you to our home to complete your recovery after you're dis-charged from the hospital."

"Are you sure?" Justina timidly asked, as she staggered for the proper words. "I mean,…I'd really appreciate it. If you don't mind… it would be temporary, of course. The doctor said I will only need a few weeks of bedrest before my condition returns to some type of normalcy," she added.

Justina thought this was a great idea, especially considering her parents' cold demeanor toward her when they visited earlier. Mr. and Mrs. Reyes were disappointed in Justina for being secretive, and for allowing herself to be put in a compromising situation.

"Enough said," Regine lightheartedly responded with a nervous smile. "You will stay with us until your condition improves." Re-gine was relieved when Guy agreed with her request to extend an invite to Justina.

Justina was not sure of her decision, considering her prolonged but fragmented feelings for Guy. However, she suddenly became empowered, knowing that Guy would be protecting her. Wickedness began to form along the crevices of her grin as she thought of the possibilities. With Guy as an ally, regaining her parents' acceptance seemed foreseeable. She further surmised, Regine had been through worse and losing Guy might be a blessing. Justina decided Guy rightfully belonged with her.

✺

It had been a week since Justina arrived at their house. Everyone was unhappy with this arrangement, except Regine. Guy stayed away from Justina's room, and Alex and Bessie made it clear that they will not be visiting as long as Justina was there. Although the twins were indifferent, they stayed away from Justina, mimicking Guy's attitude.

Regine was left to labor after Justina by herself. She lightly knocked on Justina's bedroom door before entering the room to bring her breakfast. "Good morning, Justina," she said, as she sat the breakfast tray on the dresser.

Justina was wide-awake. Her eyes instantly focused on Regine's round stomach. "Good morning, Regine. You look worse than how I feel. When is the due date?"

"I'll take that as a compliment," Regine snidely commented, as she briefly glanced in Justina's direction. "To answer your question, I'm due in a couple of months."

"Oh, that's nice," Justina replied with indifference. "Um, Regine, where's Guy?"

"He's at work."

Justina folded her arms, clearly disappointed.

Regine cautiously asked, "Did you need him for anything?"

"No, it's just…I thought I'd see more of him."

Regine was stunned by Justina's admission. "I'll tell him to stop by, when he gets home from work."

Justina had hoped to see Guy every day. She purposely woke up early every morning to apply makeup and drench herself with perfume. She had a feeling Guy was purposely avoiding her, and so did Regine.

"Why are you avoiding her?" Regine questioned, as soon as Guy came in from work.

Guy frowned. "Regine, I only agreed with this arrangement to appease you. I'll do anything to make you happy."

"Can you at least speak to her tomorrow?"

"Okay, only for you," Guy said with a negative attitude. He did not like Regine taking care of Justina, especially while she was pregnant. Regine did not seem to understand that having Justina in the house made him uncomfortable. He was working hard to keep everything copacetic until Justina left their house for good.

The next morning, Guy slowly strolled into Justina's room. He thought it was strange that she had on makeup and her hair was nicely styled. "Good morning Justina," he flatly stated.

Justina smiled and in a seductive voice, she said, "Good morning, handsome."

"Ugh…how are you feeling?" Guy asked, ignoring her compliment.

Batting her eyes, Justina continued in the seductive voice. "Fine, now that you're here."

Guy's nostrils flared as he exploded. "Enough already! I'm not going to let you disrespect my wife!"

Justina lightly put her hand to her chest. "What...what are you talking about?" she bashfully questioned, pretending to be hurt by Guy's insinuation.

"You know damn well what I'm talking about!" Guy yelled, then attempted to constrain his anger as he looked toward the bedroom door. He turned to Justina and in a hushed voice, he sternly said, "Let me make myself clear. I love Regine. I'll never lose her for you or anyone, so get that through your thick head!"

"I didn't....I mean," Justina stuttered, trying to find the appropriate words or excuse for her behavior.

"Save it!" Guy barked, before he quickly exited the room, running into Regine in the process. "I want her out of this house now!"

Regine was stunned by Guy's demand. She was outside the door eavesdropping, and could not believe Justina was continuing with her callous and deceptive ways. She angrily walked into the bedroom with a hyped stance. "Justina, it's time for you to go!"

"But...I have another week or so before I am fully recovered," Justina weakly explained.

Regine strongly declared, "I don't care where you go, but you have to get the hell out of my house!" Without waiting for Justina's response, she turned on her heels, slamming the door behind her. Distraught by what just transpired, Regine immediately called Justina's parents to have her transported to their home.

Justina was surprised by Regine's anger. She wondered if Guy told her what happened. She knew her attempt to lure him from Regine was doomed, so she was ready to go.

Guy was furious with Justina, but not enough to stop the investigation. He was curious to know what Big Mike was able to find out. He was elated when he received his phone call a week later.

"Man, it's good to hear from you," Guy explained. "In case you didn't know, Justina was attacked in her office garage."

"I heard about it," Big Mike confirmed. "Does she know who attacked her?"

"No. What did you find out?"

"I have a lead, but I need to ask Justina some specifics before I give you a full report on my findings."

Guy paused before explaining, "Justina's stayed at our house for a week, after she was discharged from the hospital. It's a long story...don't ask."

Big Mike laughed in response. "Man, you're going to learn that a leopard never changes its spots."

"Whatever man, just call me back and tell me what's going on."

Under the watchful eyes of her parents, Justina was unusually quiet for an extrovert. "I'll be out of your house in one week," she softly whispered to her mother.

"This is your home too. Stay as long as necessary." Seconds later, Mrs. Reyes answered the ringing phone in Justina's bedroom. "Justina, there's someone on the phone named Big Mike. Do you want to take the call?"

"Yes, Mom. Thanks." After Mrs. Reyes handed Justina the phone, she told her mother in a stern voice, "That'll be all. Please close the door on your way out."

Mrs. Reyes complied with Justina's wish. She did not understand why Justina remained secretive, and kept pushing her away.

Justina waited until her bedroom door was closed before she put the phone to her ear. "Did you find out anything?"

"Yes, I found some information about the fake Calvin Calloway," Big Mike explained. "According to the leasing agent, the house he rented was also in your name. The man you married is not Calvin Calloway. His name is Richard Randolf, *AKA* Slick Rick."

"What?!" Justina asked, as she quickly sat up in bed.

"Justina, there's no court record that shows you were ever married."

"Did you contact Chris, my investigator?"

"I'm almost one-hundred-percent sure he was also involved in the scam."

Justina's forehead wrinkled, clearly confused. "But it's so extreme. Why would this Richard person do this to me?"

"I don't think he had a personal vendetta against you. I think he was hired by someone else to do their dirty work."

"What are you saying...?"

"Can you think of any enemies you may have in Atlanta?"

"No, not really. Most of my relationships are on a civil and professional level."

Big Mike thought, *Yeah, right.* "What about your partner?"

"Roger? He would never be involved in this," Justina said with uncertainty. She noticed he had stopped returning her calls after she became hospitalized. Thinking about her conversation with Thorny, the man Roger referred her to, made her weep. Justina had a feeling she would not be hearing from him again, either.

"Everything's going to be just fine," Big Mike tried to assure her.

"I don't know," Justina continued to sob. "Everything I worked so hard for has been taken from me."

"When are you going to realize money and material things can be replaced, but your life cannot? What's more important to you right now?"

Justina dried her eyes and in between sniffles, she said, "Getting out of this jam, of course."

"Now we're getting somewhere. First, you need to file a restraining order against Richard Randolf. Secondly, you need to stay put and let your parents look after you."

"I know, but I can't stay here. There's too much tension."

"You need to think about it."

Chapter 32

Unknown Territory

*W*hen Justina was in the hospital, Big Mike followed up on the police report and discovered that her case was not on file. In fact, the detective who interviewed her, acted like he did not know anything.

"Let me get this straight," Big Mike said to Detective Jones, "you never interviewed Justina Reyes, who came in here with Roger McCarthy?"

"I would've remembered if I had," the detective smugly replied.

"And your name is Vincent Jones, correct?" Big Mike asked, as he eyed the detective's nametag.

The detective folded his arms and exhaled loudly. "Yes, that's me."

Under Big Mike's piercing gaze, the detective unfolded his arms and began fidgeting with his hands. He did not know Big Mike had already called the Lieutenant earlier. The Lieutenant verified Justina had arrived at the police station on the day in question, and thought it was strange that her report was not on file.

Big Mike took Detective Jones through the motions to determine if he took the report but forgot to file it. In the process, he realized he was possibly dealing with a crooked cop. He stared at the detective and determined the obvious. "How much were you paid?" he finally asked the detective.

"What are you talking about?" the detective nervously replied.

"Never mind." Big Mike saw the Lieutenant approaching them. "Lieutenant Carson," he said, as he stood up and greeted him with a handshake. "I appreciate your help, but it looks like you have another matter on your hands. It seems Detective Jones claims he never met Justina Reyes."

As Big Mike packed up his briefcase, he turned to the Lieutenant and said, "I'll be in touch." He did not wait around to see what was going to happen next. He assumed the detective would be interrogated and eventually suspended, indefinitely. Big Mike was certain the interrogation would yield more information about Justina's case.

✹

Big Mike wanted to pay Roger and Chris a visit, but first, he stopped by Justina's office to interview her secretary. He walked into the office and noticed a heavyset woman sitting at the front desk, filing her nails.

"Hi, my name is Mike Solomon. I'm a private investigator, and you're Kathy Little, right?" he questioned, after looking at the name plate on her desk.

"Yes," Kathy confirmed, as she put her nail file down to give Big Mike her undivided attention.

"If you don't mind, I'd like to ask you some questions."

"About what?" she asked with apprehension.

"Justina."

"Oh, okay," Kathy cautiously said, picking up her nail file to resume filing her nails.

"Did you know she was recently attacked in the garage?"

Kathy slowly shook her head, avoiding eye contact.

Big Mike eyed her suspiciously. "I was hired to find out who attacked her. Do you know if she has any enemies?"

Kathy stopped filing her nails, then rolled her eyes. "I'm sure there's a long list," she curtly replied. "Ms. Justina isn't the friendliest person. If it weren't for the extra paycheck I get every week, I would've left this job a long time ago," Kathy added with an attitude.

"Extra check?"

"Oh, um…never mind." *Damn! Me and my big mouth.*

Big Mike raised a brow. "No, you need to tell me about this extra check. Otherwise, I'm going to have to report this bit of information to the police."

Kathy looked up with fear in her eyes. "Please don't. I have children to take care of."

"Talk to me," Big Mike firmly said, "or talk to the police. It's your choice."

Kathy sighed. "Well, I was working for this temp agency and they referred me to this man, who arranged an interview with Roger McCarthy, Ms. Reyes' partner. This man promised me an extra $1000 a week for however long I stayed and worked here. I just had to send a weekly report on Ms. Reyes' comings and goings, and report if she was dating anyone."

213

"Can I have the address of where you send the reports?"

Reluctantly, Kathy opened her desk drawer and gave him the business card with the contact information.

"Have you ever met the person who sends you the checks?"

"No, I just met the man who arranged my job interview."

"Do you happen to have one of those checks with you?"

Kathy sighed before pulling an envelope out of her purse. It contained a payroll check with Trowne Key Estates and Resorts listed as her employer.

"Do you mind if I get a copy of this check?"

Kathy did not answer. She took the check and went to the copier. "Am I in trouble?" she nervously asked, as she handed him a copy of the check.

"No. I just need you to be here in case I have further questions."

"Are you going to tell Ms. Reyes about this?" Kathy fearfully asked.

"No, it will be our secret for now," Big Mike said, as he winked at her.

Kathy breathed a sigh of relief. But she submitted her letter of resignation right after Big Mike walked out of the office. She was afraid of being implicated for a crime she had nothing to do with. Once she began receiving the extra checks, Kathy had feared being implicated in a conspiracy against Justina.

An hour later, Big Mike called the phone number on the card Kathy gave him. "Yes, I need to speak to Timothy Carter."

The secretary asked, "May I ask who's calling?"

"Tell him it's a personal friend of Kathy Little."

Seconds later, Tim picked up the phone. "Who is this?!" he anxiously asked.

"Your worst nightmare," Big Mike replied in a harsh tone. "We need to talk."

"Talk about what?!"

"I tell you what," Big Mike threatened, "you have a choice. Either you talk to me, or you talk to the police."

Tim immediately became cooperative. "What do you want to know?"

"Why did you plant Kathy in Justina Reyes' office?"

Tim starting pacing back and forth, as he became defensive. "I didn't plant her or anyone, anywhere! All we did was help Ms. Little find a job. That's not a crime," Tim explained with a hint of cynicism.

"It is, if it had anything to do with Justina's assault."

"Assault?! I don't know what you're talking about!" Tim barked.

"I believe you do. Tell me what you know."

Tim exhaled loudly before he responded. "Jeanine Benedict was scouting a law firm to represent Trowne Key Estate and Resorts. I arranged an interview for Kathy Little after seeing the vacancy posting for their law firm. Since Kathy was qualified for the job, we figured she could give us more insight about the Reyes and McCarthy Law Firm."

Big Mike frowned. He did not believe Tim, especially since Justina's law firm solely dealt with civil and criminal law, not corporate.

"So who are you to Jeanine Benedict?" Big Mike asked.

"I'm her private investigator."

"What type of information has Kathy provided you about Justina Reyes?"

"Basically, her comings and goings, including her relationship with Attorney Calvin Calloway."

"Oh, I see. If your story checks out, you're off the hook. If not, you'll be hearing from me again."

Big Mike became alarmed at the mention of Attorney Calvin Calloway's name. When he contacted the leasing agent listed in the investigative file Guy gave him, he stumbled upon Attorney Calvin Calloway's imposter, Richard Randolf. The leasing agent gave Big Mike the signed rental agreement in exchange for one-hundred dollars. Calvin and Justina were listed as the lessees, and a New York address was listed as their former residence.

After conducting an address search online, Big Mike found two phone numbers associated with the NY address. The second number yielded the results he needed. He dialed the number and a woman answered.

"Hi, I'm looking for your husband," Big Mike casually said.

"Richard's not here," she said with an attitude. "He hasn't been here for quite some time. I don't know how to reach him, so you can stop calling."

Big Mike knew she was lying. "Wait a minute, Mrs.?"

"Randolf. Again, my husband isn't here and don't call here anymore." She hung up, but Big Mike received the lead he needed.

The person he was looking for was Richard Randolf. Within twenty-four hours, he learned all about Richard. Justina had no idea she was dealing with a professional con man. He wondered if Jeanine and Tim knew Richard was Calvin Calloway's imposter, or if they were just as oblivious as Justina.

Next, Big Mike headed to Justina's office where he spotted the security guard standing near the entrance of the building. He introduced himself, then asked the guard if he knew about Justina's assault. The guard told him a couple detectives had been by earlier, but they did not have any leads.

Big Mike looked around the ceiling in the garage, then asked the guard, "Can you tell me if the garage has some type of surveillance system?"

"Yes, it is monitored twenty-four-seven, but Ms. Reyes' attacker had a mask on," the guard explained. "I watched the video with the police."

"Can I see the video tape?"

"The original is with the police, but we have a backup," the guard explained, as he rewound the tape.

Big Mike and the guard watched Justina's attack on a thirteen-inch TV monitor in the guard's station. On the video, the garage was dimly lit and isolated, and her attacker wore black and had a mask on. It also showed Justina was caught off guard because she was attacked from behind.

After watching the attack scene, Big Mike asked, "Was there anyone else in this area that looked out of place on the day of the attack?"

"No, not really. But there was a young man who asked me if the Reyes and McCarthy Law Firm was located in this building. He asked if I was sure Justina worked there."

"Did he go to the office?"

"No, he never went inside. He walked to his car and drove in the direction of the garage, out back. I'm not sure if he went into the garage."

"Do you think the video will show if the young man entered the garage?"

"I believe so." The security guard rewound the tape to an earlier time, then fast-forwarded it to the car and the young man he spoke of.

"That's him," the security guard said, as he pointed to Alex, Guy's brother.

Big Mike tried to contain his shock, as he asked the guard, "Did you report this to the police?"

"No, I just remembered the young man, because his car was red, and it looked like he was too tall for that little car he was driving. He was blasting Lil Wayne's new CD on his stereo," the guard added with a chuckle.

There was no doubt about it; Alex was in the vicinity at the time of Justina's assault. Justina was attacked fifteen minutes after he pulled into the garage. Big Mike wanted to know what Alex was doing in Atlanta. He stepped aside and placed a call to Guy on his cell phone. "I need to talk to Alex. How can I reach him?"

Guy became alarmed at the mention of Alex's name. "Why do you need to talk to him?"

"It's a long story." Big Mike abruptly hung up after Guy gave him Alex's cell number. He wanted to avoid Guy's questions until he spoke with Alex first.

Alex answered on the second ring.

"Hi Alex, this is Big Mike. I need you to explain why you were in Atlanta on the day of Justina's assault. And don't lie to me!"

"How...do you know?" Alex fearfully asked.

"That's not important. I need answers, now!"

"I went to Atlanta to confront Justina," Alex timidly admitted. "I wanted to tell her in person, to leave Regine alone. I was in my car waiting for her when she drove into the garage. After she parked her car, I was going to approach her, but a black SUV drove up next to her car from the opposite end of the garage. I ducked down and watched someone attack Justina with an object. Then they jumped back into the SUV and drove off. I left the scene immediately afterward. Am I in trouble?" he finally asked.

"No, but sit tight. I'm going to view the video tape again, to check out the black SUV you told me about. And do me a favor - the next time you want to confront someone, do it over the phone."

Big Mike reviewed the tape again, and discovered Alex was right about the SUV. He could not get a clear view of the tag number but noticed the Florida Sunshine State emblem. He told the guard to keep quiet about what they discussed.

When Big Mike left the security guard station, he noticed an Irish pub on the corner, up the street. He assumed this would be the type of place Roger would frequent. He walked into the pub and sat down at the bar, casually looking around.

The bartender instantly approached him. "Hey buddy. It looks like you're on the wrong side of town."

Big Mike smirked. "How do you figure?"

"The cowboy hat and jeans gives you away, for one. And you're carrying a briefcase."

Big Mike looked down at his attire and smiled. "Okay, you got me. How long have you been working here?"

"Long enough to know when someone is trying to find out some information."

Big Mike held up his hand and playfully surrendered.

"What do you want to know?" the bartender asked.

"About the Reyes and McCarthy Law Firm, and its owners."

"It's right up the street. I've only seen Justina Reyes in here a couple of times. But her partner, Roger McCarthy, has been coming in here for the past year or so. He's a nice guy, but the lady he's been hanging out with looks like trouble."

"Lady?" Big Mike curiously asked.

"Some bimbo he met in here several months ago."

"When was the last time you saw him?"

"Roger was in here a couple of weeks ago with his friend, Chris, and the bimbo. He told me Chris was a private investigator for their law firm. Did I tell you his lady friend was black?"

"Yeah, I believe so," Big Mike lied.

"Well anyway, another black lady was with them this time. It was strange seeing two white men sitting with two black women like that. Roger wasn't himself that day. He kept looking over his shoulder as if someone was following him."

"Can you give me more information about the ladies?"

"One was a little shorter and darker than the other. But if I had to guess, they look like sisters."

"Thank you for helping me out. I'd appreciate it if you'd keep this conversation private."

"No problem. I figure we have to look out for our own. If Roger is in any trouble, I want to help him. He looks like he's caught up with the wrong kind of blacks."

Big Mike was offended but refrained from responding. He decided the bartender might be a reliable source in the near future.

After Big Mike looked up Chris's address on the internet, he drove to Decatur, Georgia, and parked his car a couple houses down from Chris's. After two hours of non-activity, he knocked on the neighbor's door. An elderly woman answered.

"Hi, is Chris here?" Big Mike asked, knowing he had the wrong address.

"There's no one here by that name," the elderly woman replied.

Big Mike pretended to be confused. "Oh. I thought Christopher Townsend lived here."

"Oh, Christopher lives next door, but he's out of town."

"You know where he went?"

"His wife told me they had a family emergency. She said they'll be back in a couple of days. What's your name?"

"I'm just a friend. I'm going to leave a note on their front door."

Big Mike walked onto Chris's front porch and noticed the air conditioning unit was running and the porch light was on. He presumed Chris had not left town on a permanent basis.

Prior to driving to his house, Big Mike conducted a background search on Chris. He knew Chris could easily be lured by money, considering his poor financial history. His recent credit report showed several revolving accounts with negative balances. The only account that seemed to level off and remain current was his mortgage.

Two days later, Chris and his family returned home. Big Mike was strategically parked a couple of houses away witnessing Chris, a woman, and two young boys exiting a car. After retrieving their luggage from the trunk of the car, they went inside the house. Minutes later, the woman returned to the car and backed out of the driveway.

Big Mike presumed the woman was Chris's wife and decided to follow her; she went to Wal-Mart. When she walked into the store, he exited his car and followed suit. Big Mike stood behind her in the checkout line after grabbing random items from the shelves.

"I can't believe how much prices have gone up," Big Mike said to Chris's wife, even though she had her back to him.

She looked around and assumed he was talking to her. "Prices on what?" she asked, still not sure he was talking to her.

"You know, in general," Big Mike said, while looking at the items in his shopping cart.

"Yeah, I know what you mean. Luckily my *husband* takes good care of me and my family," she said, hinting to Big Mike that she was married.

"Good for you. I hope my wife feels the same way about me," Big Mike responded with a friendly smile.

Chris's wife turned around and smiled back. "I'm sure she does. You live around here?"

"About twenty minutes away. I stopped in here to pick up a couple of things for my wife. She's not feeling well," Big Mike explained, while eyeing the cough medicine in his cart.

She followed Big Mike's gaze to his cart. "Oh, my husband hasn't been feeling well either. I've been trying to get him to go to the doctor."

"What's the matter?"

"I don't know. Lately, he's been so jumpy. Every time the phone rings, he goes berserk," she said with a worried expression.

"Why don't you take the phone off the hook?"

"That's what's strange about it. He doesn't want me to. Oh, what am I doing?" she rhetorically asked, while putting her hand on her chest. "I'm so sorry to bother you with my problems. You go head on and see about your wife."

"But it's no trouble at all," Big Mike anxiously replied.

Chris's wife turned to him and smiled. "Thanks for your concern, but go home and take care of your wife."

Based on Chris's suspicious behavior and the information Justina provided about him, Big Mike contacted the Lieutenant and explained that Chris may have been involved in the scam against Justina. He went to the police station, where he and the Lieutenant arranged a call to Chris's house.

"Hello," a raspy female voice answered.

Big Mike knew it was Chris's wife after spending some time with her at Wal-Mart earlier. "I'm sorry if I called you at a bad time, but I need to speak with your husband," he said in a disguised voice.

"Who is this?"

"A long-time friend of his. Tell him it's regarding a mutual friend of ours, Justina Reyes."

"Hon, wake up. Some man is on the phone. He says you're a friend of some woman named Justina Reyes. Who is Justina?"

Chris grabbed the phone from her. Then he put his hand over the mouthpiece, and asked his wife. "Did he tell you his name?"

"He didn't say. He sounds creepy."

Chris's eyes grew bigger. He reluctantly answered the phone, trying to sound hard and in control. "Who is this?!"

"What's up with your tone of voice?!" Big Mike demanded to know, continuing with his disguised voice.

"Is this Calvin?" Chris fearfully asked, as he put on his robe and walked out of the bedroom.

Big Mike remained quiet as Chris continued without further prompting. "I did everything required of me. I told you Justina doesn't know about you. What more do you want from me?" he whispered in a constrained voice. "What I can't understand is - why you made me do this to her? What has she ever done to you?"

Big Mike immediately disconnected the call. "You got that?"

"Yes," the Lieutenant replied. "How stupid can this guy be? He just incriminated himself."

"This is going to be easier than I thought," Big Mike said.

"My men are on it," the Lieutenant stated. "They're on their way to his house right now."

"Good. I'm going to Roger McCarthy's apartment. I'll call you if I find out anything."

Chapter 33

Love Never Fails

Alex made it his business to call every day and check on Regine. He returned home after her last false alarm to the emergency room, and was relieved when the doctor confirmed Regine's pregnancy was coming along fine. He figured the false alarm had something to do with Justina.

After visiting with Regine in her bedroom, he walked outside where he found Guy sitting on the deck. He sat down next to Guy, to address his concerns. "Guy, why are you and Regine still dealing with Justina? I don't understand your logic for helping her."

Guy was searching for the right words, trying not to sound accusatory. "Alex, I've thought about this for a long time. I need you to be honest with me. Did you have anything to do with Justina's assault? And why did Big Mike call you out of the blue the other day?"

"No!" Alex angrily replied, averting his eyes downward and purposely ignoring the second part of Guy's question. "I did not have anything to do with it."

Guy sat up on the edge of his chair, and slowly asked, "Are you sure you don't have anything to tell me?"

Alex heavily exhaled out of frustration. "Listen Guy, I gotta go. Please call me if Regine goes into labor."

"Will do. Drive safely," Guy said with great sadness in his voice. He wanted to protect his brother, even it meant finding a way to discount him as a suspect. Guy did not tell Regine about his suspicions because he did not want to alarm her.

After Justina left Guy and Regine's house, Bessie happily returned to Florida to look after Regine. She was on the phone in the kitchen when Regine called for her from her bedroom.

When Bessie did not respond, Regine slowly got out of bed and went downstairs. Her mouth flew open after she overheard some of Bessie's conversation. She quietly hid on the opposite side of the kitchen wall, eavesdropping.

"Now Kevin," Bessie firmly said, "this has gone on long enough. All these killings have to stop. You can't go around hurting everyone who hurts Regine."

"But Bessie...." Kevin tried to explain.

"But nothing! I find it hard to believe that you didn't have anything to do with PJ's disappearance when Regine had an abortion. Then there was Earl Banks, who was killed in a car accident; and Samuel White, who was found in the bottom of the Chesapeake Bay. And now, Justina."

While listening to Kevin's response, Bessie casually turned around and came eye to eye with Regine. She seemed to freeze in place. "Let me call you back," she whispered into the mouthpiece, before putting the phone on its cradle.

"Who was that?" Regine knowingly asked.

Bessie's voice trembled. "Regine...."

"That was my father...wasn't it?"

Bessie reached out to her with both arms. "Yes, but baby, let me explain."

Regine turned her back to Bessie, stifling her tears. After a few seconds, she turned around with fire in her eyes. "I want to see him! I need to see him now!" She briskly returned to her bedroom and immediately picked up the phone to inquire about PJ.

PJ's partner, Ulysses, answered on the first ring.

"Hi, this is Regine."

"Who?" Ulysses heard her, but wanted to be sure.

"Regine. Um...me and PJ. Well, um, we used to ....."

Ulysses interrupted her in a high-pitched voice. "Oh, I know who this is! Why are you calling?!" he asked with an attitude.

"I need to know if you had any luck finding PJ."

Ulysses broke down crying. "We haven't seen or heard from PJ in six years," he sobbed. "I can't talk to you now," he softly whispered, before he hung up the phone.

Regine was heartbroken to learn that PJ was still missing, but needed to make another phone call that would probably add fuel to the fire. Earl's girlfriend, Sara, answered on the second ring.

"Hello, this is Regine. I need to ask you about Earl."

After a long pause, Sara sighed before responding. "Regine, you don't have to feel guilty. It was an accident."

223

"An accident?!"

"Yeah, I thought you knew Earl was killed in a car accident."

Regine was speechless.

"Regine, are you there?"

"Yes," Regine sadly responded. "I'll call you back." She hung up the phone in a daze. She was angry, confused, and scared at the same time.

The next day, Bessie arranged for Regine to meet her father at a local restaurant. Bessie and Kevin were already seated when Regine walked in. Her eyes instantly connected with the eyes of the man she resembled.

Kevin had on a black godfather hat and dark shades. He bore a big smile as he got up from the table and embraced her. "Have a seat, baby."

Regine nervously sat next Bessie, while Kevin sat across from them. Kevin provided a thorough explanation for being absent most of her life. He did not hold anything back. He even told her about the whole custody arrangement with Mr. and Mrs. O'Neal, her god-parents. More importantly, Kevin told her about her three younger sisters, and explained how he made sure they had everything they needed.

"You also have a trust account," Kevin stated, as he pulled out the bank statement and handed it to her, "so you never have to worry about money."

Regine was very surprised to learn of her newfound wealth. Her voice cracked as tears flowed down her face. "Kevin...Dad. I needed you more than you will ever know."

Kevin gave her his handkerchief. "Baby, I've always been here for you. I made sure no harm ever came to you. I love you. I was even at your wedding," he said with a chuckle.

Regine looked up with a bewildered expression. "You were there?!"

"I wouldn't have missed my first-born's wedding for anything in the world," he proudly admitted.

"But you were not there for me when I needed you the most; not in a physical sense," Regine pouted, still hurt by his absence. "As far as I'm concerned, you're no better than my mother. I gave you a pass my entire life because I thought you were dead."

"I was only trying to protect you. I live a dangerous life, and couldn't risk losing you because of my actions."

"Why couldn't you give up this life you speak of, for me?"

Kevin sighed. "I wish it were that simple. I'm in too deep."

Regine was overwhelmed by his admission.

Kevin stood up to leave. "I gotta go, but if you ever need me, your grandmother knows how to reach me."

Regine hurriedly reached for his hand. "Wait! Before you go, I need to know if you had anything to do with Justina's assault, and PJ, Earl, and Sam's deaths."

Kevin kissed Regine on the forehead. "No one will ever hurt my baby and get away with it," he softly declared. As he walked in the direction of the exit, three burly men arose from their seats in every corner of the restaurant and followed him out.

Regine's eyes grew bigger as she gazed at the men.

Bessie said, "Don't worry, suga'. They're with him."

Regine cautiously turned to Bessie. "Why did you lie to me? You knew he was alive."

"I couldn't see myself putting you in harm's way. Everything we did, we did because we love you," Bessie admitted, as she placed her hand on top of Regine's.

Regine pulled her hand away from Bessie's. "I need some time by myself. I'm not sure what to say or how to feel."

"I understand," Bessie said, as she reached inside her purse and pulled out a business card. "Take this. Whenever you need to reach your father, call him at this number."

Regine reluctantly took the card, then turned and walked out of the restaurant. She was worried her grandmother could be implicated as a potential suspect in Justina's assault, and the killings. Though, Regine was not worried about her father, as it seems Kevin does not have a problem with disappearing. As far as she was concerned, everything her grandmother ever told her about him was a lie.

Bessie watched how Regine walked away from the table without looking back at her. She was worried about their relationship.

Over the next week, Guy noticed Bessie and Regine moping around the house, and not talking to each other as much as they used to. "Regine, what's going on between you and your grandmother?" he finally asked.

Regine was very unhappy with Bessie, and did not know how to make things right between them. "Nothing," she lied. "Why do you ask?"

"You two are normally very talkative, but everything is different now. Even Dana and Cassandra suspect something is wrong."

Regine did not want to talk about it, so she decided to change the subject. "Have you heard anything on the status of Justina's case?"

"No, Big Mike is still in Atlanta. I'll call him and get a follow-up," Guy said, as he saw fear in Regine's eyes. "Don't worry about Justina. I'm sure she's fine."

Regine anxiously asked, "Will you let me know if you hear anything?"

Guy embraced Regine, then looked into her eyes. "You shouldn't concern yourself with this."

"I suppose you're right. Please tell my grandmother I need to talk to her."

Bessie walked into the bedroom moments later, with her head held low. "Baby, you called for me."

"Grandma, I'm worried about you. I don't want anything to happen to you."

"Don't worry about me. I'm going to be just fine," Bessie assured Regine, as she sat next to her on the loveseat in the bedroom.

"I love you. You're all I have," Regine affectionately admitted, while tears flowed down her face.

Bessie cried in response. "I love you too, baby."

"Promise that you and my father will stop intervening on my behalf. I believe God has a plan for all of us. You can't stop the inevitable."

"I know," Bessie weakly admitted.

They hugged, and shortly after, resumed their usual rapport. Dana, Cassandra, and Guy were relieved the tension in the house had disappeared.

☼

Bessie did not tell Regine that she suspected her mother, Sue, was involved with Justina's assault. She vividly reflected on the conversation they had a month earlier.

"Hi Sue. How are you, baby?" Bessie asked.

"I'm fine, ma. How's Regine?"

"She's fine. How are things going with you?"

"Ma, every day is a struggle. I haven't thought about using drugs since I left rehab, though." Then Sue perked up when she said, "I met someone. Ma, he's so good to me."

"That's good, baby. I'm so happy for you."

"And ma, my new girlfriend has been very supportive. Every time I want to give up, she's there for me. She's like a sister to me," Sue genuinely admitted.

"That's good, baby. But how much do you know about her, and where is she from?"

"I think she's from Florida, because her kids live in Jacksonville with their stepfather."

"Good. Does she visit her kids? You all are right there in Tallahassee. Jacksonville is only a skip and a hop."

"Ma, we sort of moved to Atlanta."

Bessie became alarmed by this news. "Atlanta?! What's in Atlanta?!"

"I had to take care of some unfinished business," Sue hesitantly admitted.

Bessie put her hand on her hips and narrowed her eyes. "Does this have anything to do with Justina?"

Sue's voice cracked. "Ma...she hurt my baby." Just the thought of someone hurting Regine overwhelmed her.

"Sue, you need to leave Atlanta now. You've been through enough already. Don't worry about Justina. The Lord will fix it."

Sue paused, then finally said, "Ma, I wanted Justina to hurt, just like she hurt my baby. But after I got here, I found out someone else was in the process of getting even with her. I want to stay here and make sure he carries out his mission."

"I don't like the way this sounds. Please come home, now," Bessie insisted.

"No ma. I can't. Rowena and I have to take care of some business first," Sue defiantly countered.

Bessie raised a brow. "Rowena? That name sounds familiar. What's her last name?"

"Williams. Why?"

"It makes me uncomfortable knowing you are living with someone I never met, that's all," Bessie lied. She thought Rowena's name sounded too familiar.

"Ma, don't worry, she's nice. We have a lot in common. You know, everywhere we go, people say we look alike," Sue said with a big grin.

"Describe her," Bessie curiously requested.

"She's a little lighter in complexion and a little taller than me. Oh, and we have the same smile and dimples."

Bessie's mouth flew opened as she dropped the phone from shock.

Sue panicked when she heard the phone drop. "Ma! Are you all right?!"

A few seconds later, Bessie picked up the phone. "Yes…baby. I'm fine. Just be careful," she breathlessly replied, as she cut the conversation short.

Within seconds, Bessie hurriedly dialed Lucy's number. "Hi, Lucy."

"Hi Bessie. It's been a while since I last heard from you."

Bessie tried not to let on why she was really calling, so she patiently replied, "I know. I've been in Florida off and on, helping Regine when I can."

"I hope she have a girl," Lucy proudly confessed.

"Yeah, me too. Um…I just called to see if you've heard from Rowena."

Lucy frowned. "Have I heard from her? She and her kids live with me. Why are you asking about Rowena? You want to talk to her?"

"No. Do you think she knows about Sue?" Bessie asked with caution.

"I doubt it. She would've asked me by now if she did. Why do you ask?"

"Maybe it's nothing," Bessie said with uncertainty. "I'll keep in touch with you about Regine and the baby." She hung up the phone in a daze. Bessie had a weird feeling about the woman Sue befriended.

After Lucy hung up, it dawned on her that she had not heard from her other daughter, Katie, in a while. She tried calling her cell phone, but the call went directly to voicemail. Then she called her office, but the secretary told her Katie had gone on an unexpected vacation, and would not be back for another month or so. Lucy thought this was strange because Katie would normally tell her if she was going out of town.

Chapter 34
Survival of the Fittest

*I*nternal Affairs interrogated Detective Jones for two hours before he finally cooperated. The detective told the interrogator that Roger McCarthy paid him to destroy Justina's report.

The interrogator asked, "Do you believe Roger had anything to do with Justina Reyes' assault?"

"Yes, I believe Roger McCarthy assaulted her," the detective admitted.

"But that doesn't make any sense," the interrogator pointed out. "Roger was with Ms. Reyes when she came in to file the report. It seems he would have wanted to be more discreet."

The detective looked skyward, as if remembering. "Oh, I could be wrong, but I don't think Roger likes her. When he came in here, he had shifty eyes and couldn't sit still. He excused himself at least three times to go to the restroom. When he finally sat down, he avoided eye contact with her. Yeah, that's what I remember."

"What do you know about Richard Randolf?" the interrogator probed further, even though he realized early on that the detective was lying or exaggerating throughout the interrogation.

Caught off guard by this question, the detective winced. He slowly replied, "I believe he's a con man."

"How do you know this?"

"Roger McCarthy told me."

"When?"

Detective Jones was momentarily silent. "I don't remember."

"You're lying," the interrogator determined.

Detective Jones squirmed in his chair, and his voice trembled. "Listen, I told you…everything I know. So, do I get immunity or what?"

"Let's see if your story holds up. If we find out you're lying, we'll make sure you stay in jail for the rest of your life," the interrogator sharply answered.

The Lieutenant walked in from another room where he witnessed the interrogation. "We're done here, for now," he said to the officers that were with him. "Take him away."

Detective Jones was handcuffed and placed in a cell away from the other inmates. He knew he had lost his job, but was making sure his life was spared. The truth was, he was forewarned of Justina and Roger's visit, and went along with the scam because he was already paid for his participation. He knew what to say and when to say it. He could not wait to share more information about Roger, to sweeten the deal. It was just a matter of time before he would be granted immunity. He looked forward to being released from jail a free man.

Shortly after Justina was attacked, Roger, Chris, Rowena, and Sue met at the pub to discuss what happened. "I'm getting nervous," Roger professed. "What if Justina finds out I was involved?"

Chris puckered his brows as he gazed at Roger. "Why are you worried?! By this time next month, you'll be out of here working for a law firm in Ohio."

"Okay, guys," Rowena intervened, "everyone needs to stop bickering. We just need to lay low for a while."

Chris shifted his eyes to Roger. "I'm just saying…if it weren't for you, I wouldn't be in this mess."

Roger looked at Chris with narrow eyes before exploding. "Me?!" he questioned with malice. "I didn't put a gun to your head! You told me Richard threatened you and your family if you didn't go along with his plans!"

Chris looked perplexed. "You must be mistaken. I never said that. Besides, I don't know anyone named Richard. Don't you mean Calvin Calloway?"

"Are you serious?!" Roger sharply asked with disbelief, knowing Chris knew Calvin's real name from the beginning. Though, he was still kicking himself for inadvertently telling Rowena Calvin's name, figuring that was how Sue found out.

"All I know," Chris timidly said, "is that he told me his name was Calvin Calloway. But now you're saying his real name is Richard." Chris did not look at Roger or anyone else when he sought clarification. Instead, he looked down at his drink and took a sip, while everyone looked at him with questioning gazes.

Rowena shifted her focus to Sue. "Have you heard from Richard?"

"No, not yet," Sue lied. She did not tell them she met with Richard not long after Justina was attacked.

"Have you tried calling him again?" Roger impatiently asked.

"Yes, but he did not answer," Sue truthfully admitted, trying not to let on that she was worried about him.

"Well, we all know what that means," Roger said, "and I'm not going to jail for this asshole."

Sue and Rowena knew Roger had the motive. Everyone, except Justina, knew how much Roger detested her. Even the patrons at the pub were in earshot of his daily complaints about her.

Rowena looked at everyone at the table. "We have to keep it together," she firmly said. "If one of us goes down, we all go down. I think Richard should take the fall for this."

Perplexed, Sue's neck quickly snapped in Rowena's direction. "Richard?!"

"Yes," Rowena and Roger said in unison.

"Sue, Richard is long gone," Rowena explained. "I think you should quick deed the condo to someone else and leave town with me."

"What do you mean?" Chris inquired, while gazing at Sue.

"Oh, no one told you," Roger cynically interrupted. "Richard signed over Justina's condo to Sue. I don't know who thought of that crazy idea." He still could not believe Richard arranged this transaction without discussing it with him beforehand. He would have talked him out of it.

Chris incredulously asked, "How did that happened?"

When Rowena elbowed Roger, he realized he may have said too much "Oh, it's nothing," Roger lied. "I'm just speculating, that's all."

Chris turned to Sue and asked, "Is it true? Do you own Justina's condo?"

Sue was about to answer until Rowena intervened. "Chris, I think you should worry about yourself. You're in this thing knee-deep. What are you going to do?"

Chris held his head down in despair. "I'm going home to tell my wife and kids we're moving, I suppose."

"Good," Rowena said, satisfied with Chris's plans. "Just lay low and stay off the phone. It's possible that the police may be on to you."

Chris's voice trembled. "But how…can I reach…all of you?"

"That's not possible," Rowena said. "From this point on, we have to refrain from communicating with one another, at least until things die down," she added, eyeing everyone at the table.

"I suppose you're right," Roger conceded.

Chris looked at his watch. "I gotta go. Everybody, watch your backs," he said, as he quickly got up to leave. He was worried and had good reason. Chris did not know Roger threw him under the bus, by encouraging the real Calvin Calloway to file a stolen identity claim, and by supplying him with a copy of the investigative report.

Roger panicked as soon as Chris left the table. "I don't trust him. I think we should follow him."

"Don't be ridiculous," Rowena said. "Chris has more to lose than we do."

"I hope you're right," Roger countered.

Sue was speechless. She had a feeling things had taken a turn for the worse.

Rowena noticed Sue fidgeting with her napkin, which clearly showed her nervousness. "Sue, go on home. I'll catch up with you later. Things are going to turn out just fine, I promise."

Sue was unsure. The last time she saw Richard, he was on his way out of town. She believed Richard loved her, and would not forget to call her unless something was wrong.

After the meeting, everyone parted and went their separate ways. Rowena went with Roger to his apartment, and Sue went to Justina's condo, hoping Richard would call her there.

Rowena knew Roger was distraught, especially when he began blaming everyone else for his predicament. "Sue must get rid of that damn condo!" he exclaimed.

"Come on, baby," Rowena cooed, "it's not that serious."

Roger sat on the bed and covered his face with his hands before looking into Rowena's eyes. "You don't understand. When Justina signed the Power of Attorney agreement, I took care of the legal issues, including the sale of her condo. This was supposed to be a clean-cut transaction. What if Justina shows up at her condo by coincidence?"

Rowena did not know Roger was so deeply involved with the scam. She assumed he was just an unknowing bystander. "Roger, calm down. Justina will never find out about the condo. And why are you worried? I'm your alibi," she said with a wide grin. Then she slowly took off her blouse and removed her bra.

Roger instantly perked up, physically and emotionally.

"See baby. I love you," Rowena said in a seductive voice. "I will never let anything happen to you." On that note, she began kissing Roger in all the right places.

Roger laid back and enjoyed the pleasure Rowena gave him. For the moment, he stopped worrying about Justina and his predicament.

Chris left the pub and walked toward the waiting van. When the van door opened, he was pulled inside by a police officer.

"What's going on?" Chris nervously asked.

The police officer patted him down and found the hidden microphone before responding. "We wanted to make sure you didn't get away."

"This isn't necessary. I told you I'd cooperate."

"We'd rather be safe than sorry," the police officer said, replaying the tape-recorded conversation Chris just had with Rowena, Sue, and Roger. "Why didn't you do as you were told? You were supposed to ask Roger if he attacked Justina."

Chris blinked and shifted his eyes downward. "But I got Roger to admit he was involved in the scam."

"But you didn't tell us Richard threatened you. And according to Roger, it seems you already knew Richard claimed Calvin Calloway's identity. What else haven't you told us?"

"I....I didn't know what to expect. Roger was acting belligerent and jumpy. What do you want me to do? I'll do anything. You want me to call him?" Chris anxiously suggested.

"No, Roger's already on to you."

Chris frowned. "But how?"

"We had another microphone planted at the table, just in case you chickened out. Roger suggested they follow you."

Chris's eyes grew bigger. "He did? You reckon he wants to kill me?"

"It sounds that way."

"Where to now?" Chris pensively asked.

"Protective custody, as we agreed on. Your wife and children are waiting for you at the hotel. From there, you and your family will be taken to a secret location."

"What about my house?"

"You can forget about your house, and everything in it. From this point on, your life will never be the same."

In a way, Chris was relieved. He had a feeling things would go down like this. It did not surprise him when the police detectives showed up at his house after that infamous phone call in the middle of the morning. Although his wife was upset with him, she told him she loved him and would never leave him.

By chance, Richard found out about Justina's assault when he called Thorny for the rest of his money.

"She's still alive," Thorny said in a harsh voice. "The police have been guarding her hospital room all week."

Richard could not admit that he did not know what Thorny was talking about. "I'll take care of it," he finally said. "When will I get the rest of my money?

"Justina is still alive, and you're asking about your *damn* money!"

"But...."

"Just do the job we paid you to do!" Thorny yelled, before he slammed the phone on its cradle.

Doubt overwhelmed Richard. He thought about contacting the police, but he was overcome with fear of going to jail again, fear of becoming a murder victim, and fear of the unknown. For the first time in his life, he wanted to live. He was in love with Sue, and wanted to spend the rest of his life with her.

He became confused about his mission, especially after Justina was assaulted. It freaked him out to know someone else was probably paid to carry out his first mission. Now Richard figured he would never see a penny of the money Thorny promised him.

Richard reflected on how he got into this situation in the first place. His loan shark directed him to Thorny to pay off his $25,000 gambling debt. The job sounded easy at the time. Thorny told him if he would make Justina disappear by any means necessary, he would pay off his $25,000 gambling debt in advance and pay him another $25,000 when the deed was done.

Richard could not stomach killing anyone, so he asked Thorny if he could marry Justina, instead.

"Are you in love with her?" Thorny curiously asked.

"Nah man, it's a part of the plan," Richard convincingly said. "I figured I'd marry her, take her for every dime she has, and leave her for broke."

"I like that," Thorny cunningly said, as he played with his beard. "Let me think about it and I'll get back to you."

One week later, Thorny and Kevin agreed to Richard's plan, as long as he could provide proof his plan was working. However, they did not know about Richard's side deal.

The idea of marrying Justina actually came from Tim Carter, Jeanine's private investigator. Tim thought Richard was genuinely dating Justina when he approached him and offered to pay him

$50,000 if he married her. Tim had no idea Richard was already married, and had assumed Calvin Calloway's identity. The money was too good to pass up, so Richard arranged a fake wedding to make it appear legit. Tim insisted on being present to witness it, and stood in as his best man.

Richard was given the money Tim Carter promised when he returned home from his honeymoon. After Justina gave him a hard time about the house, he decided to go visit his daughter, Victoria. He immediately booked a flight to New York.

When he walked through the door, Victoria ran into his arms. He picked her up and felt the love. That is, until his estranged wife started quizzing him about his whereabouts. He successfully evaded her questions. He did not want to spend precious time arguing; he had a feeling this was the last time he would see either of them.

Richard warmly embraced Victoria. "Baby, you know I love you," he said, as she gazed into Victoria's eyes.

"I know, Daddy. I love you too," Victoria softly replied.

"Be good to your momma."

"I will," Victoria happily replied, hugging the teddy bear Richard surprised her with.

Richard hugged Victoria again then kissed her on the forehead. "Now, I got to go away for a while. Even if I'm not here in the present, know that I'm always thinking about you."

When Richard looked up, his wife was staring at them. Richard approached her, then pulled a manila envelope full of money from his coat pocket and handed it to her. "I know I didn't do right by you, and I'm sorry. Please use this money wisely."

"Where are you going?" his wife inquired.

"I'm not sure, but if I stay any longer, your lives will be in danger. Take care of yourself, and take care of my baby."

There was no love lost between Richard and his wife. They had been estranged for over two years. When they were together, it was always sporadic and short-lived. They had one thing in common: the love for Victoria, their only child.

After Tim Carter got off the phone with Big Mike, he conducted his own research, and was livid when he discovered Calvin Calloway's imposter had deceived him. He called Big Mike and asked if he could assist in the investigation.

"I'm glad you called," Big Mike said. "In case you didn't know, Calvin Calloway's imposter's name is Richard Randolf. He also goes by Slick Rick."

"Are you serious!"

"I'm afraid so. Are you still in touch with him?"

"I know how to reach him," Tim replied.

"Good, I need you to get him on the phone and find out his whereabouts."

Within minutes, Tim was on a three-way call with Big Mike as the silent third party.

"Hello, Calvin," Tim flatly said.

"Who is this?" Richard inquired.

"This is Tim. I just wanted to know if you were satisfied with the payoff. You know, the $50,000 we paid you for marrying Justina."

"Oh yeah, it's cool. Thanks man."

"And I take it that Chris is satisfied with the salary we paid him to pose as Roger's private investigator."

"Yeah, he's straight. Thanks for looking out."

"Can I ask you a question?"

"Shoot."

"Are you still happily married?"

Richard did not anticipate this line of questioning. "Yeah, why do you wanna know?" he defensively asked.

"Well, I just need to know if our investment was worth it. I'd like to meet with you and Justina tonight."

"Ugh…that's not possible."

"Why not?"

Richard was trying to think of a good lie, but decided the truth was more plausible. "Justina was attacked in her office garage. She's recuperating."

"Oh my…is she in the hospital?" Tim dramatically inquired.

"Ugh…um…let me call you back."

"Calvin, let me make this easy on you," Tim coyly said, "or should I address you Slick Rick, or better yet, Richard Randolf?"

Richard was speechless.

Tim smirked before he digressed. "A little birdie told me some interesting things about you."

"I don't know what you're talking about," Richard said, after a brief pause.

"You know exactly what I'm talking about!" Tim sharply retorted.

"Listen, man, I don't have time for games."

Tim tersely said, "You've placed me in an awkward situation. I hired you to marry Justina, but I didn't know you were an imposter. I believe you were hired by someone else to hurt Justina."

"I didn't attack her, if that's what you're implying."

"I don't know what to believe. All I know is you swindled her out of all her money and possessions, and I'm not taking the fall for you. You will contact whomever hired you and tell them to turn themselves in, or I will go to the cops."

"Are you crazy?" Richard incredulously asked. "This guy is not afraid of the cops."

"Well, you better find a way to make him believe you, or else."

Richard suddenly heard the dial tone. He waited fifteen minutes for Tim to call him back. Then he tried calling Tim on his cell phone, but there was no answer. Figuring it was time to get out of town, Richard got into his rental car and drove north with no particular destination in mind. He was continuously looking around for anything or anyone out of the ordinary. He had a feeling someone put a hit on his life.

Tim hung up on Richard, while Big Mike remained on the line. "Now, are you convinced?" Tim asked Big Mike. "Jeanine and I didn't have anything to do with the scam against Justina, or her assault."

"Yes, but I still don't believe your story about Jeanine planting Kathy in Justina's office because she was scouting a law firm for her company."

"Off the record?" Tim asked.

Big Mike agreed.

"Jeanine Benedict is Guy's stepmother. She found out Justina was causing friction between Regine and Guy, and ordered me to make sure it doesn't happen again. She loved them as if they were her very own."

Big Mike was perplexed. "Why did she choose this route? Guy and his siblings would've been happy to know she wanted to be a part of their lives."

"It's very complicated. Put yourself in her shoes. Looking at Guy and Alex would've been a constant reminder of her late husband's affair with their mother." Tim paused before continuing, "I'm going tell you this because you're Guy's best friend. Mrs. Benedict was diagnosed with terminal cancer. She listed Guy and Alex as the sole beneficiaries of her estate, and wanted to make sure they were stable enough to take over the business after she's gone."

Big Mike's mouth flew open. He was shocked to learn of Guy and Alex's newfound wealth.

Chapter 35

All is Forgiven

*B*ig Mike phoned Guy and brought him up to speed on his findings, including the mini-version of Jeanine's connection to Justina's secretary. He purposely left out the details involving Alex, hoping Alex would tell Guy himself.

Guy was in disbelief as he hung up the phone. He was thinking about what Big Mike had just told him about Jeanine, and wondered why she had resurfaced after all these years. When he contacted the headquarters of Trowne Estates and Resorts in Tampa, which was one hour north of St. Petersburg, Jeanine's secretary told him she was not available.

"Is there any way I can reach her?" Guy asked.

The secretary hesitated, before asking, "May I ask who's calling?"

"Guy Simmons. I'm her stepson."

The secretary was stunned by this new revelation. "Hold on. I'll put you through to her assistant."

"Thank you."

Fifteen-seconds later, the Vice CEO was on the line. "Yes, this is Sidney McKinley. How may I help you?"

"Hello. I'm trying to reach my stepmother, Jeanine Benedict."

"Stepmother?"

Guy sighed. "Yes. It's complicated. Charlie, her deceased husband, was my father."

"Oh, I see. Well, I'm sorry to tell you this, but Mrs. Benedict is in the hospital."

"Which hospital?"

"Tampa Bay Unity."

Guy thanked Sidney for providing the information. Then he asked his secretary to contact the hospital. Seconds later, she connected him with Jeanine's nurse.

"Yes, I'm calling to obtain Jeanine Benedict's prognosis," Guy requested.

"What is your relationship to the patient?" the nurse asked.

"I'm her stepson, Guy Simmons."

The nurse searched the hospital database. "I'm sorry, but you're not listed on her admittance record. We cannot release any information about her condition over the phone."

"Can you put the call through to her room?"

"Sure, hold on."

After the tenth ring, Guy hung up. He told his secretary to clear his calendar, deciding to drive to the hospital to see Jeanine. First, he called Alex and brought him up to speed. Alex told Guy he would be there on the next flight out of Miami.

Guy entered Jeanine's hospital room and found her asleep. When the nurse walked in a few minutes later, he asked, "Is she going to be okay?"

"Yes, she suffered a mild stroke," the nurse admitted. "But…she has breast cancer. The doctor will be coming in to check on her in another hour or so. You can stay in the room until he returns."

Guy was unsettled by this news. He pulled up a chair, sat next to Jeanine's bed, and observed her physical appearance. To him, she still looked the same, but was much thinner than he remembered.

Jeanine was still asleep when Alex walked into the room two hours later. "How is she?" he timidly asked.

"I don't know yet," Guy said, looking at his watch with worry. "Her doctor should've been here by now."

Alex sat in the chair next to Guy. "Man, this is crazy. Explain how and why she's connected to Justina."

"I don't know any more than what I told you."

Alex meditatively looked at Jeanine, then turned to Guy. "Do you think she had anything to do with Justina's assault?"

"I don't think so," Guy muttered, before he gazed into Alex's eyes. "I know you said you didn't have anything to do with Justina…."

Alex held his hand up and blurted out, "I lied to you. I'm sorry, but you gotta believe I didn't hurt Justina. I just wanted to talk to her. I was there when someone attacked her. I saw her get beat down, but it wasn't me. You gotta believe me," he pleaded.

"I do, but you should've trusted me enough to tell me," Guy sharply said, trying to control his anger.

Alex lowered his head. After a short pause, he lifted his head and faced Guy. "I didn't want to disappoint you. Man, it freaked me out. Initially, I was happy someone else did what I wanted to do.

But the more I thought about it, the more I realized Justina wouldn't have been worth it. I'm sorry."

Guy shook his head in despair. "It's okay. Can we prove you didn't attack her?"

"I told Big Mike what I knew. You think I should turn myself in?"

"No, I'll handle it," Guy assured Alex. "If you were a suspect, the police would've contacted you by now. Don't worry; I'll take care of everything. I love you. I won't let anything happen to you."

"I love you too," Alex sincerely admitted, as they embraced in a brotherly hug.

Jeanine was alert but kept her eyes closed while listening to Alex and Guy's conversation. She felt the love. At that moment, she decided to take the blame if Alex turned out to be a suspect. Jeanine figured she had nothing to lose, and sparing Alex's life from imprisonment would be worth it.

Her doctor entered the room a few minutes later, puzzled by Guy and Alex's presence. He turned to them and asked, "Who do we have here?"

"We are her stepsons," Guy professed. "How is she?"

"Luckily, it was a mild stroke, but she's not out of the woods yet. Did they tell you she has cancer?"

Alex looked alarmed.

Guy quickly turned to Alex. "I'm sorry. I forgot to tell you."

Surprised by this news, Alex curiously asked, "What stage?"

The doctor flipped through his chart, then told Alex, "She is in stage IV, which is considered terminal."

Guy asked the doctor in a hushed voice, "How much longer does she have to live?"

"Only God knows. She was receiving chemotherapy until the stroke compounded her problems."

Jeanine slowly opened her eyes and tried to talk. "Doc... doc...tor," she stammered, heaving and gasping for air. "I... I....want...."

The doctor quickly went to Jeanine's bedside. "Mrs. Benedict, please do not to talk. You need to save your energy," he said, as he poured some water in a cup and let her sip some through a straw. Then he gave her a pill to relax her. Minutes later, she closed her eyes and seemingly fell into a deep sleep.

The doctor stayed a little longer to explain Jeanine's prognosis to Guy and Alex. "Mrs. Benedict will be able to go home in a couple of weeks, and chemotherapy will resume at that time. I suggest you both come back in an hour or so. Mrs. Benedict needs her rest. I gave her a mild sedative to mitigate any discomfort she may have."

Before they left the room, Guy walked up to Jeanine's bed and held her hand, then stooped down and whispered in her ear, "Even though we don't know each other well, I feel as though you've always been a part of our lives. Regardless of what happened, *all is forgiven.* Alex and I will give you an hour or so to rest, but we'll be back." He gave Jeanine a kiss on the forehead before he walked out the room.

As soon as Jeanine knew they were out of the room, tears began flowing down her cheeks. She did not stop crying until the medication kicked in. She drifted off to sleep, thinking she dreamed of her stepsons' visit.

When Guy and Alex returned to the hospital room two hours later, Jeanine was fully alert. She looked somewhat better, and more refreshed. Her private investigator, Tim Carter, was in the room with her.

Guy solely focused on Jeanine. "How are you doing?" he asked, as he approached her bed.

"I'm fine...now that my sons are here," Jeanine proudly professed in a hoarse voice.

Alex winced because he was uneasy with Jeanine's reference. He slowly approached Jeanine's bed and looked into her eyes. "Can I ask you a question?"

"Sure," Jeanine said in a raspy voice, "but I believe I already know your question. I figured you would want the full story so I called my friend, Tim Carter."

Tim greeted Alex and Guy with a handshake.

Jeanine pointed to two chairs strategically placed in front her hospital bed. "Well, it's a long story, so both of you need to sit down." Then she deferred to Tim who explained everything from beginning to end.

Alex and Guy remained speechless. That is, until Guy took a closer look at Tim. "You're the same man I met when I was in high school," he said with amazement.

Tim smiled and nodded his head.

Guy looked at Jeanine and figured it out. "It was *you* who gave us the money?"

Jeanine nodded.

"You've been there for us all along," Guy softly admitted.

Alex frowned as he turned to Guy. "What are you talking about?"

"Remember the man I told you about. The one who would always give us money and ask how we were doing?"

Alex looked at Tim. "That was you?"

Tim nodded.

"This is so extreme," Alex stated in disbelief.

"Yeah, you should know," Jeanine said with a smug grin.

Alex slowly turned to Jeanine with narrowed eyes. "What do you mean?"

"You were in the vicinity of Justina's assault," Jeanine explained. "So tell me why you were there?"

Alex sadly muttered, "Because...we lost Regine once...and I didn't want Justina to disrupt our family, again."

Guy put his head down in shame. He felt bad for almost driving his brother to do the unthinkable.

"I felt the same way," Jeanine admitted. "I only want the best for you and Guy. I wanted to make sure Guy did not repeat your father's mistakes." Her eyes shifted between Alex and Guy before she asked, "Can you ever find it in your heart to forgive me?"

"Yes," Guy and Alex said in unison, without reservations.

Guy took her hand in his. "We want you to be a part of our lives, so we can all get to know you. Besides, you're almost a grandmother," he added with a soft chuckle.

Jeanine cried tears of joy in response.

Chapter 36

My Sister's Keeper

A year earlier, Katie was home from California visiting her mother, Lucy, when Bessie showed up one day. Normally, Bessie and Lucy would go sit on the patio in the backyard to talk. During this particular visit, Bessie was extremely distraught and began talking to Lucy in the kitchen. Katie was in the living room and detected fear and worry in Bessie's voice. She turned the TV volume down to listen closely.

"Lucy, I'm worried about Sue!" Bessie exclaimed.

"Is she still messing with drugs?"

Bessie frowned. "You know she's in rehab!" she defensively replied. "Sue told me she was done with drugs, but she can't do it by herself."

Lucy sighed. "Well, you have done all you can for her, and I sure appreciate it. Now she needs to figure it out on her own."

"Don't act like you don't care!" Bessie yelled. "She's *your* biological daughter! We need to find a way to help her."

Lucy quickly turned in the direction of the living room, and whispered, "Come out back so we can talk in private. Katie's here."

Katie's mouth flew open. *What?! I have another sister?!* As soon as Bessie and Lucy went outside, she decided to do a little investigating of her own. Katie went into her mother's room and rummaged through her top dresser drawer where she kept all of her important papers. Finding her and her siblings' birth certificates was fairly simple. Finally, she stumbled upon a manila envelope and pulled out a legal document. Kate became teary-eyed when she saw her mother's name listed on Sue's birth certificate. The father's name field was blank.

As soon as Bessie left, Katie confronted her mother. "I need to know if we have another sister," she said, speaking on behalf of her siblings.

Lucy closed the front door and stood still. "What are you talking about, child?" she nervously asked. All these years she had successfully kept Sue a secret, until now.

"I overheard you and Mrs. Bessie. Is her daughter yours?" Katie boldly asked.

Lucy averted her eyes downward, while wringing her hands. "Now you know…that's not possible," she stammered. "How… could a child…have two mothers?"

Katie stared at Lucy in disbelief as she held up Sue's birth certificate.

Lucy gasped and briefly stood still. "Why did you go through my things?"

"Because I knew it was the only way I'd learn the truth. Do I have another sister?"

"Yes, but it's a long story," Lucy nervously admitted.

Katie folded her arms and twisted her mouth. "I'm listening."

Lucy gestured for Katie to have a seat at the kitchen table. She had fear in her eyes when she took the seat next to Katie. "I had an affair with Sue's father, Kenneth," she regretfully admitted. "Your father shot and killed him after he found out about us."

Katie's eyes grew bigger.

"Katie, you have to understand…I had four children to feed at the time, and I couldn't afford another child. So when I found out Bessie didn't have any children, I thought it was best to let her raise Sue."

"So you gave your baby to the woman whose husband you cheated with? Ma, how could you?" Katie asked in disbelief.

Lucy sighed. "We were struggling. Kenneth left Bessie enough money to take care of Sue. Not a day goes by that I don't think about her. I love her. She's my own flesh and blood," she stressed with a mixture of compassion and guilt.

Curious to find out more information about Sue, Katie asked, "Do you have a picture of her?"

Lucy smiled. "Yes, I have a lot of pictures, but they were taken when she was much younger." She walked to her bedroom and returned several minutes later with an envelope filled with pictures of Sue, from grade school to high school.

Katie looked at the pictures and gasped. "She looks like me."

"I know. She looks like her father too," Lucy guiltily admitted.

"Tell me about her."

Lucy smiled as she reflected aloud. "Sue was book smart like you, and she enjoyed writing poetry. She went to Howard University in Washington, DC to become a teacher, but she never finished college. Things took a turn for the worse when she became hooked on drugs," Lucy sadly acknowledged.

"Where is she now?"

"She's in a rehab center in Florida because she wanted to be closer to her daughter, who lives in St. Petersburg. Sue's been clean for over six months, and will be released in another month or so. She has a hard time coping with life. Every time she gets clean, she begins feeling guilty for not being there for Regine, and ends up on drugs again."

"What's the name of the rehab center?"

"Why?"

"I need to find my sister and bring her home."

"You can't do that," Lucy firmly replied. "Besides, she'll never leave Florida as long as Regine is there. Please promise that you'll never mention this to anyone, not even your brothers and sister. It'll break Bessie's heart if she knew I told you."

Katie promised, but she had already made up her mind to find her sister. She went online to research the rehab center in Tallahassee before admitting herself. They tested her for drugs as soon as she arrived. When the results came back negative, Katie explained she had not been on drugs for quite some time but was having a hard time resisting temptation. They admitted her under the premise of relapsing.

The stay in rehab was expensive, but Katie was well off. She was CEO and owner of one of the largest consulting firms in California. She was not married, nor did she have any children, so she was able to take a leave of absence from her company without the added responsibilities. She left her Vice-CEO in charge, and requested that she only be contacted for emergencies.

When the admittance clerk asked for her name, Katie adopted her sister's, on a whim. 'Rowena' was the first name that came to her mind, at the time. Two months earlier, Rowena returned home to live with their mother after she was physically abused by her husband.

Katie was fed up with Rowena's husband, so she devised a plan to get even with him. While in the presence of five thug-looking gang bangers, Katie told Rowena's husband, "If you ever come near my sister again, your children will be fatherless. You understand?!" she sharply asked, as the gang bangers looked on in a threatening manner. Then they roughed him up a little. The threat worked because the abuse stopped. Katie figured the $1500 she paid the struggling actors was well worth it.

On the day Katie entered the rehab center, the residents were discussing their bouts with drugs. She strategically sat next to Sue

during the session, then introduced herself. Sue eyed Katie and noticed how much they resembled each another.

When the group session ended, Katie pulled Sue aside and asked
if they could sit together to eat lunch. Sue readily agreed. Soon after,
they quickly bonded, and went through the rituals of eating meals
and actively participating in counseling and prayer sessions together. They were drawn to each other, sort of like kindred spirits. So,
when Sue asked Katie to come with her to Atlanta, it did not take
her long to decide, especially when she saw determination in Sue's
eyes. She figured Sue would go to Atlanta, with or without her.

Prior to Justina's attack, Katie overheard Sue crying and talking
to herself about making amends with Regine. Fearing Sue would
turn back to drugs, she wanted to do something so Sue could finally
move on with her life.

Katie left the house early that morning, dressed in black, and
drove to the Burlington Coat Factory to purchase a black ski face-
mask. Then she retrieved the crow bar from the trunk of her car and
threw it in the front seat of her SUV. Later, she went to Justina's
office garage and waited.

As soon as Justina parked her car, Katie put on the ski mask and
grabbed the crowbar. She drove up behind Justina's car, jumped out
of the SUV, and charged at Justina with the crowbar. Katie struck
Justina three times in the back of the head, then stopped after realizing what she was doing. Suddenly, she thought she saw someone
watching her and got scared. She hurriedly jumped into her SUV
and drove home.

Overcome with remorse, Katie called the hospital to inquire
about Justina's status. She was relieved to find out Justina was still
alive. She never told Sue or anyone else what she did. After the attack, she was not herself. This was the first time in her life she had
ever hurt anyone. Minor spats with her siblings, when they were
younger, was the extent of her violent side. She was shaking and
inconsolable when she returned to the apartment and rushed to the
bathroom, locking herself inside.

Sue observed Katie's half-hazard appearance as soon as she
rushed through the front door. She stood up and quickly rushed to
the bathroom door, wildly knocking. "Rowena! Where have you
been?!" After Rowena didn't respond, she worriedly asked, "What's
the matter?!"

Katie was breathing hard and sweating profusely. She did not
look good. She was so ridden with guilt, she did not hear Sue's
questions.

"Are you okay?" Sue asked, through the closed door.

"I had some business to take care of," Katie weakly replied.

Sue asked with caution, "What did you do?"

"I'd rather not talk about it." Katie turned on the faucet and threw water on her face. She was shaking uncontrollably.

Sue stopped asking questions when she heard Katie crying and mumbling something about wishing she had not done it. Sue said through the door, "If you ever need someone to talk to, I'm here for you. I love you." She walked away, wondering what happened.

Katie never broached the subject.

A couple of days later, Sue received the phone call she had been waiting for. She smiled when she heard his voice. "Hi Calvin, it's so good to hear from you."

Richard paused at the mention of his fictitious name. "Same here. Did you know Justina was attacked in her workplace garage?"

"Yes, I found out. Did you have anything to do with it?"

"No, that was not part of the plan. Listen, I have to go out of town for a little while. I'd like to see you before I leave. Meet me at Bennigans, off exit 10."

"Okay, I'll be there in an hour."

Richard was sitting in a booth, at the back of the restaurant when Sue walked in. Upon seeing each other, they embraced and kissed, passionately.

"Oh Calvin, I've missed you," Sue cheerfully admitted.

He briefly lowered his head, then looked into her eyes as he admitted, "My real name is Richard Randolf."

"Richard?" Sue knowingly asked. Rowena had already told her his real name, after Roger slipped and told her. She figured Richard would eventually tell her the truth.

Richard sighed. "It's a long story…it was part of the scam. Listen babe, things got out of control when Justina was attacked. I believe I am the primary suspect, regardless of whether I have an alibi. The people I'm dealing with, think I did it. When they find out I wasn't involved, they'll be coming after me."

"What are you going to do?"

Richard sighed. "First, I'm going to check on my wife and daughter."

Sue raised a brow. "Wife?"

"Yeah. I've been married for five years, but we've been estranged for the last two. We have an understanding, though. She went on with her life, and so did I," Richard professed, while looking into Sue's questioning eyes. "Over the past several months, I've been very happy. You filled that void in my life. I love you," he whispered.

"I love you too. Thanks for coming clean with me, but now I have something to tell you," Sue reservedly admitted.

Richard interrupted her. "Baby, I already know about your past. I don't care."

"But how?"

"I don't have physical proof, but from one former drug addict to another, I can relate to you."

Sue was shocked and confused.

"I don't care about all that," Richard nonchalantly stated. "I'm just worried about you. I don't want you caught up in my mess. Had I known things were going to go down like this, I would not have put the condo in your name."

"You can't blame yourself, completely. I have a confession to make, and please don't interrupt me this time," Sue softly requested.

"What is it?"

Sue averted her eyes downward, as she whispered, "I'm HIV positive."

"I know...I am too. I found out after I left my wife, a couple of years ago."

Sue was stunned. "What...but how did you know about me?"

"I assumed you were, especially since you insisted we used a condom every time we made love."

"I have another confession," Sue said, after she took a deep breath and slowly exhaled. "I...knew about Justina. I mean...I knew about her before you and I met."

Richard quickly sat up in his chair. "What are you saying?"

Sue slightly lowered her head. "Justina was my daughter's best friend," she softly admitted.

"Who's your daughter?"

Sue lifted her head and met his gaze. "Her name is Regine. You attended her wedding."

Richard grinned, then shook his head. "Start from the beginning."

Sue explained how she met Rowena in rehab, and how she wanted vengeance after Justina betrayed Regine. "We came to Atlanta to confront her."

"What were you going to do?" Richard curiously asked.

"At the time, I just wanted to kick her behind. But when Rowena met Roger, everything changed."

"Why didn't you tell me?"

"Rowena said it wasn't a good idea, especially after you told me about your plans to scam Justina."

Richard chuckled. "So you were using me?" he teased.

"No, not intentionally. I didn't mean to fall in love with you. Every time I wanted to confess about everything, you found a way to discourage me. Why?"

"Because the truth hurts. Don't worry about all this nonsense. Take this," Richard said, handing her a wad of cash. "Go back home to Virginia."

Sue's forehead wrinkled as she gazed into Richard's eyes. "How did you know I was from Virginia?"

"Let's just say your mother has a unique way of finding people," Richard said with a chuckle. He thought about the conversation he had with Bessie, and still could not believe she threatened to chop off his manhood if he ever hurt Sue.

She raised a brow as she exclaimed, "My mother?!"

Richard held up his hand in response. "Ask her. She's a tough woman. I gotta go. Take the money and leave Atlanta." He thought about it and added, "If I were you, I'd distance myself from Rowena. I have a feeling Roger is going down and will likely try to take her down with him. You were an innocent bystander as far as I'm concerned. By the way, lose my cell number." He stood up, leaned over and kissed her with vigor. "You take care of yourself. Whatever happens, know that I love you."

"Wait! I want to go with you," Sue pleaded, as she stood up, reaching for him.

"I wish you could, but I don't know if I'm being followed. I don't want to put your life in danger."

"How can I reach you?"

"I have a feeling you won't be able to." Richard looked at her worried expression and gave in. "I'll call you; I promise."

When Sue first told Bessie about Calvin, Bessie would not let her off the phone until she had a number and address of where she could be reached. Shortly afterward, Bessie conducted her own research. She even had her boyfriend, Deacon Alfred Franklin, drive to Atlanta to retrieve more information about Richard. The Deacon was smitten with Bessie, and was willing to do anything for her.

The Deacon pulled up in front of Sue's apartment complex and witnessed Richard exiting her apartment and heading toward his car. Then he followed Richard to the Irish pub.

Richard entered the pub and spotted Roger sitting in a corner booth. "Hey Roger, what's going on?"

"Hi Richard," Roger nervously said, looking around. "You know, Justina is on to us? How are we going to get out of this mess?"

"Just chill out. Aren't you leaving next month?"

"Yes, but I have a bad feeling about this."

Richard sat on the stool next to Roger. "Why are you so worried? You were paid $25,000 for your part."

Roger shook his head. He was glad he gave the entire amount to Justina; but it did not lessen his guilt. "I wanted revenge, but I never imagined things would go down like this. What if Detective Jones threw me under the bus?"

"Don't worry about the detective. We have the same employer."

"Who's your employer?" Roger cautiously inquired.

"You're asking too many questions. When you leave Atlanta, never look back."

Roger was worried as he shook his head in disbelief.

The Deacon sat at a table within earshot of their conversation. After Roger left the pub, the Deacon took Roger's abandoned seat.

Richard glanced at the Deacon and asked, "What can I do for you, old man?"

"I know someone who needs to talk to you," the Deacon said, as he pulled out his cell phone and called Bessie. He handed it to Richard after Bessie answered.

Richard reluctantly took the phone.

"I don't know who you are," Bessie harshly said, "but I'm not going to sit up here and let you run a game on my baby."

"I don't know what you're talking about," Richard said, as he eyed the Deacon.

"Are you sweet on my daughter, Sue?"

"Yes, but Mrs.?"

"My name is Bessie."

"Mrs. Bessie. I love Sue. I promise, I will never let anything happen to her."

"You better not!" Bessie fiercely responded. "Otherwise, you will have to deal with me!"

After listening to Bessie's ten-minute explanation on how she would destroy him, Richard hung up the phone and smiled. He wondered if Sue knew she had such a feisty, overprotective mother. Coincidentally, while he was on the phone with Bessie, Justina was being attacked in her office garage.

Two weeks after Justina was attacked, Roger was still on edge. Rowena had a feeling he would eventually crack under pressure. When she left his apartment, she returned home and told Sue that she would be leaving Atlanta, permanently. Shortly afterward, they broke their lease and cleared out the apartment. Sue had already moved most of her things into Justina's condo after Richard signed the condo over to her. She was surprised when Richard had furniture delivered the same day she moved in.

"Yeah!" Katie cheerfully boasted. "Justina didn't know what she had coming to her."

"Yeah, I know!" Sue responded in kind. "Hopefully she learned a valuable lesson from this." Then she eyed Rowena's opened suitcase, and asked, "What are you going to do?"

Katie wanted to tell Sue her real name, but realized the truth would lead to more questions. "I'm not sure," she finally said. "I'm thinking about going to one of the islands for a little rest and relaxation," she said, as she packed up the last of her belongings. "Where ever I decide to go, I'm leaving from Florida to cover my tracks. Why don't you come with me?"

Sue knew that would be the most logical choice, but she had some unfinished business to take care of. "I'd love to, but not now. I'll catch up with you later."

Katie knew Sue was waiting to hear from Richard. After failing to convince her to come along. She prayed Sue would be okay. She had already established a plan to check up on her.

Katie dropped Sue off at her condo, and helped unload the rest of her things. Shortly afterward, Sue walked with Katie to her SUV.

"I'm going to miss you," Sue sincerely said.

Katie had sadness in her eyes when she replied, "I'm going to miss you too."

Sue quizzed, "What about Roger? Have you told him yet?"

"He'll be fine. I told him to meet me at your condo this evening. I was hoping you could break the news to him for me," Katie sadly suggested. "You take care of yourself, and my niece. I love you lil' sis," she affectionately admitted. This time, Katie purposely used family references. She loved Sue and wanted it to be known.

"I love you too," Sue sincerely admitted.

They embraced and bid each other farewell.

Chapter 37

Basic Instinct

*T*horny conducted his own research after picking-up some bad vibes from his last conversation with Richard. He paid a visit to Justina's office building to find out what happened, stopping by the security guard booth, first. After he gave the security guard two hundred dollars for information about Justina's assault, the guard told him everything he knew, including the discussion he had with Big Mike. The guard also told him Big Mike walked up the street to the pub after he left the building.

Thorny instinctively went to the pub and questioned the bartender. Initially, the bartender would not cooperate, but readily became accommodating when Thorny put five one-hundred-dollar bills on the counter. "Do you know Richard Randolf?" Thorny asked, as he slid Richard's picture in front of him.

"Oh, that's not Richard. That's Roger's friend, Calvin. They were in here together; the same day his partner, Justina Reyes, was attacked. I remember they sat in the booth on the end over there," he said, pointing to the back of the bar. "After Roger left, Calvin stayed here a while longer. An old man approached him and they talked for a little bit, then the old man got up and left. That's when I noticed the ambulance and the police cars surrounding Justina and Roger's office building."

"So where did Calvin go?" Thorny asked.

"He stayed here. Didn't leave until much later that evening. He got wasted. It looked as though he had a lot on his mind."

Thorny thanked the bartender, then returned to the waiting sedan. He got into the backseat and brought Kevin up to speed. "The bartender told me Richard was still in the bar when Roger walked back to the office, which was shortly before Justina was assaulted. You reckon Roger did it?"

Kevin offhandedly said, "I don't know, and I don't care at this point. Someone's gotta take the fall. Roger is convenient, and he has the motive."

"What about Chris?" Thorny asked.

"He's in the witness protection program. I don't know all the details, but he didn't rat us out," Kevin replied with confidence.

"How do you know?"

"Man, you know how this works. My place would've been swarming with cops by now if he had snitched."

"What about Rowena?"

"Rowena's cool," Kevin said with assurance. "It looks like she's on her way to Florida. I had someone tail her until she reached the State line,"

"So it's Roger," Thorny said, as he sat back comfortably in the car seat.

Kevin nodded in agreement as he flipped opened his cell phone, dialed a number, and barked into the mouthpiece, "Follow Roger until instructed otherwise!" Then he closed the phone without expecting a response.

Thorny also made a call on an untraceable cell phone and ordered a hit on Richard, figuring Richard could implicate him if caught. However, Thorny was alarmed when he learned Richard had met with Sue Croswell before he left town, driving northbound.

Thorny hung up the phone in a daze. Then he turned to Kevin. "You're not going to believe this, but Richard met up with a woman named Sue Croswell before he left town. Isn't that Regine's mother? I thought she was still in rehab."

Kevin was shocked. He immediately phoned Bessie. She answered on the second ring. "Hi Bessie, this is Kevin. You heard from Sue?"

"Yeah, I heard from Sue. She's living in Atlanta with her new friend, Rowena. She's also dating someone named Calvin."

"On the real?"

"But something is not right about this Calvin person. My friend overheard someone else call him Richard."

"Your friend?" Kevin curiously asked.

"I asked the Deacon at my church to go check Calvin out for me."

"What's your friend's name?"

"Alfred Franklin. Why?"

"Where is he from?"

"Los Angeles. He relocated to Virginia a little while ago to get his life back on track."

"Has he ever been to prison?"

Bessie paused before answering. "Now Kevin, whatever he did in the past, doesn't matter. He's a changed man."

"Just be careful," Kevin said, before he hung up. He had a feeling Bessie didn't know her friend well, and guessed he was quite possibly a former gang member or fugitive. While making a mental note to check the Deacon out, Kevin was still thinking when he closed his cell phone.

"What's up?" Thorny inquired.

"Richard was seeing my ex."

Thorny looked at Kevin with a bewildered gaze. "Kevin, man, you're losing me."

"It's simple," Kevin said with humor. "Richard swindled Justina, then Sue swindled Richard. I wouldn't be surprised if Sue took everything Justina owned." He laughed at the thought.

Thorny smiled. "Do you think Richard knows who she is?"

"Nah, I doubt it. He would've told us," Kevin confidently admitted. "Let's go check it out for ourselves."

An hour later, they arrived at Justina's condo. Kevin stayed in the car while Thorny knocked on the door. When Sue casually opened the door, Thorny apologized and told her he had the wrong address. Kevin was floored when Thorny confirmed his suspicion about Sue's new residence. He ordered one of his men to keep an eye on the condo.

After staying with her parents for a week, Justina returned to Atlanta in an attempt to get her life back on track. She went to her office and noticed it had been vacant for quite some time. Kathy's letter of resignation was on her desk, but she did not bother reading it. Instead, she remained focused on finding Richard Randolf.

Justina sat her desk, browsing through the investigative report to try to connect the dots with the information Big Mike gave her. The only thing she had was Calvin's real name: Richard Randolf. She thought, *Why does that name sound familiar?* She went through the file again with no success. She took a break and decided to run some errands.

She went to the post office to retrieve the mail from her new mailbox. It was filled to capacity. She perused the mail and found her bank statements, which all showed negative balances. Justina was becoming furious, until a light bulb went off in her head. *Randolf! I believe that name is on my marriage certificate.*

Justina immediately went to the bank and opened her safe deposit box. Inside the box, she found her marriage certificate. Bishop

William Randolf was listed on the marriage certificate with a corresponding address. *Oh my God! He was the pastor who married us!*

Justina drove two hours to Conway, Georgia to talk to Bishop Randolf. She did not contact him in advance for fear he would notify Richard of her visit. When she knocked on the door, an older woman greeted her.

"Hi, I'm looking for Bishop William Randolf."

"And you are?" the older woman curiously asked.

"I'm Justina. Bishop Randolf married me and my husband almost three months ago."

"Honey, that's not possible," the older woman confidently replied. "My husband died two years ago. I'm Mrs. Randolf, his wife."

Justina was surprised by this revelation. "Oh, I'm so sorry. It's just...."

"Come on inside," Mrs. Randolf said with the wave of her hand.

"Thank you. I'm confused. His name is on my marriage certificate," Justina said, as she held up the marriage certificate for Mrs. Randolf to see.

"Let me see that!" Mrs. Randolf sharply demanded, as she snatched the marriage certificate out of Justina's hand. After viewing her husband's name, she angrily asked, "What kind of sick joke is this?!"

"Ma'am, do you know Richard Randolf?" Justina feebly asked.

"That buzzard! Yes, I know him. Why do you ask?" Mrs. Randolf asked, returning the marriage certificate to Justina.

"We're married. I mean...."

Mrs. Randolf gasped. "You married that shyster? Richard is my deceased husband's younger brother. He came around here after my husband died and cleaned out the tool shed. Richard even took my husband's '76 Buick. My husband loved that old car. When I confronted him about it, he said it was his brother's and dared me to do anything about it," she explained, as tears formed along the crevice of her eyes. "Honey, if you know what's good for you, you ought to divorce him right away."

"That's not necessary," Justina ashamedly admitted. "Richard stole someone else's identity. His real name is not on my marriage certificate," she said, as she pointed out Calvin Calloway's name listed in the groom's field.

"You poor dear. Sounds like you've had quite an ordeal."

Justina sighed. "You don't know the half of it."

"It doesn't surprise me, though. Richard and his brother-in-law have always been partners in crime."

"His brother-in-law?"

"Yes, his sister's husband. I have a picture of both of them in an album around here." Mrs. Randolf rummaged through a couple of picture albums on the bookshelf. "Here they are right here," she said, as she pulled the pictures out of the album.

Justina gasped. "That's his brother-in-law? But that's the man that posed as the pastor at my wedding."

Mrs. Randolf shook her head, feeling sorry for Justina.

Justina returned the pictures to Mrs. Randolf, and asked, "Do you know how I might reach Richard?"

"I haven't seen Richard since he stole my husband's car. I heard he's living with an older woman in Stone Mountain."

"As in Stone Mountain, Georgia?" Justina asked with astonishment.

"Yes, that's the only one I know of."

"When and how did you hear that?"

"He stays in touch with his sister, Mary. She doesn't deal with him much, though. Mary told me he purchased a house there not long ago."

Justina thanked Mrs. Randolf for her help and decided to conduct a search online for Richard Randolf. What she discovered shocked her. Richard had served time for check fraud, and was released one year later. She went into whitepages.com and typed in Richard's name. The Georgia addresses associated with his name instantly appeared, along with her condo address. *This can't be! It's not possible!*

Justina did not waste any time driving to her condo. She called Big Mike on his cell phone and conveyed her findings. He told her to stay away from the condo, and to wait for the police. Justina did not listen. She grabbed her purse before she got out of her car, then briskly walked to her condo and knocked on the door.

Sue opened the door with a big smile on her face.

Justina was stunned. "You...you were at my wedding," she acknowledged in disbelief.

"Sure," Sue replied with a smirk on her face, placing her hands on her hips. "If you look a little closer, we know someone in common."

Justina looked closely at Sue's features. "You look like a friend of mine."

"You mean a friend you betrayed. But, you're getting warmer," Sue said, as she encouraged Justina to take another guess.

"Are you....Regine's mother?"

"Yes! In the flesh!" Sue joyously shouted out, holding up both arms like she just won a wrestling match.

Justina gasped before asking, "What are you doing in my condo?"

"Come on in so we can talk. Have a seat," Sue mischievously insisted, pointing Justina toward a leather sofa.

"Oh…okay." Justina thought it was strange being invited into her own home. She looked around, recognizing her furniture she had stored in the storage unit. She wondered how it got here.

Sue grinned. "I bet you're very curious why I'm here."

"Yes. Why are you here?" Justina asked, as she sat down on her own couch.

"Well, I figured since you screwed Regine, somebody ought to screw you," Sue boldly admitted. "You see…it was because of you, my baby was upset right before and after she married Guy. And it was because of you, she almost lost her baby when you embarrassed her at the baby shower. So, when Richard came along and told me about his plans to destroy you, I went along with it. I didn't know you had so many enemies. Anyway, I figured I might as well get something out of it."

Justina's eyes grew bigger. "Wha…What are you talking about?"

"You pissed someone off! They were out for revenge long before I came into the picture. By the way, how do you like my new place?" Sue asked with a wave of her hand. "My boyfriend, Richard, signed the deed over to me. I'm sure you know him as Calvin Calloway," she casually said, as she picked up her glass of wine and took a sip.

Justina grew furious and charged at Sue, knocking over her glass of wine in the process.

Sue quickly moved out of her way, then sideswiped Justina with her fist. When Justina fell forward onto the floor, face down, Sue straddled Justina's back, grabbed a fist-full of her hair, and repeatedly banged her head on the floor, cursing her out in the process.

Roger drove over to Sue's condo as soon as he got her message. Just as he was about to knock on the door, he heard the commotion going on inside. When he realized the door was unlocked, he rushed in and was puzzled by what he saw.

"What are you doing?!" Roger hysterically asked Sue, who was still on top of Justina.

"I'm making this heifer hurt, just like she hurt my baby," Sue replied, as she shoved Justina's head against the floor, once again.

"At this rate, she will be dead and I'm not going down for murder," Roger harshly said, pulling Sue off of Justina.

As Roger and Sue argued, Justina struggled to gather herself. After spotting a heavy steel vase on the coffee table, Justina grabbed it and slowly stood up. With all her might, she swung the vase over her head and flung it on the back of Sue's head.

Sue fell forward, crashing through the coffee table before hitting the floor. She did not move. She was badly cut from the broken glass, and her blood was quickly staining the carpet.

Roger looked on in disbelief.

Justina breathlessly turned toward him. "So you were in on this too?"

Roger panicked. "No! No I wasn't! You have to believe me," he pleaded with clasped hands. "I didn't want any part of this. I swear... it was Richard," he insisted, shoving his now sweaty hair away from his face.

Justina headed toward the phone. "Roger, I'm calling the police. You can tell them your side of the story when they get here."

Roger lunged toward Justina to keep her from getting to the phone. Justina held the vase up ready to strike again, but Roger was too quick for her. He yanked the vase out of her hands and threw her down on the floor.

"You cannot call the police!" Roger exclaimed, as he jumped on her back and wrapped her wrists with an extension cord he yanked out of a wall socket. "I'm not going to jail because of you!"

"Roger, what are you doing?!" Justina screamed, struggling to get her hands free.

"I'm putting a stop to this! I'm taking you some place no one will ever find you," he harshly said, wiping the sweat from his forehead with the back on his hand.

"Roger, please! Don't do this!" Justina cried out. "Somebody, help me!" she screamed.

Roger quickly silenced her with a scarf he found in Sue's bedroom. Then he made Justina stand up while he aggressively forced her to get in his car. Next, Roger got behind the steering wheel and drove to his family's vacation cabin, which was an hour north of Stone Mountain, Georgia. He escorted Justina inside and tied her to a chair in one of the bedrooms.

Justina's eyes were glued to the floor when Roger appeared before her. She looked up at him with questioning eyes.

"Why, you ask?" Roger mocked. "Well let me start from the beginning. First of all, you are a proven self-conceded tyrant!" Then Roger explained how he hated the way she belittled him, especially in front of his clients.

Justina was stunned when Roger recited all the terrible things she had done to him and others. She instantly regretted pushing Roger to this extreme. His statements had her questioning her attitude and vowing to make changes for the better. That is, if she ever got out of this situation alive.

Sue's neighbors heard the commotion and called the police. Big Mike and the police arrived at the condo fifteen minutes after Roger pulled off. They discovered Sue's limp body lying in the middle of the living room floor.

"She's still alive!" one of the officers yelled, after finding a light pulse. "Get an ambulance here! Pronto!"

Sue had slipped into a coma by the time she arrived at the hospital.

Chapter 38

Surrender

Mr. Reyes woke up to a ringing phone at three-thirty a.m. Fearing it was an emergency, he quickly turned on the nightstand lamp and answered on the second ring. "Hello."

"Is this Mr. Reyes, Justina's father?" Thorny asked.

"Yes, why?"

"Your daughter was kidnapped."

Mr. Reyes quickly sat up in bed, and frantically asked, "What ….who is this?"

"Don't worry about all that. I just called to tell you where she was taken. Do you have pen and paper available?" Thorny hung up immediately after he gave Mr. Reyes the address.

Mr. Reyes did what he was told, but first he wanted to see if this call was a hoax. He called Justina's cell phone, but there was no answer. Fear immediately overcame his whole body as he vigorously shook his wife awake. "Honey, get up! Justina's been kidnapped!"

"Wha…oh my God!" Mrs. Reyes cried out, as she sat up in bed, crying hysterically.

"It's going to be okay," Mr. Reyes said with uncertainty, as he embraced his wife. Then he called the Atlanta police department. The officer told him he would send someone to the cabin immediately.

Mr. and Mrs. Reyes did not wait for the police to confirm whether Justina was, in fact, kidnapped. They took a red-eye flight to Atlanta. Then they rented a car and drove straight to the police station. Mr. Reyes spoke with the Lieutenant, who confirmed Justina's kidnapping.

"Don't worry," the Lieutenant said, "we have the cabin surrounded, and our negotiator should be there any minute."

Mrs. Reyes went ballistic. "Why are you wasting time?! Our daughter could be dead by the time the negotiator gets there!" She shuttered at the thought, then fell into her husband's arms. Mr. Reyes gently put her in a chair and wrapped his arms around her.

"Ma'am, you have to calm down," the Lieutenant explained. "We know she's alive. Her kidnapper has her tied up in a spare room, which is visible to our S.W.A.T team. If he tries anything, our sharp shooters have been ordered to take him out."

"We're going to the cabin right now," Mr. Reyes firmly stated.

The Lieutenant warned, "I wouldn't advise that if I were you. Stay here and let us do our job."

"This is our baby we're talking about," Mrs. Reyes pointed out. "We are going!" She stood up and held her purse under her arm. Mr. Reyes stood next to her with the rental car keys in his hand.

The Lieutenant figured they would not listen to reason, so he told them to follow him to the cabin.

Justina remained tied up and uncomfortable. She was afraid Roger was going to kill her. She started crying as she bowed her head and prayed, for the first time in years. *Oh God, please help me! This man is a lunatic!*

Roger was rambling and pacing back and forth in the next room. "I wish I had never met Calvin, Richard, or whatever his name is. God, how do I get out of this mess?!" He stopped in his tracks when he heard the police sirens. Then he rushed in to check on Justina, making sure she was securely tied to the chair. He looked at her with disdain, then angrily said, "Look at this mess you got me into! I should kill you for ruining my life!"

Justina looked at Roger in bewilderment as he continued ranting. "I had everything going for me, until I met you. You never knew this, but I didn't have to work for you, or anyone. I'm rich. Well...my family's rich," he boldly professed. Roger held his head down in despair and muttered, "All I had to do was return home after I graduated from law school. But nooooooo..., I let you talk me into staying in Atlanta." He picked up a large stick and slowly approached her.

Justina shook her head back and forth, continually crying, as Roger approached her. But he lost his focus when he heard a knock on the door.

"Open up! It's the police!"

Roger stood still.

When the S.W.A.T team busted down the door, Roger immediately dropped the stick and held up his hands to surrender. Three police officers rushed into the cabin and threw him to the floor, then handcuffed him.

Roger began crying as he was thrown into the backseat of the police car. While sobbing, he said in a barely audible voice, "I didn't kill her. I'm a law-abiding citizen. You got the wrong person."

One of the police officers untied Justina. She had a fresh set of noticeable bruises and injuries from the fight and scuffle she had with both Sue and Roger. She was distraught when she was escorted out of the cabin, but perked up when she saw her parents standing next to the police car. She ran to her mother, first. They embraced and cried tears of joy.

Her father was stunned. Mr. Reyes noticed his little girl's face was disfigured, and her hair and clothes were soiled. There was also a huge red lump on her forehead. He broke down crying when she walked over to hug him.

Through tears and pain, Justina said, "Daddy, I'm okay. I should've listened to you. You were right about everything."

"Don't beat yourself up," Mr. Reyes weakly replied. "We'll help you get through this. We love you." Then he lightly kissed her on the forehead.

Justina paused and took a deep breath. "I'm sorry for all the pain I've caused you and mom."

Mr. Reyes never thought he would hear an apology from Justina. "I know baby."

Justina was escorted to a waiting ambulance, then taken to the nearest hospital to have her injuries examined.

Roger was taken to the police station where he was booked and had his mug shots taken. He was thrown in jail, and later given the opportunity to make one phone call. Contacting his parents, Mr. and Mrs. Eugene Salvador, was something he dreaded.

"Hi, Mom, this is Roger," he somberly said.

"Roger, it's good to hear from you!" Mrs. Salvador cheerfully replied. "We're all excited you've finally come to your senses. We can't wait until you come home," she added with great enthusiasm.

Roger dryly admitted, "Mom, I'm in jail."

Mrs. Salvador dropped the phone. She was in shock. Her husband asked her what was going on, but she remained speechless. When Mr. Salvador grabbed the phone, Roger told his father he was in jail and his bail request had been denied. Mr. Salvador told him not to worry; he would hire the best attorney money could buy.

Mr. and Mrs. Salvador booked the next flight to Georgia, to visit Roger. Their attorney flew with them.

The next day, Mr. and Mrs. Salvador and their attorney were escorted to a private room where Roger was already seated. Mrs. Salvador rushed to Roger and hugged him after kissing him on the cheek. "How are you, dear?"

"Considering the circumstances, I'm okay," Roger sadly replied.

"Roger," Mrs. Salvador solemnly said, "we just cannot understand how you were involved with such scrupulous people."

"Listen mother...," Roger tried to explain.

"No! You listen!" Mr. Salvador interjected. "We accepted the fact that you didn't want any part of the family business. Then we supported you when you wanted to live in Atlanta. We even paid for law school, and continued to give you a weekly allowance. We've given you more than you deserve."

"But dad...." Roger tried to explain.

"And what about this Rowena girl?" Mr. Salvador asked. "You told us she was your alibi," he mocked, "now she's nowhere to be found."

"Dad, it's not like that."

"Oh," Mrs. Salvador intervened, "so you tell us how an upper-class citizen like yourself, became involved with such low class people. You brought shame to our family."

Roger gave up trying to reason with his parents. He turned to the attorney while his mother was still talking. "Can you get me out of this mess?"

The attorney sighed. "It's going to be difficult, especially since your alibi is missing. Do you have another alibi?"

"No, but no one can place me at the scene of Justina's assault. I did not attack her in the garage, or otherwise," Roger weakly admitted.

"But you kidnapped her," the attorney replied. "And I just learned the State has a witness that's willing to testify against you."

"Who?!" Roger frantically asked.

"Chris Townsend. Does that name ring a bell?"

Roger nodded his head. "Yes, he was our private investigator," he somberly confirmed.

"Roger, I'm afraid I have more bad news for you," the attorney said. "Detective Vincent Jones is also blaming you for Paul James and Sam White's murders. He copped a plea deal, and will be granted immunity for his testimony."

"Who in the hell are they?!" Roger exploded.

"Unsolved murders. Paul James, *AKA* PJ, disappeared over seven years ago in Orlando, Florida. Even though his body was never discovered, Detective Jones is willing to testify that you admitted to killing him and dumping his body in the Atlantic Ocean. The Atlanta S.W.A.T. team searched your apartment and found PJ's wallet. Also, Samuel White's body was discovered when he drove off the Chesapeake Bay Bridge in Virginia. Detective Jones stated that you planned his demise. Now you're faced with several charges, including murder, kidnapping, assault with intent to murder, assault with a deadly weapon, and activities associated with swindling Justina."

Roger shook his head in disbelief. "Are you serious?! He's lying! They're just going to take his word?!" he shouted, as he banged his fist on the table.

His attorney retorted, "For a plea deal of immunity, I'm afraid so. The bartender at the pub you frequent, is also a State's witness. He told the police investigator that you detested Justina. The motive is there."

"Has the State offered me a plea deal?" Roger curiously asked.

"Yes, you can avoid the death penalty if you agree to life without parole," his attorney assured him.

Roger's life flashed before him. The little light at the end of the tunnel all but vanished. He knew he could not survive in jail with hardcore criminals. He began crying uncontrollably, while his parents looked on in despair.

Mrs. Salvador softly said, "There's still hope."

Roger sniffled as he looked into his mother's eyes. "What do you mean?"

"Sue Croswell is out of her coma," Mrs. Salvador whispered. "We were thinking you can strike a deal with the State. You know... turn the tables on her."

"Mother, you don't understand. I really don't know her. I only knew her through Rowena."

"It doesn't matter!" Mrs. Salvador snapped. "Do you want to get out of here, or not?!"

Roger nodded in the affirmative.

"Dry your eyes and just listen to our attorney," Mrs. Salvador whispered in Roger's ear. "Do exactly what you're told. You understand?"

Roger averted his eyes toward the floor, as he said, "Yes mother."

"Fine. Your father and I are going to step outside." Mrs. Salvador turned to the attorney. "Make sure he understands what is at stake if he doesn't go along with this plan."

As soon as Mr. and Mrs. Salvador left the room, the attorney digressed. "Roger, I understand you're telling me Sue Croswell coerced you into attacking Justina in the garage, because she threatened your life. She was also attempting to extort money from you, right?"

"What?! Is this your plan?"

The attorney was exasperated but continued, "Do you know anything about Sue Croswell?"

"I already told you! I don't really know her."

The attorney removed his glasses and frowned. "Let's get this out the way. Okay?"

Roger nodded.

"Now you were telling me Richard and Sue worked together. You were an innocent bystander who got pulled into this scam after your family was threatened, right?"

Roger looked at his attorney in disbelief. "I can't do this. Tell my mom and dad I love them. I'll take care of this myself." He got up and walked away from the attorney, feeling as though his life was doomed.

Chapter 39

On a Mission

*D*riving northbound, Richard called his wife to check on his daughter. He was relieved to hear his wife's voice. "Is everything okay?" he nervously asked.

"Hi Richard, someone just called here asking about you."

"What did they say?"

"I didn't give him a chance to say anything. I told him I hadn't seen you and hung up on him."

So as not to cause her alarm, Richard calmly asked, "Has anything strange happened around the house?"

"Not really. But there's a black sedan with tinted windows hanging around. It's been parked on the side street for the past three days."

Richard gasped. He knew he would die if something ever happened to his daughter. "Listen to me," he firmly said. "I need you and Victoria to pack a suitcase and go stay at your mother's house for a little while. Are your brothers still living with her?"

"Yeah, they're there. Why?"

"Just trust me on this," Richard pleaded.

Detecting worry in his voice, she said, "Richard, what did you do?"

"You don't want to know. Just do what I tell you. When you get to your mother's, send me a text message to let me know you made it safely."

Richard did not want to take any chances. Initially, he thought he was being paranoid when he looked in his rearview mirror and saw a black sedan behind him. When he sped up, so did the sedan. Curious to see if the car was following him, Richard turned off at the next exit, then stopped at a red light. Three burly men exited the sedan and ran toward his car. Richard floored the engine and got back onto I-95, zigzagging in and out of lanes trying to get away. When he looked in his rear view mirror again, the sedan was nowhere in sight.

He drove for the next thirty minutes until the low fuel indicator lit up. At the next exit, he pulled into a gas station. A text message appeared from his wife. *Richard, we made it. Don't worry about us. I told my brothers and they're watching the house.*

Richard was relieved. He knew his wife has three crazy brothers with violent pasts. All of them have served hard time in prison for crimes, including 'assault with intent to kill.' They were not afraid of the police, or guns.

While Richard pumped gas into his car, the sedan pulled up next to him. One of the men took the pump from him, and said, "I got this. Go have a seat in the car over there."

Richard was apprehensive but did as he was told. When he entered the backseat of the sedan, he asked the driver, "Where are you taking me?"

The driver peered at Richard through his rearview mirror. "You know what time it is."

"Can I make one phone call?" Richard asked, realizing he left his cell phone in the rental.

The driver briefly glanced back at Richard. "Man, what's wrong with you? You're not entitled to a phone call," he added with a hearty chuckle.

"Please man," Richard pleaded. "This is important."

The driver pulled out his cell phone, and asked, "What's the number?"

After dialing the number, the driver handed his cell phone to Richard. There was no answer, so Richard left a message on Sue's voicemail. *"Baby, I love you. You take care of yourself. Don't worry about me. I'll see you in the next life."* He handed the phone back to the driver, and prayed his death would be quick and painless.

Chapter 40

Long Awaited

*W*hen Kevin discreetly visited Sue's hospital room in the middle of the night, he learned that Bessie had not been notified. He anonymously left her contact information at the nurse's station. Immediately, the nurse phoned Bessie. "Ma'am, are you related to Sue Croswell?"

"I'm her mama. Why?"

"I'm a nurse at Atlanta Regional. I'm afraid we have bad news. Your daughter is in a coma."

"Oh my God!" Bessie frantically shouted. While whimpering she got the name of the hospital and its location. Then she immediately called Lucy.

Lucy answered on the first ring. "It's Sue, isn't it?"

"How did you know?"

"As her mother, I had a gut feeling. What happened?"

Lucy did not take the news well. She fainted after she hung up the phone. Luckily, her daughter, Rowena, was there. When Lucy came to, she told her daughter they had to go to Atlanta to go to see her sister.

"What is Katie doing in Atlanta?"

Lucy sighed. "No, not Katie…you have another sister, named Sue." She averted her eyes from Rowena's questioning gaze. "It's a long story. I'll tell you about it on the way there."

Regine panicked when she saw her grandmother sitting at the dining room table, crying. "Grandma, what's the matter?"

Bessie dried her eyes with a handkerchief. "Baby, sit down, I need to tell you something."

"What is it?" Regine nervously asked.

"Your mother…she's in the hospital."

Regine broke down crying, hysterically repeating, "Oh my God, oh my God…."

Bessie stood up from the table and wrapped her arms around her. "Regine, you have to be strong. Strong for the baby, and strong for what I'm about to tell you." She pulled a chair out for Regine.

Regine sat down, wiping away her tears. Then she took a deep breath and looked into her grandmother's eyes.

Bessie sighed. "Your mother is in a coma."

Regine rested her elbow on the table and placed her hand on her forehead, sobbing profusely.

Bessie sniffled as she placed her hand on Regine's shoulder. "Baby, it's going to be okay."

"We have to go see her," Regine insisted, as she looked at Bessie.

"But baby, she's in Atlanta. I don't think you should travel in your condition. I'll go see about her, and call you when I get there."

"I'm going and no one is going to stop me," Regine firmly said.

Bessie decided not to press the issue. "Do you think Guy would drive us?"

"Guy isn't here," Regine explained. "He's in Tampa with Alex. They're visiting their stepmother."

Bessie raised her brows. "What are you talking about, child?"

"Oh, I forgot to tell you. It's a long story. I'll tell you about it on our way to Atlanta. We'll take the twins with us."

Regine booked four tickets for the next flight to Atlanta, then left a message for Guy on his voicemail.

Almost four hours later, Dana and Cassandra sat in the hospital waiting room, while Regine and Bessie went to visit Sue in the Intensive Care Unit.

Bessie broke down crying when she saw Sue in the hospital bed. She walked over and kissed Sue on the forehead. "Sue, baby, you got to fight to survive," she weakly said. "I need you...your baby needs you. You're going to be a grandma soon, so we need you to survive. Squeeze my finger if you hear me," she said, as she placed her finger in Sue's hand.

Sue remained unresponsive.

Regine went over to the other side of her mother's hospital bed and stooped close to Sue's ear. "Mom, please be okay. I love you."

"I...love you...too," Sue said in a barely audible whisper.

Regine looked up as Sue slowly opened her eyes.

Bessie yelled out, "Praise Jesus! Praise Jesus!"

Regine gently brushed her mother's hair with her hand. "Mom, save your energy. I'll be back. I need to go let the doctor know you're awake."

"I'm so glad you're okay," Bessie said, as she washed Sue's face with a damp hand towel. Seconds later, Bessie was startled when Lucy and Rowena walked into the hospital room. "Baby," she said to Sue, while holding her hand, "you remember Ms. Lucy, don't you? Well…she's your real momma."

Sue looked at Lucy in astonishment. She realized she was looking at an older version of herself. Then she looked at the other woman standing next to Lucy.

Bessie followed Sue's gaze. "Oh, that's Lucy's daughter, Rowena. She's your sister."

"Rowena?" Sue whispered.

Rowena slowly approached the bed. "Hi sis, nice to meet you," she awkwardly said.

Regine returned to the room just as Bessie made the introductions. She noticed Sue's blank stare and her resemblance to Lucy and Rowena, then understood why.

"Sis?" Sue asked again, before drifting off in a deep sleep.

The doctor walked in and looked at Sue's vitals. He told them she was no longer comatose, but needed her rest. Then he suggested they come back in an hour or so.

As they walked out of the room, Regine looked at Bessie for an explanation. "Baby, it's a long story," Bessie told her. "Let's find a private room to talk."

Regine was speechless when Lucy told her she had asked Bessie to raise Sue. Lucy further explained, "I had four kids already and could not afford to raise another child by myself, especially after my husband went to prison. He was sentenced to life without parole, for murder. Unfortunately, he died five years later."

Regine remembered her grandmother telling her about the man who killed her grandfather because he caught him having an affair with his wife. She was shocked, beyond belief, to learn that Lucy, Bessie's best friend, was the woman he was having the affair with. On the other hand, she was elated to learn that she had two aunts, Katie and Rowena; three uncles, Wilford, Robert and Andrew; and ten first cousins. Everyone, except Katie, was married and had children.

Lucy and Bessie explained the same thing to Sue when they returned to the Intensive Care Unit. Lucy held Sue's hand and asked, "Can you find it in your heart to forgive me?"

Sue thought about the number of times she asked Bessie to forgive her. She also thought about her relationship with her own daughter and knew she would be asking Regine to forgive her as well. Sue looked at Lucy and smiled, before she sincerely said, "I forgive you." Then she briefly glanced in Bessie's direction and added, "Thank you for giving me a wonderful mother who loves me unconditionally."

At that moment, Sue knew her life had changed for the better. She learned about the power of forgiveness, she learned to forgive herself, and she learned that she had two mothers, who loved her abundantly. She knew she was in trouble for her involvement with swindling Justina, but decided, regardless of the outcome, she would not have done anything differently.

Lucy and Bessie's revelation was not such a big surprise after all; it actually tied the pieces of her life together. After Katie left for Florida, Sue discovered Katie's letter in her journal.

Dear Sis,

I'm sure you're wondering why I'm addressing you in this manner. Well, the truth is, you're my real sister. We have the same mother. I have not been honest with you about my past, so let me set the record straight. When I admitted myself into rehab, I was determined to help you and eventually bring you home. You and I know it did not happen the way I expected, but I am glad things turned out the way they did.

Everything I told you about being on drugs, and having a husband and children was all a lie. And, I am not as wayward as I appeared. I own a consulting firm, which is based in California. By the way, I prefer suits as opposed to the skimpy outfits I wore in your presence. So, I bet you're wondering why I went through such extremes. Why all the lies? For one, I love you. You are my own flesh and blood. I wanted to protect you. Secondly, I was afraid you would relapse. I wanted you to be comfortable with me, and feel as though you could relate to someone who has been in your shoes. And lastly, I followed your lead because you would have gone to Atlanta without me. I could not risk losing you again. I wanted to make sure, in the end, you would be all right. I'm proud of you. I'll be in touch soon.

Your Big Sis,
Katie

P.S. You have another sister. Her name is none other than Rowena. Now destroy this letter. ☺

Sue was puzzled after reading the letter. However, she finally understood why Katie kept referring to Regine as her niece, and would sometimes fail to respond to her alias name, Rowena. She shredded the letter into tiny pieces, then wondered if she would ever see Katie again.

Chapter 41

The Saga Continues....

Sue had been in the hospital for three days, when two detectives walked into her hospital room and questioned her about the physical altercation she had with Justina. They also asked her how she ended up in possession of her condo. Sue did not answer any questions, per her attorney's advice. The detectives read Sue the Miranda rights and took her into custody.

Sue was then transferred to a hospital inside the jail facility. Kevin, Regine's father, anonymously posted Sue's bail, which was set at $100,000. Sue was released the next day in Bessie's custody. Kevin had also discreetly hired an attorney for Sue.

"Ms. Croswell," the attorney stated, "the District Attorney is using circumstantial evidence to charge you."

"What does that mean?" Sue asked.

"It means they really do not have a strong case against you. Ms. Reyes admitted that she struck you first, so the assault charges have been dropped. Also, the prosecutor cannot prove you knew Richard Randolf stole Calvin Calloway's identity, nor can they prove you knew the condo belonged to Justina. But...."

"But what?"

"The district attorney is willing to reduce the charges if you agree to become a witness for the State. They are going after Roger McCarthy."

"What if I don't agree?"

"You go to prison for a minimum of twenty years if found guilty. But, if you take the plea deal, you will only serve the maximum sentence of three years."

Sue thought about what Richard told her. She knew without Richard, the State did not have a case. "Let's fight it," she finally said.

"What?" her attorney asked in disbelief. "Sue as your attorney, I would advise you to take the plea deal."

"Have they been able to find Richard Randolf?"

"No," her attorney hesitantly admitted.

"Then I'll take my chances."

"So, you're betting your life on Richard Randolf not being found. Ms. Croswell, if you do not take this plea deal and you're found guilty, you could get life without parole. All you have to do is testify against Roger McCarthy."

"I know exactly what I'm doing," Sue confidently replied.

The attorney thought Sue was being irrational, while Sue thought about what Richard told her, right before he disappeared. *"Sue, you're an innocent bystander. If they catch me and they never will, I will deny you were ever involved. I love you. Trust that I will never put you in harm's way."*

The one person that could clear Roger's name, is the same person that threatened to harm his family. He vividly remembered the one and only conversation he had with Thorny, which was after he took Justina to the police station to file a fraud report. Roger was walking to his car as Thorny came up from behind him.

"My man," Thorny said, as he aggressively placed his hand on Roger's shoulder. "Follow me. I need to talk to you."

"Who are you?" Roger nervously asked.

"Don't worry about all that. Let's just say we have a mutual friend," Thorny said, exposing his gun inside his jacket. He led Roger to the waiting sedan, opened the back door, and watched Roger get in first while he followed suit.

Once Roger climbed in, he came face to face with Kevin. He was not nearly as intimidated by Kevin as he was with Thorny. Kevin spoke first. "I heard you nutted up at the police station."

"Who are you?" Roger asked.

"That's not important," Thorny said. "Tell us what happened at the police station."

"I was nervous, that's all," Roger timidly replied. "Let me go now, or I will go to the police," he weakly threatened. He felt Thorny's gaze and grew uncomfortable. It did not help that Thorny stood 6'7 and weighed 350 pounds of pure muscle.

Kevin figured Roger would be the first to snitch. "We were prepared for this," he said, as he looked into Roger's eyes.

"What….what do you mean?" Roger nervously asked.

"Well," Kevin said, "we did a little background research on you, *Roger Salvador.*" Roger was alarmed at the mention of his real name.

Kevin gave Roger a synopsis of his entire life, from childhood to adulthood. "We also know your family owns a dynasty. You never had to work. How did you end up at a rinky-dink law firm?"

"I....I wanted my independence," Roger weakly admitted.

"Nah, I find that hard to believe. So you were jealous of your younger brother, huh? His name is Corrie, right?"

"Please don't harm my family," Roger pleaded. "Leave them out of this!"

"Oh. Now you're acting like you have a backbone," Kevin said with a light chuckle. He pulled out his iPod and showed it to Roger.

Roger panicked when he saw a picture of his family portrait taken in front of his parents' fireplace. Then Kevin showed Roger a picture of his younger sister, Alice. She was sitting by the pool, unaware someone had taken her picture. The next picture was of his father on the phone at the headquarters of the family business. The other pictures were of the cars they drove, the properties they owned, and angles of every segment of their estate.

"How did you get these pictures?" Roger fearfully asked.

Kevin smirked. "I'm glad we got your attention. So, this is what we're going to do. We will leave your family alone, but if we find out you're a snitch, you will regret it. You got it!" Kevin chose to threaten Roger opposed to killing him, after considering Roger's high-profile family. He could not risk drawing attention to himself, especially since he figured Roger's family would have the entire S.W.A.T. team looking for his body.

Roger started rocking back and forth. "My God, my God....please stay away from my family," he begged.

"As long as you play your cards right," Kevin said, "you have nothing to worry about. From this day forward, you never met us."

"What about Justina?" Roger nervously inquired. "She's not going to drop this."

"Let us take care of Justina," Kevin said. "In the meantime, we need you to give her Thorny's number."

Roger shifted his eyes from Kevin and Thorny, then shook his head from worry.

In response to Roger's uneasiness, Kevin said, "Suggest that you know someone that can help her with her problems."

"What if she asks me questions about Thorny?"

"You never had a problem with lying to her before," Kevin smugly replied.

"That's all I have to do?"

"Just don't make any more mistakes," Thorny interjected, while clutching his gun.

Roger knew Kevin and Thorny meant business. His gut feeling told him once he gave Justina Thorny's contact information, things would take a turn for the worse. He believed Thorny assaulted and tried to kill Justina.

After his parents and attorney left, Roger returned to his cell and fell into a deep state of depression. Two weeks later, he decided to do the unthinkable. After recess, he walked back to his cell and looked at the sheet on his cot. Two hours later, the guards found him dead, hanging upside down from the top bunk bed. He left behind a note. It was simple and clear.

Mom and Dad,
I did this for you. I love you.
Roger

At the onset of the trial, Sue pled the fifth for her involvement. The State's case against her had weakened with Roger's unexpected death. Also, since Richard Randolf was one of the main culprits and nowhere to be found, the State could not prove Sue's involvement. The State eventually dropped the charges against Sue, but ordered that the condo be returned to Justina.

After the judge rendered his decision, Regine rushed to Sue and embraced her. "I love you, Mom."

Sue smiled. "I love you too, baby. Can you ever find it in your heart to forgive me?" she softly asked.

"Yes, but promise you will stay off drugs and continue being a part of my life."

"I promise."

Sue and Regine got into the backseat of Guy's car, while Guy drove and Bessie sat up front. Regine whispered to Sue, "Is Aunt Katie the sister you always wanted?"

"And then some. I feel as though I've known her all of my life."

Regine noticed that her mother suddenly looked sad. "What's the matter?"

"I just wonder if Katie's all right. I hate that I'm the reason for her disappearance."

"Mom, you know she's safe. Aunt Katie's just a phone call away. When things die down, she'll return. She covered her tracks. No one knows her real name, or that you are related."

"But what if...."

"Mom, don't worry. Things will turn out fine, you'll see.

Sue suddenly perked up. "Your Aunt Katie convinced me to go back to school to get my degree. She also offered me a job with her consulting firm. I just have to report to the Vice CEO. She arranged everything."

"Mom, please go. This would be a great opportunity for you to start over. I am so proud of you." Regine leaned over and kissed Sue on the cheek."

Sue began to cry. All of her life, she had been waiting to hear those exact words from her one and only daughter. "I'm proud of you too," she beamed. "Oh, by the way, have you heard from your father?"

"No, and I don't expect to," Regine said with an attitude.

Sue noticed Regine's reaction. "Regardless of how you feel about your father, he's a good man. Kevin will do anything to make you happy. He loves you and has been there for you ever since you were born."

"I know, but I've never known love like this before."

"His actions may be a little extreme, but everything he does for you, is in the name of love." Sue smiled, then asked, "Have you had a heart-to-heart conversation with your grandmother yet?"

"Which one?" Regine asked with a chuckle.

Sue laughed softly. "Yeah, that freaked me out too. I have two mothers."

"Is there anything else I should know?" Regine curiously asked.

Sue mischievously smiled. "Well, I was at your wedding. And you were absolutely beautiful."

Regine's mouth flew open. "You were?!"

"Nothing could keep me away from my only child's wedding," Sue proudly declared.

"Did you know my father was there too?"

Sue nodded her head. "No, but it wouldn't surprise me."

Chapter 42

The Grass is Greener

October 2008....

Guy rushed Regine to the hospital for the birth of their baby boy, Kevin Charlie Simmons. He was named after Regine's and Guy's fathers. When the new proud father walked into the waiting room and told everyone the news, they all cheered with excitement.

"Is the baby okay?" Jeanine asked. "I mean, is he healthy?"

Guy happily announced, "Yes, your seven-pound, six ounce grandson is very healthy."

"When can we see him?" Dana asked.

"The nurse is transporting him to the nursery. He should be there in a few minutes."

"When can we see Regine?" Bessie asked.

"She's resting now. I'll let you know."

Several minutes later, everyone walked to the nursery. Jeanine and Guy stood next to each other with a clear view of Kevin Charlie.

"Wow!" Jeanine exclaimed. "He looks just like his daddy."

"You think so?" Guy all but knowingly replied.

"Yes," Jeanine said with a smile. "Thank you so much for allowing me to be a part of your lives."

Guy wrapped his arm around Jeanine's shoulders. "We wouldn't have it any other way. Thank you for all you've done for us."

Jeanine beamed. "Guy, I just want you and Alex to be happy."

Guy looked at her with concern. "I've been meaning to ask you about that. Why do you always single me and Alex out? What about the twins?"

"I don't know how to tell you this...."

"I already know they have a different father, but that doesn't make them less a part of my family. If you can't accept them, then you can't accept me and Alex."

"You're right. I'm so sorry. My behavior is inexcusable. What I need to tell you may explain everything." Jeanine pulled Guy aside, out of earshot of the others. "You never have to worry about the twins," she softly whispered.

Guy winced. "I don't understand."

"Their deceased grandfather owned the Toils and Day Toilet Paper Company. Your sisters will receive an inheritance on their 21st birthday."

Guy raised a brow. "They don't even know who their father is, let alone their grandfather."

"Before their father died, five years ago, he told his father about the twins. Their grandfather did a little investigating through the court system and found them. To make a long story short, he contacted me after he discovered I was your stepmother and you had custody of the twins. He did not want to confuse the girls by inserting himself into their lives. I guess he figured they'd been through enough."

Guy took a deep breath and slowly exhaled. "Wow, more surprises. This is amazing."

"Guy, you did a wonderful job raising them. But soon, you won't have to worry about their financial needs. Please know that I love them just like I love you and Alex, so don't get it wrong," Jeanine added with a smirk.

When they returned home from the hospital, Guy spotted a black sedan parked across the street in front of their house. He asked everyone to go inside, then cautiously walked toward the car and knocked on the window. The driver's window automatically rolled down and revealed a familiar face. Guy knew it was Regine's father based on their resemblance.

"I need to talk to you," Kevin firmly said. "Get in."

Guy hesitantly got into the passenger side of the car.

"So she had a baby boy," Kevin acknowledged with a light chuckle.

Guy smiled. "Yes, and I assume this is your first grandchild."

Kevin smiled and nodded. "Kevin Charlie. I like that name. Thanks for naming him after me."

"No problem."

"Take care of my baby."

"For the rest of my life," Guy said with assurance. "I love Regine. I will never let anyone hurt her."

"I believe you. But let me warn you; if you hurt her again, you will regret it," Kevin firmly said.

"I understand." Guy was not afraid of Kevin. He knew if Kevin wanted it to happen, he could have easily disappeared a long time ago.

On that note, Kevin bid Guy farewell and drove off. Guy figured he would never see Kevin again, so he decided to keep Kevin's visit a secret.

Six months later, Sue and Regine paid a visit to Lucy's home, with the baby. Bessie, Lucy, and Sue's siblings, along with their children and spouses stood outside as they pulled into the driveway. Everyone took turns hugging and welcoming them into the family. Bessie and Lucy did all the cooking. It was one big happy family reunion.

Bessie stood back and observed in awe while Regine and Sue were showered with love. Everyone took turns asking them questions about their lives. Sue soon discovered she had overprotective brothers, who catered to her every need. In the midst of all the excitement, she suddenly focused on someone she never expected to see.

"Richard?" she softly asked with a bewildered expression. "But how did you...?"

"Your mother has connections," Richard said, as he approached her. "She looked out for me. I can't stay long. I just wanted to see you one more time."

Sue looked over to her mother with a questioning gaze. Bessie smiled in response, then turned and walked inside the house. Everyone else followed suit, to give Sue and Richard some privacy.

"I thought you were dead," Sue whispered as Richard embraced her.

"Your mother made a phone call to one of the men I was dealing with. They took me to Mexico to hide out." Richard looked at his watch. "I can't stay long. I just wanted to see you one more time and to tell you I love you."

Sue held onto his hands. "Can I come with you?"

"To Mexico?"

"Yes," Sue firmly said.

Richard thought about this. His heart said 'yes' but he knew he was not completely out of danger. "You just reunited with your family. They need you more than I do. If you were with me, I'd always be looking over my shoulder, worrying about your safety. I love you too much for that. Stay here and embrace the love and attention you're receiving."

Regine approached them with caution. "Mom, who is this?"

Not sure how to introduce Richard, Sue simply said, "He's a friend of mine." Then she lightly touched Regine's shoulder. Baby, go back inside. I'll explain it to you later."

Richard waited for Regine to go back inside the house, then leaned over and kissed Sue, passionately, on the lips. He gave her a number where he could be reached. Suddenly a black sedan appeared in front of the house.

"That's my cue. I love you, baby," Richard said, after he gave Sue another peck on the lips. As he turned and walked to the car, he looked back and threw her a kiss. Sue pretended to catch it, then stood there until the car drove away. Sadly, she entered the house where she was faced with yet another surprise. It was Katie.

"It's about time you came inside!" Katie exclaimed. "I thought I was going to have to go out there and pull that man of yours off of you. Come here sis; give me a hug."

Sue cried as they embraced. "I thought I'd never see you again," she sobbed.

Katie grinned. "Well you thought wrong. I love you, baby girl. We all do."

"I'm so sorry about Roger," Sue belated admitted.

"It's okay. Blood is thicker than water," Katie replied with sadness in her eyes. It was apparent that she still loved Roger.

"Now, everyone grab hands," Katie insisted, as they formed a circle around Sue. " Sue, you're in the circle of love. In this circle, you're surrounded by people who love you and vow to protect you. Whenever you need anything or anyone, you never have to go outside this circle. We're family. God reunited us and we won't lose you again." Afterward, everyone took turns embracing Sue.

When they left Lucy's, Sue told Regine she had something to give her.

"What is it?" Regine asked.

Sue said, as she held up three, three-ring binders, "Everything you've always wanted to know about me is in these journals. Even on drugs, I wrote down all my sorrows and feelings, so I could remember the good and the bad. I recently browsed through my journals, and must admit, I'm ashamed of a lot of things I've done in the past. Unfortunately, I lost or misplaced some of my journals throughout my crazy life."

Tears formed in Regine's eyes. "Mom, you have the opportunity to create a new future. Don't dwell on the negative. I will help you."

"I know baby. I'm so glad you're in my life."

"Me too, but you deserve to be happy. This is your time to live for yourself."

At that moment, Sue knew what she had to do. One week later, Sue called Richard and told him she wanted to be with him. Reluctantly, he eventually gave in to her pleas and paid for her flight to Mexico City. She did not want to tell Bessie and Regine what her plans were because she was afraid she would change her mind. Instead, she left a letter for them.

When Sue finally arrived, Richard was overcome with joy. "Baby, I wasn't sure if you would make it," he said, scooping her up into his arms.

Sue laughed softly. "Not a second or minute went by that I didn't have you on my mind," she convincingly said.

"Let's go to our new home," Richard happily said. It was actually a one-bedroom bungalow, situated off the Gulf Coast of Mexico in Ciudad Victoria.

Sue fell in love with the town's people, and was surprised at how friendly they all were. She even talked Richard into seeing a doctor on a regular basis. He loved her so much; he was willing to do anything to make her happy. For the first time in their lives, they were free to love, openly and completely.

Bessie found Sue's letter and read it with great sadness. Unbeknownst to Sue, Bessie gave Richard her blessings long before she decided to go to Mexico. Bessie knew Sue and Richard were truly in love with each other. She told him, "If you're going to mistreat her, send her back home. I will deal with you later." Richard chuckled in response. He knew he would never allow anything to happen to Sue.

Bessie was also bitten by the lovebug. Deacon Alfred Franklin had won her heart. He was the one person she could always confide in about what was going on in her life. Bessie knew he loved her, and would do anything to show it. She finally let the Deacon spend the night when he proposed to her, and was pleasantly surprised he was so frisky at his age.

After they made love, the Deacon nervously looked into her eyes while smoothing her hair from her face.

"What is it, Alfred?" she asked with worry in her voice.

"Baby, you know I'll do anything for you, don't you?"

Bessie softly chuckled. "Yes suga'. That's what I love about you."

Alfred quietly rolled over and stared at the ceiling.

Bessie suddenly became alarmed. "What's the matter?"

"Baby, I have a confession to make," he solemnly replied.

Bessie instantly sat up in bed and turned the light on.

Alfred averted his eyes when he admitted, "I killed PJ when he wronged Regine."

Bessie looked at him with a questioning gaze.

His voice trembled. "Baby, I was worried about you. Whenever you are worried about Regine, you are not right."

Bessie sighed, then slowly exhaled. "Did you kill Earl and Sam too?" she fearfully asked.

"I may have done something to Earl's brake line that caused his car accident, but I didn't kill Sam," he nervously admitted.

She sighed again. "What about Justina?"

"No, I didn't have anything to do with her," he convincingly replied.

Bessie was frozen in place. She did not know what else to say.

"Baby, are you changing your mind about us?" Alfred timidly asked.

"No, it's just going to take some time for me to digest all this. Roll over and get some sleep. We'll talk more about it in the morning."

Alfred could not sleep. He was debating on whether he should tell Bessie about his past life as a gang leader. He had murdered and hurt so many people in his life; killing PJ and Earl so Bessie could have a peace of mind was a cakewalk, by comparison.

The night Sam took Regine out on a date, Alfred was only a car length behind Sam's truck. When Sam pulled over to put Regine out, he was going to follow him but he saw two other cars following Sam's truck. He presumed it was Kevin and his crew, and was relieved when his suspicions were confirmed, especially since Sam was found dead the next morning. So he closely tailed Regine until she got into a cab and made it home safely. He would not have thought twice about taking Sam's life, considering what he did to Regine.

Bessie also stayed awake, thinking about the times she told Alfred what was going on in her personal life, especially when it came to Regine. She knew he loved her, but never dreamed he would commit murder to lessen her worries. Bessie prayed Regine would forgive her father for the deeds he did not do. That is, in respect to PJ and Earl. She had a feeling Kevin had taken care of Sam.

One month later, Bessie and Alfred had a small wedding at their church. They decided to keep Alfred's involvement with PJ and Earl's murders a secret.

Chapter 43

Flop Flip

Justina returned home to live with her parents after selling her condo. She knew she had blown any chance of ever being with Guy, and still could not understand how he had gotten over her so easily. Even more shocking, was the news he had become a millionaire over night, upon inheriting Trowne Key Estates from his stepmother.

Lately, she had been doing a lot of soul searching. Justina thought about the things Roger told her when he kidnapped her, and could not understand how or why she became so unbearable and unlikeable. After experiencing all the consequences of her actions, she vowed to make changes in her life, starting with her attitude.

Upon relocating to Florida on a permanent basis, Justina had her mail forwarded from Georgia. She was very surprised one afternoon, when she received a letter addressed to Richard with no return address. It was originally dated two days before she was kidnapped, and returned several times before it was forwarded to her new address. She quickly opened it.

Dear Richard,

I found out I was HIV positive a couple of years ago. The doctor suspects that I have had the virus for a while. I think you need to get tested. I'm sorry to give you news like this in a letter, but I thought you should know.

Your wife,
Benzola

Justina dropped to the floor and cried. She was overwhelmed with grief, figuring Richard must have known he had the virus all along. Sadly, she was the one who had convinced him not to use a condom in one instance.

She finally gained the nerve to get tested, and broke down crying again when the test results revealed that she was HIV positive.

Her doctor told her she could live a long healthy life, as long as she took her meds and practiced safe sex.

"But Doctor Thompson...you don't understand," Justina tried to explain. "The man I contracted the virus from did not look sick. He looked healthy. What should I have known? I know he wasn't gay."

"That's an old stigma. Gay men are not spreading the virus nearly as fast as heterosexuals. The fact is, in major metropolitan cities, black women are being infected at a faster rate than any other demographic group. Unfortunately, no one ever knows their HIV status until they are tested."

Justina held her head down and cried.

The doctor consoled her. "Justina, you are not unique. There are many women in your situation, from preachers to teachers and lawyers. You cannot let this virus define you. There are medications you can take that will prolong your life." The doctor paused, then continued, "I have an idea. Why don't you use your legal expertise to become an AIDS advocate for women like yourself?"

Justina did not respond. She gathered her belongings and went to the library to conduct her own search. After learning all about the AIDS virus and the progress made to prolong carriers' lives, she felt a little better.

She dreaded telling her parents, but thought it was necessary. Initially, they were overwrought with fear, but were somewhat relieved when Justina told them all about the AIDS research and its findings.

Eventually, she took her doctor's advice and became an AIDS activist. It was not an easy road. She met with a group of professionals, who had been infected with the virus for ten or more years. They helped her cope. She did everything her doctor told her to do. However, she constantly worried about how to broach the subject when she would go out on dates. It seemed much easier to just blurt out her HIV status and watch their reaction.

Justina's status did not dissuade Aaron Bishop. He wanted to continue seeing her. Aaron was a good-looking businessman, who was very vague about what type of business he owned. On their third date, he told her that he, too, was HIV positive.

"So where do we go from here?" Justina asked.

Aaron smiled. "I think we could be good together. Let's take it slow and see how things work out."

"That sounds like a good plan."

They dated for five months before Justina realized Aaron was wealthy. He owned two franchised restaurants, and lived in a modest five-bedroom house in West Palm Beach, Florida.

Justina was totally oblivious of Aaron's stature as his attire and car did not exude wealth, but instead, mediocrity. She gazed into Aaron's eyes, as she asked, "Why didn't you tell me you were well-off?"

"I needed to know if you were into me. There are so many women more interested in my money than getting to know me. I decided to change my approach."

"Did I pass your test?" Justina asked, knowing she used to be the woman Aaron described.

Aaron smiled. "With flying colors! You are also the first woman I ever dated who was upfront about her HIV status. That took courage. I admire you for that."

"Well, this is all so new to me. How did you confront this issue on your dates?"

"To be honest, I rarely ever got beyond dinner or a movie. Don't take this the wrong way, but unlike you, I'm a very private person."

Justina raised a brow. "But you've been attending AIDS rallies and fundraisers with me for the past month or so."

"I know. This is the first time in my life that I have been comfortable with my status. I owe it all to you."

Justina was overwhelmed by his admission.

"I know it's too soon," Aaron softly said, "but I think I'm falling in love with you. I love everything about you."

Justina felt the same way, but after dealing with Richard, she had a hard time trusting anyone.

The next day, Justina talked to her father about her dilemma.

"I think you should give Aaron a chance," Mr. Reyes said. "It's obvious that he loves you."

"But I don't know if it's for all the right reasons."

"Listen to your heart. Do you think about him every second of the day? Do you miss him when you don't hear from him? Can you see yourself living without him?" Mr. Reyes quizzed.

Justina answers to her father's questions were a resounding, "Yes, yes, and no." She knew she loved Aaron, but she had doubts. Her father knew it too. However, Justina did not know Mr. Reyes had already given Aaron his approval to marry her.

Two days later, Aaron took Justina to a five-star restaurant, where a live band entertained them while they ate. After they finished their meals, Aaron requested a bottle of Chardonnay.

"Wow, what's the occasion?" Justina asked.

Aaron smiled. "Do you like the band?"

"I love it. They're playing all of my favorite love songs."

Aaron grinned in response, thinking of how quizzing her father about her favorite artists and love songs had been a great idea. As if on cue, the band stopped playing, then a bright spotlight hovered over their table.

Justina became alarmed as she looked around the room, blinded by the bright light. Then she turned to Aaron. "What's going on?" she asked, as she looked down and saw the ring box on the table. "What is that?"

Aaron opened the box, revealing a five-karat-diamond engagement ring. "I love you. I want you to be my wife. Will you marry me?"

"Yes, I will marry you!" Justina merrily shouted, as she jumped up and ran into Aaron's open arms.

Aaron smiled, as he knowingly asked, "Do you want a big wedding?"

Justina giggled, as she excitedly said, "Of course. I want my dad to walk me down the aisle."

Six months later, Aaron and Justina were married. Her parents were so proud of her. For the first time ever, Justina was truly happy and in love, without conditions.

Epilogue

October 2009....

After Regine graduated from the St. Petersburg Culinary Arts School, she opened her own restaurant, having it built from the ground up. It was a two-story, red brick building, highlighted with gold trim. From the outside, it looked like a mansion, but on the inside, the décor was a mixture of redwood and gray textures, aligned with beautiful redwood tables, chairs, and booths. The lighting included a mixture of skylights and miniature chandeliers hanging above each table. The top floor was designed for special events, while the bottom floor was for regular patrons, and included a bar area.

Everyone agreed that it was befitting to celebrate Kevin Charlie's first birthday during the grand opening. Regine had been up since six a.m., cooking and prepping the food. She also had the restaurant decorated with celebratory balloons and streamers in honor of the birthday boy.

Sue and Bessie flew in to help with the finishing touches, and her godparents were on-hand to give her legal advice and encouragement. Everyone was present, except Regine's father. Regine wanted to see him, despite his transgressions.

Regine returned home in time to dress for the grand opening. She stood in the full-length mirror, admiring her black, slinky, jersey gown. She thought the Flora and fauna mix, special ordered from Versace, was the perfect selection for this joyous occasion.

Guy whistled when he walked into their bedroom and saw her. "Baby, you're beautiful."

"And you, my darling, are handsome," Regine cheerfully replied, as she approached him and straightened his tuxedo tie.

Guy blushed, before he asked, "Have you seen Alex?"

"Yeah, I saw him earlier. He was with Rhaunda. They're planning to meet us at the restaurant."

"Oh, okay." Guy sat on the bed, in deep thought.

Regine raised a brow. "What's the matter?"

"I just hate for history to repeat itself," he solemnly replied.

"What do you mean?"

"Alex and Rhaunda have been dating for a while. But she recently told me about their relationship woes, and asked me for my advice."

Regine sat next to him on the bed. "What are you talking about?"

"Rhaunda has a friend who's trying to come between her and Alex."

Regine rolled her eyes skyward. "Oh Lord. What did you tell her?"

"I told her to talk to you, and I'll talk to Alex."

"Whatever you do, don't tell Jeanine," Regine teased.

"Yeah, I know," Guy said with a light chuckle. "Hopefully, Alex will come to his senses and realize Rhaunda's a good woman. It seems her girlfriend is eye-candy, if you know what I mean."

Regine frowned. "Boy, do I ever. I'm surprised he's in this situation, considering how upset he was with you when you were dating Justina."

"Have you heard from her?"

Regine bent over and slid on her silver open-toe sandals before she answered. "No, but I heard she's doing good things with her life. She's an AIDS activist."

"Good for her. You think she has learned anything from the past?"

"I think she has."

"So have I," Guy truthfully admitted, as he lovingly wrapped his arms around Regine and gazed into her eyes. "I learned that the consequences of a rebound relationship can be detrimental not only to the players, but to their families as well. I will never put you through that again. I love you," he said, as he kissed her on the cheek.

Regine smiled. "I love you too."

Guy turned to leave, then suddenly turned back toward her. "I'll see you at the restaurant. Don't worry; we'll get there on time."

Kevin Charlie, also given the nickname KC, was a bundle of joy. He had inherited Guy's dimples and Regine's black thick, curly hair. KC was a happy baby, who brought immense joy to his Grandma Jeanine. Jeanine felt very comfortable being a grandmother, and looked forward to waking up every morning and walking into KC's room.

At Guy's insistence, Jeanine moved in with them when she became weak and could not care for herself. She gave Tim Carter, her private investigator, a hefty severance package, and signed over the full operation of Trowne Key Estates to Guy and Alex. Jeanine also signed over her stakeholder shares of Lucent Technology to Guy. Guy eventually bought out the company, becoming the new owner.

Jeanine softly laughed, watching KC giggle and pull himself up on the rail of his baby bed. "I can't believe I lived to see this day," she said, as she softly touched his cheeks.

"Yeah, KC is growing up so quickly," Guy said, as he walked into the room and stood next to her.

Jeanine briefly glanced at Guy and smiled. Then she turned her attention to KC. "How does it feel to be one year old?" she asked, as she tickled him. KC smiled and giggled when Guy picked him up and placed him in his walker. KC shot off toward the bedroom door, which was blocked by a child safety fence.

"Look at him go!" Jeanine responded with excitement.

"Mom, let me take care of KC," Guy said. "You go get dressed. Everyone is waiting for us at the restaurant."

"I suppose you're right," Jeanine said, as she kissed KC one more time before departing to her bedroom. Guy looked at how much weight Jeanine had lost and could not help but feel sorrowful. He knew she would not be around much longer, and thanked God for giving him the opportunity to know her. He believed his father would have been proud of her.

The grand opening and birthday party went off without a hitch. KC smiled and laughed all evening, and everyone raved about Regine's gourmet entrees. After all the guests left, Bessie and Sue, along with the staff, stayed behind to help Regine close up the restaurant. Suddenly, Kevin appeared at the entrance.

Sue was the first to notice him. "Kevin, is that you?" she questioned, as she strained to see him from a distance.

Kevin smiled as he slowly approached her. "Hi Sue. It's good to see you," he said with a sly grin.

Sue was still in shock. "I didn't think I'd ever see you again."

"I couldn't miss my baby's big day. Where is she?"

"Regine's in the kitchen with everyone else. They're cleaning up. Is there any way we could talk in private?" Sue asked, looking at Kevin's bodyguards.

"Sure." Kevin instructed his bodyguards to relax, before he followed Sue to the bar area.

Sue asked, "Can I fix you a drink?"

"No, I'm cool. You go ahead and fix yourself something," Kevin said, checking out Sue in her red halter-top dress.

"I don't drink or do drugs anymore," Sue proudly admitted.

Kevin smiled. "I know. How's Richard treating you?"

Sue gasped as she covered her mouth from shock.

"Oh, I know about Richard," Kevin confidently admitted.

Sue eyes widened. "But how did you…?"

"He used to work for me."

Sue thought about what he was saying and put two and two together. She looked into his eyes and sincerely said, "Thank you for sparing his life."

"No problem. Just one question, though."

"What is it?"

"Why him?"

"He reminds me of you," Sue coyly admitted.

Kevin chuckled.

Sue grinned. "Now can I ask you a question?"

Kevin nodded.

"Why did you spare his life?"

"Bessie called me after you told her you were worried about Richard. She asked if I could locate him. It just so happened, he was in my custody at the time."

"Are you serious?" Sue incredulously asked.

"Yeah, Bessie didn't know he was working for me, but I figured it out. Your boy, Richard, is very lucky to be alive."

"Now what?"

"We move on. Tell Richard he better not cross you. And don't send me an invitation to your wedding. You know I still love you," Kevin softly admitted.

Sue was shocked by Kevin's admission. She stared at him in disbelief.

"Don't look at me like that. You've been my shadow for years. I regret ever introducing you to drugs."

Sue was taken aback. "Is that what you thought? No Kevin, you're wrong. The drugs were my doing, not yours. I was introduced to drugs long before you came into the picture. You can relax now. You owe me nothing."

For over twenty years, Kevin had been waiting for Sue's explanation. He leaned over and kissed her on the cheek.

Regine walked out of the kitchen with KC on her hip, and stood still when she saw her parents talking. For a split second, she wished things could stay like this. She slowly walked in their direction. "Dad?"

Kevin smiled as he stood up and embraced her. "Hi baby. I just wanted to be here for your grand opening. I'm so proud of you!"

"Thank you, Daddy!" Regine said with glee, before grabbing his hand. "Let me show you around."

"But first, can I hold my grandbaby?" Kevin asked, as he reached for KC.

"Of course." Regine handed KC to Kevin, then stood back and beamed. She never thought this day would happen. To know her parents loved her, even though they were absent for most of her life was overwhelming. All of her dreams had come true.

Fatal
Vengeance

Part II of the Fatal Trilogy

(An Excerpt)

A fictional story about the boomerang effects of getting even at all costs. Guy Simmons finds himself protecting his siblings, Alex, Dana, and Cassandra, from the pitfalls of life. Unfortunately, he has his own set of problems when his perfect marriage to Regine Croswell falls apart. A culmination of murder, lies, and deception become the central theme as the siblings seek vengeance on one another's behalf, but no one knows what the other is doing. The question of '*Who did it?*' leaves you in suspense until the very end.

"Rhaunda, I love you. I would never do anything to hurt you," Alex whispered, as he cupped her face and looked longingly into her hazel brown eyes.

"Baby, I love you too," Rhaunda softly cooed, "but I refuse to share you with another woman, especially with Alicia." Then she kissed Alex with vigor, while brushing her free hand gently across the side of his face.

Alex had completely forgotten about his houseguest as he closed his eyes, kissing Rhaunda back with fierce passion and desire.

Rhaunda was not distracted by his kiss and roving hands over her back and buttocks. She placed one arm around Alex's waist while seductively kissing him back. Then she used her free hand to withdraw the gun from her purse, which hung from her shoulder. She smiled as she held the gun up near his face.

When Alex heard the gun cock, he slowly opened his eyes and stood still. He lifted his head and shivered at the sight of the gun. "What are you doing?"

Rhaunda bore a wide grin. "Let's just say I'm fed up with your crap."

All the color drained from Alex's face as he took a step back, holding up his hands, as if surrendering. His voice trembled, "Baby...let's talk about this. You don't want to do this," he fearfully added while literally sweating bullets.

Rhaunda was unmoved by his pleas. She stood in silence wondering whether she should follow through with her plans. While briefly closing her eyes to contemplate her next move, Alex swiftly reached out with trembling hands to wrestle the gun away from her.

He wasn't quick enough. Rhaunda reflexed, then blinked each time she fired the gun. Alex fell backward as blood oozed out of his abdomen. He was fading away rapidly, gasping for his last breath before his eyes finally rolled to the back of his head.

Rhaunda was frazzled by Alex's seemingly lifeless body. She started shaking as tears streamed down her face. "Oh God! What have I done?!" she cried out, as she dropped to the floor, frantically touching his arm for a pulse. Then she became alarmed when she heard a whimper coming from the closet.

Rhaunda dried her face with her hands and became furious. "Come out, now!"

Alicia stood still, peering out the closet opening and hoping Rhaunda would leave her be.

"If you don't come out now, I will drag you out by your hair weave," Rhaunda threatened.

Alicia slowly opened the closet door, and timidly came out with her arms wrapped around her shoulders. Her voice trembled. "Rhaunda, please don't do this."

"Do what?" Rhaunda asked, as she lifted the gun and pointed it toward Alicia's head. "You did this. I told you to leave Alex alone, but you wouldn't listen. Now look at what you made me do," she said, as she briefly waved her hand over Alex's body.

"Please don't kill me," Alicia pleaded with clasped hands.

Rhaunda chuckled. "I'm not stupid. Why would I kill you? You're the murderer."

Alicia frowned and squinted her eyes. She looked at Rhaunda like she was crazy. *Are you serious?!*

Rhaunda grinned. "You don't think I killed Alex without a plan, do you?"

"But, I thought you were in love with him," Alicia softly whispered.

Rhaunda's smile broadened, exposing her pearly white teeth. "Oh, but I do. I love him to death! Now I can have him all to myself." She lightly laughed at the thought.

Alicia was alarmed by Rhaunda's demeanor. She wondered what caused her to turn into a crazed lunatic. "Just let me go," she begged.

"How?" Rhaunda asked with a sly grin. "Your car is um….how should I put this lightly? Oh, I know….*dead*, just like Alex. Or, should I say, *burned*, just like you burned me by sleeping with Alex. Or, what about *doomed*, just like you will be while rotting in jail," she added with venom.

Alicia gasped.

"Bitter sweet, bitter sweet," Rhaunda repeated with a smile. "How do you like those odds? I'm going to let you live and at the same time, let you die slowly, in jail. How awesome is that?" she sarcastically asked.

Alicia eyed the gun wondering if she should try to wrestle the gun from Rhaunda.

As if reading her thoughts, Rhaunda said through clenched teeth, "Don't even think about it."

Alicia thought, *Oh God, this is the devil right here on earth.* She began to cry a river a tears.

"Shut up that whining! And dry your damn eyes!" Rhaunda forcefully said. "Now, this is what you're going to do. You're going to go to the phone, dial 911, and tell the operator you just murdered Alex Simmons. You can tell them that it was in self-defense for all I care. But, I can assure you that it won't work, especially since you unloaded three bullets, ensuring his death." Then she looked at Alicia's half-naked body in disgust before continuing, "I'm sure the State Attorney will wonder what Alex could have possibly done to make you angry enough shoot him, since it's obvious that you were screwing him earlier tonight."

"But Alex told me you were out of town," Alicia nervously explained. Rhaunda placed her right hand over her chest and laughed heartily in response. Her reaction freaked Alicia out. Alicia thought, *What's up with the cussing? I thought she was a holy roller, round here toting her bible and acting like she better than everyone else. I wonder if Alex knew he was dealing with a psycho!*

"Go to the phone, now!" Rhaunda demanded.

Alicia looked at the phone, then turned to Rhaunda. "I can't...."

"You can, and you will," Rhaunda matter-of-factly said. Cocking her gun, she twisted her mouth, keeping the target on Alicia's head.

Alicia slowly walked over to the phone and picked it up. She paused as she kept her gaze focused on Rhaunda and the gun pointed to her head.

"Do it now!" Rhaunda ordered.

Alicia's hand shook as she pressed the buttons on the phone. She did not think to pretend to dial 911. Her voice cracked. "Hello, operator... I... ugh...um...um." She looked at Rhaunda from the corner of her eyes, and continued, "I...um...killed, Alex."

Rhaunda waived the gun as a gesture for Alicia to hang up the phone.

Alicia complied, then asked, "Now what?"

"You wait!" Rhaunda opened the cradle of the gun and removed the remaining bullets. She threw the empty gun on the bed. She wasn't worried about handprints because she purposely wore gloves. Then she looked up at Rhaunda and softly chuckled. "Though, I suggest you put on some clothes. You look like a killer hooker," she said with a hearty laugh.

Alicia looked down and suddenly felt exposed. She quickly covered up her private area with one hand, and used her free arm to cover her breasts.

Rhaunda turned to walk out the door, but briefly turned back. "I may pay you a visit in jail," she said, as she walked out the door and sprinted down the street to the next block over. She arrived at her car in record time. She was breathing heavy as she opened her car door, then flopped behind the steering wheel. She sat in her car and listened out for the sirens before turning the ignition and driving away.

(Fatal Vengeance will be released April 2011)

About the Author

Dorothy J Morris was born and raised in Fort Lauderdale, Florida. *Fatal Rebounds* is her first novel. She is currently working on the sequels, *Fatal Vengeance* and *Fatal Blow*. She earned a Bachelor of Arts degree in Psychology from Florida International University in Miami, Florida, and a Masters degree in Human Resources Development from McDaniel College in Westminster, Maryland.

She lives in Maryland with her husband and two daughters.

To learn more about the author and her upcoming novels, visit www**dorothyjmorris.com**. Or if you wish to provide feedback, send an email message to the author at contactme@dorothyjmorris.com.

www.ingramcontent.com/pod-product-compliance
Lightning Source LLC
Chambersburg PA
CBHW021505240626
47154CB00002B/515